Breathe AGAIN

*The Breathe Series
Book Three*

Rachel Brookes

Breathe Again
Copyright © 2014 Rachel Brookes

All rights reserved.

No part of this publication may be reproduced, stored in or introduced into a retrieval system, or transmitted, in any form or by any means (electronic, mechanical, photocopying, recording or otherwise), without the prior written permission of the copyright owner, except by a reviewer who may quote brief passages in a review.

This book is a work of fiction. Names and characters are the product of the author's imagination and any resemblance to any person, living or dead is purely coincidental. Any actual places, products or events mentioned are used in a purely fictitious manner. The author acknowledges the trademarked status and trademark owners of various places/products referenced in this work of fiction, which have been used without permission and is by no way sponsored by the trademark owners.

Editing: Mickey Reed
Proofreading: Tink's Typos
Cover Design: Wicked By Design
Photography: Perrywinkle Photography
EBook and paperback Formatting: Champagne Formats

ISBN-13: 978-1496116604
ISBN-10: 1496116607

Other books by Rachel Brookes

The Breathe Series
Just Breathe
Breathless
Breathe Again

The Crawford Brothers
Be My December
Be My Temptation

Dedicated to those who never thought they deserved a second chance. . . .
Everyone deserves a second chance; it's what you do with it that counts.

Part One

WHEN YOUR PAST MEETS YOUR PRESENT AND YOUR PRESENT THREATENS YOUR FUTURE, REMEMBER TO **JUST BREATHE.**

Prologue

Tate

IT HAD BEEN TWO FUCKING months. Two long, tortuous, mind-numbing months since I'd left New York to return to the loneliness and solitude Los Angeles now offered. Two months since Savannah Rae had asked me to leave.

For two months I moved through life with no concern, no reason, no expectation, no anything. Sleep, eat, and work was all I did. It had become my routine, my livelihood, my ultimate distraction. That was my life now, the life I had been given because of a vindictive bitch named Chelsea. The life I was now living without Savannah.

Tanzi had tried to get me out of my rut, Jack had been taking me surfing more than usual and Mom had even hand delivered red velvet cupcakes to me, but despite their best efforts, there was nothing that was able to shift my mood. Like an impending storm rumbling over the Hollywood hills, my mood darkened with every new day that passed. The intensity of this whole situation was frustrating the shit out of me and I constantly asked myself what the hell I could do about it.

The ever growing pit of unanswered questions was taking over every inch of my existence, and the slowly twisting knot in my stomach from walking around not knowing whether I still had a girlfriend was expanding by the second.

This shit had to stop. Right. Fucking. Now.

I, Tate Connors, never ever did this. I didn't sit on the beach contemplating life with my surfboard beside me and sand wedged in places it shouldn't be, and I sure as shit didn't pine over or allow my life to come to a half for a fucking girl.

But the girl in question wasn't just any girl. She was *my* girl.

The stubborn as fuck, sexy as sin, and sweet as candy Savannah Rae.

My girl.

"You thinking about Sav again?" Jack's amused voice rumbled beside me.

A growl escaped my dry throat as I shot him a *don't fuck with me* look. Observant fucker he was.

"She is the only fucking thing I think about Jack."

It wasn't a hidden fact that I loved Savannah with every part of my being. Every time my eyes landed on her, I drank her in like it was the last drop of water my desperate mouth could find in an abandoned desert. But now, as I was on a forced Savannah hiatus, I was craving her like a junkie craved every last bit of smack they could summon. I needed my hit, but no matter the intense life-alternating, mind-shattering effects of the drug, there would always come that time when the junkie questioned their addiction. That time when they were locked in the solitude of their turbulent mind, battling the fears, insecurities, highs, and lows brought on by their drug-induced haze. The moment when they questioned whether the addiction was really worth it all.

For me, my moment of clarity happened barely an hour ago after I'd paddled out behind the waves to Jack's and my secret surf spot in San Diego. As the ocean calmed around me, my brain rumbled like a freight train. The peace of the ocean made everything shimmer and gleam as painful reality swept through me. As heart breaking as it was and as much as it felt like my heart was ripping out of my chest, I was slowly coming to the realization that I couldn't wait for her to make up her mind. I was either worth it or I wasn't. What else could I possibly do to prove to her that I was hers and hers alone? How could I possibly get her to believe in me when it was clear she didn't believe in us?

In the middle of the serenity of the Pacific Ocean, I made the decision that would make or break us. I would give this, us—Tate and Savannah—one last fight, one last earth-defying attempt to shake it into her that we were forever. I'd fight for her. I'd fight the fucked-up situation we found ourselves, and I'd fight for the life that I deserved, that we deserved, that Jellybean deserved.

"What are you going to do about it?"

"What can I do, Jack? She made her decision. We have barely said two words to each other since I left. The only thing we talk about is Jellybean, and I am fucked if I can go on living like this. I fucking love her. I know that, you know that, Tanzi knows that. Hell, she knows that, but what can I do?"

"Go to her? Tell her exactly what you are telling me. You

have walked around with the world on your shoulders for the past two months. I love you, man, but you have been fucking hell to live with. You can fix this."

Of course I could fix this, but I was becoming tired. There was only so much my heart could bear, and as I sat on my favorite beach as the world turned around me, I made the life-changing decision.

Our future was in her court now. She held the future of Sav and Tate in her beautiful hands and the choice was hers. One simple word would change everything. Yes or no. Did she want us or didn't she? An answer that I would be gaining soon.

The face I had been dreaming about, the body I craved, and the heart I wanted to save was coming back to Los Angeles in two weeks and she had no clue I knew.

Chapter One

Savannah

2 weeks later.

TATE HAD BEEN RIGHT. My one-month stay in New York turned into a three-and-a-half-month stint. My time in New York would have been incredible if I wasn't fighting the constant battle of emotions over whether I missed or despised Tate. My thoughts were turbulent to say the least. One moment I was crying for what I had potentially lost and the next I was furious at what I had seen and the independent woman roared within me. Most days were bearable because I threw myself into work, starting before the sun rose and finishing long after the sun set, taking on new projects and attending after-hour functions—anything to keep my mind active and away from the reality I faced. But once work finished, I was back with the solitude of New York, the isolation from the world that I had so carefully built around myself, the world that offered a comfort I had been craving since I was ten years old. It was those lonely late nights that were the hardest. The time just before I would drift off to a restless sleep. Those few minutes before sleep engulfed me when my mind was filled with nothing but Tate.

I couldn't deny that our time together in New York had been anything but perfect. Having Tate with me, sharing my pregnancy together, having copious amounts of amazing sex, and having him within arm's reach was what every girl wanted. But perfection never seemed to stay in the life of Savannah Rae for long, and it had soon been shattered to a million sharp and violently jagged pieces when Hurricane Bitch-Face-of-the-Century Chelsea decided to tear through our lives, destroying and upturning everything in her path.

What a fucked-up situation I now found myself in. Just thinking of her made my blood boil. A hatred simmered inside me, a hatred I had never felt for another person before. As if life were trying to twist the knife currently wedged in my heart just a little more, my mind ran through the events of that fateful day time and time again. It crept into my thoughts when I was wide awake and haunted me when I was fast asleep. The image of her and Tate having sex felt like it was tattooed on my eyes, engrained in my memories to forever torment me and remind me that she had him first.

My reaction at seeing the video had been brutal, and instinct had kicked in without any consideration of facts. My defenses had shot up and the wall that Tate had smashed through had reappeared within seconds, brick by brick, blocking my heart from his. My words *"Just leave, Tate"* still echoed in my ears, tormenting and haunting. Tate had kept a promise to me on that day though, a painful promise I wished we had never made. He had promised that he would always do what I asked of him, and he had done exactly what I'd asked. He'd left and we hadn't spoken about that day since.

My heart ached when I awoke each morning to find a text message from Tate. His concern and love for our unborn child was incredible. Questions about how I was feeling and whether I was eating and drinking enough were filling my inbox, and most recently he had taken it upon himself to send random pregnancy facts. That was all we talked about—my pregnancy and Jellybean. He hadn't mentioned what happened once, and I hadn't brought it up either. The thought of having that conversation over the phone and not being able to look him in the eye as we spoke killed me. His eyes had always been the key to seeing his truths, and they'd spoken to me so many times when words had failed him.

The moment Blake had brought me back to the hotel room after I had fled, I had been slapped in the face by the hard hand of reality and the seriousness of what had just happened. Chelsea had been long gone, but her path of destruction had been far from over. She'd had one goal in mind and she'd gotten exactly what she'd wanted. Her pitiful and hateful desire to drive a wedge of mistrust between Tate and me had exploded around us.

In my haze of tears and spiraling emotions, I had taken a nervous step into the empty room and immediately noticed two things—the scent of Tate still lingering in the air and the plain white envelope that rested on my pillow, with Tate's perfect scripted handwriting on the front. Why did everything about him have to be perfect? Reading his words had destroyed me and I'd collapsed on the floor, sobs echoing through the air. I had soon been in Blake's arms, being lifted to the bed that only hours earlier had witnessed the love Tate and I had for each other.

Perfect and intense was the only way to describe the relationship Tate and I had been handed, and that was how it had been since day one. Intensity and Tate and Sav went hand in hand with jealousy, trust issues, frantic, earth-shattering sex, and unimaginable love. Never again would I ever experience that kind of love with anyone but him, and that was what terrified yet exhilarated me.

Tate was it for me, like a ray of sunshine that had lit up my constantly cloudy days, but here I was, on the other side of the country, petrified about going back to Los Angeles because of what could be waiting for me. The unknown scared yet energized me. I had a fierce independence, but I wanted nothing more than for my independence to be taken and owned by Tate.

My body came to a sharp halt as my eyes caught my reflection bouncing off the mirror on the far wall of the bathroom. My eyes grew wide as they traveled down the length of my body and focused solely on the soccer ball that had decided to attach itself to the front of me and the impressive set of boobs that had taken ownership of my chest. My girls, as I called them, were always fabulous, but holy shit these were freaking amazing! I was five months pregnant, and my body was proudly showing off my pregnancy to the world. There were days when I still couldn't believe I was pregnant, but then I would feel the tiny little butterfly kisses within me and then the tiniest of kicks and I knew that Jellybean was with me. I often found myself cradling my precious cargo, and my baby was my constant company in the loneliness that was New York. Jellybean, Mr. Davenport, Lucas, and surprisingly Blake.

Since everything had blown up with Tate, Lucas and Blake had become my biggest supporters. They checked in with me every day, sometimes more than once. Blake and I were friends, and we both knew that. I knew I was going to get hell for being in contact with him, but I saw the way the whole Chelsea incident had affected him. I had seen the way he had looked at Tate as it all had unfolded around us, and I couldn't put my finger on it but I knew he needed a friend. Blake's main concern was for Tate, and he constantly asked if I had spoken to him. He and Chelsea had been long over. Blake wouldn't tell me, but I knew she was holding something over his head. All he would tell me was that it was something he needed to talk to Tate about.

Tearing my gaze away from my stomach, I rushed through the room at a million miles an hour, throwing the last of my belongings into my brand-new suitcase. My shopping addiction and being on my own in the city meant that my time had been spent buying too many clothes for myself and Jellybean. Seriously, my kid was going to be the best dressed kid around.

I picked up the tiny white jumpsuit I had found that proudly displayed the Australian flag and smiled. My baby would always know that Australian blood was running through its veins. My pride for my country would not be lost on my child, and the thought of taking Jellybean to Australia to experience the beaches, the weather, the meat pies, and the Tim Tams excited me. *My child*—fuck, what a mind trip.

I cradled my stomach and lowered my voice. "Well, Jellybean, we are going home today. We are going to see Papa and we are going to see your aunts and uncles." I swallowed hard and slammed my eyes closed. "And we are going to see Daddy."

Goodbye, New York. Thanks for the memories.

"Well look at you, sexy momma."

My cheeks flushed the moment the words left Lucas's lips and floated through my ears. Without a second of hesitation, his arms enclosed around me tightly, forcing the suitcase I was wheeling out of the exit of LAX to thud to the tiled floor below me. I fell hard against his firm body, my head resting over the thumping of his heartbeat. Tears threatened to spill over as the emotions of being back in Los Angeles flooded me. The flight had been uneventful, and now, as I stood in the California sun, I was beaming.

I was home. I was back to familiarity. I was back to the chaos of Los Angeles. I was safe in Lucas's arms.

"You like my new accessory?" I asked, stepping out of his arms and rubbing my hand over my expanding stomach with a raised eyebrow.

"It looks good on you. It really brings out your . . ." His eyes traveled down from my face, and with a smirk that lit up his entire face, he took in my ever growing boobs. "Eyes."

I snorted. "Oh yes. My eyes are looking amazing, even if I do say so."

"The guys back at the apartment will have a field day looking at your *eyes.*" Lucas's laughter echoed around us as he grabbed my suitcase from the floor and started to dodge through the raucous crowd of recent arrivals who were standing in what seemed like a never-ending line, waiting for a cab. I followed diligently behind him, laughing softly to myself.

Suddenly, I stopped as his words finally hit me. Guys? Apartment? "What do you mean back at the apartment?"

"It's Jack's birthday so there is a small get-together planned for this afternoon at his place and then I'm sure we will move to Red Velvet tonight."

Fuck! Jack's birthday. His place meant Tate's place, and Red Velvet meant Tate Connors. I felt the color drain from my face, dripping and flooding the floor below me. My heart beat furiously in my chest, and my ears were swamped with white noise. I felt like I was thirteen years old and going to a birthday party where my crush would be. *Pull yourself together, Savannah.*

"Do I have to go? Can't we pretend that I'm not here?" I dropped my eyes, hoping that my best attempt at puppy-dog eyes was working.

Lucas shook his head and chuckled. Obviously my attempt had failed. "If Jack knows you are back in LA and didn't come to his party, shit will go down."

He was right.

Whether I liked it or not, I had one option and one option only. I was going to this damn party and there wasn't anything I could damn well do about it. Independent Sav hated this, but the time had come for me to shuffle through my suitcase and locate my big girl panties. Swallowing hard, I stopped at Lucas's car and watched as he lifted my suitcase into the trunk.

Slamming the trunk shut, he turned towards me and immediately his eyes swam over my face and narrowed in hard.

Damn my face and its constant need to show the world what I was thinking. He put his hands on my shoulders and held me still. "It's so good to have you back, Sav."

"It's good to be back. I've missed you." I dropped my eyes as my voice cracked. "I've missed everyone."

"You need to speak to him." Lucas lowered his voice calmingly, knowing exactly who I had been referring to. "You know that I haven't always been Team Tate, but he is struggling big time. You don't have to do anything tonight, but please think about it."

Was I hearing this correctly? Was I suddenly in an alternate world where Leprechauns and Centaurs roamed free through deliciously green fields of a fairytale world—a world where Lucas and Tate were friends?

Lucas dropped his hands from my shoulders and moved quickly around the front of the car and slid into the driver's seat while I climbed in the car and buckled up in the passenger's seat, still trying to comprehend the thought of Tate and Lucas having any form of friendship.

"Everyone is going to freak the fuck out when you turn up."

I twisted in my seat, directing my attention to him. "Is Ali going to be there? I've missed that gorgeous little pixie."

"Uh, no she isn't." His eyes ripped away from mine and focused on the road ahead as he pulled away into traffic. It was as clear as day that he was refusing to look at me. The distance in his voice immediately grabbed my attention. What the hell had happened since I had been away? First Tate and Lucas and now Lucas and Ali.

I narrowed my eyes at him. "Why the hell not?"

"She is working."

"Lucas Evan Douglas, do not lie to me. Where is she?"

He swallowed hard, eyes darting to mine quickly before looking back on the road ahead of him. "She is staying with her parents for a few days. A lot has changed since you've been gone Sav."

What the hell did he mean?

"I've been gone three months and I talk to you almost daily. Why didn't you say anything to me? I may be pregnant, Lucas, but I'm certainly not made of glass. I'm not going to shatter at the first rumbles of bad news."

"I know, I know. I will explain everything. Can we just enjoy you being home first?"

I folded my arms across my chest and pouted. "Fine, but I'm not happy about this, and we WILL be talking about it soon. I will be coming to your apartment tomorrow."

"Uh, I'm actually staying in a hotel at the moment. My apartment fell through."

"What!" I shrieked, looking back at him with wide eyes. "Right. You are coming to stay with me. Sleep in my spare room until you work out what's happening." He started to object but my words interrupted him. "Don't argue with a pregnant woman, Lucas. It's final."

I clasped my hands together, resting them on my stomach, and sat back, letting the leather of Lucas's seats caress my body. The dull hum of the engine instantly brought on a comforting mood to sweep through my exhausted body while my mind played tricks on me. So much had changed since I had been gone.

My thoughts suddenly traveled to Mr. Davenport. I

missed him more than anything. This had been the first time we'd been away from each other for any extended period of time. It was scary. He was and always would be my family, my comfort, my protector. Being away from him had cemented what he truly meant to me, and in the loneliness of New York City, I had come to the knowledge that he had been in my life longer than my parents. He was my constant. The realization had stung me like a thousand bees attacking my body, and it had taken me days to truly get a grasp of it. He had been taking care of me my whole life and I had done nothing but given him hell. I would forever be in debt to him.

I shifted in my seat and shot a pleading look at Lucas. "Can we swing by the Beautify office? I really need to see Mr. Davenport."

His eyes flicked with concern before he nodded slightly. "Sure, but this doesn't mean that you will get out of coming to the apartment. If you aren't at your apartment in an hour, I'm coming for you."

Walking through the Beautify LA office felt somewhat awkward. I hadn't been here in over three months, and now, as I strode through, I heard the whispers and comments about my expanding waist line.

"New York certainly didn't do her any favors." "Did you know she was pregnant?" "Whose baby is it?" "I knew she'd slept her way to the top."

When I left Los Angeles, I'd had a flat stomach and had been going to New York for a month, but now, I was five months pregnant and returning after an extended stay in New York. The office gossips would have a field day with this. I wondered how long it would take for someone to ask when Mr. Davenport and I would become parents. I shuddered at the thought. He was like my father.

The rumblings of an argument seeping through the walls of Mr. Davenport's office stopped me mid-step. I knew those voices. I swallowed hard and increased my pace until I was standing just outside the closed door. Mr. Davenport's and Tate's voices floated aggressively through the air as a heated discussion bellowed between them. I grabbed the door handle but froze on the spot, my ears pricking up at the conversation.

"I didn't do a thing with Chelsea. Why would I touch her when I have Savannah? She is the mother of my child for fucks sake. Sav is the one who owns my heart and who I'd do absolutely anything for. Do you really think I'd jeopardize losing her and our life together for a cheap fuck?"

"Well I don't know, would you? Your track record isn't doing you any favors Tate. I warned you about this. I warned you that she couldn't handle something like this and still you fucked it up."

"I didn't do it." Tate's voice increased as my heart stopped. "I know I've fucked up in the past, and I know my reputation doesn't do me any favors, but everything changed when I met Sav. Every single fucking day I want to make her happy. Every breath I take is for her and our baby. I'm never going to be good enough for her, am I?"

"Sav told me what she saw. A fucking video. Really, Tate?"

"I am a lot of things, but a wannabe porn star fucking on

video is not one of them."

"Do you realize I'm the one she calls and cries to every night? I'm the one she tells all about the baby, and I'm the one she called when she felt the baby kick. Me, Tate. It should have been you."

"My baby has kicked?" Tate's voice was barely audible and saturated with pain.

With a shaking hand, I opened the door and my eyes shot to Tate as I slipped into the room without a word. Their eyes shot to the door at the intrusion, their faces filled with frustration and anger, but as soon as they gazed at me, wonderment and shock drowned out their irritation.

I stood silent, like a statue on display to them both. My hand protectively cradled Jellybean as my eyes dropped and focused on a section of the carpet below me. Making eye contact with Tate would destroy me. I wasn't strong enough to deal with his piercing eyes right now, but still I could feel the pull of everything that was Tate Connors, just like that very first day in the elevator.

Mr. Davenport rushed across the room, his eyes never leaving me and before I could say a thing his arms engulfed me in a crushing hug. The intensity of the situation and knowing that Tate was only meters away from me caused my cravings to overcome me and my eyes instinctively found his over the broad shoulder of Mr. Davenport. My heart beat frantically in my chest as I searched his face for any sign of what he was thinking, I hated that his face was blank, unreadable, impenetrable.

The blue of the eyes I got lost in so many times and adored was shaded and barely recognizable. All I was seeing was pain. He looked exhausted, the spark in his eyes replaced with struggle and rimmed by dark circles. My urge to comfort him was so strong, and all I wanted to do was wrap him up in my arms, to soothe, love, and caress him, but I knew I couldn't. I still needed answers. I was desperate for answers even if those answers would give me what I didn't want to hear. Our eyes locked for what seemed like eternity before he broke away. For the first time in our relationship, he was the one to break our connection, and I felt the distance instantly.

"I will leave you to it."

Tate hesitated briefly and shook his head, refusing to look at me. Mr. Davenport's grip loosened around my waist and he grabbed my hand, pulling me towards the couch in his office. The tension in the room was blinding. Without another word, Tate slipped through the door, closing it behind him and leaving me in the office with Mr. Davenport.

"He didn't do it, Sav."

I swung around, looking at Mr. Davenport with wide eyes. Wasn't he just in here blasting Tate for cheating on me? I gripped the edge of the couch and sat down, sinking into the plush, cream leather. My body and mind were exhausted, desperately trying to comprehend everything happening around me.

"How do you know?" I whispered, my eyes pleading at him for answers.

Slowly walking towards me, he sat beside me, grabbing my hand and looking at me with pride. I felt my chest tighten and my eyes flood as an onslaught of tears cascaded over my cheeks.

"Hey, come on, Sav. You are home. What's going through

that head of yours?"

"I love him."

"And he loves you. He didn't do it, Sav. Yes, he had sex with her and it was filmed, but it's not new."

"How do you know?"

"Did you not just hear our conversation? That is a man who is desperately in love with you, who is trying to gain your love and respect. He is remorseful. Not because of anything he did but because you had to see that."

"I fucking hate that bitch," I spat, venom dripping off my every word. My hatred for her was at an all-time high. I didn't like the word hate but I didn't think hate was even a strong enough word for what I was feeling. "I'm willing to lose my visa to show her what I really think of her."

"Jesus Christ." Mr. Davenport ran his hand through his hair and a deep growl sounded. "I am not bailing you out on an assault charge, so get that fucked-up thought out of your head and watch your bloody language."

"You are a hypocrite." I smirked and pushed him slightly. His brow creased as he looked at me.

"You are going to cause a man to go grey before his time. Now tell me all things Jellybean. I've missed this little person."

"Well, I have an ultrasound tomorrow, so I'll be able to get you a photo."

"Tate should go with you."

"Back on the Team Tate bandwagon I see?" I questioned with a raised brow.

"I am far from Team Tate, but he hasn't done a thing. You need to explain things to him. Give him that much. And he deserves to see his child. Tanzi has been keeping tabs on him. He is a wreck."

I sat in silence, watching Mr. Davenport frown and scratch his chin. This man sitting in front of me only wanted happiness for me. He had never asked me for anything, but I felt obligated to give him the world. He saved me—it was as simple as that. I scooted across the couch, wrapped my arms around him, and held him for dear life. I collapsed against his chest as tears continued to fall. My tears were my relief. I cried of sadness and happiness, of fear and achievement. My life was a mess, but there were so many other people worse off than me. I was healthy. I had been given the gift of a child, the gift of everlasting love, and a family I so desperately craved.

"Sav, you need to go through the storm before you get your rainbow."

Mr. Davenport's words stung my heart and hit home.

I was one of the lucky ones. I had survived.

Lucas was true to his word. An hour after he dropped me off at the Beautify office, he was pounding on my front door. Opening it quickly, I secured the towel tightly against my body, ushered him in, and walked back to my bedroom. Clothes were strewn over my bed and spilling out of my suitcase, and my frustration levels of what to wear was skyrocketing with every second that ticked by.

"You should get changed back into the top you were wearing earlier. The guys will love it."

"I saw Tate," I spilled without consequence.

"What? Where? How?"

"He was at the office when I turned up. He and Mr. Davenport were in a somewhat heated conversation about me. He didn't say a word to me and left."

"Shit!" Lucas sat beside me and grabbed my hand tenderly. God, it was great to have my best friend back. "He is waiting for you to make the first move."

I shook my head while my mind filled with memories of Tate and me. I missed him. There wasn't any doubt about that, but could I really get the images of him and Chelsea out of my head?

"I should get ready if I am getting kidnapped and taken to the apartment." I smiled slightly and grabbed my new maternity skinnies and a shirt that was snug against my stomach. "I will just change and I'll be good to go."

"Put back on the top you were wearing before," he repeated.

I rolled my eyes in his direction but couldn't help but smile. "You really need to stop checking out my boobs." I looked down at the top I had just put on and smirked. "If you think the shirt I wore before was good, just wait 'til you see the one I'm wearing now."

"I doubt that very much."

I pulled open my makeup bag, applied my favorite lip gloss, and swiped bronzer over my cheeks. I could be girly when I wanted, but this was my go-to make up application—a bit of gloss, a spritz of perfume, a swipe of bronzer, and a lashing of mascara and I was ready. Satisfied with how I looked, I moved back into the bedroom to find Lucas reading the latest copy of Beautify I'd left on my bedside table.

I coughed softly to grab his attention. "So what do you think?"

Lucas's eyes lifted from the magazine and nearly popped out of his face. "Fuck me dead, Savannah. You can't just lay that on a guy. I'm sorry, I am not your boyfriend, and it is probably not my place to say this. Actually, I know it's not my place, but girl, the thoughts going through my head right now would cause Tate to fucking kill me." His smile filled up his face and I shook my head at him, knowing full well that my cheeks were flushing.

"Well I think I'll take that as a good sign. Can we please just go and get this over and done with?"

CHAPTER Two

Tate

I COULDN'T CONCENTRATE ON ANYTHING BUT the thought of seeing Savannah. She looked stunning. My thoughts flickered back to the instant my eyes had landed on her, standing there in that gorgeous and quite revealing top that allowed my eyes to enjoy the treat of seeing her newly enhanced boobs. And fuck, her stomach was perfection. The shield that offered protection to my child.

"What's up with you, man?" Jack's slurred words soared through the air as he pushed a beer into my empty hand.

Shaking my head, I slammed back the beer and tried to distract myself and move away from Jacks inquisitive mind. This was not a conversation I wanted to have with a highly intoxicated Jack.

The craziness of the apartment should have taken over every sound floating through my mind, but all I could hear was that sexy Australian accent that made me fall to my knees.

Fuck, it had been too long. I wanted her in my arms. I wanted her in *our* bed. My need to explain was first and foremost. I needed her to listen to me as I spoke nothing but the truth to her—one last chance, one last shot. Savannah had always told me that she could tell if I was telling the truth by my eyes, and my eyes were now ready to show her that she was it. There was no one else.

My head swung towards the front door as I heard the familiar squeak as it opened. My breath caught in the back of my throat, and the feeling of my heart stopping mid-beat hit me. Lucas stepped through with Savannah huddled closely behind him. Her eyes flew around the room, trying to reacquaint herself with my apartment. I lifted the beer bottle to my lips and took a desperate gulp, but my eyes never left her. Her eyes hadn't seen me yet.

"Savannah motherfucking Rae!" Jack's voice roared through the apartment as I watched him rush towards her, wrapping his arms around her in a bone-crushing hug. Fuck, I wanted his arms to be mine.

"Jack motherfucking Hayes!" Sav retorted, and I couldn't help but smile. I was watching her like a hawk and I didn't give a shit who saw. Her eyes rose over Jack's shoulder and finally her eyes met mine. I felt like the world stopped spinning, like the world went silent for us. My life had stopped the moment I'd left her in New York. Now, here she was. I wanted nothing more than to rush across the room, throw her over my shoulder, and lock her in my room for hours while I ravished and loved every part of her body, but I knew the ball was in her court. I would wait patiently. Fuck it—patience wasn't one of my strongest qualities.

Her eyes never faltered from mine, and I refused to break. I heard voices floating around me but nothing mattered except her. She had visited me so many times in my dreams, but having her here was the best fucking gift in the world. Nothing was ripping me away from this moment; I had waited too long to see her.

Her eyes found Jack's again as he leaned in and whispered something to her. My breath stilled. Without a moment's hesitation, both sets of their eyes found mine across the room and Jack moved quickly back to where Tanzi was watching the scene unfold in front of her, her mouth agape and her eyes wide.

Fuck this. I took off and walked across the room towards her. Her eyes widened quickly before dropping down to the floor.

"Savannah?" My voice hitched. Without restraint, my hand rose and cupped her cheek before reality punched me in the guts. I couldn't touch her—not without her permission. I ripped my hand away from her and took a step back. It killed me.

"Hi, Tate," she breathed out. Her eyes traveled over my face and she tugged her bottom lip between her teeth. Awkwardness soon rushed around us, and I lost all ability to speak. What the hell was wrong with me? I had a thousand things I could say to her, a thousand words I was desperate for her to hear, but I was totally mute.

"Tate, get your ass over here. We are having shots and there is a tequila shot with your name on it." Jack's voice sounded, breaking the trance I was currently in.

"I miss tequila," Sav whispered, and a smile rose on her

lips. The tension between us dissipated for a brief second, and suddenly it felt like everything was normal.

"Want me to have one for you?"

"Have two." Sav smiled before she broke away and rushed over to where Lucas was sitting on the edge of the couch, chatting with Tanzi. My eyes followed her and I finally took a breath.

The afternoon continued in a blur of tequila shots and Long Island Iced Teas. It had been the consensus of all the guests that Jack and I would drink Savannah's share, and considering that her drink of choice was tequila and Long Islands, there was no chance in hell I wasn't getting plastered tonight.

My eyes fixated on her for the whole afternoon, and all I wanted to do was escape into the confines of her heart and sort out the shitstorm that was surrounding us. As day soon turned into night and the party guests started moving over to Red Velvet, it ended up just being the five of us left in the apartment, waiting for Jack's beloved pizza to arrive.

Slipping into the tub chair in the corner of the living room, I narrowed my attention to where Sav was sitting close to Lucas on the couch. It almost looked like she was craving protection from him.

I was desperate for her to look at me. I knew my eyes had the potential to lock her in, and I was willing to try anything and everything to get a moment in her soul, in her thoughts, and in her memories.

"What about that chick that was all over Tate in Vegas?" Jack laughed, chugging back his beer, totally oblivious to what a statement like that would do to a highly volatile situation.

Sav's eyes flew to Jack's as the color drained from his

face as guilt swamped him.

"Nice one, dickhead," Lucas growled beside Savannah before turning to her protectively.

Without a second thought, I rushed towards her and grabbed her hand in mine. Screw the 'don't touch her' rule. "It's not like that, Sav."

She snatched her hand from mine and her eyes went blank as she looked at me. "It's not like I have any say about what and who you do anymore, Tate."

Tension-filled silence drowned the air.

"Are you really going to sit there and say that?" I felt my frustration levels rising by the second, and it didn't help that I had a stomach full of alcohol. "Do you really think I would fuck around on you? Do you honestly think that little of me that I would fuck some random chick in Vegas while my pregnant girlfriend is on the other side of the country? Do you really think that low of me?"

Tanzi's gasp filled the air. Savannah's eyes fired into mine and the strength of her face didn't falter.

"I don't know what I think, Tate. I can't think of anything but the video I saw. That's the only thing I see when I close my eyes at night and it's the only thing I have thought about for the past two months." Her eyes suddenly left mine and dropped to the hem of her shirt, which she was now playing with. "But you know what? You can screw whoever the hell you want."

You have got to me kidding me. "Look at me, Savannah," I growled.

"Tate, just shut up. I can't look at you because as soon as I do you will suck me in again. You will do that thing where you dive so deep into my soul and rip it apart. You will read every single thought that is running through my mind. That's why I can't look at you."

"Look at me so you can see what I can't seem to say to you."

"Tate, there is nothing that needs to be said."

I took a step towards her so that there was barely an inch between us, my voice lowering. "Like fuck there isn't."

Suddenly Savannah stood from the couch in front of me, rushed through the apartment towards the balcony, and disappeared through the glass door and out of view. I had pushed her too far.

"I'll go and sort her out," Lucas said, giving me a nod and following in the direction of Sav. Tanzi offered me a weak smile and Jack remained silent, guilt still evident on his face.

I couldn't just sit there.

I walked towards the balcony and stopped as I heard the soft echo of Sav's and Lucas's voices. Nausea rolled within me, my stomach flip-flopping as I feared what I might overhear.

"What's going on in that pretty head of yours, Savannah?" I swallowed hard, awaiting Sav's reply. "Hey, don't cry. What's wrong?"

"Oh, you know, just your typical Savannah saga . . . I go to New York, I lose my boyfriend, I come home to find out that some skank was all over him in Las Vegas, and I am getting fat and none of my clothes fit me anymore. It's like I am in some screwed-up soap opera."

"You haven't lost him."

Good on you, Lucas. Tell her what she wouldn't allow me

to say.

"What?! Are you drunk, Lucas? Because that could be the only excuse for your ludicrous statement! Have you not heard about the video that was shown to me of my boyfriend with his dick down the throat of slut-mole Chelsea?"

"You and I both know that video wasn't new."

"And how would you know that, Lucas? Enlighten me."

"If you gave Tate two minutes to talk to you, he would tell you."

"I can't."

"Savannah Maree Rae, you and Tate are not over. You are just both as stubborn as fuck and won't talk. I feel sorry for your spawn. He or she is going to have hard-as-nails parents. Thank fuck Uncle Lucas will be around." I heard a shuffle of feet and chanced a look around the door to find Savannah locked in a hug with Lucas.

"Did my makeup run?" Sav asked in a quiet voice.

"You look gorgeous. Now let's go and eat pizza."

Rushing back to the living room, I collapsed on the couch and fidgeted with the beer bottle that was now warm. Tanzi and Jack both looked up when the sound of the glass door leading to the balcony slid open. My eyes finally looked at Sav and my heart pounded in my chest. Her eyes were glassy and anyone could tell she had been crying. Sav glanced around the room as hesitation rolled within her and she reluctanty sat on the only vacant seat in the room—the couch beside me—her eyes never finding mine. Lucas took a seat across from me and offered a weak smile. For someone I despised for so long, he had now somehow become a needed support.

"We ordered your favorite pizza," I said softly, daring to

attempt to start a conversation. All she did was nod.

Chattering filled my ears and the smell of pizza caressed my senses. The conversation I overheard between Sav and Lucas had struck a part of my heart, and I desperately wanted to talk about it. I needed to talk about it, but at this rate, I was barely getting one word out of her.

Out of the corner of my eye, I watched as Sav began eating slice after slice of pizza. I zoned into the conversation around me, listening as Lucas talked about work, Jack talked about his recent shifts at Red Velvet, and Tanzi talked about the new neighbors who had decided that sex in public places was a prerequisite of living in the building.

"You inhaled that, Sav!" Jack laughed, throwing his crust towards her.

"I am eating for two, you know. I've gotta feed this little one." Sav patted her protruding stomach before grabbing for another slice. "This is the one time I can eat whatever the hell I want. I will deal with the consequences later."

"Let's go have birthday shots before we go to Red Velvet," Lucas announced. Tanzi and Jack hollered a resounding, "Yes!" before the three of them rushed to the kitchen, leaving Sav and me in an uncomfortable silence. My phone buzzed on my lap and I saw that it was Mom. As soon as I said hello, Mom went into a spiel about having to find out that Savannah was back in Los Angeles from Tanzi and then the questions about Jellybean started.

"Yes, she is. Jellybean is fine. Savannah is great." At the sound of her name, Sav's questioning gaze found me. "Sure. Okay. Hang on."

With a deep breath, I turned and handed Sav my phone.

"It's Mom. She wants to talk to you."

Sav nodded and began speaking softly to Mom. I couldn't help but smile as I heard Sav answer Mom's questions. I could only imagine what she was being asked. The words *morning sickness, cravings, and baby clothes* floated through the air. The first thing I noticed was Sav's eyes glistening before hearing her voice crack. My need to comfort her was so strong, but I remained still. I couldn't risk pushing her further away. Her green eyes found mine and the softness that fired back at me made my heart finally start beating again. When the call finished, Sav handed me my phone, a small smile covering her lips.

"Shit!" Sav suddenly cried out, her hand flying down to her stomach.

Fear swept through me. "What's wrong?" I begged, my eyes wide.

My eyes shot a look of distress between her eyes and her stomach as I tried to work out what was happening. Hesitation flickered over her face as if she were questioning her next move. In one swift movement, I turned to face her, crossing my legs under my body.

"Your baby is very active and decided to kick." Massaging her stomach seemed to be the only way to calm down Jellybean's recently acquired athletic skills.

"Does Jellybean move a lot?" I asked, unable to hide the sadness I felt of not yet being able to feel my baby move.

"We have a very active baby."

Sav suddenly grabbed my hand without showing any signs of doubt and gently placed it on her swelling stomach. "It's better if you touch my bare skin," she whispered, giving me permission to lift her shirt.

I felt the heat tear between us as my bare hand rested on her skin. Suddenly, my heart began pounding hard in my chest as the heat rose from her skin through to me.

"I'm sorry about losing my shit earlier," I apologised, shooting a pleading look at her.

"Let's not."

All of a sudden, as if Jellybean knew that it was time to interrupt Mommy and Daddy time, Sav's stomach rippled as a strong thud vibrated from her skin to my hand.

"Holy shit," I whispered, drawing my eyes from my hand to look at her. The moment our eyes connected, I felt our flame burn between us. We had unfinished business, and there was still the devastatingly powerful feeling of love simmering between us. I hoped my eyes showed the thousand unspoken words I was so desperate to say.

"Come to my place tonight and we can talk," Sav spoke so softly that I thought I imagined it.

I hope to the heavens above that I didn't.

Chapter Three

Savannah

TIME STOOD STILL, EVERYONE EYEING me with expectation. I was exhausted, overwhelmed, and scared of what my body was doing to me; the same body that was begging me to completely and utterly throw myself at Tate's mercy. I had just gotten caught under the Tate Connors Effect once again and had invited him to my place later. What the hell was wrong with me? We had just argued and thrown accusations at each other and now all I wanted was him alone in my apartment. Damn hormones.

Jack's eyes narrowed in on me in anticipation and hope. "Please come out with us, Sav." He took a step towards me and lowered his mouth to my ear. "I missed you, Sav. We all have. Please come out, even for just an hour."

My eyes bounced between Tate, Lucas, Tanzi, and Jack, their expressions matching each other's. How could I say no? Tanzi had just announced that the party was moving to Red

Velvet, and it was life or death that I made an appearance.

"An hour. You get me for an hour. I've got to go and rest this weary body. I need my bath and my candles."

A glimmer of a smile flashed over Tate's lips and I didn't miss it. I noticed everything about him. I nervously ran my fingers through my hair as my memories flashed back to Tate's and my adventures in the bath in New York City. Fuck, that had been hot, and my body still remembered every single kiss and caress and the way his fingers had taken my body to places I'd never thought existed. I was like a dog in heat. Pregnancy was causing my sex drive to go into the catastrophic zone. All I thought about was sex, and two months without it was killing me.

"I know exactly what you are thinking about, Sav. I know I am stepping over the line saying this, but thinking of the way my fingers were so deep in you has made the last two months bearable. You were amazing," Tate's voice hummed in my ear as he stood so closely that his scent caressed my senses. My eyes closed tight as heat rose deep inside of me. An impending explosion rumbled within me by a simple couple of sentences spoken from him. *Arsehole.* His torturous assault on my increased libido thankfully ceased as he stepped around me and slipped through the door and out to the foyer.

No, Savannah, you needed to talk and sort things out before you even think about having sex with him.

It was going to be a long night.

Walking into Red Velvet pregnant caused a wave of insecurities to blast through my body. I felt people's eyes follow my every move as I made my way through the swollen crowd with my ever-swelling belly on full display.

"People are staring at me," I spoke softly to Lucas, who walked beside me. His arm was draped over my shoulder, and I felt as he shifted beside me to look in the direction of Tate.

"If anyone gives you any shit, tell me and I will have them removed. Whether you like it or not, Savannah, this is your place just as much as it is mine," Tate stated with authority beside me.

I twisted in Lucas's arms and came face to face with Tate. Our eyes connected like magnets and I knew he had me locked in. His brilliant blue eyes were showing a command and intensity that fired a truth towards me that I had never witnessed before. My body's instant betrayal at the sound of his ownership over me caused a scorching heat to flame deep within me, and as our eyes locked together in silent discussion, his words filtered through me with promise. The noise, people, and space around us disappeared and I was hit with the realization that he would always own me. Even if I fought for the rest of my life, I'd never win the battle.

"Come on, Sav. Let's go to our table."

"Uh, yeah, sure," I choked out, my gaze with Tate broken as he took off towards the table in the far corner of Red Velvet. I glanced at Lucas, who stood beside me with a smug looked plastered on his face.

"You two are like a pair of horny teenagers."

"Shut up, Lucas." I rolled my eyes and tried to think of anything that would extinguish the heat flooding my body. I couldn't allow my sexual cravings for Tate to overcome the emotional needs I longed for.

Lucas grabbed my hand and we maneuvered ourselves through the crowd, heading towards the familiar table that had become ours. My lips curved into a smile at the sense of comfort this table provided. This was the place where I'd had my first argument with Tate, where I had joked around with Jack and Lucas, and where Tanzi and I had shared each other's inner most feelings and fears.

"The memories I have of this table are insane!" I chuckled, pulling out a seat and collapsing in a heap. All heads turned to me and I felt three sets of eyes latch on to my boobs that were spilling out of my top. "Seriously, guys, are you going to be checking out my boobs for the next four months? Tanzi, I know you are jealous of the girls."

"Your boobs are fucking insane," Jack howled before receiving a punch in the shoulder by Tanzi. "If knocking up a chick gets me this, then shit, I should have knocked you up a year ago, Tanzi."

My laughter filtered through the air. The inappropriateness of Jack was what made me love him even more. Tanzi collapsed onto Jack's lap across from me and he whispered something in her ear, something I could only guess was sex related by the look Tanzi got in her eye.

Lucas sat beside me, and the feeling that someone was missing hit me. Instinctively and desperately, my head spun around and my eyes darted through the bar in search of Tate. I was quickly losing control of my body and actions. I was heading into dangerous territory.

"He went to get drinks," Lucas said beside me. My embarrassment rose from my neck and took over my face. I was still *THAT* girl when it came to Tate. "When are you going to speak to him? I know for a fact that he wants to talk to you, but he is giving you time." He paused. "Fuck it. I'm just going to say it out loud. You realize that he didn't do anything with Chelsea, right?"

"Did you just say bitch face's name?" Tanzi snorted from across the table, her eyes suddenly overcome with a mixture of anger and intoxication.

"I know he didn't do anything,"

It was true. I knew he would never cheat on me, but the moment I had seen that fucked-up video and the moment I had been surrounded by Chelsea and her spiteful words, I had been thrown back to face the insecurities I had been battling since Cory cheated on me. I should never have sent Tate away, but the fear and the uncertainty had overcome me.

"Well what the fuck are you doing here? Go and tell him!" Tanzi shrieked and started clapping excitedly. My eyes found my best friends and they glowed with excitement.

Nodding in agreement, I stood from the chair, my eyes darting around every corner of Red Velvet in search of Tate. If I was going to do this, I needed to do it now before my confidence ran for the hills. My heart rate increased as my eyes landed on him slumped against the main bar, talking to a regular of Red Velvet. I maneuvered my way through the bar, apologizing as I bumped into people. Regulars stopped me and offered their congratulations, but my eyes remained firmly locked on Tate's back.

As I stood behind him, my memories flashed back to when I had first told him I was pregnant and finding him slumped over at this very bar after drinking himself into oblivion at the thought of becoming his dad. The feelings were still so raw. I placed my hand on his back and felt him stiffen under my touch.

"Tate, it's me."

He swung around and faced me. He eyes scanned over my face as fear swam in his eyes, a fear I could only assume was about what I was about to say to him. Whether I would be ending our relationship for good or whether we could move past the atrocity of Chelsea. My heart jumped in my chest. It was all on me now. I was holding our future in the palm of my hands.

"Sav, I didn't do anything. I would never touch her. That video was filmed—without my consent, I might fucking add—months and months ago. Before you. Why would I cheat on you? I'm drunk, Sav, but I'm not lying to you. I'd never lie to you." Tate took a step towards me with eyes firing with truth.

"I know, Tate."

"Well why didn't you trust me? Why didn't you tell her to fuck off? Why didn't you hold my hand and tell me that you believed me?"

"Tate, it's easier said than done. We both have history. We both have insecurities. I couldn't handle being bombarded like that. She had a video. The images of her fucking you are constantly on my mind. I can't forget that, no matter how hard I try."

"I am sick of talking about that fucking video," he barked. "I am sick of allowing her to control us."

"Well what do you want me to do? Forget what I saw? Forget that you fucked her?"

"What about you, Savannah? You've fucked around. Why

is it so different that I have? What makes me so different to you? I've fucked a lot of pussy and you've fucked a lot of dick."

"Uhhh, guys? You might want to take this somewhere private."

Both Tate and I swung around to find a sheepish Jack standing with his hands in his pockets, swaying slightly on his feet from the effects of alcohol. My eyes darted around the bar to find a small group of revelers now witnessing the dissolution of Tate and Savannah.

"Come with me," Tate grabbed my hand pulling me through the bar towards his office, not giving me any chance to retract my hand from his. He swung open the door and ushered me in, slamming the door behind us and shutting out the noise of Red Velvet.

I tore away from him and looked around the office. He had completely refurbished it. There wasn't a single thing that looked the same. A new, larger mahogany desk filled up the main space. An off-white leather couch was pushed along the far wall, bright red cushions splattered on it. There were new polished floorboards below my feet and the walls were now a deep red.

"You renovated?" I walked through his office, my fingertips running along the top of the desk.

What the hell? I stopped suddenly as my eyes trained in on the photo frame that was sitting on his desk right beside his opened laptop. A photo of Tate and me was looking back at me. In the photo, Tate and I had happiness oozing off us. He was standing behind me with his arms wrapped around me, resting on my stomach. I knew exactly when the photo had been taken. It was the day that we had officially told people about Jellybean, and there in my hand in the photo was the ultrasound picture. Tate had called this photo our first-ever family photo.

"I got rid of the past."

I spun around and looked at him as the anger from earlier quickly returned. "You mean you got rid of all the furniture you fucked other chicks on."

Tate's hand shot out and grasped my arm tightly, spinning me around so I was flush hard against his rigid body. If I thought he was pissed before, now he was about ready to explode. His eyes glared bottom-of-the-ocean blue at me while his jaw clenched tight.

"Seriously, Savannah? Is this how our relationship is going to be? Are we constantly going to discuss who has fucked whom? You want to know my number? Is that what this is about? I've fucked a lot—a shitload, actually." He dropped his face dangerously close to mine, his breath tickling my lips as he spoke. "But there is one major difference between you and them, Savannah. You are the only one I've made love to. The only one. Not even Candice got that. It's you, Sav. We fuck each other senseless but we also make love, and that's what is important to me. I don't want to keep going around on a roller coaster with you. Yes, I fucked Chelsea, and yes, she filmed it, but it was before you. Way before you."

My head spun dangerously out of control and my eyes became fuzzy as I realized that I wasn't breathing. Tate's words tumbled around my head, colliding with every thought and emotion I'd had jammed in there since that fateful day in New York City. I gasped deeply, begging for air to fill my empty lungs. There was absolutely no denying his love for me. His heart and soul were a on a platter for me, available for me and me only.

He had changed everything he once had been for me. His past was his past, and mine was no better than his. I had been a slut—there was no denying it. I had fucked for therapy. I had fucked for relief, desperate for a few minutes away from my tumultuous memories. But now, love was helping me more than I could ever have dreamed of, and the man in front of me my second chance.

"I fucking hate that bitch."

"So do I, but can we just not talk about her? All I can think about right now is bending you over that desk and christening it."

"I'm not just going to jump right back into fucking you, Tate," I groaned, trying desperately to hide the smile begging to shine. I clenched my legs tightly together, silently pleading with my body not to come undone. The smirk that spread over his face was a clear indication that he didn't believe a single word I was saying.

"Wanna make love then?" he asked with a sly grin.

"If I'm not fucking you, then I'm certainly not making love to you."

"Really? Well that's not what your flushed cheeks, jagged breathing, and increased heartbeat say." He placed his hand directly over my heart, and I knew for a fact that it was thumping dangerously hard. His eyes flashed over my face and dropped to take in my heaving chest against his hand. "Let me make you forget her. Let me fuck the memories of her and me out of your head. You and I need to take up every space in your pretty mind."

What the hell was he trying to do to me? Every inch of my body was alight for him. My heart was defrosting for him. And as he looked at me with hooded eyes full of devotion and anticipation, I knew this was it. This was my choice. He was giving me this moment, one last chance to move forward, make a future together, and laugh in the face of the past or throw our relationship into the hot pits of hell for the world to no longer include Tate and Savannah.

For two months, I fought emotions I'd never known existed and every thought I'd suffered was desperately trying to derail everything that was Tate and Sav. This whole situation could have been stopped if I had just been confident in our relationship. We were in this fucked-up situation because of my insecurities, yet here he was, standing before me, giving me the potential of having his entire world.

"Tate," I breathlessly and painfully said.

"Yes, Savannah?" His breath tickled my lips as he hovered closely to me. One measly step was all I needed to take to be chest to chest with him.

"I'm so sorry. I should never have asked you to leave. I was scared. I thought it was—"

My words were swallowed the moment Tate crashed into me. Within seconds, my ability to choke out any words of retraction was taken and I was pushed against the edge of his desk, my jeans swiftly removed at the impatient hands of Tate Connors.

Holy fuck. My body was on fire. Never had I ever felt this turned on. My body hummed and begged for him, craved him. With lips of want, he attached himself to my neck, sucking and nipping my sensitive skin, and my moans soon filled the empty space of the room. My head fell back and I leaned back on my elbows as pleasure swarmed my body.

"This is us, Savannah. You and me—no one else has this." His voice vibrated with promise and certainty against my throat.

It was true. There was no one like him. There would never be anyone like him. I shifted my body under his, allowing my hands to run over his broad shoulders and move their way to his hair. Roughly pulling on the back of his head, I forced his mouth to mine. For a brief moment, I hesitated, my breathing heavy, broken, and deep.

His breathing was increasing with want and his eyes hooded with mine. Dropping his forehead to mine, he whispered, "What do you want from me, Sav?"

What did I want from him? I wanted him inside me. I inched my face forward, allowing my tongue to trace his perfectly plump bottom lip. Under my soft touch, his eyes hooded and fluttered shut. He was beautiful and completely at my mercy. Sucking his bottom lip into my mouth, I bit down softly, and as if I'd turned on a light switch, my Tate was back. His tongue invaded my mouth, sweeping through, tasting everything I was. Our tongues danced together feverishly, needing and in pure ownership. I needed air, but I wouldn't break.

Tate's hand ran up the length of my thigh, stopping dangerously close to where I craved him most. My panties were saturated and I knew they had been for a while. I wanted them off. I felt the air move as he ran his hand up my thighs before lifting his hand and placing it on my hip, missing my desire. I paused and groaned in pain. I was aching.

"Tate, please," I moaned, lifting my hips from the desk and pushing myself against him. He stilled, his hips rocking painstakingly close, allowing his cock to grind against my panties.

"What do you want, Sav? You said no fucking. You said no making love."

"Fingers," I begged.

"That would mean I was fucking you. You said no fucking. That means no fingers, no mouth, no cock." He continued to tease and grind himself devastatingly close to my now throbbing and hungry pussy, and my eyes rolled into the back of my head as a symphony of moans escaped me. The sound of his heavy breathing and the feeling of his heavy cock against me made me feel as if I were swinging like a pendulum on the brink of crashing into a deep sea of pure ecstasy.

"Fuck me, Tate. Make me forget her. Make me think only of us." My eyes shot open to find him looking at me with eyes of intention and lust.

His hands swept down my hips, his fingertips sliding in the elastic of my panties and, with rushed fingers, moving them down my now sweaty thighs. He took a step back to take a moment to admire my new body.

"You are so sexy." His voice was hoarse and full of need.

His hands snapped open his fly, and within seconds, Tate stepped out of his pants and prowled towards me. His eyes never left mine. My hands, full of intention and want, grabbed him, caressed him, squeezed him just the way I knew he liked. He knew every pleasure point of my body just as well as I knew his. That's what made him mine. I knew him. I owned him. I loved him.

My fingertip swirled on the tip; massaging the drop of liquid showing he was ready for me. I lifted my fingertip to my mouth and swirled my tongue, tasting him. The rumble that escaped the back of his throat penetrated deep within me, and my body clenched with excited anticipation.

"Just you and me, Sav. Just us," Tate whispered. With one swift movement, he eased me down, my back flush against the desk. The sensation of the cold timber against my heated body was incredible.

Without a sign of hesitation, Tate slid deep inside me, filling me with what I had desperately missed. He stilled above me. Two months without him had led to instantaneous pleasure soaring through every inch of my body. My body clenched around him and the smirk sweeping over his face made my confidence soar. Pulling out and pushing in slowly, he gently rocked his body above mine, holding himself up with his hands. Confusion swept through me. This wasn't my Tate.

"Are you going to fuck me?" I moaned in desperation, raising one of my eyebrows in his direction. His eyes flashed to my stomach and I realized at that moment that he was scared of hurting me and Jellybean. I couldn't help but giggle. "Tate, if you aren't going to fuck me hard, then what the hell are we doing here?" I shifted down the desk and wrapped my legs aggressively around his hips, pushing his body closer to mine. "You won't hurt me."

I watched as his jaw tense and then the beast was unleashed. His hands encased around my waist and he pounded into me like it was the first time we had ever had sex. Every inch of my body shuddered and felt his desire with every thrust of his body. He was so deep. I bit my lip to stop the scream of pleasure soaring through the air. The sound of the desk shifting on the floor under the intensity of Tate's pounding increased the roar of my impending orgasm. Fuck, I had missed him.

"Come for me, Sav." His voice, his demands, his words unleashed a flood of desire inside me and I exploded into a rush of stars and heavy breathing as I came around him. Tate's body became rigid and stilled inside me like a statute as he came deep within me. Our breathing crashed together as our foreheads rested against each other's in a blatant attempt to be as close as possible. As I breathed out, he breathed me in. Within seconds, I felt him relax against me and finally we were as one again.

Tate pulled out slowly, his concerned eyes never leaving mine. Did he think I was going to freak out? My body finally felt relief after being wound so tight for the past two months and only Tate could relieve that.

"Thank you," I whispered.

Tate grabbed a tissue from his desk and softly and gently started to clean me up. My eyes slammed shut as the simplest of touch sent shudders through my body. His hands ran down my legs, sweeping his fingertips along my inner thigh. It was so innocent, but every hair on my body stood to attention. I was hopeless. Tate slid my panties up over my legs followed by my jeans. There was no way I wouldn't have the *I just got royally fucked* look plastered all over my face.

"You're blushing." Tate laughed softly. His hands gripped mine and pulled me to my feet. My protruding stomach grazed his, and I sighed in contentment and satisfaction.

"I know you wouldn't cheat on me, Tate. I was just scared. I felt ambushed. I felt like it was happening to me again and I can't handle that. I should have trusted you. I do trust you. And it's foreign for me to trust someone as much as I trust you. I should have told Chelsea to fuck off. I'm so sorry."

His strong arms wrapped around my waist, pulling me taut against his body. His scent flooded my nose, a mix of cologne, beer, and sex. He was perfection. My bump poked his abs, and I finally felt like I was home. The unease, the loneliness, and the confusion of the last two months were washed away the moment I was in his arms and, well, to be honest, the moment he took me on his desk.

His perfect lips splashed soft kisses on my still-sticky-with-sweat neck as he buried his face in my hair, his breathing calm yet deep. "I love you, Savannah Rae. Always." Tate words vibrated against my skin as his grip on my waist intensified.

"We are each other's forever, right?"

"You are my forever. We need to trust each other. I shouldn't have reacted the way I did about Blake and I regret it so much. You are my everything, Sav. If I have to chase you around the world, I will. If I have to shout it from the rooftops, I will. Just please stick with me. I'll prove my love every day if I have to. You are it for me. No one else."

"You are swooning again." I laughed softly, nuzzling into his chest and enjoying the rhythmic sound of his heart.

"So can I come to your place tonight?"

"Our place," I corrected. "I still want it to be our place."

"Can I move in tonight?"

Running my fingers through his hair, I kissed him quickly and pulled out my best bedroom eyes. "Um, Tate, while you are happily fucked and clearly boozed, I have something

I need to tell you."

"Should I be nervous?"

"I may have offered Lucas our spare room for a few weeks."

Confusion swept over his face. "Why isn't he staying with Ali?"

"Have you been drunk the whole time I've been gone and missed that Ali and Lucas are no longer together?"

"What the fuck? I saw them together . . . Oh. That was a month ago. Why? Where is she?"

"He hasn't said anything to me about it."

"Come on. We are finding him."

Tate clutched at my hand and hauled me out of the office and through the crowd as I protested. Two massive fears swam through me. One was how I looked. I still had the sated look of pleasure on my face and I knew my hair and makeup were an atrocious mess. And two, Tate plus copious amounts of alcohol confronting Lucas wasn't a good combination.

Lucas sat at the bar, talking to a new member of the Red Velvet staff I hadn't met yet. His eyes drifted towards Tate and me, and I gave him a pathetic smile in reassurance.

"Lucas, can I please have a word?" Tate asked in a surprisingly calm tone when we finally reached the bar.

Lucas shot a look at me before turning to Tate. "Uh sure."

"Not here. In my office." Tate squeezed my hand quickly and pulled me back towards his office.

Lucas looked at me with questioning eyes. I mouthed, "He knows you and Ali aren't together." Lucas's eyes widened and he looked over my shoulder at Tate.

I sat on the edge of the desk when we got to Tate's office.

Tate closed the door and crossed the room to stand beside me. Lucas shifted on his feet nervously, his gaze darting between Tate and me. Silence filled the air. As every second passed, the intensity increased.

"So you and Ali have broken up?" Tate asked in a low tone.

"Yes. We are on a break."

"Why?"

"Tate, that's none of our business," I objected, shooting Tate a *what the fuck* look and Lucas an *I'm sorry* look.

"Ali is my cousin, Sav, so it is certainly my business, and if Lucas is going to be staying with us, then I need to make sure someone who didn't hurt my cousin is moving in."

"You two are moving in together?" Lucas asked with a huge smile taking over his face.

"Focus, Lucas!" I shot, not hiding the smile I had on display.

"I asked her to marry me. She said no. I know we haven't been together long, but she is my future and I wanted to snap her up before someone else did. She said she needs time apart so I moved out."

"You asked her to marry you!" I shrieked and clapped like a baby seal. "Lucas, that is so sweet. How did you do it? Where were you? I want to know everything. Fuck it, I am crying."

Lucas and Tate both turned to me and smirked as warm tears cascaded over my cheeks. My emotions were a mess. Damn pregnancy hormones. I was now notorious for crying at the drop of a hat. I'd even cried in Starbucks the other day because I heard a song and because they didn't have my favorite mint chocolate Frappuccino available that day. Seriously, I was an emotional wreck.

"Don't you two laugh at me!" I warned with a hint of a smile being heard in my voice. "It's your fault I'm crying all the time." Moving towards Tate, I stood before him, my eyes scanning his face. He seemed to have sobered up quickly. I wanted to give him and Lucas time to talk. They needed to talk. "I am going to go and find Tanzi. Will you be okay in here?"

"We will be fine. We are just going to talk," Tate said softly, kissing my lips lightly and playfully slapping my arse as I turned and made my way out of the office.

An hour passed and there was still no sign of Tate and Lucas. To say I was worried was an understatement. To be honest, the thought of them brawling and now both lying unconscious in Tate's office had crossed my mind more than once. I sat with my glass of ice water, sipping it occasionally with my eyes glued to the closed office door. Talk about being on edge.

Suddenly, the door swung open and the sight before me nearly had me falling out of my chair. Tate and Lucas walked out of the office laughing, neither of them bleeding. My eyes bugged wide and I knew my mouth was hanging open. Tate shot a wink at me as he moved through the crowd towards the bar and Lucas walked towards me before slumping on the chair opposite me.

"That guy is too much." Lucas almost swooned.

I choked on my water. "What the fuck just happened?"

"All will be revealed. Let's just say I apologized for oogling at your boobs earlier and then we spoke for a good ten minutes about your girls." Lucas smirked at me and folded his arms over his chest. I looked at him wide-eyed and in shock.

Tate and Lucas were fiercely competitive with each other, but now it seemed they had skipped being friends and were now best friends.

"Oh and, Sav, you and that damn office smell of sweaty sex."

Chapter Four

Tate

WAKING UP WITH SAV IN my arms was hands-down one of my most favorite things in the world. Sex, surfing, and Mom's red velvet cupcakes were up there, but this . . . this was abso-fucking-lutely perfect. My eyes were still closed and I felt her shift in my arms. I knew exactly what she was doing when I heard the soft sigh escape her lips.

"Staring at a person while they are sleeping is creepy." My rough voice bounced off the walls of what I could now call *our* bedroom.

Her giggles filled my ears and I grabbed her tightly around her waist as she buried her face in the crook of my neck. We lay in silence, but I felt the increasing beat of her heart against my bare chest and I groaned as her nails ran through my hair. She pulled away and looked at me with eyes of intention and instantly my dick came alive.

"You have that look on your face again. Seriously, girl, you are going to fuck me to an early death."

"Now wouldn't that be a way to die?"

My laughter roared through the room. "I'd like to see my baby before you kill me though."

"If you are lucky, Mr. Connors. You are my personal sex toy, remember."

I rolled to my side as my eyes fluttered open for the second time today. My stomach growled and my head had a slight pounding from the alcohol I had drunk the night before.

The warmth of Sav's body against mine calmed me, but the growling of my stomach ultimately won. I slipped out of bed, found my boxer shorts, and silently walked out the room, closing the door softly behind me. The soft hum of the television and the smell of coffee filled the air and my senses came alive.

"Morning."

Lucas sat on the couch, eyes glued to the television, with a bowl of Lucky Charms resting on his lap. Ahh, that's right—we had a houseguest.

I collapsed on the couch beside him and flicked over to the surfing show I loved watching on Saturday mornings. We sat in silence, neither wanting to speak. I glanced at him out of the corner of my eye. This whole scene was too amusing. A deep chuckle rumbled from deep in my chest causing Lucas to look at me in confusion.

"What's so funny?"

"This. You and me sitting on a couch while Sav is in bed. We are actually talking civilly, I don't want to punch you in the face, and you aren't flirting with her. Can you believe we are here?"

"It's pretty funny. Don't worry. The only girl I want to flirt with now is your cousin, but like her cousin, she is too damn stubborn. Seriously, does stubbornness run through the veins of anyone with the Connors surname?"

"If you are planning on joining my family, then you better stop dissing our awesome qualities." I shot with a laugh.

The sound of the bedroom door opening startled us and we both turned. I couldn't help the smile taking over my face. Sav stood before us in her cute bright blue pajama shorts and tight cami that was covering her stomach. My eyes roamed every curve of her body in silent appreciation.

"You have a very active child this morning," Sav yawned as she lowered herself on the couch between Lucas and me before grabbing the bowl out of his hands and proceeded to shovel Lucky Charms down her throat.

"Is the baby kicking?" Lucas asked with a raised eyebrow.

Nodding, Sav handed the bowl to me and shifted on the couch towards Lucas. Taking one of Lucas's hands she rested it on her lower stomach after lifting her cami to reveal her bare skin. His eyes grew wide and his gaze didn't move from his hand.

"Holy fuck," Lucas stammered. "Was that . . . ? Was that a kick? That is amazing! Tate you need to feel this."

A low laugh escaped as I watched Lucas's face dissolve into a smile. "I had plenty of Daddy and Jellybean time last night. This is Uncle Lucas time." I shot him a grin, sat back on the couch, and watched as Lucas was overcome with the amazement of Jellybean. To be honest, it made me super proud of my kid.

Hospitals were one of those places I had no opinion of. I spent plenty of time in the emergency waiting room during the years. Memories of the time I broke my hand in a bar fight, the time Tanzi sprained her ankle trying to re-enact the Baywatch opening scene on the beach at home, and the time my family and I sat for hours waiting on news of my grandfather, who had fallen ill, flooded me as I now sat beside Sav. Today we were going to see Jellybean and I couldn't wipe the smile off my face but by the way that Sav's hand was strangling mine, I didn't think she shared my excitement.

"I hate hospitals," she grumbled, practically forcing herself onto my lap.

"The next time we are here will be the moment we hold little Jellybean, so then hospitals will be amazing," I cooed. Seriously, where the fuck had my balls gone? Since when had I begun talking all this soft shit?

She swiveled beside me and narrowed her eyes as amusement swept over her face.

"Since when did you become a guru of inspiration?"

"I am a changed man, Sav." I fired a suggestive wink at her. "I am now a sensitive new-age guy." The roll of her eyes that I received made it clear that she didn't believe a word I'd said.

"You are delusional. Please don't change too much. I like

you just the way you are."

My eyebrows rose. "Is this an invitation to keep being an asshole?"

"That's my favorite part of you."

"Stop flirting with me. You know I love it when you talk dirty."

"You think this is dirty? Just you wait." Sav licked her lips seductively and my cock jumped at the thought.

"Until?"

"Savannah Rae, the doctor is ready to see you now."

Sav's smirk filled her face and I squeezed her hand in warning. She was such a fucking tease at times.

We followed the woman through winding hallways and entered a surprisingly fresh and inviting room with a single bed and a machine that I knew would allow us to see Jellybean. A wave of anxiety rolled over me and my fears for the future rushed in like the biggest waves I'd ever ridden. I was about to see the person who would rely on me for protection, for unconditional love, and for safety.

My fears of the future hadn't dwindled, and for the past two months, a small piece of paper had been burning a hole in my wallet. That small piece of paper held the phone number of my father, the man who had helped create me but who had also made me the shell of a man I was today.

"Tate, where has your mind taken you?" Sav's soft voice ripped me from my thoughts. I blinked and offered her the best smile I could muster, but I knew my face was showing my deepest fears.

Would I ever feel like I wasn't going to fuck up? What should have been the happiest moment of my life was turning to shit because of a prick of a man I hadn't seen for twenty-three years. Sav's thumb swept over my knuckles before she lifted my hand to her mouth and lightly kissed each knuckle. A simple gesture to some, but to me it was a gesture of faith.

"You aren't him."

My eyes moved away from Sav's as my emotions bubbled inside of me. I never wanted her to ever look at me as anything but strong and protective. I had already let my defenses down once in New York and I needed to keep them in check here.

"You aren't him, Tate," Sav repeated, her voice laced with promise and reassurance. Her tiny hands gripped at my forearm, and with a little hesitation, I allowed my eyes to find hers. There was no fear or agreement looking back at me. Her eyes spoke to me with hope, understanding, and most importantly, a look of us. She had a faith in me I'd never known could exist, and that scared me the most. If she believed in me, then that meant I had to believe in myself, right?

Nodding slowly, I stepped towards her and wrapped my arms around her body. The body that was my comfort.

"Savannah, it's good to see you. Let's get this show on the road and see this little one."

I stepped away from Sav as, who I assumed was, Doctor Johnson walked into the room holding a bright blue file and a smile on his face. He was a middle-aged man with a head full of grey hair, deep laugh lines around his eyes, and a bushy white beard. If I'd believed in Santa, I would think he was Sav's doctor.

After placing the file on his desk, Doctor Johnson directed at me, "You must be the father?" Before he shook my hand confidently. I simply nodded, suddenly mute, and matched his grip. "Okay, Sav. If you want to hop up on the bed and lift your shirt over your stomach, we will get started."

I followed Sav across the room like a puppy dog and stopped just short of the bed. Sav turned towards me, firing a heartwarming smile and handed me her bag. My nerves were running rampant, and my eyes jumped from Sav's gorgeous greens to the bag she had placed in my hands. It was almost like my brain had dissolved to mush and I had no idea what I was supposed to be doing.

"Put my bag on the table and then come and hold my hand while we see our baby."

The doctor squeezed the gel onto Sav's stomach, causing her body to jump slightly from the bed at the cold sensation. Her free arm wrapped around my waist and her hand rested on the small of my back, her fingertips lifting the edge of my shirt and sitting so softly on my bare skin like she was locking me in.

My hand tightened on the hand I was gripping for dear life the moment the doctor swirled the weird-looking stick on her tan stomach. The silence of the room was deafening, but then out of the darkness on the small television screen in front of us came the image both Sav and I were waiting for.

My eyes widened and my throat suddenly felt dry as he or she appeared. I was looking at absolute perfection, and at that moment, it was like the world was giving me a giant slap in the face, everything became real.

I realized in that moment what it felt like to be living entirely for another human being, what it felt like to love another human being more than the air I breathed, what it felt like to be so protective and devoted to a person that wasn't even here.

My eyes burned into the screen, overwhelmed with the emotion of the miracle I was witnessing. I wasn't one to often cry, but I felt an onslaught of tears just begging to be unleashed.

Out of the silence, the most amazing and life-changing sound saturated the room—the fast beat of our baby's heart. I knew my hand gripped Sav's too tightly, but she didn't complain. Sav was letting me have my moment, a moment I would never forget. When Doctor Johnson started talking, I tore my eyes from the screen and looked at Sav and his words soon disappeared because all I could focus on was Sav and the look of complete happiness on her face.

I had always known she was beautiful. I had always known she was sexy as hell. But seeing her here with the look of contentment on her face, her blonde hair feathered on the pillow behind her, and her face makeup-free and utterly glowing, I had never met such an exquisite beauty.

"I will go and book your next appointment, so feel free to clean up and I will meet you in reception."

Doctor Johnson walked out of the room, leaving Sav and me on our own. She smiled as she unleashed her lock on my body and grabbed the tissues from the table beside the bed.

"Let me," I stated and took the tissues from her hand.

Slowly, I pushed her shirt up higher and tucked it under the bottom of her bra. I could feel her eyes watching me closely, and the sound of her breath hitching under my touch made my body react immediately.

"You are giving me the greatest gift a man could ever ask of a woman. You are giving me a child, a new beginning, a new love—something I never thought I could ever deserve," I admitted effortlessly, my words were the most honest part of who I was. "I love you so much, Sav."

Our eyes locked as I continued to clean up her stomach without another word. We were a walking contradiction. Both of us had promised ourselves during the darkest times of our lives that we would never give our hearts to another, but here we were, promising our hearts to the other to keep or break, offering our souls to love or crush, and handing our insecurities to the other to comfort or destroy. But what I was quickly learning was that the love we shared wasn't like others. We had our own crazy, fucked-up way of loving, and finally, I was totally okay with it.

CHAPTER
Five

Savannah

I KNEW MY DAY WASN'T GOING as planned when I receive a memo from Mr. Davenport requesting my attendance to an urgent meeting in the boardroom five minutes after I turned up for work.

I had been back in LA for a month and I'd jumped straight back into work. I loved my job, and the office gossips had finally realized that I wasn't carrying Mr. Davenport's love child, so things were semi back to normal.

Standing from my desk, I grabbed my morning hot chocolate and waddled through the office in all my six-and-a-half-month pregnant glory towards Mr. Davenport's office to await my fate. What could I have possibly done? The mind boggles.

For once my life seemed to be in perfect alignment. Tate and I were blissfully in love, Lucas and Ali were back together after having a heart-to-heart that had resulted in a very loud make-up session in the apartment—much to Tate's disgust—

and Jack and Tanzi were enjoying making their apartment their own. The events of New York City seemed so far in the past, and thankfully my insecurities about my relationship with Tate had all but vanished.

As I moved through the office, I was stopped at every desk. Questions about how my pregnancy was going were fired at me, and more recently, the question of whether I knew the sex of Jellybean was the most popular topic of conversation. I was desperate to find out, but Tate was adamant that he wanted a surprise; he wasn't one to plan, so he didn't want our baby's life already planned before he or she was born. He didn't want Jellybean's room painted. He didn't want all of the clothes to be picked. He just wanted the surprise. I had to admit that it was freaking adorable.

My hand grabbed hold of the boardroom door handle and I froze as I heard three distinct voices through the door. As I opened it slowly, my eyes landed on Mr. Davenport, Tate, and Chelsea. Tate was dressed in the black pants and crisp Red Velvet shirt I had seen him walk out of the apartment in this morning. He looked business-owner chic, as I'd told him this morning while lying in bed with an aching body and ragged breathing from yet another sex marathon. The further along my pregnancy I got, the more adventurous we had to get in the bedroom.

"Hi again, Savannah. As always, it's a pleasure." Chelsea, wearing red patent stripper heels, took a step towards me and glared at me.

"Don't fucking talk to her, Chelsea," Tate demanded from across the room.

I protectively wrapped my arms around myself as I stared

at Mr. Davenport for answers. Why the fuck was she here? Instantly, my walls went up as the feeling of betrayal etched within me. I refused to be hurt again; I refused to let this bitch cause any more drama in my life. Both Tate and Mr. Davenport knew how much I despised Chelsea, but still here she was, at one of my safe places, wearing jeans that were a size too small and a shirt that was barely holding in her overinflated fake boobs, looking like a two-dollar hooker. The moment my eyes landed on Chelsea, a torrent of flashbacks hit me. The visuals of her riding Tate made vomit rise from the pits of my stomach and threaten to spill out over the plush carpet of the boardroom.

"Does someone want to explain what the hell is happening because I am about to walk out of this room if I don't get answers." My words spat out with venom while my eyes threw daggers across the room at her. The smirk that painted her lips only fueled my fire.

"Savannah, can I have a word?" Mr. Davenport's strong voice boomed beside me.

Oh yeah. Leave Tate and Chelsea in a room together, on their own. Nice thinking, Einstein.

I followed Mr. Davenport out into the open floor plan of the Beautify office. Thankfully we moved just outside of the glass wall of the boardroom so I could still watch her like a hawk. Tate stood on one side of the room, his face buried in his iPhone. He didn't acknowledge anything she was saying to him. I couldn't help but feel my ego shoot through the roof. *That's right, bitch. He is mine.*

"So are you going to fill me in? Why the hell is *she* here? Why is Tate here? You know I want to scratch her eyeballs out and feed them to her."

"Yes I am very much aware of your wanted acts of violence towards her, but she is under contract with Beautify London and for some fucked-up reason that means I have to play nice with her. She is the feature model in the lingerie photo shoot next week."

"I refuse to work on the shoot."

"You are running the shoot."

He has got to be kidding me. I would rather punch myself in the face than be anywhere near her. "I'd rather quit."

"You are such a drama queen. You are running the shoot and you are going to excel at it. This is your time, Savannah. What I am about to say is me being your family and not your boss, so listen carefully and make it known that I will deny everything if it comes out." He looked around and leaned in close to me. "You have *FULL* control of this shoot. One wrong move and she is out, and I don't mean just this shoot. She will never work with Beautify again, and we are the biggest magazine around at the moment. She may think that her shit doesn't stink but you have the brains, the means, and the retaliation. Just make sure you are professional while you do it."

"So I can't punch her in the face?"

"Let me check with our lawyers." Mr. Davenport winked at me and ushered me back into the boardroom without answering my question.

Tate looked up the moment I walked into boardroom and rushed across to me with pleading eyes. His hand grabbed mine and pulled me close enough that my senses were overcome by his scent. My eyes closed briefly as I became lost in delight and memories of only a mere few hours ago. An obnoxious scoff from the other side of the room ripped me back and my mood soured instantly.

"Don't go back there, Sav. Remember you and me, only ever you and me. Remember this morning." He dropped his face to my neck, and the feeling of his breathing and lips on my skin as he whispered, made me forget everything that was happening in this room. "I can still feel my cock so deep in you that I saw stars. Remember the way your body felt as you came undone around me. Every time with you is perfection. Forget her."

"Are we going to get on with this?" Chelsea bitched. "Or are you two going to keep pretending everything is perfect in your little made-up world?"

That was it. Professionalism could get screwed. I spun around out of Tate's arms with fire roaring through my body. "Wanna know what perfect is, Chelsea? Perfect is the fact that Tate and I are talking about how we made love this morning and how we are probably going to again at lunchtime and probably again tonight. That is perfection, Chelsea, and if it is made up, then I'm living the best fucking fairytale I could have ever created."

As a standoff of epic proportions began between Chelsea and me. My hackles rose, and I knew I would never back down from her. I wasn't a revengeful person, but as soon as someone starts hurting the people I care about and throwing around half-arsed accusations, they will see the wrath of Savannah. This could be the very reason I chose to have limited female friends. It was easier than having to deal with the bullshit games girls were notorious for starting, and clearly this was why I never hid my intentions when it came to men in the past.

Be clear as day and no feelings came to the surface. I felt Mr. Davenport sigh beside me and I swallowed hard. *Professional, Savannah. For him.*

I still didn't back down as I spoke. "So I am assuming the—"

"Um, excuse me? I was told that I needed to be here."

Our heads snapped to the door opening slowly, and I couldn't believe who I was looking at, could this day get any weirder? Blake freaking Ryan had just walked through the door looking all rock star-ish. This was the first time we had seen each other since he had left New York for London.

His eyes widened to the size of saucers as he took everything in. Dressed head to toe in black, he was wearing a shirt that sat snug against his body, and his tattoos were glistening under the boardroom lights. He was born to be a rock star.

His eyes bounced between Tate and me and dropped to my hand gripped tightly in Tate's and a smile tugged at his lips. Tate's body stiffened against mine and his hand squeezed mine to the point of hurt like he was making his claim on me.

"Stop it," I hissed and shot him a pleading look.

"Sorry, just habit," he whispered then peppered my jaw with a kiss.

"Thanks for coming in, Blake." Mr. Davenport shuffled papers on the large conference table and looked towards Blake, holding out a pen and what looked to be a contract. "So you have been booked for the shoot next week and we are now just finalizing details. Savannah will be running the shoot on behalf of Beautify and Chelsea will be the female model for the campaign. If you can just sign here, we are good to go."

Blake shook his head and shot a disgusted look at Chelsea. "Are you serious? I can't work with her."

"See? I told you, Savannah. Even Blake doesn't want to work with you in your pathetic little fairytale world you are supposedly living in," Chelsea spat before she threw her straw-looking hair over her shoulder and strutted towards Blake. I watched Blake closely; the look sweeping over his face was priceless.

"I wasn't talking about Savannah, you idiot. I cannot work with you, Chelsea. I tend to not want to associate with fucked-up, conniving bitches."

I couldn't hide the smile of victory tugging on my lips. *Blake Ryan, you genius.* The look of utter devastation Chelsea was wearing made me feel like a million bucks. I still had no clue of the history that Chelsea and Blake shared.

"Well isn't this going to be a fun shoot," Mr. Davenport mumbled under his breath.

"Since when did you become a model?" Tate suddenly asked Blake.

"My band got signed. The record company believes I have a certain look and decided to book me for this shoot. Believe me, I am not impressed. This is the first and last shoot I'll be doing. Sucks that it has to be with her."

Mr. Davenport walked towards the door and closed it loudly, causing me to jump. I suddenly felt like I was fifteen and getting in trouble for the one and only time I smoked a cigarette. My laughter filled the air as I tried to pull myself together. Yep. Here I was, laughing at the most inappropriate of times. Four sets of eyes turned to me, which only caused my laughter to grow louder.

"And what is so funny, Sav?" Mr. Davenport asked with

a chuckle in his pathetic attempt to hold some authority in the boardroom.

I glanced around at everyone again, swallowed my laughter, and wiped the tear that had escaped my eye. "This whole situation is hilarious. Fine, I will run this shoot but under my terms. I am assuming the shoot is at Red Velvet and that's why you are here?" I turned to Tate, who nodded in agreement. "Chelsea, this is my shoot. You fuck up once and you will never work with Beautify again. Blake, if I am going to do this, you are too. Tate, I want Jack working on this shoot, and Mr. Davenport, Tanzi is working with me."

Silence filled the room before they all agreed.

"I'm done. I'll be at my desk."

I walked out of the boardroom and strutted through the office with determination in my step. My emotions simmered just below the surface but I refused to show how I was truly feeling. Being near her, seeing her looking at Tate like she was fucking him in her thoughts caused my heart to twist and literally ache. I needed to forget that video, but every time I thought of it, I was taken back to that moment in New York. I knew I needed to forget or at least push it aside. I dropped my head in my hands and sighed deeply as I slumped into my office chair. The air around me shifted as someone stood by my desk.

"You okay?" Tate's deep voice questioned. I raised my head from my hands and looked at him. He was painfully beautiful. His eyes begged for truth, but this wasn't the time or place, especially knowing that Maureen, Beautify's main office gossip, had her ears pricking up at the desk across the room desperate for the scent of fresh scandal.

"Yep. I'm great."

"You are a terrible liar."

"Tate, I just want to get my work done, forget about her, and try and stop thinking about what is filling my head."

He swung my chair around so I was facing him and he crouched down so his face was opposite mine. We were in the middle of the Beautify Office and I know our hushed voices were drawing people's attention. Next thing I knew, I'd be getting accused of cheating on Mr. Davenport.

"You and me. Not her. I know, no matter what I say, it won't get those images out of your head, and I wish I could climb in your head and tear them to shreds, but I need you to tell me that we can get past this, that you and I are stronger than her. I need that, Sav. You are the strongest thing in my life. I can't let that strength be destroyed."

I leaned forward and placed my lips on his. His hands grabbed hold of the chair and pulled me closer to him before his hand moved to the back of my head and hauled me deeper into the kiss. My tongue ran the length of his bottom lip before I tugged on it with my teeth. Tate's tongue ploughed into my mouth with ownership. If I could kiss him for the rest of my life, I would die a happy woman.

"Remember where you two are." Mr. Davenport's voice hovered around us and I pulled away quickly as my cheeks flushed. My eyes bounded around the office, but thankfully no one was looking.

"Well, blushy, I've gotta get back to work. Seriously, your blushing is the cutest fucking thing ever." He kissed me hastily one last time before taking off through the office, his laughter heard until he disappeared into the elevator.

The world was a miraculous place, sometimes beautiful and sometimes utterly fucked up. The fact that I was about to run a shoot with Chelsea made my anxiety soar to a whole new level. It made me question why the world had decided to fuck me over. All I wanted was for her to disappear into the deep black pit of a hole she came from and never return, but here I was, on this cold and rainy Tuesday night, sitting on my living room floor with my peanut butter and banana sandwich and looking through promo photos of her. If I was able to drink, I'd be pissed off my tits right about now.

My mood was as dark as the thunder rumbling outside my windows and my anger intensified with every photo that I held in my hands. I wondered how long it would be until I tore her photos in half and set them alight with the candles burning around the room.

Tate was at work and I knew he wouldn't be home until well after midnight, so I had hours of solitude on my own, hours of time for my mind to play games with me. My eyes moved down my body and landed on my stomach just as Jellybean decided to kick and remind me of he or she's existence.

As I flipped through photo after photo of Chelsea in lingerie I knew I couldn't be on my own. I tossed the photos I was holding out of my hand and found my phone hidden under one photo in particular of Chelsea in some skimpy black lingerie, boobs and arse hanging out everywhere. I could swear I tasted vomit just looking at it.

"Tanzi, can you come to my place and bring Chinese food and chocolate?" I begged on the phone.

"You okay?"

"I need my best friend and greasy food."

"Be there in ten."

I smiled down at the cell in my hand and thanked my lucky stars that Tanzi Connors had decided to email a stranger on the other side of the world all those months ago. What had started as a random email from a girl who I thought had the coolest name ever now had turned into a friendship that I'd always wanted and never thought I'd get. I was never one of those girls who had a lot of female friends but Tanzi was refreshing, crazy, and hilarious. Our first email was the generic 'congratulations, I look forward to meeting you, blah blah blah' but the second email was when it all started. The moment she mentioned tequila and the beach, I knew I had found my first friend in Los Angeles, and as they say the rest is history. The fact that my child is going to have her as an aunt and that the love of my life is her brother just made it so much more special.

The door of my apartment swung open with a thud. "Savannah, where are you?"

"Down here," I replied.

Tanzi came into my vision and waved the chocolate I had demanded in the air with a smile. She stood before me and looked at the photos splashed over my floor, her eyes wide as she worked out what she was looking at, her smile instantly dropped.

"Why the fuck are you looking at photos of slut face? Seriously, Savannah, you need to stop torturing yourself. This is not going to help. You are a masochistic bitch." Tanzi's face went stiff, her eyes narrowing at the particular photo of Chelsea that I was holding.

"It's for work."

"Look, Mr. Davenport may be the man I fantasize about meeting in the mailroom at work and fucking his brains out while stamps stick to my ass." She winked at me as my face screwed up. "But he has no fucking clue if he is making you do this. Seriously, what the hell is going through his head?"

I swallowed the bile that rose from the pits of my stomach and shook my head, desperate for the images Tanzi had just painted so vividly to leave my brain. "Firstly, please do not ever talk about fucking Mr. Davenport and secondly before you joke about becoming my stepmother again, I would never allow it."

Tanzi took a place on the floor beside me and leaned back on the couch, her legs out in front of her. As she ripped the picture out of my hand, I watched as her eyes scanned over the photo before looking at me and rolling her eyes. "She doesn't even have good tits, Sav."

"Look at my girls. They are so much better. At least I didn't have to spend thousands of dollars to get these bad boys." I grabbed my boobs softly and squeezed them together, almost choking on my double D's. "You're thinking of motor-boating them right now, aren't you?"

"Don't tempt me, woman." Tanzi smirked.

"Nuzzle right in there, Tanzi. I won't tell Tate. It can be our little secret."

CHAPTER
Six

Tate

Tell Sav you love her

A RANDOM MESSAGE WAS WAITING ON my phone when I got back to my office after doing my final before-close check of Red Velvet. What the fuck was Tanzi talking about? Shoving my wallet and phone deep into my pockets, I walked through the now empty bar, switched off the main lights, and exited the front door. My thoughts jumped over different scenarios about what the hell could have happened in the eight hours since I'd left Sav at Beautify.

Walking into the darkness of our apartment, I smiled at the familiar scent of Sav in the air. Throwing my keys down on the bench, I opened the fridge, grabbed an apple juice, and headed to the couch with all intentions of winding down in my solitude.

I loved my job, I loved Red Velvet, but shit, it could be

tiring at times. Tonight had been slow, and usually I'd love a slow night at work because I could catch up on the mountain of paperwork and organize upcoming launch nights and expansion opportunities, but tonight it allowed me to think about things way too much.

Tomorrow I was hoping my balls would drop and I'd grow a set and contact my father. I needed to get it over and done with, and I needed to get it done before Jellybean arrived. I hadn't told Sav of my plans yet and I knew I had to wait until the right moment. It wasn't something I wanted to drop on her without knowing if I'd actually go through with it, it was a stress she didn't need.

Finding the remote, I flicked on the television and fell back into the over-plush cushions on the couch. Thankfully, instead of having to sit through my mind-numbing infomercials, a replay of last year's Super Bowl came on as the screen as the television burst to life. Loosening my tie and pulling my shirt out of my pants, I felt the wanted feelings of relaxation arrive. After I threw my tie on the couch beside me, my hand brushed something and my eyes couldn't believe what they were seeing.

My fingers flipped through photo after photo of Chelsea in various poses and wearing nothing but lingerie. Why did Sav have these and why had she been looking at them? Suddenly, Tanzi's voice appeared. 'Tell Sav you love her.' Was Sav feeling insecure and questioning our relationship? Was she having doubts about us? Was she punishing herself for something she had absolutely nothing to do with?

I stood from the couch and looked towards the closed door of our bedroom. My urge to show her what she meant to me was burning within me, but I couldn't always show her with sex. Making my way through the apartment, I quietly opened the bedroom door, and the light from the candle slowly burning on the dresser allowed a soft life to bounce of the walls and swamp the dark space.

Sav lay cuddled up to my pillow with the sheet barely covering her body. The door that led to the balcony was open and the cool Los Angeles air cushioned the air. Her hair surrounded her beautiful face on the pillow, I could only hope that our child got her looks.

I sat down softly on the edge of the bed and watched over her. So peaceful, so beautiful, and all mine. I still had no clue how the hell I'd gotten this girl.

"Sav, wake up," I whispered and ran my fingertip down her cheek. She squirmed in bed, and slowly her eyes fluttered open. A smile appeared on her lips as she looked up at me.

"Tate what's wrong?" Her voice was husky from sleep, her words spilling with concern.

I grabbed her hand and pulled her up until she was sitting. "I need you to get out of bed for a minute."

Sav nodded slowly, her eyes never leaving mine as she swung her bare legs over the edge of the bed and stood before me wearing just one of my t-shirts.

"I saw the photos in the living room," I whispered. My fingers interlocked with hers, and the sound of her breathing increasing hit my ears.

"Tate, I don't know—"

"Don't say anything." My finger rested on her lips and her head nodded in agreement. Once I was satisfied that she wouldn't speak, I dropped my finger and brushed my lips softly over hers. "Just trust me, okay?"

My hands ran up her bare arms. Instantly, goose bumps spread over her cool skin and her eyes closed at the sensation. She was so reactive to my touch and I loved every second of it, but this wasn't what this was about. I needed her to see herself how I saw her.

"Look at me, Sav."

Her eyes pried open and looked at me with heated hesitation. Our eyes searched each other's for unspoken words. I didn't break our contact as my hands moved down her body, searching for the hem of my shirt that looked so fucking perfect on her. She gasped as my hands moved inside the material and skimmed the delicate skin of her hips. I felt the smirk form on my lips as my hands brushed her bare hipbone, showing me that she wasn't wearing panties. So fucking sexy.

"Lift your arms, Savannah."

Without a word, Sav raised her arms and I slipped the cotton t-shirt over her head. She shook her head and her hair swished around her face. She stood before me in all of her naked form. My goddess. My Savannah. Her mouth twitched as if she were going to say something, but she closed it tight while her eyes finally smiled at me. I silently walked to her drawers, knowing exactly what I was looking for. I pulled out the black and baby pink panties, suspenders, and bra that had turned me on many times in the past. Her eyes followed wherever I was, but she remained still and didn't say a word.

Moving back towards her, I gently placed the lingerie on our bed and stood before her. I couldn't stop my hands from moving to her naked skin. It was as if it were silently begging me to take ownership. My hands cupped her face, pulling her lips to mine. Our kiss wasn't frantic. It wasn't full of lust and need; it wasn't aggressive or dominating. It was soft, pure, loving, and gentle. With the back of my fingers, I traced every inch of her skin, outlining her lips, sweeping across her collarbones, caressing the bare skin of her breasts and expanding stomach, and cupping her hips gently.

"I love you, Miss Rae."

Dropping to my knees, I gazed up at her and was met with her eyes burning into mine. Grabbing the panties from the bed, I placed them on the floor beside me before turning my full attention back to Savannah. I lifted each of her feet, softly placing a kiss on each of the soles. Sliding the panties over her ankles and up her calves, I kissed the delicate skin as I moved the panties slowly up her toned legs. I stopped when I reached her knees and spread her legs wider so they would hold the panties in place.

I shuffled forward and let my lips fall to her bare skin and traced the length of her thigh with the tip of my tongue while my fingertips swept over the other, giving it just as much attention. Her breathing became heavy, and suddenly her hand found my hair and her fingertips moved through it, her nails scraping my scalp with a soothing sensation that stopped me momentarily.

My mouth continued its assault on her thighs, splashing kisses on every inch of her beautiful skin. I moved swiftly but softly to where I knew I wanted to go. I needed to taste her. I needed her to feel me. The moment my mouth connected with her, Sav went rigid against me. I wrapped my arms around her hips, stopping her from collapsing to the ground. She was standing before me, naked and submitting entirely to me.

My tongue traced every inch of her heat, my senses tumbling into overload. Her taste, her smell, and her noises were taking over every part of me. I knew she was close. The tightness of her grip on my hair was a clear indication. I moved in closer, my tongue sweeping over every inch of her now soaking pussy. When I felt her gasp loudly, I nibbled on her clit and she shuddered around me with the sound of her moaning my name over and over again falling from her lips.

The warmth and intensity of her orgasm flooded around me and I refused to move until I had enjoyed every last drop. Savannah Rae, could she be any more perfect for me? My breathing increased rapidly as I pulled away from her. I was losing control of this whole situation and I knew I had to pull it in. This wasn't about me; it was purely about her. Grabbing hold of my wildly growing need to be inside her, I continued sliding her panties up over her thighs and gave her a suggestive tap on the ass, loving the sound of her raspy giggle. I turned on my knees, grabbed the suspenders that were bunched with the bra beside me, and repeated the tortuously slow process.

With every sweep of my fingertips on her reactive skin, she gasped. I dragged my fingers up her legs, skimming over her knees and tracing her thighs, and followed with my lips. This time, I dragged my tongue, sweeping over her skin, tasting the deliciousness of the body wash she had used earlier that night. I leaned in and placed my lips on her panties, the wetness soaking through the lace, and instantly my eyes closed as I was overcome by the scent of my perfect Aussie.

Her hands found my hair again, and she gripped it for dear life. The pain of her grip and the smell of her arousal almost made me forget what I was doing. I pulled my face away, breathing in deeply as I did and shot a look of pure lust at her. The thought of being buried deep inside of her caused my now hard cock to ache.

"Savannah, I never knew perfection until I met you."

I fumbled around the floor, patting the space for the bra I had left there, not wanting to break the trance her eyes had on me. My fingers brushed across the satin and I grabbed hold. I rose to my feet in front of her, her eyes moving with mine. I ran my hands up the side of her body, a shiver ran down her sides, and her eyes closed under my touch, breaking our contact.

Lifting her arms one at a time, I slipped her arms in the straps of her bra. Moving around her, I didn't remove my fingers from her skin. My eyes were locked with hers through the reflection of the mirror. I stood behind her, staring at her, drinking in her body. I hooked her bra and my eyes ran the length of her body.

"Stay there," I whispered before grazing her shoulder blade with a soft kiss. She nodded in response.

I ran out of the bedroom in desperate search of my phone. The ache in my shorts was almost to the point of pain, and I needed release fast.

"Fuck!" I hissed to myself.

I grabbed my phone from the couch and rushed back to the bedroom to find Sav standing exactly where I'd left her. Her eyes rose from the carpeted floor and a shy smile formed on her lips. I could see the faint tint of embarrassment cover her cheeks.

"You are blushing again." I winked at her and lifted my phone up.

"What are you doing?" she gasped in horror as the sound of a photo being taken echoed through the room. Her hands shot up as she attempted to cover her almost naked body.

"Do you trust me?"

She nodded slowly. Her hands and arms remained firmly over her body and her head dropped, her hair falling over her face.

"Trust me, Savannah."

Slowly she lifted her head and her eyes met mine. Hesitation greeted me. I took a step towards her, my face millimeters from hers and I spoke against her lips. "Just you and me."

Stepping back, I lifted my phone up so that she was on full display to me. Like a goddess standing before me, she allowed me to snap away on my phone. There was a point to this. I wasn't just being some sleazy creep. When I finished, I slid my phone in my back pocket and moved so I stood behind her. Wrapping my arms around her waist, I rested my open palms on her pregnant stomach and we stood before the mirror, our eyes meeting in the reflection.

"You, Savannah, are the only person I want to look at in lingerie. Those photos you were looking at in the living room are nothing compared to what I am looking at now. The way you glow in the candlelight, the curves of your body I cannot refuse to touch, and the taste of your skin on my tongue are all I'll ever need. If I have to remind you every day, I will."

"Tate, you need to take me to bed now. I know you have just dressed me but you need to have me naked within the next few seconds. I've kinda wrecked the panties anyway." She grabbed my hand placing it at the front of her thoroughly soaked panties. "That is all your doing."

As quickly as the words had left her mouth, my hands were unfastening the hook of her bra and I moved to stand in front of her and my mouth gently fell on her peaked nipple. A deep groan escaped her lips as the moment of ecstasy swept over her. Giving her what she wanted was my ultimate pleasure.

"Tate, that is amazing."

I moved from one nipple to the other, stopping the onslaught on her beautiful tits only when I felt her hand slip in the front of my pants and grab hold of my aching cock. Her fingertip swept over the tip of my cock, and I groaned in a frenzied state of abyss as her hand wrapped around my length, gently squeezing as she ran her hand up and down painfully slowly.

"This is mine," Sav breathed deeply.

With my cock about ready to show her exactly how much she owned me, I regretfully pulled away and dropped to my knees in front of her. With eager fingers, I unclasped her suspenders and slid them down her legs, throwing them to the corner of the room. I sat back on my heels to take a moment to admire the view in front of me—my girlfriend standing before me in nothing but her panties, with the flicker of light from the candles dancing over her skin, her breathing heavy and her eyes hooded with desire.

"I want you to make love to me tonight, Tate," her words begged as her eyes craved.

I stood quickly, wrapped my hands around her waist, and lifted her to my hips. A soft giggle escaped her lips as I carried her to the bed. After I lowered her softly, she crawled back, her eyes never leaving me. I slowly started unbuttoning my shirt and slid it over my shoulders, chucking it to the end of the bed.

"Fuck, I love your tattoo," Sav sighed from the bed. I looked down at my Connors tattoo, and before I could say anything, Savannah crawled to the edge of the bed. Her lips were kissing every letter etched on my skin. Her tongue magnificently slid along every stroke of scripted writing while my hands got lost in the flowing blonde mane down her back.

"You are going to have that name one day."

Just as quickly as she had started caressing my body with her tongue, she ripped her body away from me and sat back. There was no way in the world that I could even attempt to read the expression swamping her face. Was it desire, hesitation, need, or fear?

"Whether it takes a month, a year, two years, or ten, you will become a Connors."

We were in the room staring each other down, Sav completely at the mercy of the thoughts circling her mind and me completely at the mercy of her. I hadn't hidden the fact there would be no one else but her. She knew my idea of a future included her and Jellybean, and that meant all of us having my surname. Marriage! Fuck! I was never the guy who thought of marriage. My idea of a future had been full of loose women, booze, and jumping from one bed to another. But that was until Savannah had crashed into my world and made me believe that I could have a different future. Now all I wanted was to run away with her to a chapel in Vegas and put a ring on her finger, buy her our dream house, and spend our days filling it with memories.

The shrill of my phone barreled through the air, and both Sav and I jumped. Who the hell was calling me at this time?

'Security' flashed on the screen and I cursed under my breath. "I have to take this." I held up my phone. "We aren't finished here though Sav so get ready for me."

After walking through the apartment in complete darkness after being on the phone for twenty minutes while someone walked through Red Velvet and found nothing, my frustration levels were through the roof and all I wanted was to be in bed. As I stepped through the bedroom doors, I sighed at the sight before me. Savannah lay curled up on my side of the bed, back to hugging my pillow and being sound asleep. She hadn't dressed and was wearing her panties, the rest of her body exposed. I laughed softly to myself and undressed, slipping in beside her.

She rolled towards me and snuggled in close to my chest. "I fell asleep," she muttered against my skin.

I wrapped my arm around her. "Go back to sleep."

Lifting her head from my chest, she opened her eyes and gazed at me. "I love you, Mr. Connors."

And at that moment, I knew she would definitely become Mrs. Connors one day.

Chapter Seven

Savannah

MY BODY WAS HIS TEMPLE, and boy, was I enjoying every second of it. After the events of the night before and then him finally allowing me to satisfy him in the early hours of this morning, I was ready to take on whatever Chelsea could throw at me today. Even though he wasn't going to be with me, I sure as hell made it so I could feel him deep within me, and now my body was deliciously achy in all the right places.

Pulling a brush through my hair, I looked in the mirror and smiled at Tate as his body filled the bathroom behind me. His hair was all over the place, his eyes puffy from sleep, and the stubble I adored graced his perfect jaw. The man was pure sex.

"Hey." He kissed my shoulder softly, his arms wrapping around my waist and pulling me close to his chest as he nuzzled his face into my neck.

"Will you be at the club today?" I asked, softly knowing that I had requested Jack run the event.

"I'll be locked away in my office with a pile of paperwork." He kissed my jaw before nibbing on my ear. "But I'll leave the door open for you."

"I'm working today, remember?"

"A woman needs to have a break though, especially one carrying my prized cargo."

I laughed and fumbled through my makeup bag, looking for my favorite lip gloss and bronzer. Tate stayed glued to me, watching me in the mirror. "Are you going to stand there and watch me?" He simply nodded with a cheeky grin. "You could be making me vegemite, avocado, and cheese on toast for breakfast. You know, the person carrying your prized cargo is hungry."

His hands flew off my hips in protest as he began to violently shaking his head. "There is no way in hell I am going anywhere near that devil's food. I still have nightmares about the taste."

"I hope your son or daughter loves it and asks you to make it for them all the time."

"You, Savannah Rae, are evil." He winked at me as a short laugh escaped his throat.

"I may be an evil, but I rocked your world this morning."

"Oh, and you are cocky." He took a step towards the shower before looking back at me. "Yes you did rock my world. Pregnancy certainly is befitting of you and your pussy."

My mouth dropped open in shock at his blatant honesty. "Tate!"

"Savannah!" Tate mocked.

We stared at each other in amusement as I desperately tried to stop the smile that was pulling and begging to be unleashed on my lips. Tate's unique way with words was what legends were made of. I knew his stubborn arse wouldn't break our gaze and I knew I would be late for work if I didn't give in. Damn it.

I dropped my eyes from his and fumbled through my makeup bag to try for a desperate distraction. "Get in the shower. You stink of sex!"

His laughter roared through the room and mine soon joined him.

"Your accent still kills me," he purred as he put his fingers in the waist of his boxers and pulled them torturously slowly over his hips.

My attention was peaked and my eyes automatically focused on the deliciousness between his legs. I licked my lips in anticipation. I was insatiable. I couldn't get enough of him. I knew we have a fan-fucking-tastic sex life, but as I got further into my pregnancy, my need for sex was like my need for air. I took a step towards him, still holding my mascara wand in my hand, and my panty-clad body collided with his. His eyes darkened and the familiar Tate Connors smirk filled his lips.

"Easy, tiger. You've got to work remember," he teased against my lips. "And I'm definitely not a two-minute kind of guy. You know I'm at least a half-hour guy and well . . . You don't have half an hour."

"I hate you," I whined as I pathetically ground myself into him for any relief. I would have taken two minutes right about now.

"By the look in your eyes, you certainly don't hate me,

Savannah."

He laughed as he stepped into the shower, and soon the sound of the water running filled the bathroom. *Deep breaths, Savannah. Deep breaths.* As my body came under control, I finished putting on my face and smiled at the sound of Tate humming in the shower.

"I am contacting my father today." Tate's voice suddenly bounced off the tiled walls of the shower. I froze on the spot. I'd known this day had been coming, but I hadn't thought it would have come so randomly. The lip gloss I was applying dropped out of my hands under the shock of his words and I swung around, opening the shower door.

"What? Tate! When? How?"

"I decided at about four thirty this morning when you fell back asleep in my arms. I was happy, peaceful, and completely at ease. I want to feel that all the time and I can't when I have this cloud over me. I am texting him when I get to Red Velvet and asking him to meet me today."

"Are you sure?" I whispered, fear creeping slowly through me.

I watched as he swallowed hard, and for a split second, I witnessed doubt flash over his face. "Yeah. I have to Sav."

I nodded and moved back towards the vanity. I had no clue what to do. No matter what, I would be there for him. I would stand beside him through thick and thin. But what scared me the most was the uncertainty of it all. What explanation was Tate going to receive? What possible lies or truths was he going to be given? Was his heart strong enough for what he was going to face?

Without another word from Tate about his father, we continued our morning ritual. Coffee and Lucky Charms for Tate, hot chocolate for me, and my 'devil's blood on toast' as Tate liked to call it—AKA vegemite on toast. It was domestic bliss at its best. It almost felt too good to be true, and that's what unnerved me about the whole meeting with Tate's father. It was selfish, I know, but I didn't want anything to wreck what we had. I finally had my guy, I finally was able to give him what he craved, and I didn't want anyone else to destroy that.

Once I had enough food in me to feed a small football team, I grabbed my bag and followed Tate towards the door. Tate dressed head to toe in black, the Red Velvet shirt fitting close to his body and pants snug against his biteable arse. *Stop thinking about fucking, Savannah.* Seriously, my hormones felt like they were ignited one hundred billion percent. I smoothed out my knee-length grey skirt and played with the collar of my shirt as Tate grabbed his keys and wallet before we moved out of our apartment and through the building to the car park.

After he opened my door for me like the perfect gentleman, it was all shattered as he slapped my arse hard and smirked. "This is the first time we have ever gone to work together."

"Aren't we just a couple of business-savvy people?" I laughed softly.

Tate climbed into the driver's seat, and within seconds, we were pulling out into the morning rush of traffic and heading towards Red Velvet. The unease of the day ahead suddenly filled the space around us. Engulfing, swallowing, and strangling every miniscule piece of hope we had succumbed to our little bubble. For the past twelve hours, we had been using sex, words, and our bodies as distractions for what lay ahead of us—firstly the shoot with Chelsea and now with the uncertainty of Tate meeting his father.

Knowing that Tate was about to open up the wounds he had been trying to cover for years scared me. I was frightened about what this could do to him, but I couldn't let him see my fear. He needed my strength—strength I was fearful I was losing at a rapid rate. I had witnessed firsthand the strong, fearless Tate Connors slowly disappear before me. It had been the way he'd lost focus on everything around him, as his mind took him through some of the worst times of his life, and the way I'd watched in heartbreak as a single tear had formed in the corner of his eyes, that he would quickly swipe away before anyone noticed. I had felt the shakes of his body as a nightmare took over him in the early hours of the morning. He had always been my strength. I had needed him to be my strength, but slowly he had been losing it all.

"Are you okay to come with me this afternoon?" His voice softened as he spoke, shooting a quick look of begging towards me. I shifted in my seat to face him as much as the seatbelt would allow.

"I wouldn't be anywhere else."

"Thank you for understanding why I have to do this."

"I just need you to promise me one thing?"

"Anything."

"Don't shut me out. If you feel like you can't talk to anyone, remember you can always talk to me. There is nothing you could say that would push me away. We are in this together, right?"

"I don't want you to see me break, Sav." His voice broke under his words.

"That's what we do. We pick up each other's pieces when we break and put them back together in our own special way. Let me pick up your broken pieces, Tate. Let me make you whole again."

The moment we arrived at Red Velvet, the craziness began. I didn't even have a chance to say goodbye to Tate before my arm was grabbed and I was pulled to the back of the bar. The space around me was a hustle of models, photographers, makeup artists, and designers. I stood still, letting it all soak in as the enormity of the day hit. This was the first shoot I would manage. The trust Mr. Davenport had in me was almost too much. I opened up my bag, pulled out my iPad, and began scrolling through the schedule.

Hands wrapped around my waist and lips pressed on my cheek, I spun around. Jack stood before me dressed in his Red Velvet uniform with a smirk on his face.

"Ready to run the shit out of this photo shoot, Sav?"

"Thanks for doing this, Jack. It's pretty unprofessional of me but—"

"Don't even continue. You are my girl, Sav. I got your back. Always."

A high-pitched shriek took over all sound in my ears and I groaned loudly. She was here. An hour late. Jack scoffed beside me before taking off towards Tate's office and slipping in through the door. I wished I could hide in there all day. Taking a deep breath, I lifted my eyes from the iPad in my hand and looked towards where the shriek had come from.

Chelsea was standing near the door with a monster of a man beside her. My laughter rumbled deep with me when realization hit. She had brought a bodyguard. The bitch had brought a bodyguard to the shoot. Her eyes met mine across the room before she huddled closely to him and pointed towards me. *She has got to be fucking kidding me.* Her eyes broke from mine and moved to something or someone behind me.

Blake had arrived.

My smile took over my face as I took him in. He truly was a gorgeous specimen of man. His tattooed-covered arms, his blue eyes, his strong jaw, and his messy hair only increased the sexiness of his rock-star appeal. Blake Ryan. He was the kind of guy women flocked to but who intimidated with a single glance.

"Hey, Sav," he said shyly, his eyes darting around the room. His face clouded when he found Chelsea. "Why the fuck does she have a bodyguard with her?"

"Clearly, I am more of a threat than I realized. Look at my guns, Blake." I flexed my nonexistent biceps in his direction and winked. "You should be scared too."

"You are a fucking pussycat, Sav. This tough-girl exterior doesn't work on me."

"Ssshhh! Don't tell anyone my secret." I pushed him slightly and turned at the sound of someone clearing his voice behind me. Tate. "I'm tough, aren't I, Tate? Tough as nails."

He rolled his eyes at me and shifted his attention to Blake, who looked on nervously. Their brief moment in the boardroom was the first time they had seen each other since New York. I had a lot to be thankful for when it came to Blake, and I hoped Tate understood that. Blake was the one who had checked in on me and taken me away from the drama that had unfolded, the one who had bought me hot chocolate and sat and watched me cry over my loss of Tate. It had been Blake. My friend.

Tate moved ever so slowly towards me until his hand slightly grazed mine. I grabbed his hand and pulled him towards me until I could wrap my arm around his waist. His lips fell to the side of my forehead and I felt him relax instantly.

"I suppose I should go and get sorted for this shoot. Savannah, if you like me at all, please do not let her touch me."

"Did you fuck her?" I blurted out before thinking, my curiosity kicking it.

"Fuck no, Sav. I was never with her. She just . . ." He turned to Tate briefly and his brow furrowed. It was the same look I had seen in New York City, a look I couldn't understand. "Look, I better go and get this done."

My eyes trailed Blake as he strode towards the hair and makeup station and slumped in one of the oversized chairs. There was something he was desperate to spill but he had it locked in so tight. As the hairstylist started fluffing around with his hair, his shoulders hunched forward and he almost looked defeated. Every piece of the confident rock star was shattering before me. What was etched so deeply inside him?

His eyes flashed to where Tate and I were standing, and suddenly an uneasy feeling shot through my body. Instinctively, I grasped Tate's hand, pulled him against my body, and hugged the living daylights out of him. His face dropped and nuzzled into the crook of my neck, kissing my skin softly.

"Are you okay?" Tate's deep voice vibrated against my neck. He lifted his head and his concern-filled blue eyes danced over my face. I nodded and huddled close into his chest. Unnerving energy surrounded us. Today was going to be one of those days.

Chapter Eight

Tate

There he was, sitting at a lone table in the corner of the coffee house, flipping his phone over and over again in his hands. A coffee cup sat in front of him and his brow was pulled tightly together as if he had the weight of the world on his shoulders. Over the years, I had always wondered what this moment would be like—how I'd feel, whether I'd feel anything at all.

I felt nothing.

I didn't feel one ounce of pity for him. His DNA floated around my body and he had assisted in giving me life, but the man sitting across the room from me was also the man who had abandoned his family. In a simple text message, I had grown a set of balls and decided to face my past head-on. It was a simple message. *Meet me a Café De Sol at 3pm. It's Tate.* I didn't have time for pleasantries or empty words. His reply was simple. *See you there.*

I hated him more than anyone else in the world.

My father. I'd known who he was the moment Sav and I had walked through the doors. We shared similar eyes, similar hair—I was a mirror image of him. His eyes were blue but dull as they narrowed in on Sav and me from across the café. His gaze left me and his eyes scanned the length of Savannah. Immediately I grabbed her in protection.

Sav leaned in, her lips grazing my shoulder as she spoke. "You don't have to do this, Tate."

"I can do anything as long as I have you. I need to do this for us, Sav."

Sav dropped my hand and wrapped her arm around my waist, holding me as close to her body as possible. Comfort swarmed me. Sav tried so desperately to be the strength I needed, but her face exposed everything to me. As I'd told her of my plans, I'd witnessed fear and concern flash over her pretty face a measly few hours ago.

Tanzi was a whole other story. We had come to blows about this the moment I mentioned the text message I'd sent, and she still didn't want any part of my grand plans. Our fieriness and stubbornness matched each other's. We'd said things we shouldn't have and threats had been made, but still we couldn't agree. I did understand her reasons, but it seemed like she couldn't understand mine. I'd stormed out of the office and hadn't spoken to her since.

Tanzi wanted nothing to do with our father. He'd made the choice twenty-three years ago to abandon us, and she wouldn't give him the time of day. In reality, I probably wouldn't have wanted to either, but being only a couple of months away from becoming a father myself, I needed answers. I needed to know why he'd chosen to leave and hear what fucked up reason he could possibly give.

"I'm really nervous about this," I admitted, gripping the edge of Sav's tee and pulling her closer to me.

She didn't have a chance to respond. I heard her gasp as we both watched as my father stood from his chair and made his way across the café towards us. Finally, I got to have a good hard look at him. He was dressed in khaki slacks and a black button-down shirt. His hair was the same dark brown as mine but speckled with grey. His brow was indented with frown marks, evidence of an unhappy life. The man held no confidence; he looked like a broken, shattered man.

"Tate?" he questioned the moment he reached us. His eyes darted between Savannah and me as he awaited an answer.

I abruptly lost all ability to speak. My throat constricted as panic soared with me, and suddenly my mouth was a dry as the Sahara desert. The moment was here, right in front of me, and I couldn't fucking speak.

"Son?"

He did not just call me his fucking son. He took a step towards me, and I felt the rush of anger of the past twenty-three years boil furiously inside of me. This wasn't a good idea. The thoughts of pounding my fist in his face ran with wild abandonment through my head, the thoughts of ripping him a new asshole through words of hateful truth simmering just under the surface. Who the fuck did he think he was?

"Hi, I'm Savannah, Tate's girlfriend." Sav took a step towards him and held her hand out. He looked at her and a smile graced his face as he took her hand in his and shook it softly. Sav moved so I was behind her, allowing me to get my caveman emotions in check. This was a seriously bad idea.

"It's nice to meet you, Savannah. I am Greg Connors. Would you two like to get a coffee?"

Sav spun around to face me, putting herself between me and my father as if she could sense my increasing hostility. Taking an unsteady, deep breath, I looked at her standing in front of me with a look of worry sweeping over her face and immediately everything suddenly became clear. This girl was the love of my life, the girl who had changed everything for me, and the girl who had given me a chance to start my life again. I placed one of my shaking hands on her protruding stomach and smiled. I knew exactly why I was doing this. I had to do this.

"We can go whenever you want. You just hold my hand and pull me up and we are out of here. Whatever you want, we will do." Sav rose on her tiptoes and brushed my lips with hers.

"Coffee for me. Hot chocolate for Sav." My words showed little emotion as I spoke, not taking my eyes from Sav.

My father nodded and released a deep breath before taking off towards the counter to place our orders. Sav tugged on my hand and we weaved our way through the crowded café, taking a seat at a table in the dimly lit far corner. The sound of soft music hummed in the air mixed with the chatter of a full café, but that didn't calm me as my nerves got the best of me. My hands gripped a napkin as they shredded it into a thousand pieces in a pathetic need to find a distraction, but the urge to look at him got the best of me and my gaze drifted to him waiting in line.

Twenty-three years it had been, and here we were in a

coffee shop in Burbank having a fucking reunion. If I wasn't in a frenzied ball of anxiety, I would have found it somewhat humorous. It was almost as if I were waiting for a camera crew to jump out from behind the fake plants and start filming us for some fucked-up reality show.

My attention fell to Sav as she sat beside me, hastily flicking through her phone with the aggressive tap of her nail on the screen, a scowl plastered on her face.

"God, she is a fucking bitch!" she snarled. I didn't even have to ask who she was talking about. Without thinking, I grabbed her phone from her hands and looked at the screen to find Facebook open and what looked like Chelsea's profile displayed.

I never want to be that girl who purposely gets pregnant just to make someone stay with her. Can you get any more pathetic than that? What's worse is the girl in question has a stupid English accent and struts around like she owns the place. Puhlease, everyone knows you are a fake.

"How dare she say I'm English? I am Aussie through and through. Seriously, Tate, what were you thinking putting your dick anywhere near her?" Sav gritted through clenched teeth. "What a stupid whore!"

And there she was, my feisty, intense, don't-give-a-shit Savannah looking like she could take on an army of men on her own accord.

"Coffee and hot chocolate have been ordered." My father arrived and my smartass comment back to Sav was swallowed hard.

He pulled out the seat opposite me and slowly sat down, his eyes never leaving me. I felt uncomfortable under his gaze.

Silence filled the table, and I knew I wouldn't be the first to speak. My hand gripped Sav's hard and rested on her thigh under the table. Her thumb calmingly swept over my knuckles as my fingertips stroked the bare skin above her knee. The feeling of my hand in hers and her words, *"We can go whenever you want,"* were the only things stopping me from turning into a raging bull and unleashing my wrath onto the world.

"How have you been, Tate? How are your sister and your mom?"

My eyes burned with fire as I stared at him. I felt the snap instantly. I felt the anger of a twenty-three year old volcano within me and the lava of my emotions erupted aggressively into the air. "You have no right to speak of them. I am not here to try and make happy families and I am not here to try and repair our relationship. I just need answers and I hope to Christ that after everything you have put me and my family through you will give me that."

He nodded slowly, inhaling deeply in defeat. Did he really think this meeting would be all smiles and happy reunions? Fuck that. He put both palms on the table while I waited. A young girl walked to our table and placed my coffee and Sav's hot chocolate on the table before scurrying off. The tension could be cut with a knife. "What do you want to know, Tate?"

The million dollar question.

For the past three months, I had been asking myself the exact same question. My mind had been battling with itself daily, fighting for what was the right thing to do. My time apart from Savannah gave me ample time to come face to face with my demons and a battle of epic proportions had come to the forefront. I was slowly losing. The battles of my emotions were slowly but surely swallowing me.

Right here in the middle of a crowded coffee shop with Savannah by my side was the moment when I would allow my past to come head-to-head with my present and ultimately affect my future.

"I want to know everything, and don't hold back on the truth."

Sav's hand tightened its grip and her fingers interlocked firmly around mine as she turned in her seat to face me. I swallowed hard, my eyes quickly flashing to hers, desperately wanting to find comfort within her gorgeous green eyes. Nodding slowly in silent agreement, I reluctantly removed my gaze from my future and narrowed in on my past.

"Your mother was the best thing that ever happened to me. She was the love of my life—is still the love of my life. Our life was perfect. We were happily married with two amazing kids and I had my dream job. Everything was perfect." His eyes moved from mine to Sav's and back to mine. I could see the beads of sweat slowly forming on his brow. "There was a cocktail party one weekend at our neighbor's house. Their daughter Diana was in town. She was a Hollywood socialite and the party was in her honor. Your mother and I had an argument earlier that afternoon and your mother refused to come to the party. I sat at the bar, drowning my sorrows with expensive scotch, and Diana approached me. One thing led to another and she took me home. I cheated on your mother that night, and I am not going to lie to you. From that moment, Diana and I started an affair and I was caught up with the lifestyle, the opportunities, and everything she could offer. It was all about the limelight, the parties, and the lifestyle."

"So you just forgot about your children and your wife because you wanted to fuck some socialite all the way to Hollywood?" I spat.

He shifted in his chair before taking a massive gulp of his coffee. "Our affair continued for two years and then I found out she was pregnant."

White noise surrounded me, my heart beat frantically in my chest, and I knew my hand was crushing Sav's, but she didn't complain or tear it away from me. What the fuck was I hearing? Did I just hear correctly? He'd chosen to leave his family—his children—for a random fuck and now he was dropping the bombshell of fathering another kid? My clothes suddenly felt too tight and my hands became sweaty as panic and anxiety swept over me. I needed air. I needed to get away from this. This was too much to hear.

"Sav, we have to go." I began to stand but Sav stopped me by squeezing my hand and making me stop. I looked at her with pain filled eyes, desperate to stop hearing this atrocity. She stood from her chair, wrapped her arms around my waist, and held me. We were in the middle of a coffee shop surrounded by strangers and her arms offered a comfort I craved. I fell against her body, comforted by the feeling of Jellybean between us.

"You've already come so far, Tate. Let's stay and we can close this chapter together. I am right here, okay?" she whispered softly in my ear and pulled away.

Hesitation and what-ifs swam through me. Could I leave and be okay with what I had found out? Would it be enough to move on? Would I be able to live the life I was begging for with the information I received?

Nodding slowly, I sat back down and took a long drink of my coffee. "So I have a brother or sister out there?" My question cut a deep, gaping wound in my heart.

"You have a brother. He is two years younger than you."

"What was the woman's name?"

"Diana Ryan."

My world instantly felt like the biggest ocean in the world, an ocean whose massive waves were now crashing in around me, wiping out everything in its path. The sound of Sav gasping beside me made me realize she had heard exactly what I had. This couldn't be happening. Not this. The past twenty-three years of my life boiled down to this—a concoction of lies, infidelity, and deceit. Everything came flashing back. The neighbors, the pitiful looks they would give Tanzi and me, the way they constantly had checked in on us, and the fact that their daughter had never visited but then out of nowhere their grandson had come to live with them. The grandson who was two years younger than us. The grandson who . . .

"What's your son's name?"

"Blake Ryan."

CHAPTER
Nine

Savannah

A PREGNANT WOMAN RUNNING AFTER HER pissed off boyfriend was something I was sure the people, who were stepping out of my way and mumbling obscenities under their breath, hadn't expected to see when they woke this morning. As the evening sky of Los Angeles fell around me, I ran after Tate, out of breath, panting, my eyes locked firmly on the back of my frustratingly fast-walking boyfriend.

The moment the truth had fallen from his father's lips, Tate's hand gripped mine to the point of hurt under the table and the vein in his neck pulsated aggressively. Secrets had exploded all over the place, and all I could do was sit there in shock, wide-eyed and mouth agape. I had tried desperately to keep my emotions in check, but no matter how hard I'd wanted, I hadn't been able to help the loud gasp float from my lips the moment the truth had shattered reality.

Blake and Tate were half-brothers.

This was going to shatter him into a million pieces, a million pieces I would, until the day I died, attempt to glue back together. To be honest, I was scared of that one brutal moment when the truth actually hit him, that moment when the world would give him a massive 'fuck you' and would stamp its boot into the already bloodied shards of his destroyed heart and grind it farther into the earth. That's the moment I was scared of, and all I could do was pray to the heavens above that I was strong enough for him.

"Tate, seriously, would you wait!" I yelled after him with every last bit of energy I could summon. Finally, he slowed his pace until he was almost at a standstill, allowing me to catch up to him.

The last shards of California sun beamed from the skies above, but the cloud surrounding Tate was overshadowing everything. His shoulders were slumped and his head dropped in defeat. My strong man was crumbling in front of me. I grabbed at his arm and swung him around to face me. The face looking back at me destroyed me. His blue eyes were overflowing with fear, confusion, and what looked like embarrassment. What did he have to be embarrassed about?

My hands flung up to his face, cupping his cheeks and making him look at me. "Talk to me."

The slight movement of his head as he shook it frightened me. He was shutting down, his walls were flying up at a rapid speed, and there was nothing I could do about it.

"Please, Tate. You promised me." I pulled out the big guns. His eyes finally latched on to mine. I knew he would never break a promise he'd made to me. Trust between us was now everything, and if he didn't talk, we both knew we would be back to square one.

His Adam's apple bobbled in his throat as he swallowed hard, anxious to find the strength he needed to allow me into his inner thoughts. "This is fucked up, Sav. I share blood with Blake fucking Ryan. Or should I call him Blake Connors now? That piece of shit who made my life hell for so many years is my brother. That piece of shit who fucked Sarah and who fucked . . . you." His voice cracked under his words and my heart stilled.

Our eyes flashed to each other's in pure desperation. My greens met his blues, anxious to pierce each other's soul for a simple truth both of us craved. The rush and buzz of Los Angeles flooded around us, but the bubble we had locked ourselves in was intensifying by the second.

"Don't let your mind go there, Tate. We will get through this. Together. Your heart is mine to fix, to soothe, to caress, to love, to cherish, and I'll be damned if your father or Blake will take that from me. You thought you had witnessed stubborn Savannah before. Well you haven't seen anything yet."

A miniscule smile tugged at his lips but was taken the moment his thoughts escaped back to the nightmare he was currently living. "How am I supposed to tell Tanzi?"

How could I possibly answer that question?

Without another word, he grabbed my hand and pulled me down the street towards his Jeep, his face void of emotion, his eyes fierce, and his mouth pulled tight. When we reached his car, he opened the passenger's door and helped me in, pulling the seatbelt around me and locking me in securely. His protectiveness was adorable. I watched him like a hawk as he sauntered around the front of the car before sliding onto the driver's seat. He stilled, his hands gripping the steering wheel to the point on whiteness appearing on his knuckles. His breathing was rough, patchy, and aggressive.

Anxiety crashed within me like a massive wave. I had seen this Tate before and I knew exactly what it led to. Tate was ready to fight.

His shaking hands fumbled with the keys and the engine roared to life. Soon we were driving erratically through the streets of Los Angeles. If I hadn't had complete trust in him, I would have been fearing for my life. He weaved through traffic, muttering obscenities under his breath when he had to stop. I remained silent but my eyes never left him.

As he pulled the car to a stop at the lights, his eyes closed momentarily and then shot open with a new vigor taking over them. Suddenly he punched the screen on his dashboard and the sound of a dial tone filled the air. Moments later, Jack's voice was heard.

"What's up?"

"Is he there?" Tate didn't hold back.

"Who are you talking about?"

I didn't even need to ask who he was talking about. Swallowing hard, I turned in my seat and softly gripped his leg just above his knee. His eyes flashed to mine and for the first time since our gazes had first locked with each other's in the foyer of our apartment building, I couldn't read him. His eyes were my door to what he was thinking and feeling, and now, as I looked at him, I saw nothing. No emotion, no unspoken words, no passion.

"Blake," he spat.

"Don't, Tate. Please," I begged softly, my voice sounding

like a pitiful school girl—whiny, weak, and losing my hold on him. Slowly shaking his head, he looked away and focused back on the road in front of him. Nothing I could say would stop the torment in his head. This had fucked him completely up.

"So is he there?"

"Yeah he is. He is chatting to the photographer. The after-party is in full swing. Fuckstick Chelsea is still here."

"See you in a bit."

Tate ended the call and didn't say another word to me as he took off through the intersection when the light turned green. We weaved our way through the congestion of Los Angeles traffic and along the familiar roads I knew would lead us straight to Red Velvet. My hand didn't shift from his leg, I was desperate to offer any kind of comfort I could, but as the minutes passed, I knew I was failing miserably.

One thing I was quickly learning about Tate Connors was that if he stood in the face of trouble, uncertainty, or fear, he would do one of two things. He would either shut down completely, silence would overcome him, and he would pull away from me, offering me nothing but silence or he would fight. He would fight until he was satisfied that he'd won, that the fight was his to own, that he was the ultimate winner. The scary thing about right now was that I was seeing both. I was witnessing the silence engulf him but seeing the fight ignite within him and I had absolutely no clue what to do about it.

"Tate, please talk to me. You are scaring me." My voice was barely a whisper.

"I can't talk now, Sav. I got the answers I wanted, didn't I? This whole thing is fucked up, but now it's opened up a whole new bag of fucking secrets."

"Tate, you don't need to do this. Just talk to him. Don't do something you'll regret."

Tate turned to me and his eyes darkened to a shade I had never witnessed before. "I won't regret this. That's one thing I can promise you," he scoffed and forcefully pulled out the keys from the ignition. I didn't even realize we had stopped. My head swung around and I recognized the familiar car park of Red Velvet. Fuck it! He was out of the car before I could beg him again.

"Shit, fuck, bullshit," I muttered to myself, pulling open the door and rushing after him. Seriously, would he ever not make me run after him? My feet pounded on the gravel as I ran across the car park, my breathing heavy when I finally got to him. His hand gripped the door handle of the entrance of Red Velvet and he was just about to swing it open. With everything I was I pulled him back and pushed him against the wall beside the door. His eyes scanned my face, shock at my sudden strength covering him. Inhaling sharply at the feeling of the heavy beating of his heart against my chest, I grabbed both his hands and interlocked our fingers, gluing our hands together.

"Sav, just let me go."

"Never, Tate." I rose on my tiptoes and wrapped my arms around his waist, pulling him flush against my body. My lips collided with the corner of his mouth and instantly I felt his stiff body relax ever so slightly against me. "I will never let you go."

Tate turned his head slightly, allowing his lips to fall on mine with an insurgence that made me breathless. My hands gripped his shirt, drawing him as close to my body as my stomach would allow. The early evening shadows of Los Angeles were falling around us, but as his hips collided with mine, I couldn't give a shit what was happening around me. He spun me in his arms and pressed me firmly against the wall without breaking contact with my mouth. His tongue slid between my lips as I gasped. Our tongues began furiously dancing with one another as we tasted every inch of our months. Fuck, I loved kissing this man.

Kissing was something that I'd never enjoyed. Kissing to me had always been more intimate than sex. Kissing was tasting, caressing, delving into a person's soul, and that was one thing I'd never wanted. I had often refused to kiss the men I had been with, but with Tate it was everything I needed. I wanted to kiss him until my lips were swollen, red, and bruised, until the tingle stayed for days, until our heads were fuzzy due to lack of breathing. That was what kissing Tate Connors was like, and right now I was under his spell. Suddenly the tormenting situation we found ourselves in faded into thin air, even if it was just for a couple of minutes.

A deep cough sounded beside us and both of our heads spun around to find Steve, Tate's trusty doorman, looking at us with a grin the size of the Grand Canyon plastered on his face.

"Fuck," Tate hissed between his teeth while the heat from my reddening cheeks radiated. Without a second thought, Tate grabbed my hand and pulled me to the alleyway that ran the side of Red Velvet, and once again I found myself pushed against a graffiti-covered wall.

A silence fell between us, eyes scoping each other's, our hearts beating feverishly in our chests. I grabbed the front of his shirt and smashed my lips to his. It was my turn. My tongue traced the length of his bottom lip, sweeping delicately and giving him a teasing taste of me. His hands gripped my arse, and before I knew it, I was on my tiptoes, moments away from being in his arms. I wanted nothing more than to wrap my legs tight around his hips and grind myself up against the delicious cock that was crushing against my thigh. When I pulled his bottom lip between my teeth, his groan filled the air and the wetness of my panties became apparent. His mouth claimed ownership of mine in a struggle of tongues, lips, and teeth. We couldn't get enough and I knew I never would. This was my Tate. Rough, raw, and sensual.

"We have to stop," Tate breathed heavily into my ear before sucking my lobe into his mouth and nibbling the tender flesh. My legs felt like jelly, my sex ached for attention, and my heart was exploding in my chest.

"Why?" my voice hummed with desire.

"I love you too much to fuck in you the back alley of our bar."

"But you always say you like when I'm a dirty girl." My words dripped with lust and oozed with sarcasm.

I felt Tate's lips curve to a smile against my neck. "Yes, I love dirty Sav when she is talking dirty to me when I'm pounding into her at home or the car or my office. I have no interest to meet dirty Sav in the back alley of Red Velvet when we are probably standing in someone's piss and vomit. We are classy, remember?"

"Oh yeah. Totally classy."

His mood suddenly shifted and his arms moved from around my waist, dropping to his side. I knew I couldn't stop him from doing what his mind and body were ready to do. I just hoped he realized what this could mean.

Chapter Ten

Tate

BLAKE RYAN WAS MY BROTHER. The words of my father continued to pound in my head. Had our whole friendship been a sham? Was his aim in life to destroy me? Had his concern for me during the worst time of my life been fake? The more I thought about it, the more my anger grew. I should have listened to Savannah. I should have taken her hand and allowed her to take me home. I should have huddled in her arms with the comfort of her and Jellybean and forgotten the shitstorm that was now brewing. But I didn't.

The moment I stepped away from Savannah and she didn't follow, I knew I had made the wrong decision. Pushing open the door of Red Velvet, I was greeted with a bar full of pretty people. Models were scattered everywhere, the music was blaring, and the atmosphere was electric. On any other night, this would have made me ecstatic. I would have smothered myself in happiness and my ego would have soared. But at this moment, I didn't give a flying fuck about anything other than finding Blake Ryan. I stood just inside the main doors and let my eyes scout every corner of the bar. I found Lucas and Tanzi sitting at our usual table in what looked like a hilarious conversation, and Jack was working the bar and serving Thomas, our regular Hollywood high roller.

I jumped at the feeling of a hand pressed on my back and relaxed under the touch of Savannah. The feeling of having her near me suddenly calmed the fluctuating emotions bubbling just under the surface, and for a moment I forgot everything.

"I was wondering when you'd come back without that bitch."

That wasn't Savannah.

I whipped around to find Chelsea wearing a dangerous smile and a barely there dress. Her eyes roamed the length of my body and the unease in my stomach rose in waves of bile to my throat. She licked her over-plump lips and took an uneasy step towards me. She was completely wasted and had a face full of intention.

My jaw clenched. "You say one more word about Savannah and I swear to God, Chelsea."

"What, Tate?" she scoffed, pushing her chest into me obnoxiously. "What are you going to do about it? I'm a fucking model. She can't do jack shit."

"You are also a conceited bitch I don't want in my bar."

Chelsea's face dropped momentarily and then fire ignited. As far as I was concerned, she had chosen the wrong fucking time to go head-to-head with me and I'd take whatever she gave.

"And who is going to kick me out? You?"

"Leave quietly, Chelsea, or be embarrassed when I make the biggest fucking scene you've ever witnessed. I don't give a fuck what people think about me here, but you do. Your choice."

Chelsea opened her mouth to retaliate but then spiteful hate exploded in her eyes as she looked over my shoulder.

"I need you to leave the premises, Chelsea. You are no longer an employee of Beautify and you will not be working with us again." Savannah huddled beside me, grabbing my hand hastily. Her voice broadcast strength but her face revealed that she was being swarmed by anxiety. "Oh, and you have a life ban from Red Velvet."

"You have absolutely no fucking say as to where I work, who I work for, and what bar I visit."

Savannah's hand squeezed mine before she spoke. "One, I was running this shoot and you broke one of the terms and conditions of your contract with Beautify. Two, breaking a contract means it's instantly void. And three, I am pretty sure my boyfriend here will back me up and he owns the bar so yeah, you are shit out of luck with that one."

"You are a joke. What did I supposedly do, you fat bitch?"

"You fucked a member of the Beautify staff, Chelsea. Section 5.1 of the model contract with Beautify states that models under contract with Beautify International do not engage in any sexual relations with staff and contractors while under assignment. Guess what you did today, you fucking idiot?" Savannah's voice dripped with power.

Chelsea's face drained of all color as she looked at Savannah with wide, terrified eyes. "You don't know what you are talking about."

"There is a little thing called video surveillance cameras all around the bar, and what do you know, Chelsea? You were filmed fucking on camera again. You really seem to be making a habit of this. You should become a fucking whore." Sav took a step towards Chelsea and thrust her phone into her face with a look of satisfaction and a surge of confidence taking her over. On the screen, it was as clear as day that it was Chelsea fucking the mail guy from Beautify in the corridor leading to the bathrooms. "Chelsea you are officially busted."

You could have heard a pin drop around us. Chelsea stumbled back as realization circled her. Savannah had won. Chelsea shook her head violently and grabbed at my arm. Seriously, did she really think I was going to comfort her? Shrugging her off, I moved closer to Savannah and stood proudly beside her.

"You can't do this!" Chelsea hissed.

"Already done, Chelsea. The video has been sent to Mr. Davenport, who has since forwarded it on to the CEO of Beautify International. Your career with Beautify is done. You have no reason to ever come near me or Tate again. If you don't leave immediately, I will call the police and have you escorted off the premises."

Chelsea took a step towards Sav and looked her square in the eye before dropping her gaze to Sav's stomach and a vindictive smirk covered her lips. "You are a fat English slut and Tate will tire of you. He always does."

From the moment the venom had spat from Chelsea's lips to the impact of Sav's fist to her nose, time stood still. "For the last fucking time, I am Australian! While you are unemployed, learn the fucking difference!" Sav growled, turned on her heel, and stormed through Red Velvet like a woman possessed. I had never wanted Savannah more in my fucking life.

Chelsea dropped to the floor, clutching her nose, her fingers covered with the blood spewing from her nose. "I am going to sue you, Tate! I will destroy you! I will destroy her!"

"With what evidence, Chelsea?"

"The cameras! I'll get the evidence."

"The cameras haven't been turned back on. You got any other pathetic threat you're going to throw my way?" I looked at her and smirked. "Get the fuck out of my bar, Chelsea, before Stevie throws you out. And don't ever come back."

I didn't stick around to hear her pathetic excuse. I knew she wouldn't do a thing about her threats. She was as weak as piss, and now that she had lost her contract with Beautify, she didn't have a leg to stand on. Walking through Red Velvet, I was desperate to find Sav and make sure she was okay. She had put on her *I don't give a fuck* attitude but I knew that would have gotten to her. My priority was her.

"Sav went to your office."

My eyes slammed shut at the sound of his voice. Suddenly the reason why I had come to Red Velvet was standing in front of me. I turned to face him and the truth hit me directly in the heart. How had I never noticed before? As he looked at me, it was like I was looking into my or Tanzi's eyes. The exact same blue eyes as mine were glancing back at me. There was no denying that he was my brother.

I breathed in slowly between clenched teeth. "How long have you known?"

Silence.

"Blake, start talking now. Otherwise, my fist will connect with your face in about ten seconds."

Silence.

"Tate, come on, man. Don't do this here." Jack stood beside me with fierce eyes. "Remember where you are. We have a bar full of people." I scanned the bar. He was right. I couldn't do this here. Savannah appeared and stood beside Jack with her hand grasping his arm and her eyes bouncing between me and Blake.

"Outside, Blake."

The words left my mouth without consideration of my planned actions. Savannah took a step towards me and grabbed my hands in hers, trying desperately to pull me away, but I wouldn't budge. Mr. Tate 'stubborn' Connors had arrived and he had one agenda in mind.

"You're really going to do this?" She questioned.

"Sav, please."

"You don't need to do this," Sav whispered, shaking her head, and I saw something flash over her face that I never wanted to see. Disappointment. I was disappointing the one person who never deserved to be disappointed. She didn't let me respond. Dropping my hands as quickly as she grabbed them, she turned on her heel and rushed towards the table where Tanzi was looking on anxiously. Fuck! Tanzi!

"Tate, you've got to get your priorities fucking straight," Jack growled beside me. He was right. I rubbed my face with my hands and let out a deep sigh. I needed to get my emotions in check and fast. "What the fuck?" Jack mumbled and shot a look towards the table where Tanzi and Sav sat.

Blake stood beside Sav, leaned down, and whispered something into her ear. When the fuck had he even left? That's all it took. I stormed through the bar, all thoughts of not making a scene escaping the moment he'd gone near her. Grabbing a fistful of his shirt, I pulled him away and flung him hard against the wall near my office. Patrons scrambled out of the way and the door of my office flung open under the collision of Blake's back to the wall.

"If you want to do this, at least take me in your fucking office. Don't do this in front of them." Blake looked over my shoulder in the direction of Tanzi and Savannah, who were huddled together with fear in their eyes. I grabbed him by the collar and pushed him through the door of my office, slamming it behind us.

"How long have you known?" I spat.

"Three months."

"How did you find out?"

"My grandmother told me just before she passed. I didn't believe her at first. I couldn't believe her. The thought of you and Tanzi being my brother and sister scared me. Grandma had been sitting on this secret for twenty-three years." Blake dropped his eyes to the floor. "I admitted everything to Grandma about our past, and she hated that we were no longer friends."

"You brought everything on yourself, Blake. You fucked Sarah and then you had to go after the one girl you knew I was interested in even after I told you. I had every intention to make amends with you that first night. That's why I asked your band to play at Red Velvet, but then you had to go and take her home."

Blake moved farther into my office, his eyes traveling to the wall that held my favorite family photos. Sadness washed over his face. "I'm a fucking asshole, Tate. What more do you want me to say? When I first moved in with my grandparents, it was because my own mother had decided that I wasn't worth looking after and, well, my father was non-existent. I moved in and saw your perfect life. You had a mother who adored you, a sister who cherished every breath you took, and what did I have? I had grandparents who didn't deserve to be given the responsibility of looking after a fucked-up teenager. I was jealous. I craved affection, and when Sarah showed me affection, I took it."

The sound of the door opening pulled my attention away from Blake. Savannah, Jack, and Tanzi nervously walked in. "Get them out of here, Jack," I barked.

"We aren't going anywhere, Tate. If he is my brother, I deserve to know." Tanzi's voice hitched under her words, and I could see a wave of tears ready to crash over her cheeks. My heart ached for her.

Screw this. I rushed towards Tanzi and cupped her face in my hands, making her look at me. We stared at each other, communicating through unspoken words like we did so often when we were younger and not wanting anyone to hear us.

"You and me, Tiny. You and me," I whispered, using her nickname from when we were children. "We will get through this. I am your strength and you are my calm, remember?"

Tanzi nodded slowly as tears finally spilled over her cheeks. She took a step away from me and moved towards Jack, who wrapped his arms protectively around her. Turning my attention back to Blake, I saw that he was watching Tanzi closely.

"And Savannah? Why the fuck did you go after her? You knew I wanted her. You knew that but you still went after her,"

Blake turned to look in the direction of Sav, who had now moved to sit on the corner of my desk. His features immediately pained. Regret swamped his face and his eyes lost the spark they'd had moments ago. "For once I saw someone I was genuinely interested in. She was stunning and I knew she wasn't an LA girl. That was refreshing. That's what I needed. I saw the way she was looking at you and I saw the way you were looking at her. I am an asshole. I just wanted to forget for one night. I'm so sorry, Sav."

Sav walked across the room and stood before Blake. I waited with bated breath. Sav grabbed hold of both of his hands, pulled him to her body, wrapped her arms around him, and hugged him. Right there in front of me, she hugged him. "It was what it was, Blake. The past is exactly that—the past," she spoke softly.

"This is so fucked up," I growled, pulling Blake from Sav's grip. Every emotion I had bubbled over inside me and unleashed in a flurry of confusion. My father, my brother, my ex-girlfriend, my current girlfriend, my unborn child, my sister, my mother—who the hell could I trust anymore?

I didn't even realize what I was unleashing until Sav's piercing scream tore thought my office. Blake plummeted to the floor, clutching at his bleeding face. One punch led to two, which led to three. I laid into him, every frustration I had being released through my fists. I lost complete control. Blake didn't fight back. He let me hit him and he watched me through pitiful, broken eyes as I hit him with everything I had. My fists ached, my breathing broken, my gaze focused. It was only when I heard the faint pleas from the corner of the room that I remembered we weren't alone.

"Just stop!"

I pulled away and twisted towards Savannah. Her beautiful face was scrunched up and looking pained and confused. Her cheeks were flooding with tears. Tears that my actions had brought on. I felt like a prick. My thoughts hadn't even crossed to what Tanzi and Savannah were witnessing. What was wrong with me? My bloodied hands cupped her face and brought her lips to mine. She stilled against me.

"Savannah," I begged, needing to feel her. She opened her eyes, looking at me through tears, looking at me with lifeless eyes.

"Tate, I need to go. You two need to sort this out. I can't see this. I can't do anything to help this situation." Her words rushed.

"Sav, I didn't mean for you to see this."

"Lucas is taking Tanzi and me home. I need to ice my hand." Her eyes dropped to the floor before bouncing up and landing on her stomach, which she was now cradling. "You need to remember what's important, Tate. Sometimes you need to move on from the past in order to see the future."

She didn't say another word to me. She just slipped through the door and out to the main bar. Jack kissed Tanzi tenderly and followed closely behind Sav, leaving Tanzi, Blake, and me in the silence of my office. Tanzi shook as she crossed the room and stood before Blake. With bloodshot eyes, she ran her gaze over his face, bloodied and battered from my fists.

"You have the Connors eyes," she whispered, her eyes flicking from Blake's to mine and back to Blake's. "I need time to adjust to this. My father—our father—leaving wasn't your fault. I just need to let it sink in."

"Tanzi, I don't expect anything from you and Tate. I don't deserve that. I fucked up time and time again. I fucked up when I couldn't stop Chelsea from the hell she unleashed in New York. It's just one thing after the other with me."

My head snapped up at the sound of his words. "What does Chelsea have to do with this?"

"She found out about my connection to you. She was using it against me in New York. Tate, I was never with Chelsea. She was holding that over me and threatening to tell you. I didn't want you hearing it from her so I went along with her games. When I came to the hotel to speak to you, I was coming to warn you about her plans." He shook his head as he remembered.

I remember the exact moment I had told him to leave. All of the drama that had happened with Sav and I could have been stopped if I had listened to him, if I had given him a moment of time. He had been standing here telling me that he was with the fucked-up bitch to stop Savannah and me getting hurt and I hadn't even given him the fucking time of day.

"I still don't know how she even found out. I just got an email through the band's management about her and I had to go along with it. I only contacted Sav through Facebook to make sure I knew where she was. I didn't want you or Sav finding out from her. I thought I was doing the right thing."

Tanzi gasped and she looked at me with wide eyes.

"Thank you," I whispered, swallowing my pride. "I should have spoken to you."

"You had every right not to speak to me, but I had to try." Blake winced as his fingertips swept over his quickly bruising cheek. "I am going to go and get myself cleaned up. I have a photo shoot scheduled for tomorrow. I think it may be canceled." He laughed softly and guilt swam through me.

"I, ah . . . Sorry about that."

"You don't have anything to apologize for." Blake walked towards the office door and grabbed the handle before stopping and looking back at Tanzi and me. "When I was told that you two were my family, I finally felt like maybe I had a shot at something. It was always my grandparents and me, and then Grandpa died and now I lost Grandma. I don't expect anything from you two and I would never ask for anything, but knowing that I do have family out there and knowing that it's you two kinda makes up for everything."

I stood, mouth open, fists aching and bleeding, and my heart beating furiously in my chest as he stepped through the door and out of my office. Tanzi grabbed hold of my arm to steady herself and pulled me over to the couch in the far corner of my office. We sat in silence, staring at each other, both breathing heavily, the quiet sobs of Tanzi the only sound filling the air. Our world as we knew it had just been shifted. I had gotten my answers from my father, and in the process I'd gained a brother. A brother who for years I'd hated, despised, and wished to never see again. But in a split second, with Savannah's words floating around in my head, I started picturing a whole different world for me. A world where forgiveness was the key and certain things clearly happened for a reason.

I wouldn't have had the intensely loving relationship with my mom if my father hadn't left. I wouldn't have had Savannah in my life if Blake hadn't fucked Sarah. And I wouldn't have had the desire and urge to be the best damn partner to Savannah and father to Jellybean if my father hadn't fucked up.

Chapter Eleven

Savannah

YOU KNOW THAT FEELING WHEN your mind runs a hundred miles an hour but your body feels like its running on empty? That's how I was feeling now. Today could only be described as utter bullshit. The morning had been perfect—waking up in the arms of Tate, spending the morning flirting and sneaking into his office for make-out sessions, running the shoot and knowing that I was doing a damn fine job, spending lunch with Tate and laughing at Jellybean kicking and talking about baby names. But then shit hit the fan in the afternoon.

I'd known that meeting Tate's father would open up deep wounds for Tate and Tanzi, but I'd had no idea of the extent of the secrets that would be unleashed. It was mind blowing to think of Blake as their brother. I wasn't exactly sure how long it would take for me to be able to comprehend it.

"Where are you, Sav?"

Lucas's concerned voice filled my ears as we weaved our way through traffic and away from Red Velvet. This was a time that Tate and Tanzi needed to spend together. I would always be there for them, but at the moment, they needed their twin time and I would never come between that.

"Just trying to get my head around everything."

"It's a shock, isn't it?"

"Tell me about it." I grabbed my phone out of my clutch bag and flipped it over in my hands. "Do you think it was the right thing leaving them there?"

"Tate knows you are there for him. If I have learned anything about Tate, it's that he wears his heart on his sleeve. He puts on this macho caveman act, but he will break just like the best of us."

"I'm scared of what this will do to him."

"Just be there for him, Sav. That's what he needs."

I leaned back on the leather interior of Lucas's car and closed my eyes. My hand ached from punching Chelsea, my heart was heavy, and my eyelids were begging to close under the emotion of the day, but yet I wasn't ready to go home yet. The thought of driving around and listening to music felt like heaven.

"Can we drive around for a bit? I don't feel like going home yet," I suggested softly.

"Message Tate and tell him. If he gets home and you aren't there, he will panic."

Nodding, I swiped open my phone and hesitated briefly before tapping on the screen.

Tate, I will be home soon. Please don't wait up. Love always, me and jellybean xx

Putting my phone back in my purse, I shifted in my seat and gave my full attention to Lucas. "Tell me about you and Ali. It's good to see you two back on track," I asked, trying desperately to change the subject.

Lucas smiled as he shot me a quick look. It was clear as day that he was happy. "We had a really good talk. She was scared of getting married too young because she had seen what happened with her parents and their divorce. I love that girl, Sav, and I am happy to have her in my life as my girlfriend at the moment."

"You two will end up married with babies. You'll make the cutest kids."

"Did you think you and Tate would have kids?"

"Hell no! I thought I would just fuck him and that would be it. I fought him for weeks. That day he turned up to take me on our date when you were at the apartment? Seriously, he blackmailed me into going on that date."

Lucas and I spent the next two hours driving along the Pacific Coast highway, listening to an '80s flashback station on the radio, and singing really terrible renditions of classic Bon Jovi songs. I could tell Lucas was getting antsy about getting me home. His eyes kept flashing to the clock on the dash. I knew it was time.

Laughing at Lucas's failed attempt at hitting the high note in Livin' on a Prayer, I stopped mid-step as we walked into the foyer of my apartment building. My breath caught in my throat as my eyes landed on Blake hunched over in one of the plush black leather chairs on the far wall near the now closed coffee stand. Lucas halted beside me and grabbed my hand protectively.

"Are you okay? I can stay if you want."

"No, that's fine. Go upstairs. I need to speak with him."

Lucas kissed my cheek tenderly and nodded towards Blake, who walked slowly towards us with his face bruised from his early altercation at the fists of Tate Connors. The foyer was silent, not another soul around us. Considering it was close to midnight on a Saturday night, it was somewhat freaky.

Blake stood before me and looked beaten, reserved, and utterly heartbroken.

"I'm sorry for barging in here, but I just needed to come and see you to apologize. I'm so sorry, Savannah. I didn't mean for any of this to happen." Blake's knees collapsed from under him and he dropped to the floor as every emotion erupted within him. I had no idea what to do.

My heart broke for him. I knew exactly how it felt to grow up without a family to call your own, but thankfully I had Mr. Davenport. I wrapped my arms around him and pulled him towards me.

Here was the guy who had made my first night in Los Angeles memorable, the guy who'd had confidence oozing off him, sex appeal dripping off every inch of his tattooed body. And now he was weak, broken, fractured. This wasn't the Blake Ryan I knew. I held him as he sobbed, my shirt becoming drenched with his tears. He was Tate's brother. Tate's little brother.

And that's when it hit me, at the worst possible time, the time when I should be concerned, quiet, and reserved. It hit me. Hard. I had fucked brothers. Blake Ryan and Tate Connors. Brothers. Why I laughed when I was faced with uncomfortable situations is something I would never understand. I laughed at the most inappropriate times. It could be someone falling over, a sad scene in a movie, or here in the middle of an abandon foyer of the apartment building. Now, as I felt the familiar energy swarming through my body, I desperately tried to swallow and restrain the laughter that was begging to escape my chest. Nope, it wasn't happening.

My laughter flew out of my mouth before I could slam it shut. Blake's head snapped up and he looked at me in complete astonishment. Here he was, facing one of the worst times of his life, and some weird Australian girl was laughing in his face. *Nice one, Savannah.*

"I. Am. So. Sorry. Blake!" My words were hitched by laughter. "I. Don't. Mean. To. Laugh!"

He rose to his feet, his brow furrowing as his eyes scanned my face. My laughter continued to bounce off the walls of the empty foyer before I finally got it under control, my stomach cramping, my eyes watering, and my throat dry. Every time I looked at him I laughed. Seriously, what the hell was wrong with me?

"What are you laughing at, crazy girl?" A smile finally appeared on Blake's face. He even smiled like Tate. How had I not recognized this?

"I fucked brothers!"

Blake's eyes shot open and he bit his lip nervously. "I probably wouldn't joke about that around Tate. I don't think my face can handle any more run-ins with his fists."

My mood instantly dropped and my laughter ceased. "I'm sorry that happened."

"It's not your fault, Sav. I deserve everything that Tate releases on to me. I miss my best friend, but I know I completely fucked it up. I don't expect anything from him, but he deserved to know. I am sorry if you felt that I used you to get back at him. I promise that I didn't. You were something else, Sav, and I know we had our moment but that's done now. I see you as my, well, brother's partner now and I want Tate to know that. You will always be one of the most beautiful girls I know but we are entirely platonic now." He shoved his hands in his pockets, and I couldn't help smiling at how shy and awkward he was acting. "I wouldn't have gone there if I had known Tate was my brother."

"I am entirely and utterly in love with Tate. He owns my heart, my soul, and every part of me, so platonic would be great. It can't be weird, especially when we will be spending holidays and such together."

Now it was Blake's turn to laugh. "Savannah, you really are a comedian, aren't you? I highly doubt I'll be spending holidays with you. I will be lucky if Tate talks to me."

"Just leave it to me, Blake. I have ways of making Tate see things clearly. He is really hurt at the moment. He is emotionally bruised and he is freaking out. But if I know Tate like I think I do, he will open up to me and we will talk."

"You'll have to be a miracle worker," Blake scoffed and shook his head. Little did he know that I already had plans in motion in my head.

I watched Blake as he sauntered towards a cab before heading off to his apartment. The fact that he had turned up at my apartment building in the early hours of the morning made it clear that he wanted redemption when it came to his past. My eyes were transfixed on the fading tail lights. The peace and stillness of my surroundings made me feel somewhat comforted. The night air of Los Angeles caressed my bare arms and a shiver ran up my spine. What a day.

As I walked through the empty foyer and entered the elevator, my mind jumped through the events while my hands rested on my protruding stomach. I'd be meeting my little one in a matter of months. How my world would change. How my world had already changed! One thing I was growing very accustomed to was the unexpected. I never knew what to expect when I woke anymore. I was never a planner, but I did always like having a routine, an idea of where I was heading, but that had been shot out of the water when I arrived in Los Angeles. Men, fucking, parties, and living the LA lifestyle had been my plans for my new life in Los Angeles. However, fate had had something else awaiting me. A fate that now saw me living with the love of my life, expecting a baby, surrounded by a brand-new family and a somewhat calm and peaceful life. Life had played a weird set of cards with me.

The moment I walked through the door and made my way into the apartment, my body shivered as I sensed Tate. I always sensed him. The television projected a soft, dull hum through the still air and the light from the screen bounced off the walls, creating creepy shadows, only lighting the room momentarily. My eyes adjusted to the light as I stood by the kitchen bench. My breathing was echoing out of my chest, my palms were sweaty, and my heart was beating erratically.

Tate sat motionless on his favorite grandpa chair, the chair that had been the first thing to be moved from his apartment to what was now our apartment. His head was downcast but I knew he wouldn't be asleep. He never slept if I wasn't beside him. He would wrap his body around mine so tight, as if he feared I would escape during the early hours of the morning.

I quietly put my handbag on the kitchen bench and walked along the polished wooden floorboards towards the living room. A loose floorboard squeaked beneath my bare feet and finally he looked up at me. Our eyes connect instantly and I cringed inwardly at the shattered man looking back at me. His perfect blue eyes were circled with red from the tears he had shed in the loneliness of our apartment, his face lined and pained from the emotions that had drained from every pore of his wounded body. My strength was broken. Tate had and would always be my strength, but as I stood in silence, I was witnessing my strength fading. Now I was taking on that role. A role I didn't know if I was strong enough to take on.

"Lucas got home about twenty minutes ago," Tate said softly through fractured speech. I nodded, slowly walking towards him. His head dropped as I stood before him.

"Look at me."

Slowly he lifted his head and we stared at each other in silent conversation. Words that needed to be said were spoken in longing looks, comfort provided in the furrow of a brow, love given in the biting on our bottom lips. Words escaped me. What could I possibly say to a man whose world had been upheaved only hours earlier?

"What can I do, Tate?" I asked, finally finding my voice, my words a squeak, showing no confidence. I crawled on his lap, wrapping my arms around his broad bare shoulders. How had I not noticed that he was shirtless? Pulling him close to my chest, I silently begged him to fall into my body. His face dropped into the crook of my neck and his warm breath danced delicately, almost soothingly, over my skin. My eyes fluttered shut under the sensation.

"I don't know."

My arms encased him as I begged for comfort from my arms to engulf him. We sat mostly in silence, the sound of our breathing and the soft hum of the television the only sounds in the air. Shifting in his lap, I straddle him as best as my protruding stomach would allow. My hands skimmed gently along the ridges of his sculpted chest, my fingertips moving to his tattoo like magnets. I loved that tattoo. I had since that very first day in his bedroom.

I felt his eyes boring into mine as I concentrated on his tattoo, the intensity around us increasing with every silent second that passed. I didn't know what I could do. The feeling of Tate's fingers running through my hair, undoing the braid that had taken me an hour to do this morning sent shivers down my spine. My hair loosened and flowed down my back, the scent of my strawberry shampoo taking over my senses. Without a word, I lifted my hips slowly before sitting back down, grinding on the increasing bulge I felt swelling below me. His lips found my neck, sucking, licking, and kissing my favorite spot. I couldn't stop the moan from escaping my parted lips.

"Lucas is just in there," Tate mumbled against my throat.

"It's our apartment," I suggested with a wink. "I need you in me, Tate. I need you to feel me and I don't care who hears."

Chapter Twelve

Tate

MY FATHER—OR THE MAN I now affectionately called 'sperm donor'—had been trying to call me for the past week, and now it was getting to the point where I was either going to throw my phone against the wall, hoping it would be obliterated to a thousand pieces, or have to be an adult and change my number. How many times would someone call before they gave up? After over a hundred unanswered calls, you'd think he'd get the point.

"Are you going to answer your phone?" Jack asked from the front bar. The shrill of my phone ringing through the bar had grabbed his attention.

"Nope."

"Well turn the damn thing off then," Jack spat and turned his back to me.

I walked to my office and fell into my chair. My moods were volatile and completely hostile. I was like a firecracker, an atomic bomb just waiting to detonate. One minute I was fine, happy, content with everything, and the next I was snapping at people and being thrown into the black abyss of my thoughts. This was getting to be beyond a joke.

My poor Savannah was getting the brunt of this whole fucked-up situation too. I was working all hours of the day and night, pulling eighteen-hour shifts. My mind needed to be active because the moment it stopped I would think of him. Savannah was hurting because of this. We had barely spoken this past week. It had only been last night that it had finally blown up.

"Tate, you need to tell me what I can do. I can't keep wondering whether you are going to come home or I am going to get a call from some random bar where you have decided to drown your sorrows. This isn't healthy. You can't keep shutting everyone out," Sav grasped my arm halting me to a stop as I walked through the apartment. It was three A.M. Why the fuck was she up?

"Why are you even awake?"

"Because my boyfriend is worrying me sick, because I never see him anymore, and because I am scared something is going to happen. That's why I am awake."

I shuddered under her touch, a reminder of the effect she had on me. Our bed had been a place of pleasure for so long, but this week it had been a scene of awkwardness. What the fuck was I doing? Grabbing her hand, I led her to the couch, encouraging her to take a seat. Collapsing beside her, I felt exhaustion swamp me. I had barely slept a wink this week.

"Savannah, I don't know what to say."

"Tell me what you are thinking. I am a lot of things, but

I'm not a mind reader."

"You want the truth?" Taking a shaky breath, I unleashed my deepest thoughts to the one person who needed to know. "I feel like my whole life has been a lie. I feel like I am going to go down the exact path of my father. I feel like I can't trust anyone anymore. And I feel like this is all going to blow up in my face. I want nothing more than to be the guy you deserve. You are a fucking goddess, Savannah, an enigma, and I want desperately to be the guy who loves you forever and a day. I want to be that guy, I desperately need to be that guy because there is no one else, Savannah. You are it for me, but I'm terrified I'll be my father. My track record is fucked up. I am more like him than I could even imagine."

My chest tightened and my cheeks suddenly covered with salty tears. Her arms surrounded me with an honest security I craved. My head fell to the crook of her neck and I breathed in her scent. I despised showing weakness, but now, as I lay in the arms of my future, I was the weakest I had ever been. She scooted out from under me and moved up the couch, and my head was soon lying on her lap, her fingers soothingly running through my hair.

"Do you want my truth, Tate?"

I finally looked at her, her eyes begging for me to let her speak.

"The thought of being in a relationship scared me. It terrified me. The thought of giving my heart to someone was something I never wanted to imagine. That was until you. I want to give you my heart, my soul, my love, my life. There is no one else for me, Tate. Whether you are going through your darkest days or experiencing life-altering highs, I want to be *by your side. I need to be by your side. I will not let this destroy you. I will not let your father take you away from me. I will not let your father make you feel like you are anything but the best partner a girl could ask for and the best father our Jellybean can have. I will not allow that."*

The sound of my office door creaking open distracted my memories. Looking towards the door, I saw a furious-looking Jack walk in without an invitation. I closed my laptop and sat back in my chair, awaiting his assault.

"You gotta snap out of this and quickly." His arm folded across his chest, his eyes narrow and his voice direct. He wasn't kidding around. "I know you found out shitty news, but you know what? You have the best fucking girl in the world at home waiting for you. You have a beautiful baby that is going to be arriving in a matter of weeks, you have a family that adores you, and you have a best friend that is sick to death of watching you torment yourself. Fucking snap out of it and do something about this." Jack glared at me but then his eyes softened. "Go to him, tell him everything you want to say, and get it off your chest. If you don't, I honestly don't know if your relationship will survive this." He turned and stormed out of my office without another word.

He was right. I had been a prick this past week. Last night felt like it had been the boiling point, the point of no return. Sav loved me. She loved me with every piece of her being and I had been slowly trying to destroy that because of my fears. This had to stop. I deserved this kind of happiness. Fuck it—I had earned this happiness. I fumbled through the paperwork on my desk, locating my phone and hastily typing in a text. *Change begins now.*

Come to Red Velvet when you are free.

Satisfied, I sighed in relief and placed my phone back on my desk, leaning back in my chair. *Let's see if I get a visitor.*

Blake's deep voice bounced off the walls of Red Velvet no more than thirty minutes later. He'd actually turned up. I hadn't seen him since his face had met my fist, so to be honest, I was surprised he had shown. Swallowing hard, I pushed back from my desk and stood, stretching high and looking towards my closed door. *You can do this, Tate,* I chanted to myself.

Taking confident steps, I made my way out of my office and out into the empty bar. Standing by the main bar, Blake and Jack were in conversation. Blake looked across at me and nodded in acknowledgment. *Okay, Tate. One foot in front of the other.* I moved through the bar, my eyes dodging all over the place.

"Hi, Blake. Thanks for coming in."

"Sure thing. What's up?"

Jack watched both of us before making an excuse about having to call Tanzi.

"Want a drink?" I asked with a nod towards the bar.

"Sounds good."

We walked towards the main bar side by side and my nerves quickly made their appearance. I just needed to get through this conversation and then I could go home, wrap my arms around my beautiful Sav, and start my life again. I slipped in behind the bar, moving towards the row of my best liquor. My eyes scanned the shelves until they landed on what

I was after. Ahhh, my prized scotch.

Grabbing the bottle and two glasses, I placed them on top of the bar with a clink and held it up to Blake. "You still like scotch?" I asked.

"Wouldn't drink anything else."

I dropped my eyes and watched the amber liquid swirl in the glass as I poured, and I knew I had the beginnings of a smile on my face. Maybe this wouldn't be as bad as I'd expected. "Good to see some things haven't changed. Many of my hazy memories growing up include you, me, and a bottle of cheap scotch."

"I'm surprised I still have a working liver after the abuse I gave it with you." Blake laughed and took the glass I held out to him.

"Remember the time you tried to hook up with that Sally chick and your dick got jammed in your zipper? Fuck, that was the funniest shit ever." I roared with laughter as I was taken back to when I was nineteen.

Shaking his head, Blake grimaced. "I couldn't fuck for weeks."

Our laughter meshed together as we were both lost in the memories of a time where life seemed to be all about drinking on the beach, surfing, and picking up girls. A simpler time—a time when we were just two best friends, who were about to take on the world, one surf and one chick at a time.

"Look, Blake, I know shit has been cr—"

"Tate?"

What the fuck? My eyes moved from Blake and looked over his shoulder. What the hell was he doing here? Blake looked at me with questioning eyes, and the glare on my face spoke a thousand words. He twisted on the stool and looked towards where our father stood by the main entrance. The moment our father realized who he was looking at, he clutched a seat to steady himself. I bet he hadn't thought he'd see both sons when he'd decided to barge into my bar unwelcome and uninvited.

My eyes pointed at him as my anger increased with every passing second. "What the hell are you doing here? I suggest you turn around and leave now."

"If you answered your phone, I wouldn't have had to come here. Why are you not answering my calls?"

Was he serious? A billion responses echoed in my head; a billion images appeared in my thoughts. I heard Blake scoff beside me and the sound of his glass slamming down on the wooden top of the bar. I followed his lead, swallowing the strong scotch down my throat before turning back to face my father.

"I don't have anything to say to you. I got what I needed, and now I suggest you leave." I felt my hackles rise on the back of my neck and the panic flood me. My comfort wasn't here. The calming waves in my life weren't here. Sav wasn't here.

"I am your father. I deserve your respect."

What the hell had this guy been smoking? Respect? He could piss off as far as I was concern. Respect is earned. It was an honor to be respected, and I wouldn't piss on him even if he was on fire, so he could jam respect up his ass.

"You lost all opportunity to be respected by me the moment you put your dick in another woman's pussy and left my mother."

His eyes narrowed on me. "Watch your mouth, son."

"I'm not your son," I sneered. "You are not my father. You lost the right to call me your son the moment you abandon your children, Blake included, so get on your fucking high horse and fuck off." I shot a look at Blake, who looked on silently. I saw the vein in his neck pulse dangerously and knew any minute he would unleash his own assault of words.

"So what, you can't talk for yourself, son?" he spat, moving his gaze to Blake with a smirk on his thin pathetic lips.

Blake stood from the stool and moved beside me in a show of brotherly solidarity. "I've got nothing to say to you. You left before I was born so why the fuck should I give you the pleasure of speaking with me? You are a pathetic waste of space. The only thing you did right by me was give me a brother and sister, and as far as I'm concerned, you aren't even alive. So that's what I want to say to you. Fuck off out of our lives. You are neither wanted nor needed."

Props, little brother! I turned and gave Blake a look of satisfaction before turning back towards our father. His demeanor had changed and he knew he was quickly losing the battle he had waltzed in here trying to start. What had he really expected? If a person doesn't answer your hundreds of calls, it clearly means they want jack shit from you. Now it was my turn to let loose, and the pleasure of facing him ran rampant with me. I stood face to face with my past, a past that, from this moment on, would not affect my present and would be forgotten in my future.

"I'll tell you why you have absolutely no part in my life, not even a minuscule part. It's because within a week you have gone from fucking up my life to now affecting the lives of the two people who mean the most of me—my girlfriend and my unborn child. I have a girl who has finally healed all of the fucked-up hurt you put on me and now she is hurting because of you. And I have an unborn child I would die for but now I am so petrified of screwing up because of you." My eyes ran over his face to memorize the monster I didn't want to become. His blue eyes were void of any emotion or life. "Actually, come to think about it, I do have something to thank you for. Thank you for showing me the kind of man I never want to become. Thank you for screwing up so much that I will never inflict that on the people I love, and thank you for showing me everything I don't ever want to be. Now get the fuck out of my bar and my life before I call the cops."

I didn't wait for him to respond. "Blake, you and I are celebrating. Let's go." Making my way through the bar, I jumped at the sound of the entrance door slamming as my father left. Finally, he'd gotten the point.

"What are we celebrating?" Blake asked nervously.

I smiled at him as best I could. "Freedom."

Savannah walked through the doors and anxiously looked around the bar. Friday nights were always busy and tonight wasn't any exception. I watched her from across the bar before I moved towards her. I just wanted to enjoy her innocence. Her head darted around the bar as she tried to find me. Her eyes connected with mine and a smile filled her face. I put the empty glass I had just collected on the bar and strolled through the people towards her.

"Hey, Sav."

"What's going on, Tate?" she asked anxiously, grabbing my hands and pulling me close. I had asked everyone to come down to the bar tonight. Tonight was the first day of my new life. "Is everything okay?"

"Everything is perfect, Sav. You are perfect. This little one is perfect," I cooed, placing my hands on her eight-months-pregnant belly. "Can we talk?"

"Of course."

After I laced my fingers with hers, we moved through the bar towards my office. I halted as Sav stopped dead in her tracks. I shifted around and followed her gaze to the table where Jack, Tanzi, Blake, and Lucas were sitting. Tanzi was sitting on Jack's lap and Blake was laughing at something Lucas had said. Her eyes darted between the table and me as a questioning look flooded her face.

"That's what I need to talk to you about." I tugged on her hand and we made our way into my office. I closed the door behind us. Sav stood before me and I finally got to take in the sight before me. She looked stunning, absolutely glowing. The dress she was wearing hugged all of her curves, and Jellybean was on full display. She was so proud of showing off her baby bump. Her hair was swept into a low braid that hung over her shoulder and she had no makeup.

"Today I faced my father." Sav's eyes widened and she opened her mouth to speak. "Let me speak, Sav."

Walking towards my desk, I sat on the edge and pulled Sav between my open legs, flush against my body. My hands rested on her lower back before trailing down and cupping her perfectly inviting ass. My eyes roamed her face, taking in her invitingly pouty lips that were covered in a sheen of gloss and her wide, green eyes that were looking at me with question and anticipation. Fuck, I was a lucky bastard.

An air dense with need, want, and anxiety thickened and shifted around us the longer our eyes hunted each other's. Her arms wrapped around my shoulders and my eyes closed as her fingernails raked through my hair. The sounds of the bar beyond the closed door flitted into the office, but all I heard was the broken breathing coming from Sav.

"I love you so fucking much, Savannah."

A tormented sigh escaped her mouth as my lips crashed on hers, forcefully taking the air from her chest. Softly my tongue ran the length of her bottom lip, sweeping, tasting, and caressing her sensitive flesh. As I pulled her lip between my teeth and nibbled the flesh I wanted to devour, a moan rose from Sav and her hands gripped my hair tighter, pulling me desperately closer to her and deepening our kiss. Our tongues swept each other's mouths, claiming the loss the past week had given us, a week where our affection had been a kiss on the cheek here and there, a week I would never ever let us experience again.

"Do I have you back?" Sav hesitated against my lips, her breath dancing with mine as she spoke. Dropping my forehead against hers I drank her in. "I need you here Tate."

"I wouldn't be anywhere else. I've said goodbye to my past today, Sav, and that means I told my father I couldn't have him in my life in any way. I want my relationships with people in my life to be positive. I am going to try with Blake. He is my brother, Sav, so I need to try." I cupped her face with my hands and looked at her with a smirk begging to show. "You are my life now, this baby is my life, and your incredibly distracting new set of boobs are my life."

"Well I won't have these distracting boobs for much longer once Jellybean arrives," Sav scoffed and squarely slapped my chest.

"I'll always have the memories. Memories like those are burned into my brain. I have a month to do some serious motorboating on those bad boys." I kissed her lips lightly and groaned as another slap ricocheted off my chest.

She wrapped her arms around my waist and dropped her head to rest on my chest, just above my racing heart. Complete silence surrounded us. Everything about today, the last week, all boiled down to this moment. Every fear I had, every thought that consumed me, and every regret that swallowed me—it all boiled down to this. Finally I could smile at the thought of the future.

"I finally feel like I'm going to be the best dad in the world, Sav," I whispered into her hair.

She lifted her head from my chest and her entire face smiled at me. "I've known since day one."

Chapter Thirteen

Savannah

MY BODY FELT STRETCHED TO full capacity, like at any moment my insides were going to explode through my tightly pulled skin. Graphic, I know, but that's how I felt as the full term of my pregnancy had come and gone. This wasn't fun anymore. Sleep evaded me for what felt like days, and every time Jellybean decided to move, a wave of nausea rolled over me, which had resulted in the doctor now watching me like a hawk for fear of dehydration. And with this news, Tate had gone all protective and refused to leave my side. I had to force him out of the apartment to go to work most days, and then the hundred or so text messages would begin. To say he was invested in this pregnancy was an understatement.

All I wanted was to meet my baby. The date was marked on the calendar, circled with thick red sharpie. Today was the last day I was being allowed to go naturally before the doctor would order me to have a Caesarean. I woke today hoping that it was the first day of the rest of my life.

"Sav, where are you?" Mr. Davenport's voice echoed from the front door. I popped my head out from around the door of the bedroom and smiled as I gazed at him. He held a bunch of flowers, his eyes darting around the empty apartment in search of me. I stepped out into view and his eyes lit up when he saw me. "Well look at you!"

"What are you doing here? Shouldn't you be at work?" I moved towards him and instantly wrapped my arms around him.

We walked towards the couch and I lowered myself on, wincing as a shot of pain roared through me. It had been happening all morning, but I'd kept it to myself. No need to worry protective father to be.

Mr. Davenport sat with me for an hour, his hand constantly on my stomach, waiting for Jellybean to kick. "How are you feeling? Is my grandbaby behaving?"

"I'm nervous," I admitted, resting my hand on my stomach as a torrent of butterflies swarmed within me.

"You'll be spectacular." He genuinely smiled at me as I fidgeted with the loose-fitting top that was stretched to capacity over my stomach. "How's Tate fairing?"

Shaking my head, I laughed softly. Amazing wasn't even the word that could explain how Tate had been over the past few months. I couldn't have asked for a better partner. He was there at two A.M. when I wanted peanut butter and banana sandwiches, he was the one who sat with me in the bath when my body was aching, and he was the one who held me as we both spoke of our fears. But mostly he was the one who made me feel completely and utterly loved.

"He has been incredible. I think he is more excited than I am. He even got a little jumpsuit made up with the Red Velvet logo on it." Suddenly my phone vibrated on the table in front of me. Leaning down, I picked it up and looked at the screen. "Speak of the devil."

Hey baby momma, I'll bring you avocado and chicken sandwich home for lunch. How's my little one doing? Causing mommy grief?

"I never thought I'd admit this, and don't go around telling people, but I am definitely Team Tate. You have a good man there." He stood from the couch while I was left sitting there completely flabbergasted. "Shut your mouth, woman. You'll catch flies."

I put my hands behind me and slowly levered myself off the couch while Mr. Davenport stood above and looked at me amusingly. Bastard. I'd known there was a reason I didn't sit on the couch anymore. My amazing couch which I couldn't enjoy anymore because I would sink so far into it that I would have to be pulled out of it. Tate had found this hilarious time and time again. I'd called him an arsehole and refused to sit with him, sitting instead on the floor.

"You make sure you have Tate call me as soon as there is any news. I want to be pacing that hospital corridor like the excited grandfather I am."

Just hearing him say those words turned on the waterworks and tears spilled down my cheeks. My emotions were a mess. I didn't say a word. I just leaned into Mr. Davenport's chest and sobbed as he wrapped his arms around me and held me tight. Just us. His arms had provided me with so much comfort over the years, and now that I was about to turn over to the next chapter in the book of Savannah, there was nowhere I would rather be.

"I love you." I sobbed.

"I love you too. You are my girl, Savannah."

During my tenth waddle around the apartment, which seemed like the only plausible means of settling the dull ache that had come on after Mr. Davenport had left, I felt a sudden and brutally intense pressure ricocheting through my body. I grasped on to the kitchen bench, my eyes slamming shut and my breath hitching as I leaned over, desperate to find relief. Then out of nowhere there was an instant release and *whoosh.* My legs spread instantaneously, and soon enough, my thighs were coated in a warm liquid as my body contracted in the middle of the kitchen.

I stared at the puddle beneath my feet with wide eyes, and a sense of panic ran through my body, which was followed by fear, excitement, and exhilaration. It was eight P.M. and I was at home alone, as Tate worked the close shift at Red Velvet. I'd known my child would be a night owl, and Jellybean had just proved my point. I stood in the kitchen looking at the mess on the floor as realization hit. I was officially on my way to becoming a mum. *A mum.* My first instinct was the clean the mess, so I grabbed the mop and cleaned up as my mind ran crazily out of control. *A mum.*

Jellybean was ready to meet us. After nine months of falling in love with this little person, I could now be only hours from holding him or her in my arms. Savannah Rae, a mother, having the responsibility of this little person.

My confusion increased as I stood in the kitchen and looked down at my stomach. Wasn't I meant to be feeling different? Like, wasn't I meant to be huddled over, grasping on to the bench as pain ripped through me?

I stumbled through the apartment in an oblivious state and searched for my phone, anxious to call the hospital to find out what the hell was happening. All those visits and information I had desperately crammed into my head from the pre-birth class had vanished from my mind.

After speaking with a midwife and finding out that everything seemed to be okay, I felt a little more relaxed, but still, I needed Tate here. A sense of calm would sweep through my body but then, *boom,* panic would set it.

His panicked voice boomed down the phone when he picked up. "Sav what's wrong?"

"My waters broke." I sighed into the phone. "We are going to become parents."

"What! Okay. I am leaving now. I will be there in ten minutes." His astonished voice filled my ears and instantly I felt comforted. "I'll be home soon."

Holding my phone close to my chest, I smiled at Tate's words. He loved me, we had a home, and now we were going to be having a baby. I was about to give birth. Both Jack and Lucas loved teasing me, reminding me daily that giving birth would be like trying to fit a watermelon through a pinhole. Seriously, I had freaking arseholes as family.

I walked through the apartment towards the bedroom, where I lay down as my mind went crazy. It all came down to this. Tate and I were prepared. We had everything organized and waiting for our little one to arrive. My heart was ready to meet my next great love.

I gasped as the door suddenly flew open and Tate's panicked face looked over me. He took a seat beside me, frantically grabbing my hands and lifting them to his lips, kissing each knuckle.

"Are you okay?"

I nodded. "Did you break every traffic law getting here?"

"There is no time to think of traffic laws, Sav. I have to get you to the hospital. Have you called the hospital? What did they say? What do I need to do?" His panicked voice rang through the room.

"You need to lie down on this bed with me and let me look at you. I am alright. The midwife told me to come in when the contractions start. I am only having little ones at the moment."

"We are about to have a baby, Sav," he sang. He climbed on the bed beside me, rolling to his side and watching me. A look of panic yet calm filtered over his perfect face.

I lifted my feet up and rested them over his to ease the stab of pain that had shot through me. "We should probably call your mum and Mr. D. I know Tanzi, Jack, and Lucas will want to know," I rambled, squeezing my eyes shut as the pain rushed through me and then eased.

"Let it just be us three right now. I just need you and Jellybean."

We stared at each other in complete silence, the only sound coming from our excited breathing. With our eyes, we read each other and spoke our feelings without words. My love for the man lying beside me was immeasurable by words, and for some crazy reason he loved me just as much.

Never in a hundred years had I ever thought I would be here with the man who had saved me from myself and about to have his child. The universe had thrown me curveballs, but it all lead to this very moment, a moment where the heartache of losing my parents was slowly being repaired by this man. No, I didn't have my parents here with me, but I knew they were in my heart. They were protected away from the world and they were mine. I was one of the lucky ones. After years of feeling sorry for myself, I had come to realize just how lucky I was. I had had the opportunity to live with two families—my parents and now my current family. My heartache was nothing compared to others and I had to remember that. I had to live for my present and future, not for my past.

"Thank you," I whispered. My hands rose to his face, cupping his cheeks, and my thumb grazed his bottom lip. His eyes softened but didn't leave mine. The blueness I wished our baby would inherit glistened in front of me.

"What are you thanking me for?" he whispered back.

"For everything. You gave me a reason to love again, Tate Connors. I love you more than I could ever express to you and there is no one else in this world for me. Forever, you will be my heart. Will you mar—Holy shit!" I groaned, my hands dropping from his face to clutch my stomach as a pain I had never experienced ripped through me. Tears came to my eyes and my teeth clamped shut.

Tate shot off the bed, clasping my hand and pulling me up. I fell against his chest as he wrapped his arms tightly around me.

"I am taking you to the hospital." He ran to the room that

was going to be Jellybean's room and fetched my hospital bag before running back into the bedroom. I had never seen him this frantic.

Grabbing his hand, I pulled him to a stop. "We are about to meet our baby, Tate."

Chapter Fourteen

Tate

"TATE, I AM SO TIRED," Sav whispered as she tucked her head deep into my shoulder. I felt the wetness of her fresh tears dance over my skin as her emotions and exhaustion took their tolls. We had gotten to the hospital in record time. I was sure that I had broken numerous laws getting her here, but all I could focus on was her and our baby. Jellybean.

Pushing a strand of her sweaty, matted hair from her cheek, I kissed her forehead softly. Her eyes were tired, her face showing signs of fatigue and her body about ready to give in. This had been hell. Ten hours of hell. I hated that I couldn't do a damn thing to take away her pain. Watching her squirm, cry, moan, and scream had caused my heart to twist time and time again.

"Baby, we are almost there. We will see Jellybean really soon. You are doing so well." I kissed her lips tenderly before pulling away and taking a close look at her. Even in the middle of labor with a person trying to rip itself out of her, she was still the most beautiful girl in the world.

There was something so unique and life changing about watching the one person who was your universe attempt to give you the most precious gift. This woman lying before me in all of her pregnant glory was about to give me a child. We were about to share blood.

"Can you go and make sure Mr. Davenport is here?" Her eyes begged me. "I need him to be here."

I nodded at Savannah before shooting a questioning look at the midwife. "You have time," she said, confirming my unasked question.

After I rushed out of the room like a windstorm, my eyes darted around the sterile-smelling hallway as nurses and doctors hurried around me. The light above shone brightly, causing my eyes to squint under its annoying glare. I took off down the hall almost colliding with a lady wheeling the food cart and crashed through the door of the waiting area. My heart stopped when I found my family. Everyone was here; Tanzi, Jack, Lucas, Ali, Blake, Mr. Davenport, and mom.

Tanzi's eyes widened the moment she looked up from the magazine in her hand to find me and the loudest, most high-pitched shriek I'd ever heard escaped from her tiny body. I flinched as pain shot through my ears.

"Tate! Am I an aunt? A girl or a boy? Is Jellybean adorable?" she rattled off, rushing towards me and pulling on my arm as if she needed to get my attention. Her shriek alone had gained the attention of everyone in the room.

"Settle down, Tanzi. Jellybean isn't here yet." I smiled.

Her face dropped instantly. "Sav just wanted to make sure you were all here." Speaking generically, I let my eyes land on Mr. Davenport's, who stood silently.

"Can I have a word, Tate?" he abruptly announced and headed towards the corner of the waiting room. Obliging, I quickly kissed Tanzi on the cheek and moved towards him. Jamming my hands in my pockets and yawning loudly, I looked at him and waited for him to speak.

"How's our girl going?" His eyes showed tiredness and concern for the girl who owned both our hearts. His suit was crumpled from the hours sitting in the plastic seats of the waiting room, but his face was bursting with intrigue.

"She is so perfect. She is doing amazingly well. I think our child is going to be stubborn. Jellybean definitely is comfortable in there." I sighed, a hint of a smile playing on my lips.

"With parents like you two, what do you expect?" He laughed. "I hope your kid gives you hell."

"I'll just make sure I have his or her grandfather on speed dial for those hellish times. How will you be able to say no to spending time with your grandchild?"

"You are an evil genius Tate Connors." Mr. Davenport laughed deeply and patted my shoulder before walking back to Mom.

Our relationship had gone full circle. To think that finally he realized I wasn't going anywhere and that I was here for the long run made me feel pride swell in my chest. Mr. Davenport was the one and only man in my life I was desperate to gain respect from and finally I felt like I was slowly getting there.

A moment of clarity hit me as I stood by the window looking over the visitor's courtyard below. I was hours—possibly minutes—away from becoming a father. For the past nine months, I'd wondered when it would finally hit me, when the reality that I was going to be responsible for a little person and that every decision I made would be for them, and right now it was here.

I was already thinking of the future. I was already planning the house I wanted to buy for my little family. I needed my little one to grow up on the beach. I needed him or her to experience the freedom, the ease, and the lifestyle the ocean offered. I wanted to give the ocean to Sav and her memories. I knew her parents would be with us if we were near the ocean.

The sound of the coffee machine grabbed my attention. *Coffee. An espresso would be great right now.* Darting through the other people in the waiting room, I followed the scent of strong coffee and impatiently waited in line. I needed to get to Sav. I felt someone come up beside me, and turning to my left my eyes, I landed on my brother. Shit, that still took a lot to get my head around.

"Hi," Blake said timidly.

"Hey."

"I wasn't sure if I should come. Tanzi called me and demanded that I get my ass down here, and well, as you know, you can't argue with her. I will leave the moment you tell me. I don't want to cause any trouble," he rambled and nervously rubbed the back of his neck. I took a good look at him and felt the edges of my mouth curve.

"One thing you will learn about our sister. You will never win an argument."

"Yeah, I'm learning that fast."

We stood in silence as the line moved excruciatingly slowly ahead of us. My mind bounced back to Savannah and how desperate I was to get back to her. My foot tapped anxiously below me, my patience wearing thin. *Seriously, people, my fucking girlfriend is about to have a baby.*

"I hate not being able to do anything to stop Sav hurting." I sighed and stepped out of the line. Screw coffee. Blake followed me and sat beside me as I slumped down on the chair, a wave of exhaustion hitting me.

"Just being there is all she needs." Blake wrung his hands in his lap and finally raised his eyes to look at me. "You are going to be an awesome dad, Tate."

How in the hell had we gotten to this moment? This was the guy who'd helped break my heart, shattered it into a million pieces, but he was also the guy who had been there during my bleakest moments, the guy who was now staring at me with what I could only describe as pride. How had I not realized we were brothers? Besides the tattoos adorning his arms and the dimple in his right cheek, we looked the same. The same eyes, the same nose, the same hair.

I'd swallowed my pride a long time ago. I needed to send every negative thought I'd ever had about him to the trash. I couldn't move on with my life, a life that could only be happy and healthy, if I held on to the past. My past was exactly that, my past. A past that involved fucked-up shit, heartbreak, loss and pure and utter devastation. But what I had in front of me was a future, a future with the love of my life, a baby of my own, a new beginning, a second chance.

"Can we forget everything that happened with us? We have both said and done shit we aren't proud of, but at the end of the day, you are family. You're my brother and you are about to become an uncle. I don't want my kid being around negative shit." I held my hand out in earnest. "Brothers?"

"Brothers," he replied, grabbing my hand and shaking it hard. "You really need to get back in there. Go and meet my niece or nephew."

When I rushed back in the room, Sav's head snapped towards the door and an exhausted smile moved over her face at the sight of me. "Is everyone here?" she asked breathlessly.

I sat on the edge of the bed and entwined our fingers together. "Yeah, everyone is here. Mr. Davenport, Tanzi, Jack, Lucas, Ali, Mom, and Blake."

Her eyes widened in surprise. "Blake?"

"He is here to meet his little niece or nephew."

"Thank you." Her eyes glazed over and my heart filled with love.

The midwife moved around the foot of the bed and I watched her closely. This woman was responsible for the safe birth of our baby. The room we were in had such a calming effect. Soft music was filtering through the air, candlelight danced on the walls, and the familiar scent of green tea and bamboo took over my senses. This was what had calmed Sav down at home, so I'd needed that to be here. It was the perfect place to welcome Jellybean.

"Are you ready, Sav? Are you ready to meet our baby?" I whispered lovingly into her ear.

After ten hours of labor, numerous false starts, and doctors saying one thing but Sav's body doing another, I knew it was time by the nod the midwife had given me. I clutched Sav's hand and gave her one final kiss on the cheek. Our lives were about to change drastically.

"Just one more big push, Sav, and your baby will be here." The midwife's words were like a symphony to my ears. "Does the father want to see the head?"

What the fuck did she just ask me? No no no!

I knew my eyes were bugged out of my head at the thought of looking down *there*. Yes, I had seen *there* on more than one occasion. I loved nothing more than being down *there*. But I was usually making her scream as pleasure gripped her body, not gawking as a baby ripped its way out of her. Fuck, I was going to faint. I gripped the side of the bed as panic roared through me. I was going to be one of those fathers who fainted under the pressure. That's what I would remember of the birth of my child—lying on the floor after fainting at the sight of Savannah's pussy. Brilliant.

"Tate, your face is priceless," Sav groaned with a slight chuckle. "Go and see our baby's head. I want you to see it first."

Oh, Savannah, why did you have to say that?!

All I could do was nod. Of course I would do as she asked. My eyes bounced between Savs and the midwife, and I slowly moved down to the end of the bed, my hand gripping the mattress to hold me up. God, could I really do this?

"Another one is coming. I have to push!" Sav choked. I rushed as soon as I heard her words.

"Okay, let's do this." The midwife grabbed Savannahs legs, yanking them open wider. "If you want to see this, then stay down here. If you want to be with Sav, then as soon as she pushes and the head becomes visible I suggest you move back to the bed. It's your call."

There I stood beside the midwife, totally speechless and in complete and utter awe. I had never seen or witnessed anything like this before. The sound of Sav's painful cry filled the air around me and I cringed. I hated not being able to help her.

But then everything faded around me as I was witness to most beautiful sight in the world. As if I watching a movie in slow motion, my baby's head appeared before me. He or she was really there and barely inches away from me. Time felt like it was standing still, like everything had stopped around me. I couldn't move, I couldn't speak, I couldn't breathe. My gaze was locked on the miracle that was happening before me. My baby. I saw the tuft of dark brown matted hair and couldn't help but smile. Our baby had a head full of hair. Sav had wanted Jellybean to be born with hair for some weird reason, and she was about to get her wish.

"Tate, I need you."

All I could focus on was the look of exhaustion on Sav's face as I hurried to the top of the bed and grabbed her hand. "I'm here."

Sharing this experience with her, seeing her at her weakest yet strongest, set something on fire within me. I needed this woman for life. She was the strongest, most resilient person I had ever met and she was mine. She clutched my hand with all the strength she could muster. Her teeth clenched together as the tears of every piece of emotion bubbling through her body came to the surface.

"Tate!" she groaned and her head fell to the side as she looked at me.

"Come on, baby. You can do this. One more push and we will have our Jellybean." I leaned down and softly kissed her sweaty forehead.

Her face crumbled as a ripple effect of pain shot through her body. It was excruciating but exhilarating to watch, and then suddenly her face softened with relief.

The world I knew was shattered and my heart exploded with love as the most amazing sound glided through the air. The chaos around us echoed in my ears, but the only sound I heard was the soft, innocent, perfect cries of our baby, and the only thing I saw were the tears flooding Savannah's cheeks.

"Is the baby okay?" she choked out as exhaustion dripped from her words. "Tate, is the baby okay?"

I let my eyes leave hers and hesitantly turned towards the midwife. My heart stilled. This was the moment. The exact moment when the life I knew ceased and the life I'd craved began. This was it. The moment when I forgot everything and was able to start with a clean plate, the moment I let go of every fucked-up experience that had been dealt to me. The moment happened the second I first looked into the inquisitive eyes of my first born. I couldn't even fathom what emotion was taking over every inch of my body. Every hair on my body stood to attention, my blood ran hot, and my breathing was jagged. Everything prior to this second held absolutely no relevance.

"Sav, Jellybean is perfect."

"Your baby is perfect." The midwife looked between Sav and me. "Congratulations, you have a son."

Sav's head swung to me as the first tears streamed over my cheeks. We had a son. Sav and I had created a beautiful, healthy son. The midwife brought our bundle of love over and placed him on Sav's bare chest. His soft newborn cries soothed as he rested on his mother's chest.

My eyes were fixated. I couldn't look away from the sight in front of me. I'd never imagined that I would be a father. I'd never imagined that I would be here. But now I couldn't imagine being anywhere else. Every insecurity I'd had, every ounce of doubt that had played heavily on my mind vanished the moment my eyes locked with my son. My son. This little person was my life now. My heart beat for him and my decisions were based entirely on his safety and well-being.

"We will give you both a minute," the midwife said softly. I couldn't even acknowledge her. My eyes were latched to the perfection in Sav's arms. A head full of dark brown hair, big blue eyes, and a perfect set of lips greeted me. His eyes darted around, trying desperately to focus, completely oblivious to the extent of his arrival.

"We did it. Look at him. We have a son." Sav's voice attracted our baby's attention, and as their eyes connected, I felt a love swarm through me that I'd never thought existed.

We hadn't discussed names. We'd wanted to name Jellybean when we first met him or her. "Max Davenport Connors," Sav whispered as she ran a finger along his cheek.

"Hey, Max. I'm your daddy, and this beautiful lady is your mommy. I am so happy you are here, little man."

CHAPTER
Fifteen

Savannah

IT REALLY WAS TRUE. THE moment you hold your child in your arms and your eyes connect with them for the very first time, you forget every pain, stretch, rip, and pull of childbirth. Sure, my body was aching in all the wrong places. Sure, my hair looked like a bird had taken residence in it. Sure, my face was blotchy and puffy from all the crying I'd done. But the swelling of my heart with the love I felt overcame everything in this moment. For the past nine months, my anxiety about this moment had been sky high, but now I couldn't imagine anything besides watching my little Jellybean have the best life I could offer and being the best damn mum the world had ever seen.

Reluctantly I dragged my eyes away from my gorgeous son, who I was cradling protectively in my arms, and glanced at the door as it slowly crept open, instantly allowing the light from the corridor to flood through the room. The moment my eyes latched on to Mr. Davenport's, my emotions exploded over and tears flooded my already damp cheeks. Tanzi, Jack, Lucas, Blake, and Ali followed Mr. Davenport and Tate's mom into the room, all wearing tired eyes and sincere smiles. Jack, Blake, and Lucas made their way towards Tate and shook his hand in congratulations while Tate beamed proudly at them, wearing his own mask of exhaustion.

Tanzi's knuckles turned white as she gripped Mr. Davenport's hand while they walked slowly towards my bed. I watched my best friend and saw a look I had never witnessed on Tanzi Connors's face ever before. She was showing signs of nerves and anxiety. My confident best friend had disappeared. My curious eyes watched her closely as her eyes left mine and dropped to the gorgeous boy curled up protectively in my arms. Her eyes widened and the smile that swept over her gorgeous face made my tears rush again. Tanzi stood motionless; her grip didn't lessen as her eyes roamed her nephew's face. My son was absolute perfection with his scruff of chocolate brown hair and big blue eyes. He was wide awake and taking everything in.

The bed beside me dipped under Mr. Davenport's weight as he sat next to me and grabbed my hand after finally being free from the clutches of Tanzi. The hushed voices in the room disappeared as I watched as he took in his grandson. My throat tightened. This was a moment neither of us could have ever imagined experiencing together.

"You, my girl, are my absolute inspiration." Mr. Davenport spoke a thousand words as his fingertips swept the loose strands of hair from my cheek. His eyes glistened with love and pride at the sight of his grandson in my arms. "I have a grandson," he choked, his voice cracking with emotion.

"This little guy is Max Davenport Connors," I whispered. His eyes rose from Max in shock, as if he were trying to comprehend what I had just said. "Max Davenport Connors," I repeated with a wide smile, proud of the name my son would bear.

"Sav, you didn't need to do that." Mr. Davenport said, stumbling on his words, his voice faltering.

"He is named after the three most special men in my life. You, Tate, and Dad. He needs to have your name. He needs to know where he came from." I smiled at him lovingly as Max squirmed in my arms. "Would you like to hold your grandson?"

He hesitated for a brief moment as he focused intently on Max before slowly nodding his head. This was the proudest moment of my life thus far, placing my baby into the arms of the man who'd made me who I was today. I sighed in contentment and burrowed deeper into the mattress below me, letting the scene unfold in front of me. The way that Max snuggled into Mr. Davenports arm's and looked up at him with his big blue exploring eyes made my heart tremble.

The twists and turns of the life I had been given had made me fly by the seat of my pants my entire life, but right at this second, with my family surrounding me, every bump and hurdle life had thrown at me had been completely worth it. I would live my past a million times over if it always led to this single moment.

I rolled my head to the side and my eyes landed on Tate sitting in the far corner of the room. He sat back with his legs crossed at the ankles, softly speaking with Jack, Lucas, and

Blake. His smile lit up the room but the exhaustion taking over his body was apparent. His brown hair disheveled and sticking up in crazy directions, his clothes crumpled and his blue eyes shadowed by sleeplessness, but still he was the most beautiful sight to me.

He had been with me every step of the way. He was the one who'd gotten me the ice cubes when I was thirsty. He was the one I had gripped on to as contractions ripped through my body. He was the one who'd allowed me to call him an arsehole during the birth. He was the one who'd gotten the gift of first seeing Max. And he was the one who had whispered that he loved me time and time again.

My body was riddled with exhaustion and aching in a way I'd never known possible, but my heart was exploding with a love that was indescribable. I felt exhilarated, like I could do absolutely anything, like I could face any challenge head-on, like I was the queen of the universe. I, Savannah Rae, was a mum.

"I love you," Tate mouthed from across the room as his eyes fell on mine—the perfect blues I could only pray that our son would inherit. In all of our time together, I'd never felt this connected to him as I did in this single moment. That arrogant, self-assured, broken arsehole, who I'd wanted the moment my eyes had fallen on him in the elevator, was now the father of my child. Our love and angst had created this gorgeous miracle.

"Sav, he is beautiful," Mr. Davenport's voice rumbled beside me, breaking me from Tate.

"Can you believe I created him? It's kinda freaky." I laughed softly, sweeping my finger over Max's soft forehead.

A cocky smirk formed on his lips. "He is going to be a ballbuster if he is anything like his mother."

"You know what scares me the most? Is that this little person is a blank map without coordinates, a book with empty pages, a movie without a script. He can do anything with his life. He can be whoever he wants and do whatever his heart tells him. He has the ability to write whatever book he wants for his life and I am going to be the one who guides him. It scares me. I can't fail him." My voice hitched under my admission.

"You have been and will always be in my life, Sav. You are the one constant, the one anchor, the one fixture. Yes, you have had your falls, but when you rise, you rise with grace and a new determination. You don't ever fail, Sav. You re-emerge stronger, more beautiful, and more focused than ever. I have every faith in you, my girl. You will never fail him. This little guy is lucky to have you."

"I need to find you a woman."

As he rolls his eyes, I could swear I saw his cheeks flush crimson. "Here we go again."

"It's either a woman or you are going to have Tanzi calling you a gilf." My words played with the smile swamping my face. I had made the mistake of telling Tanzi that it was only a matter of time before the nickname gilf would be circulating the office. Little did I know that she would be the one leading the crusade.

His brow rose in question. "Do I want to know what a gilf is?"

"Grandfather I'd like to fuck."

Mr. Davenport shook his head and moved his eyes back

down to Max while embarrassment crept up his neck. Before I had a second to warn him, Tanzi slipped up next to him with a familiar smirk planted on her lips. *Oh fuck. Here we go.*

"You can be married, single, divorced, gay, or straight and I'd still call you a gilf," Tanzi purred, wrapping her arm tightly around Mr. Davenport's shoulders before directing her attention at me. "Sav, I could be the stepmom you've always wanted and I could be Max's grandma."

"Sorry, Tanzi, but I like my women blonde."

"I am willing to dye my hair," she retorted without hesitation.

"Maybe a little older."

"I am a good actress."

"Preferably not in a relationship."

Tanzi moved closer and dropped her voice. "I'm willing to leave him." Tanzi's face held still as she stared at Mr. Davenport. His eyes went wide and his mouth dropped open at her admission. Mr. Davenport's eyes darted between mine and Tanzi's, and I could sense that a billion thoughts were running through his head.

"Jack, come and get your damn girlfriend away from me!" Mr. Davenport growled in Jack's direction.

Jack's head shot up and he shook his head knowingly. "Are you trying to pick up the old guy again?"

"Who the hell are you called old? I'll let you know that I'm a gilf, alright!" Mr. Davenport said, and everyone in the room burst out laughing. God, I loved that man.

"Jack, I want a baby!" Tanzi shrieked, startling Max. "Oh shit. Sorry, little buddy."

Lucas, Jack, Blake, and Tate walked towards the bed,

their eyes firmly set on Max, who was still watching Mr. Davenport closely. An instant bond had formed. I slowly and gently moved down the bed, allowing Tate to slide in behind me. I leaned back against his chest as his arms wrapped around me and rested on my hips. He was so gentle with me. The beat of his heart thudding against my back and the warmth his body provided soothed me within seconds. His fingers found my hair, sweeping it off my neck, and his lips found the special spot he knew I loved just beneath my ear.

"Thank you for giving me the best gift in the world."

Part Two

There will be moments in life that will leave you **Breathless,** until you learn to **Breathe Again.**

Chapter Sixteen

Tate

TWO YEARS LATER

"Happy birthday, Maxey!" Savannah's high-pitched bellow ripped through the apartment. Watching our son playing with his abundant amount of toys on the floor of our living room caused emotion to bubble within me. We were surrounded by family and friends, celebrating our little boy's second birthday. Savannah sat beside Max, helping him open his presents with pride covering her face. She was the perfect mom. Everything revolved around Max and nothing was too good for him. The moment she became a mom, she'd changed but in the best possible way. She'd opened her heart to possibilities, to new beginnings, and she'd closed some of the doors of her past. But still there were ones I didn't think we would ever get closed.

For two years we had been living in pure and utter bliss.

Our days had been filled with watching Max, being completely in awe when he'd crawled for the first time, taken his first step, and said momma and dada for the first time. There were still days when we would look at each other and burst out laughing at the fact that we were parents. Tate and Savannah, two people I was sure many people would have cringed at the thought of being parents, were doing a damn good job with this little guy.

I was what Savannah so lovingly and teasingly called a 'textbook dad.' I'd read way too many books on what to expect as a new father, which had left me watching too closely for illnesses and stressing when he didn't do something the book had told me he should be doing. But he always surprised me. He did everything before he was supposed to. He'd crawled early, he'd said his first word early, and he'd walked early. And every time, I'd felt my chest swell with pride.

"You have that look on your face again?" Sav cooed as she took a seat on my lap and huddled into my chest. Shooting her a look, I unlocked my arms from around her waist and pouted. Her giggle sounded like music to my ears.

"You really need to stop with the teasing,"

"Ahh, are you upset, my little muffin?"

"And you need to stop with the cute names."

"Fine, I'll start calling you an arsehole again," she whispered with a raised brow.

I nodded triumphantly. "That's better. We don't want to become that sickeningly cute couple now, do we? If you call me muffin, I'll call you dear."

"You wouldn't dare."

"Try me, *dear.*"

Her glare caused my ego to soar. If anything, the stubbornness we'd each possessed had fueled us to the point of fiery arguments and battles that neither of us would ever back down from, but that was Tate and Savannah, and I hoped to Christ we'd never lose the fieriness of our relationship. She kept me on my toes. That's for sure.

"I hope you know he clearly gets his awesomeness from his mum," Sav taunted, looking back towards Max, who now sat with Tanzi and Jack, playing with the Thomas the Tank Engine toy they had bought him.

"Well it's obvious he gets his good looks from his dad," I retaliated.

"Whatever."

I pulled Sav towards me, wrapping her in my arms as we sat in silence, watching Max. Today was about him; every day was about him. Whether it was our early morning snuggles in bed watching his newfound addiction of Thomas and Friends, taking him to the beach and watching him hesitate by the water's edge, or moments when it was just the three of us cuddled on the couch, it was in those moments where I knew I was the luckiest bastard in the world.

As I strode through Red Velvet, ready to start my evening shift, a cold shiver of fear rang through my body. I stopped suddenly in the middle of the crowded bar as a need to scope out the bar took over my every thought. Everything looked like a normal Saturday night at Red Velvet. Bachelor parties were in full swing, the band was playing on stage, the bar was crowded with people three deep waiting to be served, and the air was thick with excitement, anticipation, and sweaty desire. It was a normal Saturday night, but something didn't feel right.

Finding Jack talking with Stevie by the closed door of my office, I marched through as the anxiety I was feeling soared to unrealistic proportions. What the fuck was going on? I spoke sternly when I reached them. "Is everything okay here tonight?"

They both looked at each other and a look of caution and understanding bounced between them. Instantly a shiver ran down my spine. Something wasn't right and these two in front of me were keeping it from me. I owned the fucking bar; I deserved to know. My temper and unease flared like a ranging wildfire.

"Who is going to tell me what the fuck is going on?"

"It seems Chelsea forgot about her ban from Red Velvet and she has brought someone along with her." Stevie admitted cautiously.

Just hearing her name was like getting stabbed in the eye with a thousand knives. Why she continued to haunt me was anyone's guess.

Slamming my clamped fists into my pockets, I narrowed my eyes at Jack, desperate to grab onto my rapidly increasing frustration. "Why haven't you kicked her out?"

"I didn't know she was here until about a minute ago," Stevie, my burly bouncer, stated with a look of failure sweeping his face.

"Okay, look, just stick with the door. I'll go over and ask her to leave . . . as nicely as I can." I took off to the sounds of Jack calling my name but I refused to wait around and allow

Chelsea to stay in my bar any longer than she already had. My only thought was getting her, and whoever the hell the poor soul she had latched on to and brought to my bar, the hell out of it. I didn't have time, and to be honest, I couldn't give a fuck about dealing with her shit. A ban was a ban.

What I found stopped me dead to the spot and suddenly a wave of nausea hit me. What the hell kind of world had I just stumbled into? There, sitting at the table that everyone knew as Tanzi and Sav's was Chelsea and my father and she was sitting on his lap, looking like a two-dollar hooker. Blake stood before them, looking like he was ripping them both new assholes, his arms flailing everywhere and the roar of his voice being heard over the pounding of the drums from the band.

"Here he is. I was wondering when you'd show," my pathetic excuse for a father spat. After more than two years of having nothing to do with him and barely thinking about him, all it took was one sentence and he had singlehandedly ripped open the gaping wounds he'd caused—the same wounds I had been desperately trying to heal.

"What the fuck could be your reasoning be for being here?" I questioned, begging every bit of confidence I had to shine through; I refused to allow him to see what he had truly done to me. "What part of never wanting to see you again don't you understand?"

Chelsea stood from his lap and moved towards me on unsteady feet. As she stood before me, I looked her over in pure disgust. She placed her palms square on my chest as she looked up at me through drunken eyes. "Where's the slut?" she vindictively questioned, a smirk filtering over her lips.

I took a step towards her, pressing my body firm against

her palms, and glared at her with fuel burning within me. It took everything in my power to restrain the thoughts running riotously in my head. "Watch what you say, Chelsea."

"What are you going to do about it, Tate? You tried to ban me and that didn't work so what the fuck are you going to do?"

This time, my father stood and moved beside her, looking at both Blake and me. Déjà vu hit me. We had been in this exact spot when both Blake and I had confronted him before, the last time he'd barged into my bar. Seriously, when the fuck would this guy get it through his head? My anger for my father bubbled just below the surface yet again. I needed to get off this roller coaster of emotions. I didn't have the strength or desire to allow any more of my thoughts to be taken by him.

"Are you happy?" I directed my attention squarely at my father. "Does this make you happy?"

"I don't know what you mean."

"Are you happy bursting into my bar, the bar that I have spent years building? The bar you are now standing in with the girl who just called the love of my life and the mother of my child a slut. Are you happy with that?" I took a step towards him so we were chest to chest. "I meant what I said. I have moved on from the days of wishing my dad would come home. I've moved on from the confusion I felt about why you left. I've moved on from everything to do with you. I only need you to do one thing for me and one thing is all I'll ever ask. Just leave. I've lived more of my life without you in it and I'm finally at peace with that. If you do one thing for me, that's all I'll ever ask from you."

His eyes flashed with regret and realization before they moved from mine to Blake, who stood beside me, silent yet tense.

"Is that what you also want?" he directed to Blake.

"Yes. You made your decision and you need to deal with that. This is Tate and me making our decision, so just leave. And while you are at it, get her out of here. No one calls one of the best girls I know a slut and gets away with it."

Chelsea snorted and shot a smirk at both Blake and me. "Yeah you would say that, Blake, seeing as you fucked her. When will you two open your eyes and see what she really is? She fucked both of you. If that's not a slut, then what the hell is?"

"Chelsea, I would suggest you shut your fucking mouth, turn around, and walk away." I knew if I didn't walk away within seconds I would say or do something that would destroy everything I had worked so hard for. That I would become the person I never wanted to be. "Blake, can you deal with her?" I shouldn't have asked him to do that, but I needed an out and quickly.

I didn't even wait for his response. I stormed through the bar, ignoring the people saying my name, and disappeared into the safety of my office. I breathed deeply, leaning over my desk with both palms resting on the mahogany top. My thoughts went straight back to that moment when Sav first arrived, the moment when Blake went for her and got her. It was a moment I'd tried desperately to forget, to move on from, to believe hadn't happened, but then moments like this would happen and I'd be punched in the face by it.

A soft knock on my office door echoed through my office, and looking towards the door, I sighed as Blake's face appeared after it opened slowly. I nodded for him to enter. In his hands, he held two glasses and a bottle of scotch from the bar. Without a word, he poured the amber liquid in the glass and handed it to me.

"They have left and I doubt we will see them again," his deep voice announced. His eyes bounced away from mine as awkwardness swept through my office.

I nodded, tipping the glass to my lips. The scotch was gone in one swift gulp. The sting in the back of my throat made me suddenly realize that this was reality. "Thanks for that."

"Is the whole Sav and me thing going to forever be something that will hang over us?"

"I'll be honest. It will always be there. It's not going to just disappear, but I need to deal with it. I know there is nothing between you and Sav any longer, and I have her. I can't let my issues of that affect my relationship with her now."

"Believe me when I tell you this. I love Sav, but I love her as a best friend. I have absolutely no feelings for her. The moment I found out you were my brother, that was it. I will never regret anything when it comes to Sav because she doesn't deserve that, but you have my word."

"Thanks, man."

"I must admit though . . . When you finally let your balls drop and propose to her, it will be strange calling her my sister. If you know what I mean," Blake said with a shake of his head. I couldn't stop the smirk that was washing over my face.

Walking through the silence of the apartment after what had

been an eventful shift at Red Velvet, I made my way down the darkened hall and straight to the protection the bedroom offered. All I wanted to do was wrap myself around Savannah and forget the rest of the world. The moment I lifted the sheet and climbed into bed beside her, she stirred and her body found mine. Sighing in pure contentment, I wrapped my arms around her body, pulling her as close as possible as she nuzzled into my chest, her lips kissing the space above my heart. There was something unexplainable about having my body covered by hers that made the rest of the world nonexistent.

"How was work?" she asked in a sleepy haze, her lips brushing against my skin as she spoke. I shifted my head slightly, allowing my eyes to find her.

It was after one A.M. and I knew our bouncing and incredibly energetic boy would be awake just as the sun rose, so the thought of discussing the events of the night was the last thing I wanted to do . . . But that was until I remembered that we had sworn that we would never keep anything from each other. It was catch twenty-two though. I knew I had to tell her, but I also knew she wouldn't like it.

"Chelsea and my father turned up," I whispered so softly.

Her head shot up immediately from my chest and she pulled herself up so she was sitting beside me, looking down at me with wide, confused eyes.

"Wha . . . what did they want?"

"Sav, I don't want to say it."

"We said honesty, Tate. I can handle it."

"She brought up you and Blake." I rolled to my side to watch for her reaction. I hated the fact that someone who was so far in my past was still fucking up our lives. I grabbed her hand in mine and brought it to my lips, but her eyes were fixated on the sheet beneath us. "Blake and I told our father we didn't want anything more to do with him and he left. I think this time he got the point."

Her face dropped but I saw fire flame within her deep green eyes. Fuck Chelsea. Fuck my father. "Are you okay?" Sav asked, finally looking at me. Was she serious? Why was she even considering me in this?

"Honestly, I am more concerned about you. Don't think that I don't know how that mind of yours works."

With my hand in hers, I pulled her back down so that she collapsed on top of me, her chin resting on my chest and her eyes looking up at me.

"I'm actually okay with everything, Sav. I learned a long time ago not to expect anything from anyone, so I don't. My only concern is you and Max. Please don't worry about what Chelsea said. Everything that happened was before us. Look, I'll be honest. I don't exactly like the thought of what happened, but it happened. He is my brother and I know he cares about you. We are a family. What happened in the past is exactly that."

"God, I love you."

"And I love you. However, I think we need to stop with the chitchat and either have sex or sleep because our spawn will be awake in exactly four hours and it's my turn to get up."

"You are such a charmer!" She giggled as her hands went down my body. Bingo!

"So I've got to go to Australia for a business meeting. Some shit is going down in the Sydney office and apparently I am the only one who can fix it." Mr. Davenport sat beside me on the bench and looked out over the ocean as we tried to regain our breathing after our now regular Saturday morning workout session. Since Max was born, this is what we did every Saturday, it was our bonding time as Sav liked to call it. "I don't want to leave Sav and Max, but I know they are in good hands with you."

"Are we having a moment?" I asked with a chuckle before throwing back the rest of my water.

"I think we are." His words showed a hint of amusement. "Don't get used to it."

"How long will you be gone for?"

"No longer than a few weeks. It should be—"

"Would you put a damn shirt on? She'll be up for sexual harassment and you'll have a stalker on your hands." Savannah's thick Australian accent sounded behind us. Turning to face her, I saw that she stood with Max sitting on her hip. Tanzi was looking at Mr. Davenport with a devious smirk crossing her face. Tanzi winked at Mr. Davenport as they walked towards us in the shadows of trees along with boardwalk.

"Oh I already stalk him. Don't worry about that. Simon Davenport is my number one favorite Google search." Tanzi sat beside Mr. Davenport, who shook his head and shot a pleading look at Sav. Seriously, my sister was something else.

"Sav, I just told Tate about my trip to Australia," he stated and Sav's face clouded immediately. "It's just for a few weeks. You won't even have time to miss me."

CHAPTER Seventeen

Savannah

THIS CAN'T BE HAPPENING.

My breath hitched in the back of my quickly closing throat as my heartbeat accelerated to the point of pain, leaving me to feel like I was going to crumble any second the moment I heard the heartbreaking words. *Miss Rae, there has been an accident.*

This couldn't be happening again. Was this karma coming back to fuck me over? Panic soared through my body and I was instantly thrown back to being ten years old—a ten-year-old who had no clue what a car accident could mean, a ten-year-old about to face life without parents. Now, at twenty-four, it was so much rawer, so much more real, so much more shattering. I actually understood what this could mean. I understood the ramifications of what ICU meant. I understood what critical condition meant. The scariest of all was that I understood that my life with Mr. Davenport could have already been ripped away from me and I was on the other side of the world, not able to do a damn thing about it.

"Sav, what's wrong?" Tate's worried voice hit me when I stepped into the living room and into his view.

I turned and stopped in my tracks. The heavy sigh escaped me as fresh tears spilled over my cheeks. Tate and Max were my life now, a life I had been fighting for years to earn, a life that finally had a sense of purpose and a future I still found hard to comprehend was mine. But even in the happiness of the future I had been handed, my heart ached for the man who had been my only family for the past thirteen years. My eyes traveled from Tate to Max, who slept peacefully propped up against Tate's shoulder as he did most days. He was such a daddy's boy.

"I've got to go to Australia. It's Mr. Davenport." I spoke quickly, hoping I was making sense through the choke of my tears. I knew my voice was heavy with emotion, cracking at every word I spoke, the words getting lost in the echo of sobs.

The color from Tate's face drained as he tried to grasp the bombshell I had dropped. Tate hurried out of the living room with Max still peacefully sleeping in his arms and headed down the hall towards Max's room. Walking towards the couch, I felt like I was floating. Like my feet were rising from the ground and I was living a dreamlike existence where none of this could possibly be real. This couldn't be real.

My chest tightened with emotions I had spent years desperately trying to lock away. I hadn't wanted to ever feel like I was ten years old again, but now, as I collapsed onto the couch, I felt like I was back to being the small child who had just lost her world.

The feeling of Tate's strong arms wrapping tightly around my body brought me back to reality. Max was no longer to be seen. "I put him in his bed," he explained, answering my unasked question. He pulled me close to the comfort his chest could provide and looked at me, the pain evident in his eyes. "Tell me what happened?" he whispered, rubbing small circles on my back. "Talk to me, Sav."

"There has been an accident. They found his car in an embankment just outside of Sydney and he is barely alive. He isn't breathing on his own." A devastating sob ripped out of me and his arms tightened around me. "It's happening all over again. I can't go through this again. I can't lose him." Tears flooded my face as the ability to breathe became harder. Crawling onto Tate's lap like a small child begging for love and comfort, I wrapped my arms tightly around his neck and dropped my face into his shoulder as tears dampened his shirt.

"Who can I call, Sav? We need to find out what's happening." Tate's usually strong voice shattered. The relationship between Mr. Davenport and Tate had turned twofold. Since the birth of Max, Mr. Davenport's acceptance of Tate had been phenomenal, and now every Sunday afternoon was known as *Boys Only Sunday,* a day where Mr. Davenport, Tate, Blake, Jack, and Lucas would take Max somewhere, just the boys, and I never knew where they went. He knew that Tate wasn't going anywhere and he saw how amazing Tate was to me and Max. I think that was all he wanted for me.

Tate's hand gently moved from around my waist and ran over my hips before slipping into the front pocket of my jeans in search of my phone. I pulled my face away from his shoulder and painfully watched as he scrolled through my last received calls and pressed the call button.

"Hi, this is Tate Connors calling on behalf of Savannah Rae. Could I please ask about the status of Simon Davenport and the condition he was brought in today? Yes, ma'am, what's his condition? Okay, that sounds good. Is he stable?"

Time stood still as Tate spoke softly into my phone and my eyes didn't falter from him. I desperately tried to read his face and listen to his words, but they weren't giving me a thing.

"What's the time frame?" His eyes finally met mine, and empty pits of blue looked at me.

Tate said goodbye to the person on the other end of the call, his gaze never leaving from mine. Leaning over towards the table in front of the couch, he placed my phone on the glass top before turning back to me and grabbing both my hands with his. The next words that were to flow out of his mouth had the potential to change the world as I knew it. I wasn't a praying person, but right now, all I could think of was begging to the heavens above to allow me this mercy.

"He has three broken ribs, a punctured lung, and head injuries, and he is in an induced coma because of the severity of the swelling around his brain. The next forty-eight hours will be crucial. He is in ICU at St. George Hospital."

The breath I was holding in released. Mr. Davenport was still alive—barely but still. He was here.

"I need to be there, Tate. He needs me. I have to look after him. I need to be there when he wakes up," I rambled as my body began shaking uncontrollably. My worst fear was swirling around me, taunting me into oblivion. Losing one of the three most important people in my life was the constant fear I lived with, and now, here in the comfort of my living room, in the arms of the man I loved, I was being slapped in the face by my fear.

After all the troubled times Mr. Davenport and I had trudged through, after all the messed-up and painful experiences we had been dealt with, and after finally overcoming all of the craziness and being given the most amazing happiness, I refused to even begin to comprehend the thought of losing him. I was not going to lose him while I was on the other side of the world.

"I can't lose him, Tate. I won't survive that." I crumbled into his arms as terrifying sobs ripped from the depths of my chest. Tate's arms scooped under me and carried me like a child down the hall and into our bedroom, where he laid me down so softly on our bed. The bed dipped behind me before Tate's body spooned me in a cocoon of his warmth and splashing kisses on the skin of my exposed shoulder blade.

"We will get through this, Sav."

As I rolled over in his arms to face him I finally looked up at him through aching eyes. He had so much unwarranted confidence in me—a confidence that I was scared of shattering. Tate hadn't seen me when my world crashed around me when I lost my parents and then when Cory's suicide was blamed entirely on me. He hadn't seen the girl who hadn't given a fuck about anyone but her own selfish needs, the girl who had gone out at night with the intent of having some random guy between her thighs, begging for those few moments when everything in the world was forgotten and she was made to feel like the most amazing thing in the world. He had never seen that Savannah. The Savannah who would rear her pitifully ugly head when the world fucked her over. The Savannah I hoped was so far locked away that she couldn't and wouldn't appear now.

Was I now strong enough to live a life without the one person who had allowed me to live all those years ago? Would I get through this if the worst happened? Yes, I was a survivor, but I wasn't a warrior. I'd survived once, but the thought of my heart breaking again and trying to rebuild a life without my one constant was unthinkable.

"I need Max," I whispered, desperate for the comfort of my son.

Tate untangled himself from my body and I instantly felt the loss of his contact. I watched him walk out of our bedroom and escape into the darkness of the hall. The rain was falling heavily outside and my aching eyes focused on the raindrops sliding down the glass of the window as I begged for distraction from my thoughts.

Tate walked through the door with Max tucked up in his arms, still fast asleep. I couldn't help but smile. He was absolute perfection.

"I can't believe he is ours."

Tate chuckled and climbed back in bed, gently laying Max on the mattress between us. We both rolled in to face our precious boy, who was totally oblivious to the chaos around him. Tate swept a piece of the chocolate brown hair from Max's forehead and looked at me.

"What are you going to do, Sav?" Tate asked quietly. I didn't have any answers. My heart ripped in two at the decision before me. The thought of not going to Australia to be by Mr. Davenport's side and staying in the US with Tate tore me apart, but then the thought of going to Australia and leaving

Tate behind broke my heart. Whatever my decision, someone would be left behind and I would have to deal with the consequence.

CHAPTER
Eighteen

Tate

LAX WAS CRAZINESS. THOUSANDS OF people rushed through departure, desperate to get to the gates of their awaiting flights, but all I wanted was for time to freeze. I didn't want time to pass. I didn't want this day to arrive, and I didn't want to be here. Today was the day that Savannah and Max were walking out of my life for God only knew how long.

The past week could only be described as living a horrendous nightmare. That phone call changed everything. I felt completely at a loss and utterly helpless when it came to Savannah, and I'd spent the past week watching as she became a shell of her former self. She'd withdrawn from everyone and everything. She had barely been functioning and had been moving through the days with a constant cloud hanging over her. Thank God for Max. Our son was the saving grace, the only one who'd had the ability to put a smile on her face, the only one who's been able to make her face light up for a split second before her thoughts were hit in the face by reality. I was losing her with every passing day and that's what scared me the most.

Mr. Davenport's condition had been moved from critical, but he was still in a serious condition. Our days had been spent locked in the apartment, frequently calling Australia for updates. Sav had been desperate to go to the Australia as soon as possible, but the small problem of not having a passport for Max had come up. Who would have thought you would need a passport for a two-year-old? After finally getting an express passport the day before, we now found ourselves in the departure lounge of LAX.

How was I going to survive without seeing Max every day? I had been ready to pack up my life and follow her to Australia, but she wouldn't have any of that. She wanted me to stay in the States because of my work. I had responsibilities, she'd said, but to me, my responsibilities were her and Max.

Sav had it in her head that she was going to fly into Sydney and go straight to the hospital and then Mr. Davenport would wake up and all would be right with the world. Then they would be back in the US within a week. I knew otherwise, but I couldn't break her heart by telling her. Even though it killed me—the thought of being away from them and not walking on that flight with them—I couldn't be the one to break her heart with the truth. I knew Mr. Davenport was far from recovering enough to come back to the States. He had been in critical condition but had only been moved into serious condition the day before. He had a serious head injury. People don't just wake up from that. Sav was in constant denial of the facts, but that was her way of surviving the shock of what was happening and I had to support her. If the last thing I did was support her, then that's what I needed to do.

The departure line filled around us as people dragged their multicolored suitcases down the maze-like lines, and the chattering was almost overwhelming. Sav pulled her phone out of her purse, checking it for the tenth time since we'd arrived. My hand grabbed hers and pulled her knuckles to my lips. Her empty eyes looked at mine and the intense green I loved was lost.

"Are you sure you don't want me to come? I can work from Australia."

"We won't be gone for long. We are going to arrive in Sydney and we are going to go to the hospital and he will be awake and everything will be fine." Her smile was weak as she desperately tried to believe the words she was saying. My heart broke for her. "We will be back before you know it."

"Okay, Sav, but make sure you come back to me. I need you. I need Max."

"You will always have us. Please understand, Tate. I need to be there for him."

All I could do was nod.

Tanzi, Jack, Lucas, and Ali arrived shortly after Sav and Max had been checked in and been given their boarding passes. Tanzi's eyes found mine through the crowds of people as they rushed towards us. In silent conversation, I told her everything she needed to know. She could read me better than I could read myself. My hand didn't let go of Sav's as we walked towards the gate. Thankfully there was still time that I could spend with them. Jack made quiet conversation with Sav while I walked beside Lucas in silence.

"You doing okay?" he asked softly from beside me.

I turned my head towards him and nodded slowly. I couldn't find the words to answer a question like that. There were no words.

Max finally woke in my arms, his little body moving around and taking everything in. This was his very first time being in the hustle and bustle of an airport, his first time around this many people. Panic engulfed his body and his eyes frantically darted to the safety of Tanzi and Ali, who walked in front of us, before he settled back into my arms, still wide awake and on guard.

"Daddy, planes," he said softly, his hand pointing to a Boeing 747 that was awaiting passengers—passengers that would include Max and Sav.

The sound of the first announcement for Flight 325 to Sydney, Australia echoed through the departure lounge and I swallowed hard as my eyes met Sav's. It was happening.

"Want to come and watch the planes, little guy?" Tanzi asked Max softly. Max shook his head and buried closer to my body. "Come on, Max."

"Daddy," Max cried and scratched at my arm, trying desperately to get a grip to hold on to as I handed him to Tanzi. It killed me.

Tanzi's soft voice soon calmed Max down as they walked towards the window to watch the planes land and take off. Jack patted my back before walking to join them, leaving Sav and me in silence in the middle of the departure lounge.

My hands cupped Savannah's face softly as my eyes burned into hers. With a sweep of my eyes, they traveled over every inch of her face, begging to memorize everything about her. I breathed in deeply, desperate to remember her scent. Her eyes closed briefly under my gaze and her lips parted.

"I love you, Savannah Rae. Never ever forget that."

As she rose on her tiptoes, Sav's lips swept across mine, kissing me ever so lightly before she crashed into my chest as my arms circled her body, pulling her close to me. Our hearts beat frantically against each other at the finality of this fucked-up situation.

"I don't want to leave you, Tate, but I don't know what else to do," she choked against my shirt. She pulled her face away from my chest and looked up at me. The first tear I'd seen all day rolled over her cheek as she looked at me with devastated eyes.

I had no idea what I could do or possibly say, so I just held her. I held her in my arms and hoped to Christ she was memorizing what this felt like because I had absolutely no clue when I would be doing it again.

We stood in each other's arms until Tanzi walked toward us with Max in her arms. Grabbing him, I held him close to my chest, desperate to hug him because my fear of not seeing him was barreling in.

"You be a good boy for Mommy, okay? And remember that Daddy loves you so much."

"Where are you going, Daddy?"

"You are going on a plane with Mommy, and Daddy is going home with Aunty Tanzi."

"But why?"

"You are going to see Gramps."

"But why?"

"You and Mommy are going on a trip."

"But why?"

"Come on, Max. Let's go," Savannah's broken voice spoke softly. Max clung to my neck, and his soft cries were like knives in my heart. After I finally pried his arms from around me, his cries were the last thing I heard. Watching them walk down the corridor and towards the plane felt surreal, like I was watching a movie where I was the star. It didn't feel real; I didn't want it to be real.

Max's eyes locked with mine until they got to the corner that would take them out of my sight. Savannah looked back towards me with tears streaming down her face. Her lips moved as she mouthed, "I love you," and then they were gone.

Jack stood beside me as my eyes fixated on the space where Sav and Max had just disappeared through. "Come on, man. You have to let her go." His words cut through me.

The problem was that I could never let her go.

Chapter Nineteen

Savannah

SIXTEEN HOURS LATER, MAX AND I stepped into the brightness and heat of the Australian sun. Being surrounded by Australian accents didn't comfort me at all. This didn't feel like home anymore. The plane trip had been tortuously long I hadn't slept and my mind had kept running through worst case scenario. What if I turned up and something had happened while I was in the air? What if he had woken up and I hadn't been there?

I'd made a decision on the plane during the tenth hour of travel. My complete focus needed to be on Mr. Davenport. No matter how long this took, I would be by his side. I had to put myself second. I needed to stop thinking about anything besides caring for Max and Mr. Davenport. All of my life, he had been the one constant. He was my family, my protector, the one who had saved me. And he was the one who had allowed me to still be alive today. At my darkest, he was my light, and now, as he was facing the biggest challenge of his life, I needed to be his hope.

I cringed at the thought of what I had put him through. Mr. Davenport never questioned any decisions I made. Yes, he might have suggested other ways, but he never left me. He had been my life since I was ten years old, and now, with a child of my own, I needed him more than ever. It was my time to protect him, to care for him, to provide him with everything he had provided me.

Tate had been my constant companion during the trip; he'd never left my thoughts. A constant stream of tears cascaded down my cheeks as I realized what I had left.

Max struggled in my arms as we waited at baggage claim. After I placed him on the ground, he held my hand and pulled me towards the door, anxious to run around and stretch his little legs. He had been absolutely perfect during the long trip. As I waited, getting antsier the longer it took. I pulled my phone out of my handbag and turned it on. A new message icon flashed on the screen as my phone came to life.

I miss you two so much already. I called the hospital and there has been no change. Call me. I love you x

I pressed the call button, not caring for one second about the international call rates, just needing to hear his voice. He picked up after one ring.

"Savannah?"

"We just arrived and I needed to hear your voice."

"How was the flight? How is Max?"

"The flight was long and Max was amazing. He had one flight attendant wrapped around his finger. We seriously have a lady-killer on our hands."

"He is doing his daddy proud."

I laughed for the first time in days.

"It's good to hear you laugh."

"I don't know how I'm going to do this without you."

"I'm always with you, Sav. You have my heart in the palm of your hands, so wherever you are, I'm with you."

Rushing through the corridors of St. George Hospital, I was dragging my suitcase and carrying Max on my hip, having come straight from the airport. Finally reaching the empty waiting room of ICU, I sat Max on one of the plastic seats besides the nurses' station and gave him his favorite Thomas book.

Turning towards the desk, I stood before a middle-aged woman with a face of thunder. She continued to tap away mindlessly on the keyboard, completely ignoring the fact that I was standing in front of her. I cleared my throat loudly and but she didn't look up.

"Excuse me."

Still she didn't look at me. My temper was spiraling out of control with every second she blatantly ignored me. It was seven A.M. and my jetlag was the worst I had ever suffered, I was starving hungry, my son hadn't had a good sleep in hours, and I hadn't slept for twenty-four hours.

"Look at me," I snarled, my hand pounding the desk.

Finally she met my eyes. "Visitors hours are not until nine A.M. Children are not permitted." Looking over at Max she unashamedly turned her nose down at him and rolled her eyes.

How fucking dare she?

Leaning over the counter, I glared at her with every ounce of my frustration. "I have just traveled sixteen hours and I will not be leaving before I get into room eight. You will let me the fuck through the doors, otherwise I will scream this place down with bloody murder. I don't need your sour face bitchy attitude. Are we going to have a problem?" I kept my voice low so that Max didn't hear me curse.

"Come with me, miss. I'll take you through." I turned at the sound of a warm, inviting voice behind me. A young woman who looked barely old enough to have graduated stood just behind me dressed in her blue hospital uniform. Her smile was genuine and her eyes were welcoming, a beautiful contrast to bitch-face mole behind the counter.

"You should learn some bedside manners. Don't be a sour bitch all your life."

I leaned down and lifted Max from the seat. After taking his hand, we left the woman behind the counter huffing and puffing as we followed the sweet girl through another two corridors, my hand holding Max's for dear life.

The closer we got to room eight, the more nervous I felt. I had no clue what to expect. My mind had been protecting itself with thoughts of walking through the doors of the hospital room and finding Mr. Davenport sitting up in bed, drinking his favorite coffee with the morning paper in his hands. That's the only thing that had kept me from completely breaking down over the past week.

"Miss, I would suggest not taking the little one in there. There are tubes and machines and it might scare the little guy. I could take him to the staff room and watch cartoons if you'd like?"

She was so damn sweet. I looked at Max and knew she was right. I couldn't let him see Mr. Davenport like this. Crouching down to his eye level, I smiled as his big blue eyes looked at me. "Maxey, you are going to go and watch some cartoons while mummy goes in that room for a little while," I said, pointing to the closed door of room eight. I looked at her name badge quickly. "This is Justine and she is your new friend, okay? You could show her your Thomas book." Max hesitantly looked between me and Nurse Justine and a tired smile swept over his face.

"I'm Max."

My gorgeous amazing boy. I followed Justine into the staff room and moved our luggage to the far corner before setting Max up on the couch with his book and favorite blanket. I knew he wouldn't stay awake for long.

"Are you sure this is okay?"

"Of course. I've been expecting you. I have been on the phone to a Tate Connors from the US all day. He has been ringing every hour for updates and asked me to take care of you when you got here."

Tate was looking after me from halfway across the world. A single tear rolled over my cheek at the amazingness of him. He truly was with me. "Thank you," I whispered.

My feet moved on their own as my mind left my body. I was shutting down in fear of what I was about to walk into. The number eight gleamed on the closed door in front of me, and with a shaking hand, I pushed down the handle and stepped into the unknown.

My hand flew to cover my mouth as I gasped and took

in the stranger in the bed in front of me. I barely recognized him. Gone was the strong, courageous man that could make fear overtake me with a single glance. Gone was the man who would bring me pancakes on my birthday every year. And gone was the man who had shed a tear when Max was born. In his place was a weak, barely breathing man who looked a shadow of his former self. A constant beep from the heart monitor filled the air and a breathing tube was secured down his throat as he clearly struggled to live.

I pulled the chair from against the wall towards the side of the bed and sat beside him. I didn't know what to do. Did I talk to him? Could I touch him? I sat like a statue, just looking at him and trying desperately to remember to breathe. After what felt like an eternity, the door of the room opened and a middle-aged man with salt-and-pepper hair walked in, startled to find me sitting by the bed.

"Miss Rae, I assume?" he asked in a deep, low tone. I stood from the chair and shook his hand. "I am Doctor Sloan and I've been the doctor taking care of this very lucky man."

Lucky? Was he looking at the same person I was looking at? My face must have shown my confusion because he pointed towards the chair, indicating for me to take a seat, and then he started with his doctor speech.

"Simon suffered a traumatic brain injury in a motor vehicle accident ten days ago and this injury is our main concern. Due to the severity of the injury, he was placed into a medically induced coma to allow the swelling and bruising of the brain acceptable time to recover without the added stress of normal brain function. We ran a variety of brain activity tests last night, which came back better than expected, but he definitely isn't out of the woods. As the swelling comes down, we will then proceed to start reducing the medication, slowly bring him out of the coma, and see if he comes through on his own and to see his level of function."

"Will he be okay?" I finally spoke, my eyes begging Doctor Sloan.

"He is a fighter, Miss Rae, and he has every chance of pulling through this. His recovery rate so far has been exceptional. I suggest talking to him, holding his hand, making him aware you are here. He may not be receptive, but studies have shown that this kind of interaction helps quicken recovery. I will ask Nurse Jenkins to bring in his belongings for you."

With a stern nod and a straight smile, Doctor Sloan walked through the door and shut it behind him. With a shaking hand, I grabbed Mr. Davenport's hand and squeezed it lovingly. I could do this. I scooted the chair closer, leaned my head on the mattress, and looked up at him.

"Max and I are here. Max took his first plane trip today and he was so amazing. He drew you a picture. He is here but I haven't brought him in to see you yet. I am scared that he will be frightened with the noise and the tubes." I felt my throat tighten and the first of my tears slide over my cheeks. "Please fight this, Mr. Davenport. We need you more than you will ever realize. You have to fight. You need to come back to us. I can't do this without you and Max needs his gramps. I promise I will not leave your side until you are walking beside me out of this hospital. That's my promise. You have spent your life caring for me, and now I will care for you, whether you like it or not."

Chapter Twenty

Tate

One Month

THIS WAS FUCKED.

What kind of karma was this?

I felt like a selfish asshole because all I wanted was for my girlfriend and son to pack up and leave Australia and come back to me, but how could I really wish for that when Mr. Davenport was on the brink of death in Australia?

So many times I had wanted to beg Savannah to jump on the next plane and come home, but I knew I couldn't. She needed to be the one to make the decision to come back to me. I wasn't going to be the cause of her leaving Mr. Davenport, because I knew she would never forgive me if something were to happen and I would never forgive myself if I were the cause of her not being there, if something did happen. All I could do was pray that she made the decision and soon.

I had never felt this extent of loneliness before. It was gut-ripping, heart-twisting and breath-consuming cruelty. It was like being in a constant state of distraction, a place between reality and fantasy, a world where you hoped that you were about to wake up from the worst nightmare of your life.

"Tate, seriously, not again." Tanzi's words ripped me from my tender thoughts.

Every morning it was the same. I'd get lost in my thoughts and Tanzi was the only one who could pull me from them.

From the stove, she quickly grabbed the pan of what was supposed to contain scrambled eggs but now was just smoking charcoal. "You need to pay attention."

"Sorry," I mumbled, grabbing my glass of orange juice from the bench top and walking out of the kitchen and towards the living room.

"Wait," Tanzi's strong, pleading voice echoed from the kitchen. Stopping in my tracks, I dropped my head and awaited her next words. "I am worried about you, Tate. It's been a month. What happens if they don't come back for a while? I hate seeing you like this. What can I do?"

"You can bring back my son and girlfriend."

I left Tanzi speechless in the kitchen as I rushed out of the apartment, desperate to get away from the inquisition. I couldn't get into a conversation where the subject was Max and Sav being away for an extended period of time. I couldn't even begin to fathom that idea. My one place of refuge over the past month had been Red Velvet. It was the one place where I could get lost in the craziness of business meetings and expansion opportunities. Now, as I worked twelve-hour shifts most days, it was my one place of solitude.

It was early when I arrived—the cleaners were still there—and I knew I had the empty bar for a few hours before I had to deal with conversation.

Sliding into my chair, I opened my laptop and looked at a blank email before beginning to tap feverishly at the keys.

From: Tate Connors
To: Savannah Rae
Time: 08.48am PST
Subject: I miss you

Hi Sav,

I miss you. It's as simple as that. What else can I say? I miss your touch, your taste, your lips, and your smell. I miss every single thing about you. You are making me into some mushy guy who is pining over his girlfriend. Fuck, I even slept with one of your t-shirts the other night just so I could feel somewhat near you.

How is the little guy doing? I hope he isn't getting into too much mischief. Thank you for the Skype call the other night. You don't realize how much it meant to be able to see and hear you both.

How is everything with Mr. D? Is there any change in his condition? What are the doctors saying?

I really do miss you both so much. I knew it would be tough but I didn't think it would be this tough. Please take care of yourself Sav. Mr. Davenport needs your strength and so does Max.

I love you Savannah.
Tate.

Chapter Twenty-One

Savannah

I was exhausted, both physically and mentally. Days were running into each other like I was in some messed-up Groundhog Day. Everything was predictable—my days, my emotions, and my reactions. My day involved waking up at six A.M. with Max jumping in bed with me. We would climb out of bed after our morning phone call with Tate. Then I'd make his favorite breakfast and watch our morning cartoons while I caught up with emails from the States. We would dress and then make our way to the hospital, where we would spend most of the day.

I had no clue what else to do. My emotions were a wreck, I was constantly on edge and my phone was always glued to my hand in case there is any change in Mr. Davenport while I wasn't around. I spent hour after hour sitting beside an unresponsive Mr. Davenport, not knowing whether my presence was even helping. My bedside vigil would remain until I saw him open his eyes, but the longer I stayed, the more my relationship with Tate suffered. There was nothing win-win about this, and I knew for a fact that I was destroying the best thing that had ever happened to me and there wasn't a damn thing I could do about it.

"Savannah."

I lifted my head from its resting position on the mattress beside my hand that was holding Mr. Davenport's to find Justine standing by the door with Max in her arms. She had been my constant companion since I had arrived in Sydney. She would look after Max while I would talk with the doctors, and she would take him to the hospital park when my emotions got the better of me. Without her, I had no clue what I would have become.

"Let's go and grab a coffee in the cafeteria."

My eyes shot to Mr. Davenport anxiously, not wanting to be away from him for a moment. It was hell leaving him at night when visiting hours were over, let alone voluntarily leaving him during the time when I could be here.

She spoke softly. "Let's take Max to grab some lunch. He misses his mummy."

My precious Max. His cuddles in the late hours of the night, his innocent giggles as he learned something new, and his sweet kisses first thing in the morning were everything I needed to calm the torrential downpour that life was throwing at me at the moment.

"Okay." Agreeing, I pulled myself up from the chair that I hadn't left for the past three hours and stood anxiously by the bed. I leaned over, taking in the still-unconscious Mr. Davenport, a stranger of himself lying before me. "Don't go anywhere while I'm gone," I whispered before kissing his forehead softly and turning to follow Justine and Max to the cafeteria.

After ordering sandwiches for Max and me and salad for Justine, we moved out to sit on the vast, perfectly green lawn that was shadowed by the twenty-story hospital that was beginning to feel like a second home. I was seeing the inside of that place more than I was seeing the inside of Mr. Davenport's Bondi apartment.

"Tell me what's going on, Savannah. I know we have only known each other a few weeks, but I see you more than I see my boyfriend and family, so if you need to talk, then speak to me." Justine opened her salad before shooting me a pleading look. Could I really talk to her about everything? Could I open up to someone who had been a stranger less than a month ago?

"I feel useless. Is sitting beside Mr. Davenport all day every day really doing anything? I am on the other side of the world doing nothing that seems to be helping while the love of my life is in the US. Everything was perfect with Tate and me before this. We had the perfect life planned for the three of us, but then I was ripped from my present life to my past life by a single phone call and all rational thought flew out of the window and now I feel like I am stuck in limbo. I want nothing more than to be with Tate, and every morning I wake up and look at my suitcase, just wanting to pack up Max and me and go back to him, but then what happens if I leave and something happens to Mr. Davenport? I could never live with myself knowing that I wasn't here. What do I do?"

"It's helping, Savannah. Even though he isn't communicating, his charts show that it's helping. Every conversation you have with him, every time Max visits is helping. I'm not supposed to say anything, but they are going to attempt to bring him out of the coma in the next few weeks. His vitals are stable, he is responding to tests, his injuries are healing, and the swelling in his brain has subsided quicker than expected. You being here is definitely helping."

My voice cracked with emotion as my eyes glistened with tears. "Really? You mean I may have him back soon? He might be awake? Will he be able to talk? When can he come home? When will I be able to see him?" I shot off question after desperate question.

"Hang on, Savannah." She placed her salad on the grass beside her and grabbed my fidgeting hands. "We are going to try and bring him back. I can't tell you exactly when but as soon as I do know, I will tell you. He has had major head trauma, so we cannot guarantee that he will come out of this the same man that you remember. We are doing everything and I mean everything to bring him back to you. I promise you that I will keep you in the loop at all times. You have my word."

I had no more words of response. Until I saw Mr. Davenport conscious, I knew my life would be tumultuous, but I had to keep going. The little boy that was chasing the seagulls and squealing in complete happiness needed his mum functioning like everything was okay. How could I explain everything to him? I knew he was missing Tate. He would talk to him constantly, gibbering and laughing at whatever he was saying. He'd brought a photo of Tate to the hospital today and kept saying, "Daddy." It broke my heart. Would he hate me for keeping him from Tate? Would Tate hate me for keeping him from Max? I felt like my heart and mind were in a UFC cage, both pounding each other to the point that one would be completely fucked over and the other would win whether they were meant to win or not.

The moment we walked into the darkened apartment that Max and I now called home after being kicked out of Mr. Davenport's room, Max shot out of my arms, ran across the living room, and launched himself onto the couch. His newfound running skills were running me rampant. He literally ran everywhere and anywhere he could. It was so damn cute but so damn exhausting. Watching him curl up in his favorite corner of the couch, I knew he would be asleep within minutes. Opening my laptop, I sat at the dining room table and began typing out everything I was feeling in a new email.

From: Savannah Rae
To: Tate Connors
Time: 20.32pm AEST
Subject: Max
Hi Tate,

Max and I just got home from the hospital and now he is curled up on the couch watching Gordy. He has seemed to have forgotten about Thomas and now everything is Gordy this, Gordy that.

Today I got news from Justine that they are going to try and bring Mr Davenport out of the coma in the next few weeks. I hate seeing Mr Davenport like this, Tate. I feel so helpless when I'm just sitting beside his bed while he lays motionless in front of me. I don't know what I can do. I talk to him, I tell him everything Max has been doing I even read him the paper. Apparently every little bit helps but it's so heartbreaking when I am seeing absolutely no change. It's not even like I am looking at him anymore.

All I want is to be wrapped up in your arms and to feel your heart beat against my chest. I miss you so much, Tate. I don't know what to do. I want to come back to you, I want to sneak into our room early one morning and climb into bed with you so I'm there when you wake up. I want to kiss you and make love to you and hear you breathing in my ear in the early hours of the morning. But then what if something happens to Mr Davenport? I would never forgive myself if I'm not here when he wakes up or if..... I can't even say it. Why does this have to be so screwed up? Please tell me what to do? Please tell me that you understand? Please tell me that I am doing the right thing?

You have my heart,
Savannah x

Chapter Twenty-Two

Tate

Two Months

THE MOMENT MY PHONE CHIMED with an incoming email notification, I knew it would be Sav. Fumbling through my pockets, I pulled out my phone, instantly unlocking it and going to my Gmail app. Sure enough, it was from Sav and just seeing her name flash in front of me made my face come alive with a smile. The smallest things meant so much now.

Sitting at the bar at the end of a busy shift at Red Velvet, I scrolled through the email, drinking in every word she had written. The longer we were apart, the more numb I got. I was moving through the days like a robot now, every day moving into one. The highlights of my days were now the emails, the calls, and the text messages I received from Savannah.

"An email from Sav?" Blake asked as he took a seat on

the stool beside me and nodded in acknowledgement to Jack, who stood behind the bar watching me closely.

"Yep."

"How's everything going over there?"

"They are going to try and bring him out of the coma. I don't think she will be coming home any time soon." I grabbed the glass of scotch that Jack had pushed towards me and slammed it down, the burn of the strong liquor awakening my senses.

"Go to her, man. Jump online and buy a ticket and get yourself to Australia. Jack can look after the bar and I am off tour for a couple of weeks, so I am more than happy to pour some drinks and swoon some ladies." He shot me a cocky grin.

"What? And get my bar mentioned in a sexual harassment case?"

"Hey! The ladies never complain."

The thought of buying a ticket to Sydney and turning up on Sav's doorstep ignited something within me, arising something I had given up on. Hope. Hope that I could see my son. Hope that I could wrap my arms around Sav and practically kiss her face off. I looked at Blake and Jack, who watched me with encouragement flashing over their faces.

"You know what? What's stopping me from going there? Abso-fucking-lutely nothing." I pushed back from the stool and walked towards the far couches that lined the walls near the stage for privacy. Collapsing on the couch, I scrolled through my phone until I got to an app that Sav had downloaded onto my phone before she'd left that allowed me to be able to text her. Checking my world clock, I saw that it was seven p.m. there. She would have left the hospital for the night.

Tate: What would you do if I just turned up on your doorstep one day?
Sav: Honestly?
Tate: Always honestly.
Sav: I would probably scream in your face while I cry my eyes out but then I'd pull you into a hug and I would fuck the living daylights out of you. I'd be hoping that Max isn't around to see mummy attacking daddy.
Tate: Jesus Sav, I'm at work and I am about ready to explode in my pants. Fuck I miss everything about you. I want to taste you, I want to be balls deep in you, I want to pull your hair until you whimper but then beg me for more.
Sav: I miss the ache of you being so deep inside me that I can feel you for days.
Tate: I'm booking a flight to see you. I will be there in two weeks. Let me finalize these details for the club opening in Vegas and have my final investor meeting and I'll be there. If I could get out of these meetings believe me I would. I will stay until the moment I can bring you and Max home.
Silence.

I checked my phone constantly, and for ten long minutes, there was no response. Did she really not want me there? Was this just her way of easing me into the thought of not being together? The longer the minutes clicked over, the more my mind rioted.

Savannah: Say that again.
Tate: I'll be with you in two weeks.
Savannah: I love you so much.

The moment I told Savannah I would be coming to Sydney, everything seemed to change. I was happier, I stopped working as much, and I was enjoying life again. Knowing that I would be seeing Max and Savannah in a matter of weeks did a world of difference. I walk walking on cloud nine.

"Tate, can I have a word?"

Jack joined me in the kitchen and I couldn't help but be aware of the hesitation in his step. His eyes darted back to the living area. He looked completely on edge. After I grabbed my coffee and nodded towards the living room, he followed me in and sat on the chair opposite me.

"Is Tanzi here?" he asked suddenly.

"No. She left about twenty minutes ago." My suspicion grew by the second. "What's going on, Jack?"

"You know I love your sister, right?" He dropped his eyes to the floor and swallowed hard. "Look, I am just going to come out and say it."

The longer he hesitated, the more suspicious I got.

"I am planning on proposing to Tanzi, but I want to ask your permission first. I love your sister, man. I worship the ground she walks on, and I want her to be my fiancée. So, Tate Connors, will you give me permission to propose to Tanzi Connors?"

My best friend was asking for my permission to propose to my twin? I couldn't hide my excitement. I had been waiting for this moment for years now. When I thought of Tanzi, the only thing I wished for is her utter happiness and for her to be treated like the princess she was, and Jack does that—daily.

Of course I had been an asshole to him when he had first come on the scene, but sure enough, he'd kept coming back. And the next thing I knew, he had been sitting on the couch in Tanzi's and my living room so many years ago. I had done the whole arrogant brother routine, warning him, threatening that if he hurt her that he'd pay—the usual brother spiel. But then we'd surfed together, we'd drunk copious amounts of alcohol together, and eventually he'd become assistant manager of Red Velvet. The rest is history.

"I would be honored for you to marry my sister. You have my full blessing," I said with pride dripping from my words.

"Thanks, man."

"So when is the big proposal happening?"

"Next weekend. I just need to organize it." He flipped on the television before turning back to look at me. "When are you going to ask the big question?"

I considered my answer. Proposing to Savannah had been playing on my mind ever since Max was born. I wanted it to be perfect. I needed it to be perfect for her.

"You never know what will happen in Sydney," I said with a smirk before turning back to the television and thinking of all the ways I could propose to Sav.

Chapter Twenty-Three

Savannah

It had been two weeks since Tate had announced that he was coming to Australia, and now, in less than twenty-four hours, he would be here. The thought of lying in bed with him, having him hold me, kiss me, and of course make love to me sent shivers skyrocketing down my spine. My body was craving the touch that only he could provide and the pleasure that he could deliver. My body knew how long it had been.

Today was going to involve all things Tate Connors. I was banned from going to the hospital as they were finally attempting to bring Mr. Davenport out of his coma and I wasn't allowed to be in the room for fear of my appearance doing more damage than good. I'd screamed, demanded, and begged, but they wouldn't have any of it.

Thankfully, I had the perfect distraction. Home and body prep for Tate. Pulling out my phone, I opened my notes app and wrote exactly what I needed to do in the next ten hours before I would be allowed to go to the hospital. I had negotiated with the doctor and he said had that I could visit at five P.M., considering how Mr. Davenport was faring.

My smile took over my face as I busily began typing my to-do list.

1. Clean apartment
2. Grocery shop
3. Wax, buff, and moisturise every inch of my body
4. Put red satin sheets on bed
5. Buy new lingerie

Satisfied with my list, I climbed out of bed, wrapping my gown around my body and putting my phone in my pocket in case any news came through. I took off through the quiet space of the apartment towards Max's room, shocked that he wasn't already out of bed and begging me to watch cartoons. It was usually our six am ritual.

Quietly opening the door of his room, I felt my heart rate quicken at the sight before me. There he was my little guy, sitting by the sliding glass door with his legs pulled up to his chest, looking out over the beach, peacefully, calmly, and contently. For a minute, I stood in silence, taking in the sight before me. Grabbing my phone from my gown pocket, I took a photo and immediately sent it to Tate with the caption "Like father like son."

"What are you doing over there, Max?" I asked softly. His head spun around quickly towards me at the sound of my voice.

"Daddy?" he asked, pointing to the guys on the beach going for their morning surf.

Walking across the room with my heart in my throat, I sat beside him on the carpeted floor and immediately he crawled into my lap, wrapping his little arms around my neck and hugging me tight. Every night he would look at a photo of Tate and talk to him. It had been my mission from day one that Max would never forget who his dad was, and knowing he would be seeing him so soon was something I was so excited to be able to give to Max.

"Okay, little man. We have a big day ahead of us. We are going to clean, go shopping, go to the hospital, and then come home because tomorrow I have a very big surprise for you."

"A surprise?" he asked with wide excited eyes.

"Yep, for you and Mummy but we have a lot to do before we get it."

Five P.M. was constantly taunting me, radiating in front of me, begging for me to completely come undone. Finally, at four thirty, Max and I got into the taxi and made our way to the hospital to await news of Mr. Davenport. Justine had been quiet all day and that only intensified my anxiety.

In some fucked-up and crazy way, I had almost felt more calm when he had been in the coma because that was one thing I'd known I could be certain about. My fears were sky high. What if he couldn't remember us? What if he had no clue who Max was? What if he couldn't talk or walk? What if he didn't wake up at all?

"Miss, we are here," a firm voice said from the front seat. Looking out of the window, I saw the bright lights of

St. George Hospital in front of me. Handing him a fifty dollar note, Max and I climbed out of the cab before I propped Max up on my hip and ambled through the double glass doors, making my way through the corridors that I knew like the back of my hand.

Justine stepped out of the room as Max and I turned the corner. Her eyes found mine and I panicked because I couldn't read them. She rushed up the hall towards me and finally the most welcoming smile I had ever wanted to see took over her face. Instantly I felt my emotions bubble over and my cheeks flooded with pent-up tears I had been holding in all day.

"Justine, what's going on? Please tell me it's good news," I rushed out.

"He is awake, Savannah. He seems to be alert. He is speaking, he has no recollection of the accident, and he is complaining of an intense headache, but that is expected. He knows you are here and he has been asking for you."

It was as if my prayers had been answered. The past two months had been a blur of tears, stress, separation, and panic, but just hearing that he was awake felt like the biggest weight had been lifted from my shoulders.

"Can I see him?" I whispered hopefully.

"Of course." She smiled before her eyes dropped their emotion slightly. "But, Savannah, please remember he has just awoken form a severe head trauma. He may be a little disoriented, so just be patient. How about I take Max to get ice cream so you can go and have some time with Mr. Davenport?"

Nodding, I kissed Max and watched as he walked hand in hand with Justine down the hall. When I turned back towards the closed door of Mr. Davenport's room, my nerves swam freely. I grabbed hold of the door handle and the door swept open quietly.

What I noticed first was the lack of the constant beeping of Mr. Davenport's breathing machines that had taken over the room at every visit. There was nothing. He was breathing on his own. At the sound of the door opening, Mr. Davenport's head rolled slowly to the side and a weak smile fell over his face as his eyes met mine, the eyes I hadn't seen for two long months. I stood frozen to the spot as every emotion I could summon swayed within me. My chest tightened and a loud sob escaped as fresh tears streamed down my cheeks. I didn't know what to do, what to say, whether to move or turn around and leave and try to wake up from this dream.

"Sav," his voice croaked from the bed, laced with exhaustion. He remembered me. His hand patted the mattress beside him softly and finally I found my ability to walk. Cautiously walking across the room, I pulled the seat towards the bed, sat beside him, and completely lost it. Every stress, worry, concern, and fear I'd had over the past two months washed out of me in a barrel of tears.

"I thought I had lost you. I thought I would never speak to you again."

"I am tougher than that. You won't get rid of me that easily. Can you pass me some water?" his scratchy voice asked. Handing him the water, I watched with wide eyes as he eased the straw to his mouth before coughing slightly. "How long have you been here?"

"Two months. I came as soon as I found out," I admitted.

"Tate?"

I swallowed hard, averting my eyes from his. "I haven't

seen him since I left."

"Savannah," he groaned.

"I needed to be here to be with you. When I got that phone call, everything came crashing back to me. I couldn't imagine what I would do if I lost you so I did what I thought I needed to do." I dropped my head to the bed as fresh tears appeared. "I need to take care of you like you have always taken care of me."

"Sav, what am I going to do with you?" he said softly, his eyes closing briefly as the need to sleep came on. "You aren't ever going to lose me. I'm a tough cookie and I'll be around annoying you for a very long time to come."

"You promise?"

"Always."

Chapter Twenty-Four

Tate

I WAS GOING TO AUSTRALIA.

In ten hours, I would be boarding a plane from LAX and flying straight to Sydney, finally be where I was meant to be—with Savannah and Max. To say I was ecstatic would be an understatement. To say I had been floating around like a lovesick fool for the past two weeks wouldn't be short of the truth.

The moment I told Sav, it had felt like everything that had been shadowing my life had lifted. Now, as I started filling my suitcase for what would be an extended trip, I couldn't be more excited. I had made sure my ticket was open ended and I would stay for as long as was needed until we could come back to Los Angeles together as a family. That was the one and only goal I had.

Everything relating to Red Velvet was under control. Jack would be taking over management during my absence; Blake would be working when he wasn't on tour, and anything relating to the expansion to Las Vegas could now be done via email, seeing as all the contracts had been signed.

The annoying buzz of my phone ringing sounded from my bed. After I lifted shirts and pants to find it, my eyes narrowed when I saw Stevie's name flash on the screen.

"What's up, Stevie?" I asked cheerfully, my mood annoyingly chipper.

"Tate, you've got to get down to the club. There are some cops here and Blake is being questioned and now they are demanding to see you."

And just like that my cheerful mood disappeared. "What the fuck? What are they questioning Blake about? What the hell do they want from me?"

"Chelsea Davison is suing Red Velvet for damages and claiming that Blake assaulted her."

The world began rapidly spinning out of control. Stevie's words hit every inch of my being. I'd never wanted to hear that name again, but here she was, haunting everything I had fought so hard for. Why the fuck was she so intent on creating misery in everything she did? Looking at my half-packed suitcase, I felt unease swamp through me. *Savannah.* Standing to my feet, I fetched my keys, wallet, and phone and rushed to Red Velvet, desperate to get to the end of whatever fucked-up story the psycho known as Chelsea had come up with this time.

Six hours later, I stumbled into Tanzi and Jack's apartment, I couldn't stay another night alone in mine and Sav's apartment. *Chelsea fucking Davison strikes again.* Her claims were completely unfounded. Chelsea was claiming that Blake had used aggressive force when he removed her from Red Velvet when she had turned up with our father and that she had sustained bruising to her arms and neck that resulted in her not being able to work. To add another layer to her stupid claims, she was also suing the club for breach of general citizen rights, citing that the reasons for her removal hadn't been justified and that I had verbally abused her, which had resulted in emotional turmoil and subsequent loss of income since there was no way that she could work. It was completely and utterly false. Knowing that this absurd work of fiction was being taken seriously only intensified my anger. The moment she had told them she had a witness—a witness, I might add, in the form of my father—the LAPD had to take her claims seriously, meaning it would be investigated and go to court unless it could be thrown out.

"Tate, is that you?" Tanzi's sleep-filled voice sounded from the hall.

"Yep. Go back to bed, Tanzi."

The light above me flickered on, illuminating the apartment. It was after two A.M. and I knew I wouldn't be sleeping for many hours to come. My head was rattled, playing what-if scenarios over in my mind, trying desperately to come up with a solution to wipe this from reality, but so far I had come up with nothing.

Tanzi walked through the apartment, sleep etched on her face. Joining me on the couch, she took my hand in hers softly and faced me, sitting cross-legged. She didn't speak. She just sat there watching me, reading me, trying to work out what was swimming dangerously fast in my head.

"I have to tell Sav that I can't come to Australia." My voice broke under the finalization of my words. "What am I supposed to do, Tanzi? I've spent the last two hours driving around Los Angeles, trying to work out a way to get around this but I've come up completely empty. If I leave the country, it could go to court any time, and if I'm not here to attend proceedings, then it will look like we are in contempt. If I don't go to Australia, I don't see Sav and Max."

"Sav will understand. I talked to her earlier tonight. Mr. Davenport is recovering faster than expected so she could be home before you know it. You two have already been separated for long enough, so if it's another month, you will handle it."

Tanzi kissed my cheek before taking off back down the hall towards her and Jack's room. I turned my phone over in my hand, knowing that the inevitable needed to happen. Pressing the call button, I waited anxiously to hear that sweet Australian accent greet me.

"I get to see you in less than a day!" Sav squealed the moment she answered and immediately my heart sank. I lost the ability to speak. "Tate?"

"Hey, Sav." I knew my voice was as weak as hell.

"What's wrong?"

Swallowing hard, I slammed my eyes shut, begging for an ounce of strength to hit me. "I need to postpone my trip. Chelsea filed an assault charge against Blake and she is suing Red Velvet for damages. It all happened a couple of hours ago and I've been with my lawyers all night trying to work out what I can do. I am so sorry, Sav. I want to come to Australia. I even have my bags packed, but I can't leave the country yet," I rambled, desperate to get everything that needed to be said out. Complete silence greeted me on the other end of the phone. "Savannah, are you there?"

"Yes, I am here."

"I am sorry. I cannot believe that she would do this. Please say something."

"You can't believe she would do this?" Sav spoke so softly I could barely hear her. "Do you realize you are talking about Chelsea? Once again she is dictating our lives."

"Sav, please," I sighed over the truth of Savannah's words. "You know that I want nothing more than to be with you and Max, but what the fuck am I supposed to do? She is suing my club. Our livelihood is in those clubs and she is threatening to go to the press about Blake. He is stressing out. I am trying to my hardest to get this worked out. Fuck, I will pay her off if it means I can get to you, but my lawyers are telling me that's the last straw."

"You need to do what you've got to do. Max and I are fine over here." Her words were laced with annoyance, sadness, and frustration. I knew I wouldn't get any more out of her tonight. "I hope it all works out and you get everything sorted. I know her threats are lies and I know she won't stop until she destroys you and me. I am learning that time and time again."

"Nothing will destroy us, Sav. Nothing."

Chapter Twenty-Five

Savannah

A WEEK HAD PASSED SINCE TATE told me he couldn't come to Australia. I felt the emptiness of being away from him rush back and I was back to going about my days with only one focus—Mr. Davenport's recovery.

The moment he told me he wasn't coming, my body had bubbled with angry emotion. The fact that it was Chelsea who had stopped him from coming ripped away at me. Why had she had to do that? Was her obsession with Tate that strong that she didn't care who she took down in the process? I couldn't let thoughts of Chelsea take me away from why I was here though and now I felt the urge and need to refocus and regroup.

Walking down the familiar corridors of the hospital, I slammed to a halt. *What the fuck?* Mr. Davenport walked towards me with a smile plastered on his face—without the help of an aid or nurse. I knew he was recovering quickly, but this completely baffled me. I took off with Max in my arms as happy tears streamed down my face.

"Gramps!" Max squealed. I flinched at the intensity of Max's excitement and noticed the look being shot to us from the nurse sitting at the nurses' station.

"When did this happen?" I asked. "You forgot to mention the fact that you are walking now."

"I have been doing extra sessions with physiotherapy for the past week. I didn't want to worry you anymore if I couldn't do this." His face suddenly dropped and his eyes narrowed in on me. "Why have you been crying?" his thick voice demanded.

Shit! "I am just so happy to see you and see that you are up and about," I lied, dragging my eyes away from him and turning to Max, who looked at us both happily.

"Savannah, tell me. These tears aren't about me. Let's go outside. Max can have a run around while you and I are talking." He took off slowly. He might have been walking unaided, but his steps were small and hesitant. He was walking!

The Australian sunshine hit my skin as we walked through the landscaped lawns of St. George Hospital. After Mr. Davenport and I took a seat on the bench, Max ran off laughing and completely carefree.

"Tate was meant to be here with us but bitch-of-the-century Chelsea has decided to stir up shit again. He was supposed to have flown here last week."

"Why didn't you tell me? Go back to LA, Sav. Go back to Tate. You can see that I am okay. I am recovered. All I have to wait on is word that I can travel and I'll be back in LA."

"When you go back is when we go back."

"Sav, stop being so stubborn. I'm not going anywhere.

You have stopped your life for me for almost three months. You did not have to do that."

"Yes I did," I whispered

"Sav, talk to me, please. What is going on in that pretty little head of yours?"

"I can't leave until you are with us, okay? The last time I left anyone I cared about in the hospital, I lost them. They died and I will never get them back again. I can't lose you and I refuse to lose you. I don't care what you say or what threats you make. I will not be going back to the States without you."

"I have never met a more stubborn person in my life. What can I do to show you that you aren't losing me? I am here, Sav. I am walking, talking and breathing. My brain is fully recovered. All I have are a couple of scars to remind me. I will be back in the States within the next month, as soon as I get clearance for long-haul travel. You can go, Sav. Take Max back to Tate."

"No. We are flying back together and that's final."

Mr. Davenport didn't argue with me again, but I could tell by the scowl etched on his face that he wasn't impressed. It was final. I couldn't leave without him. However, hearing him say that we would be back in the States within the next month excited me. It unleashed thousands of butterflies in my belly at the thought of being back in Los Angeles and back with Tate.

God, I missed him, and fuck, I'd been stubborn. I was taking out bitch-face Chelsea on him and he didn't deserve that. I was a bitch and that's all I could be called.

From: Savannah Rae
To: Tate Connors
Time: 11.00pm AEST
Subject: HI

Tate,

I know you will be sleeping but I needed to send you an email. I am so sorry that my frustration about the whole Chelsea situation got to me. It was stupid of me to let her barge in and take over our world again and for that I apologise. Tanzi told me the other night that she is starting to retract what she said. Does that mean the case will not move forward?

Today we got word that Mr. Davenport can finally leave the hospital. The doctors say that his recovery has shocked them because it's been so quick. Three weeks is unheard of. I feel like he is finally back to his usual self and the fact that he called me a drama queen this morning and has been calling me stubborn all day tells me that. He will be released tomorrow and I am bringing him back to his apartment and we are now waiting for final confirmation that he can fly.

I am so ready to come home, Tate. I want to come home. I need to come home.

I miss you.

Savannah x

Pressing send, I sighed deeply, shoved my phone deep inside my bag, and turned my attention back to the television. My bag vibrated on my lap at an incoming text message. Pulling my phone back out of my bag, I saw Tate's name flash on the screen. The five words on the screen made my heart ache and roar at the same time.

Tate: **Come back to me Sav**

Chapter Twenty-Six

Tate

Three Months

S AVANNAH WANTED TO COME HOME. Every time I talked to her she would tell me that she was ready to come home, and every time I received an email she would make sure I knew. But still I was waiting on the other side of the world for them to come back to me.

Now, as I sat on the balcony as the sun set over the pacific at the start of our third month separation, I read her most recent text message over and over again, desperate for my mind to believe them. I was reading the words but they weren't sinking in. I saw the words, but why did I feel like she would just be coming for a visit?

The false accusations from Chelsea had done a number on Sav and me, and the moment I had to cancel my trip and spend countless hours with my lawyer trying to end the nightmare of tornado Chelsea, something had shifted between us. Sav was frustrated, and I knew hearing that Chelsea had weaseled her way back into our lives had taken Sav back to a place I'd never wanted her to revisit.

Through the craziness, I did have something to celebrate though. Tomorrow we were celebrating Tanzi and Jack's engagement party and today I had decided to man up and spend the day with Tanzi, helping her organize the last few things. I busied myself annoying Tanzi with requests of what I could do to help. Fuck, I even went with her to get her nails done. Whatever she needed I would give her. She worked me like a pack mule though, and Jack soon joined me on the balcony with a huff.

"Your sister is running me ragged."

I raised my eyebrow in warning.

"Not like that, asshole. She is making me help choose what to wear tomorrow. Where the fuck is Savannah when you need her?" He laughed quickly before his face dropped. Sav and Max's absence wasn't just affecting me. I knew Jack missed his partner-in-crime, and Tanzi wasn't her usual self without her self-proclaimed BFFL—best friend for life.

"So I got another text message from Sav this morning," I admitted with a slight frown,

"And?" he asked excitedly.

"She told me she wants to come home but something feels different about this message."

"What? When? And why the fuck would you have that look on your face?" Jack's shocked expression narrowed in at me. I turned quickly, looked back towards the beach, and sighed deeply.

"I am trying really fucking hard not to feel anything about this until Max is standing in front of me. I can't allow myself the risk of getting excited for something that probably won't even happen."

"You are such a fucking girl. Get excited, you asshole! Your girl wants to come home. Your little boy is coming home. Scream the shit out of this."

"The longer she is away, the more I realize what this means. What's to say that she won't follow Mr. Davenport everywhere he goes? What's to say that one day he will up and leave and she will follow?" I admitted, knowing full well that he wouldn't let me off the hook if I didn't start speaking. Seriously, we chatted like a couple of chicks most days.

"You and Sav need to talk about this. Only you two have the ability to want to be together or not. I know for a fact that she is still totally into the whole Tate and Sav thing. She loves you, man. Don't fuck it up with your insecurities. Tell her how you feel. Tell her that you have this fear. You don't want to lose that girl. You'd be fucking hell to live with if you did."

I rubbed my hands over my face in frustration. These exact questions had been haunting me for the past month. I trusted Savannah wholeheartedly, but the fear that I would never truly have her became more apparent with every day that passed. Knowing that they would be back in Los Angeles excited me beyond belief, but it also frightened me.

"I can't believe Tanzi said yes to your proposal. You are like some fucking wannabe Doctor Phil," I taunted, popping the tops off two beers and thrusting one into his hand while his words swirled around my head.

"What can I say? I'm good in the sack, damn good to look

at, and I know my way around words."

Looking at my best friend and now future brother-in-law, I rolled my eyes dramatically and called him a few choice names. But truth be told, I was as happy as a pig in shit that he'd finally proposed. It had been long overdue. Jack had been planning his proposal for months, right down to the intricate details to the point that Tanzi had thought he had been cheating on him because he was being so sketchy. I had been with him when he bought the perfect ring for Tanzi, I had been there when I heard the shriek of excitement when Tanzi said yes, and unfortunately I had been there when I walked in on them celebrating their engagement on the kitchen table.

"Think about what I said. Don't screw this up. She is coming back for you, Tate. No one else. Listen to her. Let her explain. Don't fuck up the best thing in your life." Jack patted my shoulder as he stood from his chair before disappearing into the house and leaving me to my own devices.

Being on my own was dangerous, this was the time where my brain would decide to be an evil bastard and play mind games with me. I knew Sav was in Australia for Mr. Davenport and I understood her reasoning for going in the beginning, but I also knew that he was out of the hospital and had been on the mend for a month now. She could have been home a month ago. This separation almost destroyed me daily, but in the back of my head was the little voice telling me that one day, maybe one day, they would come back.

Taking my phone out of my pocket, I flipped it over in my hand. I needed to speak with her. I was at the stage now that I needed to give her an ultimatum. I opened up a new text message and began typing.

We need to talk when you wake up.

For the next eight hours, I checked my phone religiously, yet there was still no response from Sav.

Climbing into bed that night, I tossed and turned. I thought of worst-case scenarios. I spent the better part of the night scrolling through every photo on my phone and watching every video of Max Sav had sent while they had been away. Finally, as the orange haze of sunrise floated through my windows, reality hit me.

I still hadn't received a response from Sav.

Chapter Twenty-Seven

Savannah

Today was the day that had been twisting and turning my insides since I realized Max and I were going back to the United States. After three exhausting and life-changing months, we were heading home. I never in my wildest dreams ever thought that I wouldn't class Australia as home, but all I knew now was that home was wherever the man with the deadly blue eyes was, and that was now Los Angeles.

Sitting in my business-class seat with Max at one side and Mr. Davenport on the other, everything suddenly came full circle. The last time I had been sitting on a plane beside Mr. Davenport, he had been warning me with stern eyes to stop sleeping around when we got to Los Angeles. Thank fuck I hadn't listened to him. If I had, I might not have fallen for the effects of Tate Connors and I might not have had my gorgeous baby boy, who was now chattering away to the air hostess.

I looked at Mr. Davenport and smiled with a heavy heart. Seeing him at his weakest and bouncing between life and death had instilled something in me that had been dormant for years. I had to live. I needed to finally break down the tight walls that kept me from moving on fully to the best chapters of my life.

"Are you feeling okay about this?" Mr. Davenport questioned from the seat beside me, looking up from the emergency landing pamphlet he had been handed.

"I am nervous as f-u-c-k," I spelled out. Mr. Davenport laughed and shook his head at me. *Some things never change.*

"What are you nervous about?" he continued with a raised eyebrow. I looked at him with wide eyes.

"Is this a trick question?"

"Gramps, draw with me," Max's soft voice interrupted.

When I looked down at my son, my smile took over my face and Mr. Davenport's crazy question dissipated. Max was everything I could have asked for and more.

"Are you coming to the p-a-r-t-y with us?" I asked softly, knowing the word 'party' would set Max off like a firecracker. We were arriving in Los Angeles the day of Tanzi and Jack's engagement party, and our arrival was planned all around that. I couldn't miss my two best friends' special day.

Mr. Davenport's eyes left the page he was coloring and found mine. "I have been invited but I am not sure if I will go."

"Please come with us. We need you there." I shot him a pleading look.

"Everything is going to be fine, Sav. It's time I gave you back to the one guy who seems to be able to put up with you." He smiled lovingly at me before turning back to Max and leaving me with way too much time to think as we soared through the air at 30,000 feet. What the hell kind of world was I going to step into when we arrived?

The sun was shining brightly in California. The trip from the airport was full of Max asking questions and laughing at the driver's accent. I watched him closely. He was so much like Tate that it was crazy. There was absolutely no doubt who his father was. They shared the same eyes, the wild chocolate brown hair, and the cheekiness that I loved so much.

The cab came to a halt in front of a house I didn't know. I had simply been given an address when I received the invitation via email, the engagement party was happening at a beach house in Santa Monica. The driver was chatting to Mr. Davenport, but all I could concentrate on was the thumping of my heart and the increasing sweat forming in my palms. *Just breathe, Savannah. Just breathe.*

"You ready for this?"

"No," I admitted with a shake of my head.

Following Mr. Davenport out of the cab, I couldn't stop my hands from shaking. What the hell was wrong with me? He grabbed my free hand as if he thought I'd flee, and to be honest, the thought had crossed my mind. We slowly walked up the paved drive with Max in my arms as I felt the anxiety fill to full capacity.

"Mummy, a puppy!" Max shrieked excitedly. He wriggled his way to freedom and ran up the long drive and through the double wooden gates before I had a chance to grab him.

"Max Davenport Connors, come back here!" I demanded, rushing after him, leaving Mr. Davenport chuckling at the scene unfolding in front of him. "This is not funny!" I shot over my shoulder, firing him an amused look. Fuck, my son was fast. I hurried following close on his heels and halted as soon as I stepped through the gates.

Max Connors in all his sweet innocence had burst through the middle of the engagement party and was now pretending to be a dog, totally oblivious to the implications of his stark arrival. Every single person's attention was now firmly locked on us, and I immediately felt the world around us cave in. This wasn't the way our return was meant to go down. We were meant to quietly walk in and see everyone one on one. We were meant to make sure we were welcome. We were meant to be a subtle inclusion to the party, not this party stopper.

A gasp rang out behind me and I swung around quickly. My eyes widened as they landed on Tate's mum. The color from her usually suntanned face drained out as she looked between me and Max. Almost as if it were in slow motion, the plate she was carrying slipped from her hands, smashing into a thousand pieces as it hit the pavement below.

"Savannah?" she asked in barely a whisper.

Max's laughter grabbed my attention away from the shocked expression on her face. I crouched down and picked Max up, placing him on my hip. I watched her closely as her eyes took him in. We had our weekly Skype dates and I emailed photos regularly, but it wasn't the same as having him in the flesh. Max wiggled in my arms and was barking like a puppy, causing me to giggle and a smile to slowly come to her face.

"Max, do you know who this is?"

Max shifted in my arms and turned to look at her. Begging

tears formed in her eyes as she looked over him. He fired a killer smile and she broke out in giggles.

His little brow furrowed in concentration as he looked between me and Mrs. Connors. The breath I was holding in escaped the moment recognition hit him. "Gramma," he said matter-of-factly.

"Why is everyone so quiet? I thought this was a par—"

Mrs. Connors inhaled sharply and my eyes closed briefly as my head dropped. This wasn't how it was meant to happen. Just hearing his deep, husky voice made my breath catch. Silence fell, crushing the excitement that had been around us just moments ago. I hadn't expected our reunion to happen like this. I thought maybe it would be just us three away from the world, away from prying eyes and hushed voices, but definitely not like this. I thought I could have sneaked into the house and saw him, but now our reunion was on display to everyone.

I finally raised my face and my eyes connected with his. Tate looked at me like he was seeing a ghost, a mirage, and that this wasn't reality. But then his eyes flashed to the wriggling little boy in my arms and a lethal combination of happiness, intrigue, and confusion swam in his deep blue eyes.

"Let me take Max. Go and talk to him." I broke my stare from Tate and looked at Mr. Davenport, who had moved up beside me with an encouraging smile on his face. "Be strong, beautiful girl."

"Hey little man, do you want to go and play with Gramps for a minute." I smiled at Max who nodded excitedly and held his arms out to Mr. Davenport.

"Come on, Maxey. Let's go and find Uncle Lucas." Mr. Davenport took Max from my arms and strode towards the group of people staring at us.

My eyes flashed through the crowd and finally I found Tanzi and Jack. My eyes misted at the sight of my best friends. God, I had missed them. Tanzi's hand was at her mouth and Jack shot me a wink from across the yard. I tore my gaze from them and turned back to face the man who had given me my life back. Tate Connors.

As if the world stood still, all noise around us evaporated. Right at this moment, it was just the two of us. I felt the pull towards him the closer he got. My breathing hitched as he stood before me. His eyes traveled over every inch of my face, drinking me in.

"Tate," I breathed out into the space between us. His eyes darted from mine and moved to where Max was with Mr. Davenport. My heart broke as I watched his face crumble and a single tear roll over his cheek.

"I can't do this, Savannah." His voice was barely a whisper. He turned his back to me and stormed towards the stairs leading to the house. The screen door slamming behind him caused me to jump. I stood in front of the empty space he left and sighed deeply.

"Sav, I can't believe you are here," Tanzi's soft voice said beside me. I spun around quickly and my arms swallowed her within seconds.

"I couldn't miss my best friend's engagement party."

"Savannah Rae, you sexy momma." Jack's arm wrapped around my waist from behind and pulled my back into his chest, resting his head on my shoulder. I smiled at the feeling of love surrounding me as Tanzi, Jack, and I stood in a huddle of arms.

"Jack, you sexy beast of a man." I twisted in his arms, hugging him for dear life.

"Mummy, Lukey said we can go swimming at the beach-hhhhhhhhhhhhh!" Max squealed, filling the air and causing deep laughter to escape all of us.

The familiar feeling of being watched took over me and I froze at the intense sensation of being under the gaze of Tate Connors. It was a feeling I would never forget. I turned and looked towards the house and found him standing on the balcony, glaring down at us.

"This right here is his biggest dream coming true. He just needs to let it sink in. He has been waiting forever for this moment." Tanzi admitted, truth dripping from her words.

I smiled at her before focusing back on Tate. His gaze didn't falter. Wherever Max was, Tate's eyes followed. I took nervous steps up the stairs towards him. Standing beside him, I looked out over the backyard, not having a clue what to say or do.

"He is perfect, Savannah."

I looked at Max and couldn't help but smile. He was chasing Tanzi around the backyard, squealing with happiness, and completely oblivious to the stir his arrival was causing.

"He is happy, healthy, and a little heartbreaker. You have nothing to worry about."

"I never doubted that you'd look after him."

A tense silence fell between us. I couldn't drag my eyes away from his, and his eyes drove into mine. Still to this day, he could drag me in and make me forget about the rest of the world with one glance. I knew he would be happy to see Max, but as he stared at me with waves of anger and desire flooding his eyes, I had absolutely no clue if he wanted to kiss or strangle me.

"Tate, Savannah, get your asses down here."

"Uncy J said arse. Uncy J said arse," Max started chanting in sing-song.

"Fuck, he even says arse," Tate muttered before walking down the stairs and leaving me with a million thoughts swimming through my head.

I straightened my skirt and ran my fingers through my hair. The smell of the nearby ocean filled my senses and made me feel at peace in the turbulence of the day. Moving down the steep steps, I rushed across the lawn to where Max was now the center of attention. Jack, Tanzi, Lucas, Ali, and Tate surrounded him, watching him playing with the dog.

"Did you just say a naughty word?" I asked with a stern voice.

Max walked over to me with his head down and wrapped his arms around my legs. "Uncy J said it."

"That doesn't mean you have to say it."

"I'm sorry, Mummy." He pulled away and gave me the biggest, bluest puppy-dog eyes he could muster. I shook my head and turned towards Tate. I pointed to Max and rolled my eyes at Tate. "Those eyes? That look is all you."

Max suddenly became alerted to the fact Tate was standing with us. His face flashed with recognition as he looked at Tate and the biggest smile took over his face.

"Daddy!" With excited steps, he ran towards Tate, wrapped his arms around his legs, and held him tightly.

My heart ached and clapped triumphantly in my chest at the sight before me. Tate's fears of Max not knowing him disappeared when Max spoke that one word. Tate stilled and stared at our little boy, losing all ability to speak. Suddenly, Max took a step away from Tate and grabbed his hand, pulling on it to force Tate to lean down to his level. Out of nowhere, Max's tiny hand lifted the edge of Tate's shirt until his toned stomach was on full display to the whole party.

A high-pitched squeal shattered the air before an eruption of giggles poured out of Max's tiny body. Throwing himself on the grass, he laughed like he had just witnessed the funniest thing he'd ever seen. Max rolled towards me and pulled the edge of my skirt. I leaned over, coming to his eye level.

"Daddy has drawings on him," he whispered innocently in my ear.

My laughter joined his while everyone around us stared like we were a couple of nutbags. Tate's eyes drove into us as Max looked back at him. Max was completely in awe that he was with his daddy.

"Tell him, Max," I encouraged.

Max moved towards Tate, standing before him and looking up at him through questioning eyes. My heart skipped a beat at the vision before me. Max was the spitting image of Tate, and seeing them together like this was painfully beautifully.

"You have drawings on you," Max giggled and pointed at Tate's chest. "Mummy has a picture of you with your drawings and she always had it in her bed like a teddy."

Oh, Max Davenport Connors, you are a walking secret teller. My eyes dropped to the ground, searching desperately for a hole to fall down. Everyone now knew about my ritual I had while I was in Australia. I had the ritual of falling asleep while hugging a photo frame containing my favorite photo of Tate. It was the one thing that had allowed me to fall asleep in my loneliest days in Sydney. Now, as I watched the stormy look roll in over Tate's face, it seemed it would be a ritual I would also have in Los Angeles.

Chapter Twenty-Eight

Tate

TALK ABOUT A COMPLETE AND utter storm of emotions. No wonder she'd never replied to my text. She had been above the fucking Pacific. I needed the ocean and fast. Escaping from the engagement party, I slipped out the back gate, crossing the road until the feeling of warm sand hit my bare feet. I couldn't get my head around Savannah and Max being back.

As I took a seat on the sand, the sun beamed down on my skin and I closed my eyes, tilting my head towards the sky. My mind bounced all over the place, trying desperately to believe what was happening. Max and Savannah were here. I could touch them, I could hold them, I could see them in the flesh. This morning I'd woken up thinking I was simply going to celebrate my sister and best friend's engagement. Never in my wildest dreams had I thought I'd be seeing my son and Savannah.

I couldn't even begin to comprehend the thoughts running through my head. Was I happy? Of course I was. Was I scared? Fuck yes. Was I confused? More confused than I'd ever been. Was I dreaming? I hoped to Christ I wasn't.

Through my closed eyes, a shadow lingered over me. My solitude was shattered.

"How are you doing, man?" Jack questioned, collapsing beside me and looking out at the ocean. "Honestly? I have no fucking clue."

"You have your family back, man. Sav is back for you, Tate. Your son is looking at you like you are a fucking superhero or something. It's kinda sickening."

My eyes widened at his words as my irritation rose in my chest. "It's such a mindfuck. Do you know how hard it was not to drag her inside like some fucking caveman and show her just how much I missed her? Fuck, I would have taken her right then and there if I could but I can't and I won't. What's to say she won't run off again in a week or a month?"

"You need to get this thought out of your head that she ran. If it were Tanzi on the other side of the world, completely banged up, what would you have done?" He stared at me knowingly and I knew the answer. "You would go straight to her! Your relationship with Tanzi is the same as Sav's and Mr. Davenport's. Tanzi is your other half and Mr. Davenport is Sav's. She did what she had to do, and to be honest, I think it's the most selfless thing I've ever witnessed someone doing." Jack stood and shoved his hands in his pockets. "I probably sound like a pussy for saying this, but a love like yours and Sav's doesn't come around often, so don't lose it."

I watched with narrowed eyes as Jack strode away from

me, leaving the beach and leaving me to deal with my increasingly frantic thoughts. Jack was right. If anything happened to Tanzi, my world as I knew it would stop and I would drop anything and everything to be by her side. Everyone knew that.

The difference though was that I knew Savannah was my number one priority and my world was hers. Everything, and I mean everything, is second to her, and that's where my issue was. What I couldn't understand and was finding impossible to comprehend was that she hadn't seemed to consider me in her decision to leave. Not once. To me, it felt like I was always going to be second choice. I was always the one who was going to be left behind and I'd be damned if I would let that happened again.

Standing, I took off back towards the party, knowing full well that being a pussy about this whole thing wasn't going to make it any easier. This was my sister and best friend's engagement party and I wasn't going to let the dramas of my life ruin that. Plus, I had a son in there I just needed to see.

The moment I opened the back gate and appeared, Max ran across the yard and was pulling on my hand for attention. "What's up, little man?" I asked, finally finding my voice amongst the emotions I was fighting.

"Mummy said we can stay!" Max's excited voice said with a promise. My eyes darted around the backyard until they landed on Sav's, who stood watching us closely, her face not showing any sign of reaction. A little hand grabbed mine and Max began pulling me towards the group, talking quickly about staying over.

"Are you staying here?" I heard Tanzi ask as Max and I joined the group.

Sav's eyes darted to the house behind her and raised a brow. "Whose house is this?"

"It's yours and Tate's."

"What?" she questioned with wide eyes. "Our house? Tate?"

"Can I speak to you alone?" I didn't bother waiting for a reply. I grabbed her hand, dragging her away from the group and towards the house since this wasn't a conversation I wanted to have in front of our son.

With my hand still clasped tightly with hers, we moved through the house to the living room. Standing in the middle of the empty room, everything seemed to hit me with full force at once. Savannah was back, standing in front of me, looking at me with anticipation. I felt the familiar rumblings of my attraction for her taking over every inch of me and there was damn well nothing I could do about it. Her eyes traveled to our joined hands and immediately I dropped them, folding my arms across my chest.

"I would prefer if you stayed with us," I demanded, dropping my eyes to look at her.

"When did you buy this house?"

"About a month ago. I was planning on telling you when I came to Australia."

"Oh, the trip that Chelsea decided to wreck. Always fucking Chelsea."

I breathed in deeply, begging to keep calm. "I haven't seen Max in three months and I'd appreciate if you would stay here. I need to get to know my son again."

"I'd never keep you from your son Tate."

And just like that, the switch was turned on to the enraged

feelings I had kept locked away for the past three months. "Are you serious? Are you not aware of the three months that you were away?" I snorted.

"I'm sorry. I didn't know what to do. Do you think I enjoyed being on the other side of the world, watching Mr. Davenport almost die in front of me? Do you think I wanted to be apart from you? I didn't know what the fuck to do and I'm sorry!" Her voice rang through the living room, shocking me with the intensity of her words. "We missed you."

"Don't say that. This isn't about you," I hissed as my heart began thudding in my chest.

"I missed you."

"Well why didn't you come home?" I spat. "Why the fuck did it take you three months to decide that I was worth coming home for? I don't know what the fuck to do. I want you in every sense of the word, but why should I even bother? I can't help but feel like it will only be a matter of time before you run off again."

"Why do you have to be such an arsehole?"

I felt the boiling of emotions rip through me, stabbing me brutally with truth and fear. This woman standing before me held my heart so tight in her hands that I felt like I was bleeding for her, I would change the fucking world for her, but did she even realize that? Looking at her, I found her face crumbling as she glared back at me. I saw the hurt flying through her eyes, and without reasoning, I lost all sense of rationality.

In two steps, I pulled her towards me with so much vigor that she collided into my chest. Lifting her from the ground, my hands swept under her skirt, kneading her ass through her lace panties. My heart thumped dangerously fast in my chest as my eyes dominated hers. I thrust her against the wall with such force that the side table against the wall shook and the lamp crashed to the floor, but I didn't even care. All I wanted now was to taste her and rattle her feelings like she was rattling mine.

"Tate," she moaned as my lips crashed to her neck, biting, sucking, and kissing the delicious flesh. Fuck, I had missed her taste, her noises, and the feeling of her body slamming against mine.

Her legs squeezed around my body as my mouth finally encased hers, taking with it her breath and claiming its ownership. Three months of pent-up frustration and loneliness was forced into this kiss, and I wouldn't stop until she was breathless and panting for more. My tongue ran the length of her bottom lip, pushing its way into her willing mouth as my body ground up against hers. She whimpered into the kiss, her hands thrusting into my hair, pulling and twisting it within her fingers. Fuck, I'd missed this. I didn't have time for romantic kisses. I needed this kiss to be frantic and brutal, devouring and consuming.

"We will stay," she exhaled against my lips, pulling away to gain a desperate breath and allowing me to realize exactly what we were doing. Her breathing was ruthless, broken, and desperate.

"Thank you." I took a step back and sat on the edge of the couch, my eyes never leaving her. "This is the home I bought for the three of us, Savannah. I wanted to make a home, a place to call our own."

"Wanted?" she asked, her voice dropping to almost a whisper.

I stood and walked out of the living room and back to the party without answering her question. I was a weak prick when it came to Savannah, and my weakness was on full display. So as usual, I had let my dick decide what I wanted just as it usually did when it came to Savannah Rae.

Taking the stairs two at a time, I stepped on the grass and immediately Tanzi and Jack looked at me suspiciously. Jack's eyes jumped and looked over my shoulder and I knew Savannah had just stepped out of the door. Looking over my shoulder, I noticed that her face was still flushed and her lips were swollen. It was obvious to every single person what had happened.

"Good to see you, Tate." Mr. Davenport's low voice shocked me. I turned towards the man who had greeted death's door head-on and had come out the other side. Holding out his hand, he shook mine firmly. "He's perfect, isn't he?"

"Yeah," I said in quick response. "How are you feeling?" I asked, desperately trying to clear the lump that was forming in my throat from the sight of Max.

"I am all clear. Final tests showed no long-term damage."

"I've missed so much," I admitted softly, my eyes never leaving Max. "Can I ask you something? Why didn't she come home a month ago? You had the all clear but she still stayed away."

"I can't speak on her behalf, and you need to speak with her, but she had her reasons. My accident took her back to her darkest days, Tate, to a time where you or the life she is living now didn't exist. At that time it was Sav, her parents, and me. That was her life. Since her parents died, she has blamed herself for some crazy reason and she thought she could do something to stop what happened, and that's what she thought when I was in hospital. All I can ask is that you give her a chance to explain. Listen to her and then decide what you want to do. You do something amazing to her, and in all the time I've known her, I've never seen her more alive than when she is with you. You have given her life again and a future." He patted my shoulder quickly and moved towards Savannah, who I hadn't noticed was watching us. Her face dropped suddenly. She scooped Max up in her arms, walked to Tanzi and Jack, and hugged them both.

I stormed across the yard towards them. Jack's eyes connected with mine in silent discussion before dropping to Max in warning.

"I might actually take the little guy inside," Sav spoke softly. She took a step towards me, breaking the distance I had put between us. "I never ran from you, Tate," she whispered, her eyes showing sadness and regret before turning with Max in her arms and walking towards the stairs leading to the house.

All I knew was that my heart was still hers but my mind was telling me to be careful. I wanted nothing more than to continue what we had started inside and tell her that no matter what, I loved her, but the heart she owned was now bruised by the distance it had suffered because of her.

Chapter Twenty-Nine

Savannah

I STUMBLED UP THE STAIRS AND through the front door with Max tucked safely in my arms. I was trying desperately to keep my emotions in check, but the threat of tears was almost too overwhelming. I refused to completely lose it in front of my little boy; his questions on why Mummy was crying would crush me and I wouldn't be able to answer him. My body still hummed from the effects of Tate's aggressive kiss, the taste of him lingering on my lips and now taunting my thoughts. It scared me how easily I was so willing to submit to him.

"Mummy, where are we?" Max's tired voice asked from the confines of my chest. His head sleepily looked around the space, taking in the new surroundings.

"This is Daddy's place. How 'bout we go and have a little snooze and we can talk about it later?" I whispered, pushing back the chocolate brown hair falling on his forehead. He nodded his head slowly and snuggled back in as exhaustion took over his tiny body.

The oversized cream-colored couch taking over the vast living space being flooded by late afternoon California sunshine grabbed my attention. The bitch known as jet lag was swallowing me by the second and the couch was calling my name. Max's body was limp in my arms, and his soft, constant breathing told me that he had finally crashed out.

Taking my handbag off my shoulder and placing it on the bench I quietly moved back to the couch and lay down with my little man. He cuddled up close to my body and wrapped his little arm over my stomach. It was a peace I always loved. Within seconds, I felt the familiar wave of sleep invading my exhausted body and I was soon out to the world.

The sound of giggling startled me as I came back to consciousness. My eyes fluttered open, and for a moment in my post sleep bliss, I lost all sense of where I was. The couch beside me was void of Max and panic hit me. I shot up from the couch and my head swung around the room, desperate to find any sign of him. The unease of how quiet the house was petrified me. Max was never this quiet, and if he was, it was because he was into something he shouldn't be and his mischievous streak was barging through—something I liked to blame on Tate.

"Max, where are you?" I pleaded as I rushed out of the living room, my eyes frantically darting around the emptiness around me.

"Mummy!" The sound of Max's excited voice froze me on the spot. Turning towards the area his voice had sounded from, I hurried into the large kitchen.

My eyes anxiously searched the chrome and white kitchen, still unable to see him. As I reached the kitchen island, I heard the sound of a door opening from what I assumed was the hall, and the sound of Tate's voice echoed through the air. I closed my eyes, briefly falling into the deep, soothing voice of Tate, but then the giggle of Max ripped me from my intoxication of the man I would fight for until the day I no longer existed, and boy, did it seem I had a fight on my hands.

"Oh, Maxey, what are you doing?" I breathed out with a laugh when I finally found him near the far kitchen counter.

Max looked up at me, a killer grin taking over his precious face and those blue eyes that got me every time twinkling in front of me. Surrounding him on the floor were Sharpies in every color imaginable with lids off, his arms and chest that were now covered in squiggles, lines, circles, and different creations causing my laughter.

"Look, Mummy, I have drawings like Daddy. I have a ball and my name and a puppy dog," he stated with pride, pointing out his various *tattoos* to me. "Daddy!" Max squealed.

My body stiffened and I felt the air shift around me as the familiar feeling of being near Tate lingered in the air. My body ignited in the way only he could make it and it ached to feel him in every possible way. He had and would always have the resilient ability to make my brain turn to mush and my body to become his own without question. Once again, I was involuntarily succumbing to the damn Tate Connors Effect.

Hesitantly glancing over my shoulder, I found Tate leaning against the door frame, watching Max closely, a smile tugging on his lips, and my breath caught. His hair was wet and he wore a shirt that sat close to his perfectly toned chest, showing me the outline of the flawless canvas I had sucked, kissed, bitten, and touched so many times before. He was like a walking freaking aphrodisiac.

"They look great," Tate said softly with a hint of amusement in his voice. He sauntered past me without a glance through the kitchen towards Max and crouched down to study his 'tattoos' closer.

Max looked at Tate in pure admiration. His eyes were wide as he looked at Tate's torso, trying to see the drawing he had seen earlier. "I want to be like him, Mummy." Max announced while looking at Tate with a silly grin. Tate's damn tattoo had gained another victim.

My heart clenched at the innocence of Max's words and the fact that he had absolutely no idea how much he was already like Tate. Their similarities comforted yet broke my heart. My time in Australia had been one of the toughest times of my life and it was because this little boy had been with me that it had allowed me to feel like Tate had still been with me. They shared the deep blue eyes that made me weak at the knees and the eyes that would get me to do whatever the hell they wanted. Max's cheekiness was clearly derived from his father, but it was the look of determination and stubbornness that reminded me daily of Tate.

Tate's eyes locked with mine and my heart rate quickened as he drew me in at a rapid rate. His face showed no emotion, no sign of what he was thinking, and no insight to what he wanted from me.

"I should go and wash this off," I whispered, knowing full well that my voice was showing no sign of confidence or want to leave the lock of his gaze.

"You are welcome to the guest room down the hall. Third door on the left. There is a bathroom attached." He turned and headed towards the living room without another look.

Grabbing Max's hand, we walked down the hall and opened the door to find a large bedroom with a king-sized bed, a dresser, and an antique freestanding mirror in the far corner. The familiarity of this room hit me hard.

"What the hell?" I said in disbelief. My eyes scanned every inch of the room. This was my exact room from the apartment I had left three months ago. My bed, my dresser, my mirror, my candles, and my artwork filled the space. I was swamped by déjà vu.

I sat Max on the bed and ran my hand along the red satin comforter as I took in my favorite Andy Warhol painting Tate had bought me in New York. Max wriggled on the bed, getting comfortable on the pillows, his tired eyes almost winning the battle of staying awake.

"Come on, little man. We have to get you in the bath and into your Thomas PJs," I said softly. Max nodded silently and wrapped his arms around my neck and kissed me gently.

It was moments like this, in the craziness of my life, that I loved the most. A simple kiss from Max, a cute drawing that he would demand I put on the fridge, or the silent snuggle in the early hours of the morning was what I craved the most.

Max chatted the entire time he was in the bath; bathing was his favorite time. Bathing or going to the beach. During our time in Australia, he would spend every afternoon in the waves of Bondi Beach with Mr. Davenport. It was their boy's only time and I knew Mr. Davenport was making sure he remembered for when we got back to the States.

Once his skin looked wrinkly like an old man, I pulled him out and dressed him in his favorite Thomas PJs and chased him down the hall as he burst into the living room.

"Mr. Max! I love your PJs!" Jack's voice boomed from the couch.

Max scrambled onto Jack's lap and leaned back against his chest, focusing on the television with heavy eyes. Tate glanced at me from the couch before turning back to the television without another look.

"Pizza! I have pizza!" Tanzi announced excitedly as she burst through the front door. I still hadn't had a good chance to have any one-on-one time with her. I couldn't wait for best friend time.

Max's head lifted from Jack's chest at the sound of pizza. He truly was my son. His love of pizza had developed from a young age.

"'Rooms and pineapple?" Max's tiny voice asked.

"You've got our son eating mushrooms?" Tate asked softly at memories of my obsession with mushrooms during my pregnancy.

"Mummy, 'rooms!" Max demanded, scrunching his face up and pouting. I burst out into a fit of laughter and was soon joined by Tate, Tanzi, and Jack. Max's eyes bounced among the four of us before his giggle filled the air. "Mummy, why are we laughing?"

"You are too much, Max Connors," Tanzi said between giggles.

"Aunty Tanzi, I love you," Max swooned and crawled from Jack's lap into Tanzi's awaiting arms.

Tanzi looked at me with a completely look of love swallowing her blue eyes. "Thank you," she mouthed to me before wrapping Max in her arms and kissing his face as he giggled in her arms.

We were home.

Chapter Thirty

Tate

THE NIGHT WAS FILLED WITH giggles, catching up, and my sitting in silence while observing Max talk to Jack and Tanzi and cuddle up to Sav. It was so surreal. The exhaustion from the day and the excitement of the engagement party filled the room as yawns amongst us became more apparent. Max's little eyes kept drooping, and when Sav announced that she was taking him to bed, I knew I had to show her.

I stood from the couch and Max's eyes immediately shot open and found me. "Max, do you want to see a surprise?" I asked softly. He eagerly nodded his head and held his arms up to me. "Can you come with us?" I directed at Sav. She rose from her seat, shooting Tanzi a worried look before following me down the long hall in silence.

I stopped in front of the closed door and took a deep breath to settle my nerves. Shooting Sav a quick look, I opened the door, switched on the light, and walked into the blue room I had spent so many days in over the past month. My eyes fell shut at the sound of Savannah's deep gasp ringing behind me. I took a chance and finally turned to look at her. Her eyes filled with tears as her head swung around every inch of the room taking everything in around her. This had been my sanctuary while they had been away. The times where I'd needed my solitude I'd spent in this room, creating the perfect escape for Max.

The walls were painted a sky blue, the far wall displaying a mural of the beach and the other wall showed hand-painted pictures of the trains from Thomas the Tank Engine. A low bed ran along the center of the room and the door leading to the balcony allowed for his beloved waves to be heard in the silence of his room.

"What do you think, little man? This is your special room."

Max was out of my arms and running around every corner of his room, excitedly talking to the Thomas mural that was painted on his wall. Seeing him happy and clearly overjoyed made everything worth it.

I watched as Savannah moved around the room gracefully, her fingertips running along the bed and the walls. She stopped by the dresser and her hands found the picture frame that contained a photo of the three of us on Max's second birthday.

"This is one of my favorite photos," she whispered as she stared at the photo in her hand.

"Mine too."

"This room is amazing." She placed the photo frame back on the dresser and turned to look at me. "Thanks for bringing all the furniture from the apartment. It was crazy walking in and seeing our exact room from the apartment."

"It's not a problem."

Sav opened her mouth to speak but Max's voice interrupted. "Mummy! Daddy! I love!" Max's excited shrieks filled the tense space and he held up his arms to be lifted up. Propping him on my hip he kissed my cheek and hugged me tightly.

"I love you so much, little man."

Max pulled his face away from my chest and beamed at me.

"More than ice cream?" he asked.

"Yep."

"More than lollies?"

I looked at Sav with questioning eyes. What the hell were lollies?

"Candy," Sav replied quickly through her tears.

"Yep! Way more than lollies."

"More than Thomas?"

"Yep. More than Thomas, Gordy, and Percy."

"Daddy!" he shrieked before laughing. "You are so funny."

And in that exact moment, everything seemed perfect.

The following day, as I sat at the dining table with my laptop open in front of me, my mind drifted to only hours earlier. Seeing Savannah waltz around the house in her tiny shorts and bikini top after she and Max had gone to the beach resulted in me and my hand becoming well acquainted. Seriously, she would be the fucking death of me. I knew what I wanted, my cock knew what I wanted, but my stubborn ass was still waiting for the bubble to burst. I was slowly but surely ready to come undone.

"Tate, can I talk to you for a minute?" Her thick Australian accent filled the silent space around me.

Looking up from my laptop, I saw Savannah, who stood nervously by the kitchen counter wearing a knee-length grey skirt and a white button-up blouse with come-fuck-me red heels.

"Sure," I stated, swallowing hard, diverting my eyes from her tan legs and tight ass back to her face.

"I've got to go to Beautify for a meeting with Mr. Davenport and Max is napping so I was wondering if I could leave him here with you until I get back. I shouldn't be any longer than an hour or so. I am happy to take him if there are any problems."

Closing my laptop, I folded my hands on the table in front of me. "I'm his dad. You don't have to ask me these things."

Nodding, she looked at the floorboards below and then back towards the hall. She almost looked fearful. What could she possibly be afraid of?

Sighing, I stood from the dining room table and crossed the living room towards her. I stood before her and waited. "What's wrong?"

"Tell me what you are thinking because I getting sick of you shying away from me. You look at me like you want me but then you talk to me like you despise me. I feel like we are complete strangers." She let out a deep breath and stared at me in anticipation.

Rubbing the back of my neck, I stared at her, trying to find out what I could possibly say. "Sav, we are far from strangers.

You know more about me than anyone in this world and that will always be the case. I am desperately trying to get my head around the thought of you and Max being back. It was three long, torturous months where I was here on my own while you and my son were on the other side of the world. A lot changed when you decided to leave, Sav. The only thing I know for sure is that I am going to get to know my son."

"But that wasn't entirely my fault, Tate. You can't lay blame entirely on me." Her voice broke under her words.

"I will tell you this one thing, Sav. I love you so fucking much that it hurts. You make me weak but in the next breath you make me stronger than I've ever felt. You make me feel a love I've never thought possible but then I feel a hurt I would never wish on anyone. I want nothing more than to drag you to my bedroom and do things to your body that you could never imagine but I feel like I need to get to know you again. I need to make sure that I am what you want."

"What more can I do, Tate? I came back for you. You are the reason I am here." She took a step toward me, grabbing my hands and pulling me towards her body. "I came back for you, Tate."

Her lips dropped to the corner of my mouth, kissing me tenderly, and instantly my eyes closed under her touch. Suddenly, she pulled away and took a step towards the door before turning back to me with a look of determination sweeping across her face.

"I'll tell you what I know, Tate. I want you and I will not let you go without a fight, and that's one thing I can guarantee. I came back for you, I came back for what we are, and I came back for the future I know both of us crave. I am not stopping until I get that. Call me stubborn. Call me determined. Call me persistent."

Standing across the room from her, I knew that I was quickly getting caught up in the intense waves of Savannah Rae, and I knew that once I got lost in the swell, there was no turning back. Without another word, she stepped out of the door and I released the breath I had locked up tight in my lungs.

My body and mind were in a constant war with each other, telling me to do what the other told me not to do. I didn't know how long I could keep myself from throwing myself at her, and the thought of burying myself so deep inside her had made my lonely nights come to life. But then my mind would kick in and warn me against diving back in, warning me to take it slow and make sure she was here to stay, encouraging me to test her and play this dangerous game of cat and mouse.

Chapter Thirty-One

Savannah

PULLING OPEN THE SLIDING DOOR with nervous hands, I stepped out onto the balcony and into the cooling ocean breeze of Santa Monica. The soft hum of voices and roar of the nearby ocean greeted me, and I found Tanzi, Jack, and Tate sitting around a round table, open beers in front of them, talking softly amongst themselves.

Tanzi was first to see me, and before I could say a word, she rushed towards me and pulled me by both hands towards the table. There was no turning back now. Tate glanced up over his beer bottle without a word, but I noticed the emotion flickering over his face. Our eyes met for a brief moment before he broke the connection and shifted his gaze to the dark waves being illuminated by the full moon above us.

"Beer?" Jack suggested, holding a bottle out towards me, his eyes showing the glazed effects of one too many beers.

Grabbing it from his hand, I popped open the top and

sighed as the cold amber liquid slid down my throat.

"Sav, can I ask you something? It's kind of personal." Jack asked abruptly with a cheeky grin filling his lips. *Oh crap.* If there was one thing I knew about Jack it's that if he asks if he can ask you something, you can never know what to expect.

"When have you ever considered my privacy, Jack?" I replied nervously, chugging back more of my beer. His eyes narrowed in on mine as they flashed with excitement and intrigue. *Oh shit.*

"Have you had sex since you left LA?"

What the hell? I knew my eyes shot open in shock and my hand holding the bottle lingered just near my mouth as I took in his words. The sound of Tate choking on his beer caused a nervous laugh to escape my throat. Jack certainly had no qualms about getting right to the nitty gritty details.

"No, Jack. I haven't had sex since I left."

Jack's eyes widened and darted to Tate and then back to me. Did he honestly think I'd have fucked myself around Sydney? "Has anyone touched you since you left LA?" His voice was lower this time.

"Nope. The only hands that have been on my body are mine."

"Jesus fucking Christ, woman. What about you, Tate?"

"You know the answer to that, Jack," Tate growled. His eyes glaring at me, penetrating deep in my soul in only the way Tate Connors could. "I haven't touched or kissed anyone since Savannah and I certainly haven't had sex."

"Well fuck me sideways! How the hell are you two not ripping each other's clothes off right now? You aren't even eye-fucking! You two are notorious for that."

The intensity of Tate's glare and the directness of his words offered the kind of promise I needed. I didn't want to eye-fuck him—I wanted him. I needed to show him that he still owned me in every sense of the world. My heart was still his, my body was still his, and I would always be his.

"So, ahh, the little guy settled, okay?" Tanzi asked with a comforting smile, thankfully breaking my addiction to Tate. I turned my attention to her and smiled brightly at the talk of Max.

"Yeah, he went down without a fight. I think he was too excited about being in his new room to worry about fighting me about going to bed."

Silence fell among the four of us and the sound of the ocean roared in the distance. I felt eyes on me and finally looked up from the neck of the bottle. "Why are you crying, Tanzi?" I asked softly, finding tears streaming down her cheeks as she looked at me with a smile plastered on her face.

"I still can't believe I have my best friend back. You don't realize how much I missed you. Do not ever leave again. I will hunt you down," she warned with a short laugh.

Watching tears fall from my best friend's eyes made my stomach twist. I had missed her so freaking much. The calls, the mass of emails and text messages daily weren't the same as sitting here with her.

"It was the scariest time of my life. I thought I'd lost him, Tanzi," I admitted, deciding then and there to put my cards on the table. It was true. My life had only functioned for Max and Mr. Davenport over the past three months. Everything I had done I'd done for them, and I knew people thought I was selfish because of it. I loved Tate with my whole heart, but the fear of my past, the fear of loss, and the feeling that I was indebted to Mr. Davenport had taken control of my life. "I never wanted to leave you, but I owe Mr. Davenport my life and I had to be there for him. I didn't know what else to do." The familiar feeling of tension burned in my chest. My eyes moistened as a threat of tears appeared. "I'm so sorry. I didn't mean to keep Max from you all." I looked at Tate, knowing that I was saying these words to him, begging for him to listen to my words. His eyes blazed at me, showing regret and confusion.

"It wasn't just Max we missed," Tate spat in my direction. He was now completely facing me, watching me, taunting me.

"Well you aren't making that very clear, Tate. I know I fucked up, I know that I took your son away from you and I will regret that for the rest of my life, but I didn't know what else to do. What the fuck could I possibly have done? I tried to do what I thought was right and it's blown up in my face. I don't know what I have to do to make you see."

"Make me see what, Savannah?" He shifted in his seat, leaning over the table in my direction, allowing his eyes to penetrate me so brutally. I completely forgot that we had company, but right at this moment I couldn't give a shit.

"That I love you more than anything, Tate. Yes I screwed up, yes I know you will never fully understand why I supposedly ran, and I don't expect you to. But I want nothing more than to be wrapped up in you completely. That's what I want you to see." I was breathless and spent.

Without another word, he pushed back his seat, the screech of the legs scraping on the pavers below making me cringe. His eyes never found me again. He stormed through the glass door and into the house, leaving me in a puddle of emotions.

Breathe AGAIN

After sitting under the stars for another hour with no sign of Tate returning, I slurred that I was going to bed. Three beers had rocked me and the craziness of the past three days suddenly rushed through me in brutal force. With a mumbled goodnight from Tanzi and Jack, I walked through the house, the lights on low creating a harmonious atmosphere in the air when in reality this house was far from harmonious at the moment.

As I walked down the hall, I hesitated at Tate's closed door before shaking the thoughts of bursting into his room and demanding that we talk out of my head. I took off towards my room with my tail between my legs and headed straight for the safety of my bathroom.

"Can I speak to you for a second?"

"Shit!" I shrieked, clutching my heart as shock filled me. I looked into the reflection of the mirror and found Tate standing by the door. "You scared the bloody daylights out of me."

He didn't say a word. He just moved into the bathroom like a vision of want and need. I dropped my eyes from his and fumbled with my cleanser on the sink, desperate for anything to distract me.

"What are you doing?" I breathed out as the feeling of his body close to mine took the air from my lungs.

He didn't touch me, but his breath caressed me delicately on the sensitive flesh of the back of my neck. He didn't move an inch. He just hovered dangerously close. Like a moth to a flame, my body flickered alight. He took a step closer, the curves of his chest now sculpted against my back. With feather-like fingertips, he swept over my bare shoulder blades and neck, pushing away the hair that covered the skin near my ear.

"I need to stay away from you, Sav, because I'm scared

that you'll run again, but every part of me is begging me to be near you." He ground his hips into me. "My mind is screaming at me to let myself go to you but my heart is questioning everything." His eyes flickered to mine in the mirror. "I need you to tell me what you want, Sav. What should I do?" he asked as one hand skimmed across my stomach, coming to rest on the bare skin peeking out from the top of my jeans.

"Don't ask me that." I sighed. My head involuntarily fell to the side as his teeth raked over my flesh, nipping and gripping my most sensitive spot just above my collarbone. My body pushed back into his like a magnet, fitting so perfectly against it. This shouldn't be happening, but my body was in battle with my conscience and my body always seemed to win. My hand rose and wrapped around the back of his neck as his lips danced over my neck, kissing, sucking, stroking, and devouring me.

"I love you, Tate. I truly do."

My eyes found our reflection in the mirror and the image of him consuming me made my body hum and forget everything. His fingertips skillfully unbuttoned my jeans and his hand slid into the front of my lace panties. He hesitated and his eyes flickered to mine in the mirror.

"Have I told you lately how much I love your accent?" he whispered as his lips grazed my jawline and his fingers slipped between my folds. I gasped loudly as he pushed a finger deep within me. "We shouldn't be doing this. We have too much to discuss, but I can't stop. This is what you do to me, Sav. Even when you break my heart, I still love you."

My head flew back to his shoulder as his pace increased. Adding a second finger, he thrust in and out of me so rhythmically and so intensely. At the first sound of my moan of pleasure, he captured my sounds with his lips on mine. His tongue dove into my mouth, tasting and caressing every inch. I fell headfirst into the kiss. The sensation of being owned by Tate's body overcame me, possessed me, and ignited me.

I rocked fiercely against his hand, begging for more, needing more. Every inhibition I had about us faded the moment his thumb met my aching core. I shuddered around him, a wave of pleasure ripping through me as I came undone around his fingers in the bathroom with Tanzi and Jack barely a room away.

He spun me around, picking me up and sitting me on the bathroom counter. Bringing his fingers to his mouth, his tongue flicking over his fingers, he tasted me and made me completely and utterly fall apart. I grabbed at his belt buckle, pulling him to my body and forcing my lips to his. I could taste myself on his tongue and the lioness roared within me. As we battled each other for ownership of our mouths, his groan against my lips filled the air. Just as quickly as it had started, he pulled away and took a step back. His face froze as he looked me over with my jeans undone and my face flushed with satisfaction.

"I shouldn't have done that."

He rushed out of the bathroom without another word. Fuck this! After pulling my jeans up over my hips and buttoning up my fly, I stormed out of the bathroom and down the hall towards his now closed door. I didn't bother knocking. Opening the door, I took one step in and stopped. Tate sat on the edge of his bed, his head in his hands with his shoulders slouched. I silently crossed the room and climbed on the bed behind him, wrapping my arms around his waist. He froze under my touch before allowing his head to fall back against me.

Kissing the side of his neck, I pulled him back, his body falling against the comfort of his mattress. I took a chance. I crawled up beside him and held my breath, expecting him to ask me to leave, but he didn't. As we lay facing each other, we stared at each other, communicating by our eyes only. He tucked a piece of loose hair behind my ear and his thumb swept over my bottom lip so innocently, so calming.

I lay there for an hour as I watched his heavy eyes succumb to tiredness. My need to wrap myself in him almost overcame me and the thought of touching him, kissing him, feeling him was almost too much. Sliding off his bed, I hesitated before I walked to the door and opened it quietly.

I wouldn't spend the night unless I was invited.

Chapter Thirty-Two

Tate

THE ANNOYING BUZZ OF MY phone vibrating against the glass top of my bedside table ripped me from my slumber. Stretching my arms above my head, I was swamped by an uneasy feeling. Instantly my eyes fell to the empty space beside me and everything came flooding back like a torrent of rain.

Savannah.

My memories flashed to only hours earlier, my body coming alive with an instant heat. I thought of her unforgettable taste as I'd licked my fingers clean and the way she had completely unleashed herself under my touch. My low groan of satisfaction filled the empty space of my bedroom. Her body was once again my kryptonite and it was destroying me in the best possible way. With a heavy sigh, I fumbled for my shirt and slipped it over my head, stretching tall and allowing my bones to crack into comfort.

After I opened my bedroom door and stepped into the empty hall, my ears focused on the soft voice coming from behind the closed door of Max's room. I hesitated for a moment before slowly opening the door. Peering around the door, my face came alive with a smile as I found him lying on his bed with a Lightning McQueen figurine in one hand and a Thomas figurine in the other. The three of them seemed to be having an in depth conversation about the beach. I stood, leaning against the doorframe with my arms folded across my chest, taking in the miracle before me.

Max's head shot up and turned towards where I was standing and his face lit up in delight. Lightning McQueen and Thomas were soon forgotten as he jumped off his bed and threw himself at me. "Daddy!" I still couldn't believe how one simple word could make me so happy. Hearing him call me Daddy made me forget everything.

"Want some breakfast and cartoons?" I asked softly, trying not to wake the rest of the house.

"Pancakes and juice box?" he asked with a smile I couldn't say no to.

While we walked through the silent house and made our way to the kitchen, Max chatted animatedly about the beach and his new room. My smile said a thousand words. I placed Max on the counter and turned on the small flat screen we had on the far wall near the counter to the first cartoon channel I could find. I busied myself pulling out everything I needed to make my world-famous pancakes. Soon enough, the smell of pancakes filled the air and Max ignored the cartoons. He sat cross-legged on the counter with his juice box and started telling me how he wished he could live in a sand castle that he would make with Gramps, Jack, Lucas, Blake, and me. This kid was a riot and had the imagination of a bestselling author.

"Daddy. Listen!" he barked in frustration. Damn, he had a temper on him. Smirking at the knowledge that he had obviously gained his short fuse from me, I spun around and startled when I found Sav watching us from the living room, a sweet smile covering her face. As soon as her eyes met mine, she blushed.

"Mommy is awake," I announced softly, not breaking my line of sight with Sav.

Max spun around on the counter and instantly held his arms out to Savannah. She floated towards the counter, wearing nothing but a satin slip that showed off her deliciously tan legs. Max jumped into her arms and buried his head in her neck and the content smile that flooded her face made my heart come alive.

"How did you sleep, Maxey?" Sav questioned lovingly. "How was your new room?"

"I heard waves." Excitement bubbled in his words.

"I told him I would take him down to the beach today if that's okay?"

"You don't have to ask me, Tate."

I nodded and couldn't hide my smile. Turning my back to Sav and Max I focused on the pan in front of me and got lost in memories of the night before. The taste of her mouth and the deliciousness of her body against mine had kept me up most of the night. I'd wanted nothing more than to completely and utterly make love to her, but there was still something holding me back and it was quickly beginning to piss me off.

"Do you need a hand?" Sav's soft voice came from beside

me. *Oh, Savannah, your ability to say something that could be taken so out of context never ceases to amaze me.* "Oh crap, I can't believe I said that. I mean with the pancakes."

"You can give me a hand any time, Savannah, but I am good with the pancakes," I said with a laugh. Shaking the thoughts of her hand around my dick out of my head, I dropped the spatula on the plate and turned to look at her.

She leaned back on the counter, staring at me with question in her eyes. "I couldn't sleep last night," she admitted quietly, dropping her eyes to the tiled floor below us.

"Me either."

"I wanted to come back into your room and curl around you. I wanted to feel your breath on my skin as you slept. I wanted to wake up beside you. Yes, I've missed everything else about us, but waking up in your arms is the one thing I've missed the most." Her honesty shocked me and immediately it shattered my resolve.

"Why didn't you stay?" I asked.

"Because you didn't ask me to stay."

"You don't need to be asked to share my bed, Sav."

"I am not forcing you into anything. I want no regrets between us, Tate, and if you aren't sure about you and me, then I'm not going to force myself into your bed or your heart."

"You aren't forcing me to do anything." This was the most honest I had been with her since she'd come back and it felt refreshing. I felt the familiar rumblings of my heart coming alive in those few seconds. "To be honest, I've kind of missed your snoring."

"I have kind of missed your arsehole tendencies," she whispered with narrowed eyes. She looked over my shoulder to make sure Max wasn't within earshot. I followed her eyes and saw that he was now curled up on the couch with his constant figurine companions.

"Well I have missed your cute little ass teasing me constantly."

"What? This one?" She turned and wiggled her satin-covered ass in my direction while giving me a sexy look over her shoulder.

Fuck living life with hesitation. I needed that hot body against me—now. I needed to feel her hips grind into mine and her tits bounce against my chest. I just needed to feel her.

I threw caution to the wind and grabbed her around the waist, causing her to shriek at the sudden contact, before I pulled her forcefully towards me. Her smile completely took over her face and her body pressed firmly against mine. Her face was void of makeup and her eyes crystal clear, but the slight darkening under her eyes showed the effects of her restless night. Tucking a stray piece of hair behind her ear, I watched as her face changed from excitement to hesitation to wonder.

This was us. This would always be us. My heart was bruised but it wasn't completely broken. She had healed my heart once before, and this could be the chance for her to completely heal it.

Her eyes dropped lustfully to my lips and in that moment I needed to kiss her. Leaning in, breaking the distance between us, I felt her breath sweep over my lips and her hands gripped tightly onto my shirt.

"Mummy, what are you doing?"

We froze—Sav in my arms, my hands cupping her face,

and our mouths inches from one another while my heartbeat roared against her chest. I tore myself away from her, distancing myself and moving back towards the pile of pancakes going cold on the counter, anxious to get control of my increasing want for her.

"Come on, Max. Let's get ready for breakfast." Sav scooped Max up in her arms, rushed towards the dining room, and sat him down at the table. Like a sledgehammer hitting full force, I realized there and then in the emptiness of the kitchen that there was nothing that could keep me from her. Fuck, I loved that girl. I loved her with every inch of my being. What Sav and I had was so much stronger than any problem we faced, stronger than any outside source that threatened to derail us, stronger than even the dangerous craziness of our minds.

"Tate!" Tanzi's tired voice growled from behind me. She looked at me with sleepy eyes. "Do you have to be so damn loud when you cook? A person is trying to sleep in, you know."

"I'm cooking pancakes. I almost just kissed her. Last night we had a . . . moment," I rambled as my sister's face became a canvas of amusement.

"Why almost?" Her brow raised in question. "Would this moment have happened in the bathroom? You both rushed out like a couple of teenagers who just did seven minutes in heaven."

"Uh, Max walked in the kitchen and busted us."

Tanzi looked quickly into the dining room, where Sav was sitting beside Max watching cartoons before pulling me farther into the kitchen with force. "What else is going on in that head of yours? Remember that I can tell when you are fighting one of those internal battles you are notorious for," Tanzi probed with a stern look. Ahhh, the famous twintuition.

"Nothing."

"Like fuck it's nothing," she hissed. "Start talking, Tate."

"I want Sav to come to the club opening in Vegas."

"Have you told her this?" Her eyes softened and her tone became less brutal. "You need to man up, go in there, tell her how you feel, move her into your bedroom, and start living your lives together. I'm sick of this constant back and forth. Seriously, it's exhausting. Just fuck and get it over and done with."

Tanzi left the kitchen with me, thoroughly amused at her reaction. I knew the tension between Sav and me had been increasing by the second. Her words rang in my ears as I piled the pancakes onto a plate and walked to the dining room, taking deep breaths with every step.

"Come on, Max. Let's have some pancakes."

"Veggie?" he asked suddenly.

"Please do not tell me he is going to wreck my amazing, life-altering pancakes with the devil's food."

"That's one amazing habit he has gotten from his trend-setting mum."

I could not believe I was searching for Vegemite to put on pancakes. What the hell had the world come to? Handing Sav the Vegemite, I watched in disgust as she lathered my creation with that disgustingness. Max inhaled them like they were the best thing in the world, his mouth smeared with it. Sav chuckled from across the table at the look on my face.

"That's disgusting," I muttered as I poured copious amounts of syrup on mine like a normal person.

"Daddy, have some of mine?" Max held out a Vegemite covered pancake towards me and looked at me with the most serious puppy-dog eyes I had ever seen. Sav's giggle caught my attention and I shot her a look of disgust. How was I supposed to get out of this? "Daddy, please?"

"How are you going to say no to that?" Sav laughed softly.

"You're loving this, aren't you?"

"You have absolutely no idea." She handed me her half-finished glass of juice with a smirk. "Orange juice helps it go down. You don't want to throw up in front of your son, do you?"

"Okay, Max. Let's do this." I grabbed the pancake from his hands and took a deep breath. Even the smell made me gag.

What the hell did Aussies see in this? Give me a Tim Tam, a Mint Slice, a Caramello Koala any day, but this? What the hell had they been thinking? I looked at Max, who was gazing at me with anticipation, whereas Sav stared at me in complete enjoyment. I took this as my chance to mention Vegas. I needed her there.

"You're coming to Vegas if I do this." I didn't give her a chance to answer. I put the whole thing in my mouth and drank the whole glass of orange juice.

Shit, this stuff was bad.

Chapter Thirty-Three

Savannah

Tanzi's bedroom was what you'd see in one of those fancy décor magazines. Everything about her and Jack's room screamed Hollywood chic. Black furniture, polished floor boards, deep reds, and lamps in every corner. It was stunning. Sitting on the bed with a throw rug wrapped around my shoulders as a cool California breeze swept through the room, I watched on amusingly as she zoomed around the room talking at a hundred miles an hour. Her suitcase was open beside me on the bed and clothes, shoes, and accessories were spilling out of it, flooding the comforter with splashes of colours.

Tate, Jack, and Tanzi were leaving for Las Vegas in the morning and would be spending the weekend, celebrating the opening of Red Velvet Las Vegas while I stayed in Santa Monica with Max.

"You sure you don't want to come to Vegas?" Tanzi asked

with a raised brow, stuffing a black and white bikini in her suitcase.

I knew this was coming. "I can't leave Max."

"You can but you won't," she retaliated within seconds.

I rolled my eyes in her direction, grabbed one of the dresses she had roughly jammed into the suitcase, and began to fold it with the respect it deserved.

"Tanzi, please can we just drop it."

"Nope."

Tanzi grabbed my hand and stopped me. I risked it and looked at her. That was my biggest mistake. Her eyes were as dangerous as Tate's and I knew I was getting locked in.

"Come and have a weekend away with the three of us. I know you've always wanted to go to Vegas and here is your opportunity. I want my best friend to come with me. Tate wants you there," she pleaded.

"I don't know, Tanzi. I just—"

The door inched opened ever so slowly, causing Tanzi and me to stop mid-sentence. Tate's head poked around the doorframe with a sheepish look plastered on his face. "Sav, Mr. Davenport just showed up and wants to speak with you."

"Do you know what he wants?" I asked, standing from the bed, straightening my dress over my hips before walking slowly towards the door where Tate was waiting with intense eyes.

"We haven't finished discussing this, Savannah Rae, so don't think you got away with anything," Tanzi said in an almost teacher-like voice.

Immediately I noticed the look that flashed between Tanzi and Tate. I couldn't handle them on their own, let alone the two of them ganging up on me. Shaking the thoughts from my head, I slipped under Tate's arm, which was holding open the door, and instantly froze as I was lost in bliss of green tea, sandalwood, and the ocean. My senses thundered to life. Could it be possible to become drunk off the scent of someone? My head for a moment became woozy under the familiar scent of Tate Connors and every inch of my body became inflamed. Desire roared through my body like wildfire.

"He is in the living room with Max." As he spoke, his breath tickled my highly reactive skin.

Don't, Savannah. STOP! I silently shouted to myself. I didn't listen. I looked up into his eyes as they bored down at me. Big mistake. HUGE mistake. My breathing came to a halt as I witnessed the exact same feelings I was fighting swimming around in his perfect blues. I was locked in—hook, line, and sinker—and there was no chance in hell that I was going to be able to tear my gaze away from his.

"Hey, you two . . . Your son? Mr. Davenport? Living room?" Tanzi's snicker broke my concentration on Tate's eyes and thankfully my rapidly building pulse eased. "Sav, I have proved my point. You are coming to Vegas. Start packing." She rushed past me and disappeared down the hall before I could object.

Walking into the living room, I felt a sense of unease crowd my body. Max ran towards me with a cheeky grin on his face and his arms out in front of me. "Mummy, I'm having a sleepover and Gramps said I can have ice cream for breakfast and lunch but vegetables for dinner." Max pouted at the thought of vegetables. He wrapped his tiny arms around my legs, inviting me to lift him up. I positioned Max on my hip and turned towards Mr. Davenport.

Narrowing my eyes at them, I focused on the smirk on Mr. Davenport's face and immediately felt my brow furrow as it all came to a crashing reality. He was using my son to make me go to Vegas.

"When is this so called sleepover happening?" I scoffed, pulling Max closer to my body.

Mr. Davenport took a step toward me, resting his hands on my shoulders. My eyes drilled into his as annoyance engulfed me. Slowly, he scanned my face and I knew the moment he realized I knew about this so-called plan. Did he really think I was that stupid?

"Go to Vegas for the weekend, Sav, and have fun with your friends. Go crazy. Do whatever you want. Dance on bar tops if you have to. You'll only be three hours away." His eyes pleaded with me as he spoke.

"I can't leave Max."

"He will be here with me. I might spoil him too much and he may get away with hell but he will be with me, and I will call you numerous times a day if need be."

Max wiggled in my arms, begging to be released. Sliding down my body, he took off quickly with a giggle, running straight towards the kitchen and into Tate's waiting arms. Tate picked up Max effortlessly and held him in his arms. Tate spoke quietly to Max, who looked up at him with admiration flooding in his eyes.

Wherever we were or whatever we were doing, he always needed to be near Tate. Tate was the one who had to tuck him in at bed time. Tate was the one who was allowed to pick what book I read to him at night. And it was Tate who always got him up in the morning. A loud giggle erupted from Max's tiny body as he squirmed in his arms while Tate tickled him. My heart beat frantically at the scene in front of me.

I tore my eyes away from Tate and Max and moved through the house towards the sanctuary of the balcony. I desperately needed fresh air and space. I pulled open the heavy glass door and breathed deeply as the salty air hit my lungs. The thought of being away from Max terrified me. Panic shot through me, and I knew it was for completely selfish reasons. Max had been my world for almost three years. Not one day passed where I wasn't with him. He protected me from the world. He gave me a reality I'd always wished for. But mostly he grounded me. In a nutshell, he was my life.

The sound of the door opening and closing silenced my thoughts. Heavy footsteps thudded against the paved flooring of the balcony as the person paced towards me.

"What's going on, Sav?" Mr. Davenport's Australian accent rumbled beside me.

"I can't leave Max."

"This isn't really about that, is it?"

Why was I so damn easy to read?

Turning towards him, I breathed in deeply, trying desperately to settle my pounding heart. "I am scared, okay? I am scared that I am still so deeply in love with Tate and more in love with him today than I've ever been. I am scared that finally our lives might have the chance to be exactly what we dream it to be and mostly I am scared that maybe it's my time to finally be happy."

"Sav, this is your time. You have a man in there who has patiently waited for you while you looked after me and who is so desperate to tell you that he loves you. Talk to him. Go to Vegas. Have fun, Sav. You are still a baby yourself. I've been dying to babysit Max since he was born, but he has a mum who doesn't let him out of her sight. Let me have time with the little guy."

"I don't know." I hesitated before looking back out over the ocean and sighing in defeat. "I'm not sure what credentials this so-called babysitter has."

"Right. I'm pulling rank. You are going to Vegas. You are having a weekend with your friends. Do you not trust me to look after him? Do you not think I can look after him? Do you really think that little of me?"

I looked at him with wide eyes. "You are not using blackmail on me!" I shrieked, a laugh escaping my lips.

He winked at me. "If I have to use blackmail, I will."

"You are a bastard."

"You love me though . . . right?" Mr. Davenport's arms encased me and pulled me close to his chest, and comfort flooded my body. I still had nightmares of the first moment I saw him lying lifelessly in the hospital bed after his accident. Most of the nightmares ended with me seeing him motionless in a coffin and being lowered into the ground. I couldn't fathom the thought that I'd nearly lost this man. I froze in his arms as memories roared back to me. "Stop thinking Sav. I'm here and I'm not going anywhere," he whispered into my hair.

"Sav, Max is asking for a peanut butter AND Vegemite sandwich. Together. I need your help." Tate laughed nervously as he stepped onto the balcony. "Oh shit. Sorry for interrupting." His eyes darted to me in Mr. Davenport's arms and he started backing up, moving towards the door he'd just walked out of.

"Tate, you stay here. I'll take care of the little guy." Mr. Davenport dropped his arms from around me and lowered his voice as he spoke to me. "Talk to him." He kissed me on the cheek and patted Tate's shoulder as he walked inside, leaving me in an awkward silence with Tate.

"I can't believe you got your wish," Tate stammered as he joined me.

What the hell was he talking about? "What wish?"

"Our son loves the devil's food. Remember that morning when you wished this exact curse on me?"

I burst out laughing as the memory hit me. "He would eat Vegemite for breakfast, lunch, and dinner if he could, and believe me, there are days when he does. He has a temper on him when he doesn't get what he wants. I wonder who he gets that from?"

"Definitely his mother," he said with a knowing grin.

A silence fell between us as we both looked out over the ocean. My mind was running crazy, and I couldn't help but notice Tate fidgeting with his hands as they rested against the balcony rail. Without a word, he shifted and turned towards me, his eyes falling on me with a look of thought swimming before me. I felt the familiar effect he had on my body soon barrel in—the hard thump of my heart, the weird breathing that would attack my body, and of course the slow, intense heat flooding my cheeks. His lips curved into a cheeky smirk and he quickly rubbed his hand over his face, scratching the stubble that was gracing his jaw.

"Will you ever not blush when I look at you?"

"Probably not." I shrugged and dropped my eyes.

Suddenly his voice plunged to a serious tone. "Will you hear me out?"

"Okay."

"That means not interrupting me."

"Would I do that?"

He rolled his eyes at me as his lips turned up.

I held my breath as I knew what this conversation would be about. I had been waiting for this conversation since I'd returned, and now, on a balcony overlooking Santa Monica Beach, it was about to happen.

"Three months without you killed me, Sav. Yes we had email and phone and Skype, but it wasn't the same. Do you know what it feels like to be abandoned by the one person you never wanted to leave you? That's how it felt, Sav. It felt like you left me with no explanation. I feel like I've lost three months of my life with you and Max and we will never get that back. I need you to explain to me why you left without considering me, why you left without feeling like you could tell me how you were feeling. I know I was supposed to come over, and every day I regretted not being able to. I need you to help me understand it because it's the one thing stopping me from asking you to spend the rest of your life with me. And the one thing I never wanted for you and me was regret or hesitation and now I feel like it's swallowing us."

I dropped my eyes and inhaled sharply. "Mr. Davenport saved me, Tate. If he hadn't helped me when he did, I wouldn't be standing here. Max wouldn't be here. I didn't know what else to do, but all I knew was that I needed to take care of him. I felt like I could finally repay Mr. Davenport for everything he did for me. I didn't mean to keep you away from Max. I didn't mean for any of this, but I just didn't know what else to do," I breathed out and felt the sob that was bubbling inside my chest fly through the air. The wetness of my cheeks showed that I was finally breaking. "I thought I'd lose him like I lost my parents. The last time I saw them was in the hospital, Tate, and I was so scared to leave him there. And that's why I could only come back when he came back."

"So what does that mean? Does that mean that you'll follow him wherever he goes?" He rubbed his thumb over my cheek, collecting my splattered tears. "I can't be second choice, Sav. I can't be afraid that you are going to run every time something happens. I can't be afraid that you and Max aren't going to be around. I can't be afraid that Mr. Davenport will always come first." I started to object but he silenced me with a finger over my lips. "Let me speak."

I nodded and he removed his finger.

"You need to decide what you want. I will always be in your life because of Max. I will always be there for you no matter what, and I will always love you more than the breath I take, but I can't be questioning our relationship every day. We have a life together, Sav. You need to finally let me be your life. I can't lose you again. Sav. I would rather not have you at all than risk having to feel you walking away from me. I don't think I could survive that again."

I looked up at him through tear-stricken eyes. He was giving me an out. His hands fell to my cheeks and lifted my face, forcing me to look at him. His lips fell to my cheeks, kissing away the tears I was shedding for him, for us, for everything that was Tate and Savannah.

"You own my heart, Sav. It's yours to break."

Without another word, he turned and walked back into the house, hesitating briefly at the door to give me one last look. The sound of the waves crashing mixed perfectly with the sound of my broken breathing as I tried to control my emotions. What did I want? That was the million dollar question. Did I want to continue to live my life with the past overshadowing everything? Did I want to live a life that had everything I never knew I wanted? Did I want to love that man who had just bared his soul to me like I had never loved another man before? It was there in the solitude of the balcony that everything became as clear as the night sky above me. I was so ready to give my all to this man—every last broken piece of me, every inch of my future, and every beat of my heart. It was Tate. It would always be Tate.

Moving through the house, I didn't make eye contact with anybody as I walked towards my bedroom with Tate's words still ringing in my ears. I was still living out of a suitcase, so it wouldn't be hard to pack for a weekend trip. My decision to go to Vegas had been made the moment Tate had told me that his heart was mine to break. Tate was my great love. A great love that seemed to want to stand the test of time, a great love that no matter what bullshit we threw at it was still standing strong, and a great love I would always fight for.

I shook the thoughts out of my head and moved to the bathroom with a new motivation. I opened my toiletries bag and began piling in my necessities—perfume, makeup, shampoo and Tate's favorite red lip gloss.

"Mummy, where's my Gordy jarmies?" Max's sweet voice joined me in the bathroom. I looked in the mirror to find Max in Tate's arms. Tate's eyes fell to the vanity, saw my toiletries bag, and raised a brow in question. Nodding, I silently answered his unasked question.

I was going to Vegas.

Chapter Thirty-Four

Tate

THE SUN BLAZED THROUGH MY Jeep as music and laughter rolled through the air. Las Vegas was the destination, and after a tearful goodbye with Max when we dropped him off with Mr Davenport, we were now on the I-10 and on our way to a weekend that could possibly change everything. I sat in the driver's seat with my fingers drumming on the steering wheel in rhythm to the music. Jack was sitting beside me and Sav and Tanzi were taking up the back seat. The chance for Sav and me to talk about the night before never happened, but I couldn't help but feel my ego come alive as I continued to find her looking at me when I glanced in the rearview mirror to look at her. Seriously, we were like a couple of fucking high school kids.

"I have news," I announced between songs. Three sets of eyes focused on me. "Chelsea has dropped her case against Blake and Red Velvet. She has apparently realized that she is a conniving bitch who doesn't have a clue. She has also signed a legal document stating that she will not step foot within 300 feet of me, Blake, Sav, or Red Velvet, and if she does she will be arrested."

"What the hell was her problem? Why did she do this in the first place?" Sav's frustrated voice sounded from the back seat. "This would have saved a lot of problems."

"It's over now, Sav. We don't have to worry about her anymore. She will play no part in our lives anymore."

"I'm still pissed off. You could have come to Australia. You and I could have been . . ." She stopped mid-sentence, her eyes finding mine in the rear-view mirror. "Ah, just fuck it."

Sav's eyes ripped away from mine to focus on the scenery flying past the car as we drove through the vast desert of Nevada.

"So what's the plan for the weekend, boss man?" Tanzi asked, breaking the silence of the car. She was well aware of how much I hated being called a boss and yet she continued to rub it in every chance she got.

Rolling my eyes, I glanced quickly in the rear-view mirror and shot her a look, which only intensified her amusement. "I have a meeting to go to when we get there. I should be done by around seven, so maybe we could grab dinner and hit up the Strip. The opening is tomorrow night, so I'd say most of my day will be spent at the club. Blake and the rest of the band fly in tomorrow."

"Why didn't we fly?" Sav quizzed, suddenly coming back to the conversation.

"I remember you telling me you wanted to drive from Los Angeles to Vegas one day, so here we are."

"Tate, that was years ago!" Sav stuttered nervously, the disbelief evident in her voice.

Without a hint of hesitation or reluctance, I replied, "Yeah, but we never did it."

"That's kinda cute," Tanzi whispered. The thing with Tanzi was that her whispered tone was still loud enough for the rest of the car to hear. My eyes met Sav's and I shot her a wink.

"Eyes on the road, stud," Jack teased from the passenger's seat.

"You think you are fucking comedian, don't you?" I scoffed.

"Comedian, sex machine . . . I've been called a lot of things in my life, Tate."

"I've also heard you called fuck-stick, dick-wad, ass-wipe . . . Do you really need me to continue?" I smirked in triumph.

"Just get us to Vegas, Romeo."

The trip was long but the singing, laughing, and eating copious amount of gas station junk food made it worth it. As we pulled into the resort and all stepped out of my Jeep, my eyes instantly were drawn to Savannah. Watching her stretch her arms above her head allowed me a glimpse of her tan stomach. I could swear my pants tightened just at the vision before me.

She'd dressed in short denim cut-off shorts with a simple white tank top that fit so snug to her perfect waist and even more perfect tits—the perfect outfit in my eyes. What I loved about her most was that she didn't care what she looked like. I remember the first time she wore sweatpants to the movies one night when Jack, Tanzi, she, and I went to see a midnight showing. Tanzi had been horrified that Sav had left the house in sweatpants. Sav's response had been, "I am at the movies at midnight. Why the fuck would I get dressed in something that wasn't comfortable? You are damn well lucky I am wearing shoes and not my Uggs."

"You're staring. Shut your mouth before your tongue rolls out and you start drooling."

"Fuck off, Jack." I laughed and diverted my eyes to the valet, who looked like he was about to pass out in the Nevada sunshine. Handing him my keys, I moved towards Tanzi and Sav, who were both beaming with smiles. Tanzi had always loved Vegas and I knew she was excited to be back and ready for a weekend with Sav.

"So what are you two ladies going to do while Jack and I work?"

"Pool, cocktails, cheeseburger, massage," Tanzi fired out. "In that order too."

"Yeah, that." Sav laughed. "I also need to also buy something to wear tomorrow night. It's not often that I get a night out, let alone in Vegas. I've got to make it a good one."

"I am sure Tate has plans to make it a good one," Jack muttered under his breath.

"Huh?" Sav asked, oblivious to what Jack had said, although the smirk on Tanzi's face showed that she had heard exactly what her asshole fiancé had said.

I shook my head and walked through the double glass doors being held open by a middle-aged man dressed head to toe in maroon. Ahhh, to be back in Vegas. I did love this city. Like New York, it was one of the cities I would disappear to when life got too much. A life that seemed so far away from what my new reality was. Walking towards the check-in desk I opened my wallet, placed my credit card on the marble countertop, and smiled at the young girl looking at me with the perfectly straight and overly white teeth.

"How can I help you, sir?"

"Hi, I have a room booking for Connors?"

She tapped loudly on the keyboard and muttered under her breath, "Yes, we have your down for two king suites on the twentieth floor."

"There should be three suites."

"Oh, I'm sorry. We only have you down for two, and unfortunately due to the club opening tomorrow, all of our rooms are booked."

Fuck it!

Turning around to face Jack, Tanzi, and Sav, I cringed at the news I was about to share. Taking a deep breath, I walked across the vast foyer, plopped down on the seat beside Tanzi, and sighed loudly. Three sets of eyes fell on me.

"So we have a problem," I started, finally looking at them. "They only booked two rooms."

"And what's the problem with that?" Jack asked, completely unfazed. "There are four of us—two people per room. It's not rocket science, man."

I was more than happy to share a room with Savannah. Fuck, I'd share a shower, a bath, a bed, a life with Savannah. "Sav, what do you—"

"You two are mature enough to stay in the same room together. It might make you stop being so damn stubborn and actually do something about this." Tanzi's eyes bounced from Sav to me while her finger waved frantically between us. "Seriously, the sexual tension between you two is fucking insane. It's making me almost want to fuck Savannah."

The sound of Savannah choking on her water rolled around us, and I could feel my eyes widen at the brutal honesty of my sister. She had absolutely no filter.

"I knew I picked the wrong twin. You can fuck me any time, Tanzi. Jack, Tate, you are rooming together. Tanzi and I are getting nasty together." Savannah waggled her eyebrows suggestively. "What's that saying? What happens in Vegas, stays in Vegas?"

"So it's settled. Sav and Tanzi are fucking each other, I am watching and probably participating, and Tate, well . . . It would be kinda weird with you watching your sister fuck, so you can leave it to me."

I had no words in reply. Shaking my head at Jack, I noticed that Tanzi and Sav had taken off towards the elevator. Obviously our rooming arrangement had been decided. I grabbed the key cards from the lady at reception and headed towards the elevator and up to the twentieth floor.

Room 20F would be my room for the weekend—our room for the weekend. Sav stood nervously beside me as I fumbled with the key card. "I'm excited to see the room," I admitted, desperate to break the tension. Tanzi and Jack had taken off to their room the moment we'd stepped out of the elevator, leaving Sav and me in the emptiness of the hall.

With a beep and click, the door shifted open and I pushed with my hip, holding it ajar for Sav to slip inside. Her gasp filtered through the air. The room was immaculate. I closed the door behind me and placed the key card on the glass table in the entrance of the room.

The room opened into a vast portrait of class and chic sophistication. Three days of pure indulgence were in front of us.

The caramel-colored walls caressed the deep mahogany tones of the polished floorboards floating through the room. The bed was beyond king-sized, covered with inviting pillows, and a deep red comforter graced the mattress, making it look deliciously sexy. One bed. No couch. This could either completely blow up in my face or I was going to have the best fucking weekend of my life.

The bathroom grabbed and held my attention. Glass featured on three of the walls, and the fourth wall was a floor-to-ceiling window that looked out over the city skyline of Las Vegas. This was the kind of bathroom that allowed for absolutely no privacy, and my cock twitched with anticipation. How the hell was I not supposed to watch her? Savannah plus glass walls plus a shower equaled me jacking off constantly.

A large freestanding bathtub ran along the floor-to-ceiling window and many colorful bottles filled with what I could only imagine was girly smelling body washes outlined the double sink. Savannah's eyes found the bath the same time as mine and she nervously laughed. Why the fuck did things have to be so awkward?

"Okay, so how are we going to do this?" she asked softly from beside the bed. Lifting her suitcase onto the mattress, she sat on the edge of the bed and started shifting through the contents.

My eyes dropped to what was inside her suitcase. Dresses, shoes, lace panties, and—holy shit, she brought *the* bikini. The bikini that sat perfectly in sync with her curves and cupped her tits to perfection. The bikini I had ripped off with my teeth many times before. The bikini that was the one thing that would make me lose all sense of control. "Tate?"

"Huh?"

"This weekend. How are we going to do this?" she cooed, her lips curved into a sexy yet sweet smile as she looked at me from across the room. She knew exactly what that bikini did to me.

Fuck, this was awkward. I leaned back against the wall, crossing my arms tight across my chest. "Do you want my brutally honest answer or my PG answer?" My eyebrow rose in question.

"When have you ever not been brutally honest?"

"Okay, you asked for it," I warned, giving her one last chance to bail out, but she didn't take it. I strode across the room and kneeled before her placing my hands on her bare knees. Her eyes dropped to my hands and then found my eyes. I lowered my voice to a low growl. "The thought of sleeping next to you in this bed made my cock come to life the moment I saw it, the thought of you in that bath makes me want to jerk off, and the image of you in that bikini makes me want to cancel all my scheduled meetings and fuck you up against that window for all of Vegas to see. That's me being brutally honest."

Her breathing hitched in her throat and the tension sweeping through her body made my confidence soar. This weekend had the potential to change the course of our standstill relationship, and if brutal honesty would make that happen, then I was all for it.

"The thought of you was the only thing that kept me going while I was in Australia. I didn't even feel at home because you weren't there. Home is now wherever you are, Tate."

"I want to kiss you until your lips are swollen and love

your body like a goddess deserves to be loved." My heart beat furiously in my chest. Never again would we be separated. Never again would we be deciding if we were together. Never again would there ever not be a Tate and Savannah.

"Come on, bitches! We need to start enjoying Vegas. Sav get your hot little body into that—Oh shit. Sorry."

Tanzi 'interrupt at the worst possible time' Connors decided to barge into our room just as my lips were about to touch Sav's.

Rising from my crouched position, I looked at Sav regretfully through needy eyes and then turned my attention to my twin. "How the fuck did you get in here?"

"You didn't close the door properly, you ass-wipe." She rolled her eyes at me with a huff. "You need to get to work and I need to take Sav down to the pool. We have cocktails to drink and pool boys to flirt with."

I shifted my gaze to Sav in question. She just shrugged her shoulders and stood from the bed. Her hands gripped the bikini and I swallowed hard. *Fucking work commitments.* "Are you really going to wear that?" I groaned, my hands rubbing my face furiously. "Seriously. You are trying to kill me, aren't you?"

Sav's laughter filled the room. I couldn't stay here. There was no way in hell I would leave for the club if I saw her in that bikini, and I was afraid my sister would see something she would never recover from. I knew for a fact that she would never want to see me hammering into Savannah like the way I now wanted to. I patted my pockets, making sure I had my wallet, phone, and keys, and gave Sav one last look.

"I need to get to the club." My gaze traveled to the bikini

in her hands. "I can't witness you in that."

Tanzi's laughter grabbed my attention and I shot a look of death at her. *Laugh it up, Tanzi.*

"You might have to jerk off before you go out in public." She walked towards Sav and wrapped her arm around her shoulder, pulling her close to her body. Sav burst into fits of giggles. "Oh and, Tate. I'll be sure to enjoy seeing Sav in this."

"Fuck you, Tanzi."

Chapter Thirty-Five

Savannah

It was official. I was in love with Vegas.

I had barely been here two hours and I was already throwing my love around the place. Some things never changed. My body felt like I was finally succumbing to the effects of relaxation as I stood in the inviting coolness of the pool that had made me gasp upon seeing it.

"So what's happening with you and my brother?" Tanzi asked from beside me. Our backs were flush against the cool tiles and we both held a cosmopolitan in our hands as the refreshing water cooled our bodies under the Nevada sun. "I know I interrupted a moment upstairs."

I pulled the straw to my mouth and looked up at her, willing myself to make her stew for a bit longer. I'd known this question was going to come the moment I had agreed to come to Vegas. To be honest, I was surprised at how long she had waited.

"Well I'll be sharing a bed with him."

"And?" Tanzi prompted eagerly.

"I hope to sleep."

"And?"

"I'll probably shower at some stage."

"And?"

"I guess I'll have to eat as well."

"Savannah! Are you getting back together with him or not? I don't give a fuck about your shower and eating routine." Tanzi glared at me, the corners of her lips shaking as a smile threatened to appear. I loved messing with her head, but it was a question I had no answer to.

"I'll always be in love with him, Tanzi. What the future holds . . . ? I can't answer that." I turned and put my empty glass on the edge before signaling for another. Seriously I could get use to this kind of life.

"If he kissed you, would you kiss him back?"

"Well we would know if you hadn't barged in." I winked at her before diving under the water, allowing the cool water of the pool to caress my heated body. I wanted nothing more than for his lips to be on mine, to feel the cushion of his lips devouring every inch of mine. I missed the sweetness of his taste and the way his tongue would massage mine one minute and then completely own it the next.

I rose from beneath the water as a shadow formed above me. When I held my hand over my eyes to shun the glare of the sun, my breath caught in my throat at the sight hovering in front of me. Standing at the edge of the pool, observing me with a panty-melting smirk, was a six-foot man of pure sex. His tan body, ripped with muscles and covered in tattoos, was stopping girls in their tracks. Who was he and why was he looking at me like that?

"You must be Savannah." His voice oozed roughness and raw need. I looked around, trying to work out what the hell was happening.

"And you are?" I asked with a raised brow.

"Colby, get the fuck away from her. She is Tate's girl." Blake came into view and glared at who I now knew was Colby.

Just hearing Blake's voice caused my cheeks to ache from smiling so hard. Blake was now one of my best friends, a friend who would call me out on my shit and would mock me until it ended with me jumping on his back and a rendition of UFC happening. That was Blake to me. His life was now about his band and traveling the world. Seeing him on television was surreal.

"It's a pleasure to meet you, Colby, and it's about time you got here, Blake."

"Believe me, the pleasure is all mine." Colby zoned his eyes into me hard and dangerously before he took off towards the bar, leaving me to stare at his retreating figure in confusion.

"Drummer or bassist?" I asked, turning my attention back to Blake, who was sitting at the edge of the pool with his legs dangling in the water and a beer in his hand. His usually cheery face was shadowed with something I couldn't put my finger on. The Blake Ryan spark that was always on display was mimicked by dark circles and frown lines.

"He is our fearless drummer, but don't mind him. He is on a self-imposed celibacy bout and he has this crazy idea that he can go without sex for the entire tour. I guarantee he will lose before the end of the day. He'd fuck anyone at the moment."

My eyebrows shot up. "So I'm just anyone, am I?" I scoffed. "And here I was thinking I was something special." Tauntingly, I pouted and folded my arms across my chest.

"Fuck, shit, no, Savannah. I didn't mean that. You aren't just anyone. Every single guy here wants to fuck you. I just meant he wouldn't care whose pussy he dipped his cock into. Fuck, I didn't mean that either. Sav you're—"

Laughter roared from within me, so intense that I lost my footing and fell beneath the water. Choking and gasping for air as I rose, I focused on Blake and shook my head. "God, you crack me up, Blake. I've missed you."

"I've missed you too, but enough of the sappiness." Blake slipped into the water beside me and got straight to the point. "I need to know whether you and Tate have stopped being stubborn." What the hell was it with this family and their lack of subtlety?

Tanzi floated towards us, hugging Blake quickly and then turning to me with a grin. "See? It's not just me, Savannah. Seriously though, you are both so happy when you are loved up together. I miss the spark that I see when you two are together. I miss the happiness that I feel from both of you. You are the most perfect couple in every sense of the words. You just need to realize that."

"I suddenly feel like I am being ganged up on." I looked at Blake and Tanzi with a sly grin. "And for your information, I don't kiss and tell unless I have copious amounts of tequila in my body, and if that's the case, you'll probably hear things about your brother neither of you wants to hear."

Laughing at the looks on their face, I pulled myself out

of the pool and walked towards the lounge to grab my sheer dress. Throwing my dress over my bikini, I headed to the bar for another cocktail. My eyes latched on to Colby's tattooed back as he sat at the bar, leaning over a beer.

"So I hear you have a bet going with Blake?" I laughed, taking the vacant seat beside him. "You reckon you will win this little bet?"

"Lady, if you weren't shacked up with Tate, I would be breaking all the rules with you right now." His confidence was overwhelming yet refreshing. "But between you and me, I've already lost the bet. I'm just stringing Blake along for a bit."

Colby turned towards the guy behind the bar and ordered me a Cosmopolitan and a Whiskey Sour for himself. I sat with Colby at the bar for a good hour. He told me how he met Blake, how long he had been playing drums for, and why he was a self-proclaimed pussy destroyer.

My attention faltered from Colby as my eyes landed on Blake, who sat on the edge of the pool, his eyes glued to a stunning brunette wearing a black bikini with the most impressive back tattoo I had ever seen. Blake's complete focus was on her. His eyes were narrowed on her with an ownership I had seen so many times in the way his brother looked at me. His eyes followed Miss Stunning Brunette as she walked through the pool area towards Colby and me.

"Colby, do you know what time the club opening is?" Miss Stunning Brunette asked, her eyes quickly darting to me and then back to Colby.

"Ask Savannah. It's her club."

"Really? You own Red Velvet?" Her eyes widened as she held out her hand to me. "My name is Violet."

"Hi, Violet. I'm Savannah. I don't own Red Velvet my, um . . . Tate Connors owns it."

Chapter Thirty-Six

Tate

WHEN I'D DECIDED TO INVITE Blake's band to play at the opening of Red Velvet, I'd never expected to be now looking at a photo of their drummer with his hands all over Savannah. The photo my lovely and ever-so-kind sister had decided to send to me showed Sav in the arms of who I had learned was Colby. Luckily for my jealous streak, she looked somewhat uncomfortable and not enjoying it at all, but it did make my jealous streak rear its ugly head nonetheless. I wanted no one touching her. The caption 'Do something about this before someone else gets her' was all Tanzi had written and I knew exactly what her intentions were.

My day had been spent attached to my laptop working strenuously on the final details for the grand opening of Red Velvet Las Vegas. I had been working on this for months. I couldn't even begin to think of how many times I'd signed my signature today or how many times I had said yes or no. It had been exhausting, and now, as the clock turned over to another day, I decided that I needed to call it a night.

As the cab drove through the bright lights of Vegas, my heavy eyes strained under the impending sleep that was tormenting me. Thankfully tomorrow I had some downtime and maybe I could finally talk to Savannah. I needed her to know that she owned my heart completely. I was sick of the distance, the games, the looks across the room, and the innocent brushes of our hands. That wasn't us. I missed the intensity, the passion, the flirting, the argumentative streaks, I missed us. I wanted us again.

Slipping quietly into the hotel room, my eyes were instantly drawn to where I had hoped to find Sav. Every hope I had escaped my exhausted body the moment I found the empty bed. There was no sign that she had even been in the bed—the cover wasn't turned down, the pillows weren't showing the effects of someone lying on them. Nothing.

Shrugging off my jacket, I threw it on the floor and slumped down on the edge of the bed. My head hung in my hands while my mind took off in all directions of what-ifs and wicked scenarios. This was my one chance, my one fucking chance to make things right with us, and now somewhere in Las Vegas was the one person who had finally made me the man I wanted to be but she wasn't with me. Welcome to Fucked-Up Town—population one.

"I was wondering when you'd get back."

My head shot up from my hands as her voice floated through the air. In the darkness, in a whisper of candlelight, and in the lights coming through the windows, my eyes landed on a pure and honest beauty. Savannah lay bare, covered by bubbles in the freestanding bath. I stood from the bed, walked towards the glass wall, and leaned against the doorframe. My gaze roamed her face, untainted and clean, without an ounce of makeup, her hair pulled up on the top of her head like I'd always loved.

"I didn't think you were here," I admitted softly.

Her lips pouted as she slipped into thought. "Where did you think I'd be?"

"To be honest, I have no idea."

"I'm not going anywhere, Tate." Her eyes burned into mine with a promise of a thousand meanings. Her words echoed in my ears, repeating over and over again. She was here.

My fears of her leaving were unjustified. Her promise of a future cemented by five simple words was what I had to focus on. For once I didn't think of who she could be with. For once I trusted her completely, without reluctance. The Tate of old would have been belting down Blake's room demanding to know where Colby was, but that hadn't crossed my mind once. Savannah wasn't my past. She was my present and would be my only future.

"I figured it out," I whispered.

The black and white of Savannah and Tate was being shattered by the hope of color. I saw what it was like now. We were far from perfect, but we were perfect for each other. Why strive for a perfection that wasn't us? Our perfection was in the way we frustrated each other like no one else and in the way I missed her the second she wasn't in my sight. Our perfection was in the way my heart hadn't truly been beating until she had come into my life and in the way our demons tried to beat us but our angels joined as one to save us. That was our perfection.

"What have you figured out?"

"Us, I've figured us out." I didn't say another word. I spun on my heels, walked through the hotel room, grabbed my wallet, and escaped through the door with one focus taking over my thoughts. Midnight in Vegas didn't mean a thing. I had something special to buy and I knew exactly where I was going.

Finally, at one A.M. under the lights of Las Vegas I walked back into the foyer and made my way back to the confines of our room. Slipping out of my clothes and leaving on my boxers, I slipped under the covers and rolled to my side towards Sav. Sav's lips were parted slightly as she slept, her hair sprayed out on the red sheets. My eyes fought the flirtation of sleep as long as I could before my eyes closed to the warmth of Sav's body next to mine.

I woke to a jolt of sudden movement of the bed. Sav's whimpers and her thrashing arms grabbed my attention and I fumbled for the bedside light switch. As light flooded the room, I grabbed her as panic filled me.

"Sav, wake up." I shook her, slightly desperate to pull her from her torment. "God damn it Sav."

Suddenly, her tear-filled eyes shot open and she looked at me in fear. Her arms circled my waist as she clung to me for dear life. Without a word, she covered half my body with hers and buried her face into the crook of my neck, and within seconds, wetness from her tears greeted my skin.

"Talk to me, Sav." My fingers ran through her hair, trying frantically to comfort her as she shook in my arms. "What's going on?"

"I keep having nightmares about my parents and Mr. Davenport. They are always lying in coffins and I can't reach them. I can't bring them back to me." Her head lifted from the confines of my neck and looked at me as if something had suddenly dawned on her. "But this one was different because you and Max were there." My face must have showed my fear of her words. "No nothing like that. You were both calling out to me, begging me to come to you, trying to take me away from what I was looking at. You and Max were trying to protect me."

"I can't bring your parents back, Sav, but you should know that Max and I aren't going anywhere, and Mr. Davenport is sticking around too. You don't have anything to fear when it comes to us." I kissed her forehead softly and she slowly nodded. Her head dropped to my chest and her body wrapped tightly around mine.

The extent of her grief from her parents' death was something she dealt with daily, something she tried desperately to hide behind the tough exterior she wore. The thought that Mr. Davenport's accident had brought up painful memories hadn't sunk in until right now. What I didn't know was how I could provide her with the security she needed? All I could do was be there for her, be her support, listen when she needed to talk, and distract her when I knew her mind would be going crazy just as I knew it was now.

"Did you buy a dress today?" I asked softly, my fingertips still running through her long hair.

"Yep I did. I can't wait to wear it tomorrow night." Her voice was barely a whisper.

"Are you going to be getting every guy's attention in the bar?"

"There's only one guy's attention I want."

"Colby's?" I asked, the grin I was sporting able to be heard in my words.

"Yeah, definitely Colby's. I might run off on tour with him so don't wait up for me tomorrow night."

"That's not one bit funny, Savannah."

"You brought it up. I think it was the bikini. It seems to do things to guys. You know what I mean, right?"

"Touché."

Her muffled giggle was the last thing I heard before she fell into a deep sleep tucked up tight in my arms, and she didn't leave the confines of my body all night.

Chapter Thirty-Seven

Savannah

"Sav, are you ready?" Tate's voice boomed through the hotel room. I gave myself a once-over and nodded at my reflection. It was now or never.

My heels clicked on the polished floorboards as I moved towards the living area of our room. My hands nervously skimmed down the front of my white bandeaux dress as I waited with bated breath for Tate to see me. The theme for the evening was black, white, and red, and I was in my white dress with my red heels, my black clutch, and my blonde hair swept to one side in a cascade of curls over my shoulder.

"Sav, we really—"

Tate turned in my direction and his face stilled as his eyes raked over my body. As he shifted his gaze from my red heels, up my legs, and over my hips, hesitating at my boobs and then finally landing on my face, I felt my cheeks burn under his gaze. I seriously needed to get my blushing under control.

"Fuck," Tate hissed between clenched teeth as his possessive eyes undertook their second assault of my body.

I was getting the reaction I'd craved and the lioness began to purr within me. I strutted towards him, the sound of my heels clicking against the floorboards matched the increasing beat of my heart perfectly. My lust-filled eyes landed on his bottom lip, which he was gnawing on with his teeth, and I suddenly felt alive.

"Like what you see, Mr. Connors?" I twirled in front of him, making sure I was just outside of arm's reach.

"In a dress like that, Miss Rae, you are the spawn of Satan." He took a step towards me and I was suddenly lost under the scent only he possessed. "And for once I'm not afraid of visiting Hell to get what I want."

"Well we can't visit Hell because we have a bar opening to go to." I spun on my heel and took off through the room, loving the feeling that sassy Savannah was out to play.

My eyes felt heavy as the first signs that intoxication had begun taking over every part of my body. Las Vegas was destroying me one tequila shot at a time. This was the first time in over three years that I had really gone out, and now, as I knocked back yet another shot of tequila that Jack had thrust in my hand, it rushed through my body like hot springs.

The moment Tate and I had walked into Red Velvet, he had been pushed into the limelight and I'd made my way to Tanzi and Jack. I loved seeing him in his element, and right now, Tate Connors was on show. My eyes hadn't left him all night and his hadn't left mine.

The more the night went on, the more my body ached for him. Something had definitely shifted between us after last night. I still didn't understand what he'd meant when he'd said that he'd figured it out. I was still lost about that statement, but I knew that my nightmare had opened up my thoughts about Tate and me. And to be honest, I was now more than ready to go on the ride of my life.

"Well here comes Mr. Hot Shot," Jack taunted as Tate collapsed in a vacant chair at what was now *our* table at Red Velvet Las Vegas and flipped him off.

"This living in the limelight is exhausting." He laughed.

"You are such a dick."

"Suck it, Jack." Tate patted his crouch and shifted his eyes to me.

"So when are you two going to fuck?" Jack asked loudly over the music pumping from the stage.

Tate's eyes narrowed at Jack "What the fuck?"

"What? I know for a fact that you are right this second fucking her in your head, and I know Sav wants you between her thighs, so it's a justifiable question. Sav and I do talk about you two, you know."

Tate glanced questioningly at me, and all I could do was offer a shrug and a slight nod. "He is my 'talk about fucking Tate' buddy. I can't do it with my female bestie so I do it with my male bestie." And just like that, honest Sav had come out alive and kicking. *Thank you, Mr. Tequila.*

"And I can't talk to you about fucking Tanzi, so I speak to my sister from another mister."

Tate and Tanzi looked at each other as disturbance flashed over their perfectly matched faces.

"Aren't they just deliciously gorgeous?" I murmured, my eyes jumping between Tate and Tanzi. "How would you two feel about a foursome? No boundaries? No regrets?"

"Oh you know I'm keen, Sav. The thought of that kind of makes me think of those stories you've told me," Jack growled in response. I had to bite the inside of my mouth to stop a fit of laughter from escaping. Tate's and Tanzi's eyes shot wide and only ignited the fire of confidence roaring in my body.

"How about that time I told you about Tate fucking me against the window in New York City? Fuck, that was hot. My arse up against the cold window for the entire world below to see was such a turn-on. It was definitely one of our best times."

I closed my eyes and slowly ran my tongue along my bottom lip as my memories floated back to New York City. The way Tate's body had ground against mine, the way his voice had growled as he'd come inside me, and the words he'd breathed into my ear as I'd come around him.

"How about when I told you about the time I fucked Tanzi in the back seat of the car because we couldn't wait to get to the apartment."

"And Tate! God, he goes deep, like right up in there. I've never had it that deep before. It's like he is going to screw the last breath out of me."

"Yeah, Tanzi rides me like I am a champion stallion. Jesus Christ, it's hot."

"WILL YOU TWO SHUT THE FUCK UP?" Tanzi and Tate yelled simultaneously.

The looks on Tanzi's and Tate's faces were priceless. They

looked like they had just stumbled in on their grandparents having sex or something just as disturbing.

"God, I love you Savannah! You are the one person who can get under Tate's skin, so I am keeping you around," Jack boomed from beside me.

He grabbed my hand and we took off through the bar towards the back laughing at the torment we had just put on Tate and Tanzi. As we waited to be served at the packed bar, I rested against the bar and leaned back on my elbows, taking in everything in front of me.

Red Velvet Las Vegas was stunning. The deep burgundy on the wall, the chrome fixtures, and black and white furniture made it look classy yet chic. The roof was covered with thousands of tiny fairy lights, and the draping of material from the high ceilings made it feel like a fairytale.

I closed my eyes at the sound of Blake's voice filling the room. I was so happy knowing that Tate and Blake now had a relationship. They both had been so damaged by their arsehole father, and they'd found a common goal of proving that they could move past their insecurities over him. Humming along to one of their songs, I smiled, knowing that this was such a big deal for Tate to allow him to play at Red Velvet as part of a tour kick-off show.

"Do you like what you see?" Tate's voice flooded my ears and the warmth of his breath made a shiver run down my spine. My eyes shot open as he took a step away and stood directly in front of me, and I couldn't help but admire the hotness of Tate Connors dressed head to toe in black—black suit, black shirt, black tie. His hair looked like he had been perfectly fucked and the stubble grazing his chin was what I loved, but it was his eyes that made me fall under his spell. His perfect blue eyes were crystal clear tonight, looking like they were shining with life and contentment.

"Are you talking about the bar or what's in front of me?"

"I was talking about the bar, but I'd take anything you are willing to give. Any access to what's going through that pretty head of yours would be good."

He leaned beside me and I looked at him out of the corner of my eye. He was in his absolute element. A smile played on his lips as he took in his surroundings.

"That was a mischievous display you and Jack put on out there." He turned to me, shaking his head slowly, and I swear his cheeks flushed.

"Are you blushing?" I squealed.

"No, it just got suddenly warm in here." He turned away and looked towards the bar. "Can I have two ice waters please?" I heard him say.

"Pfft! Why are you ordering water?"

"Savannah, I need you standing by the end of the night."

"And why is that, Tate?" I purred with intention.

"Don't flirt with me, woman. I am still working and I think it's a little early to christen my office the first night we open."

"You need to live a little, Tate." I pushed his shoulder gently, dropping my head to the side and looking him over. I was blatantly flirting with him.

"I have plans for us tonight, Sav, and I really need to make sure you are one hundred percent coherent when it happens."

Swallowing hard, I heard the promise in his words and instinctively licked my lips, dragging my bottom lip between my teeth. His eyes scanned my face and his eyes burned deep within me. My body ignited under his heated gaze, and I knew my breathing had increased. What the hell was it about us and bars?

"What are you thinking right this second?"

"Honestly?" I whispered.

"Always honestly."

"You make me want to come right here at the bar."

"Fuck!" he muttered. Running his hands over his face, he looked around the bar and frowned. "Why did you have to say that?"

"You wanted honesty." I smirked.

"Yes, but now my cock is straining against my pants and I am about ready to push those damn panties to the side and fuck you 'til everyone in this damn bar knows my name."

As I was about to respond, a middle-aged man approached us with his sights locked on Tate. "Hi, Mr. Connors. I just wanted to congratulate you on a very successful launch. I look forward to meeting you regarding expansion internationally and further discussions regarding the New York and Vegas bars."

"Thank you, Craig. I look forward to discussing this in detail. I will be taking a month off once this launch is complete to spend time with my family, so let's organize a meeting then."

"I heard you had a little one. I hope your boy knows what a great job his dad has done with this place. It's the talk of Vegas."

"Max or his brother or sister will be running this place one day, so I have to set the groundwork for them." Tate's eyes flickered to mine as I stood in total shock.

Sister? Brother? Since when did Max have a sibling? Was I pregnant and didn't know? Was it some kind of Immaculate

Conception because I am pretty certain I'd know if Tate had been anywhere near me.

"Okay, I'll be in contact in a month or so to organize that meeting. Congratulations again."

"So I am thinking we should have three kids," Tate stated and leaned back against the bar beside me after he finished his conversation with who I now knew as Craig. For once in my life, I was totally speechless, and all I could do was look at him with wide eyes. "I'm thinking our daughter will want this bar and Max will run the New York bar."

"You said three kids?" I whispered.

"Yep. Two kids and a puppy."

He winked at me before stepping away and walking through the bar, leaving me with a billion butterflies bashing around in my stomach and a weakness in my knees that only he could bring on.

"You are getting so lucky tonight," Jack laughed beside me as he grabbed the drinks. When had he reappeared and what had he heard?

"Did you just hear that?"

"I have been hearing about his big old plans for the past three months, Sav. Seriously. For someone who calls himself Mr. Spontaneity, he has his dream life already planned, and it includes no one except you and Max."

CHAPTER
Thirty-Eight

Tate

THE LAUNCH WAS GOING OFF with a bang. Every inch of the club was jam-packed with people, the music was loud, and the drinks were flowing. Sav continued to torment me in that white dress. It was like another layer of skin, sitting in perfect sync with the curves of her body that I wanted so desperately to be kissing, biting, licking, and fucking. I couldn't look away. Utter fucking perfection.

When I wasn't thinking of being balls-deep in Sav, I had spent the night in business-owner mode, mingling with guests, and smiling for the camera when needed, but my attention was always drawn back to Jack, Tanzi, and Sav, who had been dancing the night away.

"You've done good with this place," Blake stated as he moved up beside me when The Fallen went on a well-deserved break. I couldn't help but be highly amused by the small group of girls that were following Blake everywhere he went and were now giggling and deciding which one of them would approach him.

"You guys are getting a good reception up there." I nodded towards the group of girls now staring at Blake. "They are about to pounce."

He shifted his sight to the hyenas and winked in their direction, the pitch of the squeals almost causing my eardrums to erupt. "Yeah, Vegas is always good to us."

Shaking my head, I knew exactly what he meant. Las Vegas had seen its fair share of man-whore Tate in his prime.

"What the fuck is Colby doing?" I growled as Sav once again took hold of my attention.

Colby and Sav were dancing in the middle of the jam-packed dance floor, her blonde hair illuminated by the lights above and her cheeks flushed from the heat in the air. Colby spun Sav around until she couldn't stand and slammed into his chest as laughter bellowed from her body. His arms wrapped around her waist and then they proceeded to waltz to a Beyoncé song the DJ was spinning.

"He is harmless." Blake laughed. "He knows she's yours."

"She isn't mine. That's the problem."

"Well, change that."

"I am planning to. I just told her that I pretty much have our lives planned out and she didn't run off screaming, so that's a positive." I laughed at the stupidity of this whole situation. Blake and I were players from way back, but here we were, talking about the future, me about my grand plans of living in the suburbs with my girl and kids and Blake looking like a lovesick puppy as he stared at a pretty brunette sitting by the bar. Seriously, what the fuck had happened to us?

"Who is she?" I nodded towards the bar. Blake's eyes followed mine and I heard him sigh loudly.

"Band manager of the band we are touring with."

"I didn't ask her profession, Blake. Who is she?"

Blake scrunched his face up and groaned loudly. "She is my perfect distraction."

"It's always the way."

Blake shook his head and glanced one last time at the brunette before taking off towards the stage, clipping Colby around the ear as he walked past. It was their final song before the opening night of Red Velvet Las Vegas was officially done. I had no idea what time it was. Tanzi and Jack had disappeared about an hour ago, and now it was just Sav and me.

When the first strum of Blake's guitar shattered the air, Savannah moved to the front of the stage. As her body swayed along with the sounds of The Fallen, flashbacks flooded through my mind of that very first night at Red Velvet Los Angeles. I had stood watching this stranger I'd only known as Tanzi's new Aussie best friend move her body so seductively, so mesmerizingly. I'd wanted her in every sense of the word that night, and now, almost four years later, absolutely nothing had changed. If anything, I needed her more now than I ever had.

Throwing caution to the wind, I did something I should have done four years ago. Weaving my way through the crowd and making my way to the front of the stage, I moved behind her and slid my arms around her waist, pulling her tight against my chest. Her head turned to look at me and a smile covered her face. Our bodies meshed together in perfect sync as we swayed with the rhythm of the music. Her head fell back against my chest and her hands covered mine. We moved to the music, completely lost in the low pulse of the bass and the feeling of our bodies locked together.

Sav twisted in my arms to face me, her arms snaking around my neck and her nails running through the back of my hair. "I need to kiss you, Tate." Her tongue swiped her lips as the look in her eyes intensified and ran over my face. Her lips caught the corner of my mouth in the most sensual way, making me forget that we were in the middle of the dance floor.

I gripped her waist tighter and dragged her as close as physically possible, needing to feel every inch of her body. My hand clasped the back of her neck, enticing her mouth to mine. Her tongue ran the length of my bottom lip, asking for acceptance. Slowly we molded together in a sea of bliss. I wanted to taste every inch of her mouth. I wanted the memories of every kiss we had to flood back. I missed this. I missed getting lost in the passion of kissing Savannah Rae. Never again would we be apart.

Breathlessly, she pulled away and smiled softly. "I've missed that."

"It's about time," came a voice from the stage. We both swung around as Blake looked down at us and fired a thumbs up towards us. Sav buried her face in my chest as a giggle rose from her throat.

"Can I take you home, my Aussie?"

"I never thought you'd ask."

As we walked into our room, Sav's hand clamped mine as she

walked unsteadily on her feet.

"You can't handle your tequila anymore." I laughed as I led her to the bed and sat her down.

She looked up with unfocused eyes. "Oh, I know it's devastating. I am the queen of tequila and now look at me. I am a bloody disgrace," she complained with a pout before falling back onto the bed with a giggle. "What are you thinking?" Propping herself up on her elbows, she looked at me and asked the question that was beginning to be our thing.

"I am having an internal battle with myself about whether I should take advantage of my drunk girlfriend. It has been a while, you know." I winked as I undid the buttons of my shirt and slipped it off my shoulders.

Sav sat up on the edge of the bed, tugged on my belt, and reeled me in towards her. "Your drunk girlfriend would be very welcoming if you took advantage of her. I hope my va-jay-jay still works."

"Your va-jay-jay? What the fuck?"

"Fine, my pussy. Jeez, Tate, I was trying to be a respectable woman. I'm a mother now, you know.

"I cannot wait to find out if your pussy still works, but it won't be happening now. I want you to remember every single feeling, thrust, scream, moan, and depth my cock goes. I want to own you when we have sex, Sav, and I need you fully functional for that."

"So you are just going to leave your girlfriend turned on and desperate?" The pout reappeared.

"Yep." I winked at her and pushed her back on the bed. She fell instantly with a huff.

As she pulled off her heels one at a time, I felt her eyes

burning into me. I counted to ten in my head, desperate to stop the blood flow flooding my high-alert cock. I could not have sex with her right now.

I motioned for her to roll over, which she obliged without a fight. Unzipping the back of her dress, I slid it down until it reached her hips. With a quick move, I flipped her over and I continued sliding the tight dress off, making sure I touched every inch of her body. She lay before me in virgin-white panties and a push-up bra, her glowing skin, tinted from the California skin, beaming in front of me.

"You are a goddess, Savannah. It is killing me not to take you right now."

"Can I sleep in one of your shirts?" she almost begged.

I walked to my suitcase, removed one of my shirts, and handed it to Savannah. She stood from the bed, removing her bra and pulling my shirt over her head. Seeing her in just panties and my shirt sitting perfectly short on her thighs was a painful turn-on. She walked uneasily towards the bathroom, turning the light on and walking to the vanity.

Pulling the comforter back, I lay down and watched her through the glass walls. Slowly she began taking off her makeup, not letting her gaze leave mine in the mirror.

I finally had her back.

Chapter Thirty-Nine

Savannah

MY HEAD POUNDED AS THE tequila I had so easily and recklessly consumed barely hours ago decided to remind me of its most recent assault. My love/hate relationship with the deliciously intoxicating spirit was now leaning towards the hate side at a rapid rate.

As I shifted in bed, a weight pressed firmly against my back, heating my skin with radiating warmth. Tate. I finally had him back in my arms. The night sky still floated through the windows, and the lights of Las Vegas allowed me to see the outline of his gorgeous face as I slowly turned to face him. Never again would I be away from him. I would stick to him like super glue.

Sliding out slowly from under his arm, desperate not to wake him, I held my breath as he rolled over with a sigh and huddled into my now vacant pillow. I quietly moved through the room towards my suitcase while my eyes remained locked firmly on Tate's sleeping form. My fingertips found the satin of my favorite black gown and I quickly removed his shirt—that had left his delicious scent tainting my skin—and panties and slipped the gown over my naked body. Giving him one last look, I sauntered back to the bed with a seductive smiling taking over my face and the sass of Savannah roaring inside.

"Tate," I whispered, grabbing his hand as I stood beside the bed. He stirred in his sleep but refused to be interrupted from his slumber. "Wake up."

Kneeling beside the bed, I leaned over his sleeping form and placed my lips softly on his. If he wouldn't wake on his own, then I'd make sure he woke with a start. Splashing his closed mouth with kisses, I ran my tongue along his bottom lip before pulling it between my teeth. The moment my teeth gnawed at his bottom lip, he came alive with a groan. His hand shot out from under the cover and moved to the back of my head, pulling my face closer to his as his lips opened and his tongue met mine frantically. Right after he started kissing me back, he pulled back suddenly and looked at me with hooded eyes.

"Sav?"

"I had to do something to wake you up." My words vibrated against his lips. "You need to get up."

"Sav, it's like three A.M.," he groaned after looking at the time on his phone.

"Tate, it's like eight A.M. somewhere," I taunted, mimicking his American accent.

"Are you teasing me?"

"Never." Standing up, I pulled back the covers, revealing his naked body. "Now get that sexy body out of bed. We are leaving in ten minutes."

"What? Where are we going?"

"Get your arse out of bed, Tate. Otherwise I'll find someone else to go swimming with!"

His eyes widened as he slowly sat up in bed with increased interest. "Are you going to wear *the* bikini?"

"I'm wearing this," I slowly ran my fingers along to sash around my waist. A gentle pull allowed the front of the gown to open and reveal my naked body. His hungry eyes swept over my bare skin. I'd finally gotten his attention. "Now, if you don't get your arse out of bed, my naked body and I will be swimming alone, and because of the way you left me earlier, I know for a fact I'll be having sex tonight—with or without you."

Tate shot out of bed in one swift movement and pulled on a pair of sweatpants and a t-shirt before I had time to laugh. Grabbing my hand and the room key, he dragged me out of the room and towards the elevator without a word.

"You do realize that I have never ever felt this turned on in my life," he growled from across the lift as the air around us grew thicker with need and anticipation.

"What better way to make up for lost time?" I hit the first floor button and started watching the numbers drop. "We have to get off at the first floor and use the stairs so no one sees us."

"How long have you been planning this?" he asked with a laugh.

"Since the moment I saw the pool." The chime of the lift door opening broke our gaze, and I impatiently pulled on his hand as we stepped out into the quiet of the first floor. In silence, we rushed down the hall and down the stairs until we reached the emptiness of the pool area. My eyes darted frantically around for any signs of life; it was just me, Tate, and the beauty of the pool.

The fairy lights around the pool were still shimmering like a billion stars in the night sky, and the translucent lights at the bottom of the pool made the crystal-clear water radiate through the air. I grabbed hold of both of Tate's hands and walked backwards as I led him to the secluded area at the back of the pool where it was almost cave like.

"I love you, Tate. Like no one I've loved before."

"I know, Sav." His words were simple but full of promise.

Dropping his hands, I undid the sash, pulled the satin robe over my shoulders, and felt it skim my body as it dropped to the floor. I had never felt as sexy as I did right this second. I moved into the water, taking one step at a time. The coolness of the water met the fire of my body as I swam away from the steps towards the middle of the secluded pool.

The feeling of Tate's eyes on me only increased the desire flooding me and the ache of my body for his. I turned back to where I'd left him and found a very empty poolside. What the hell? My eyes darted frantically around the pool edge for any sign of him.

Suddenly, hands wrapped around my bare waist, pulling me back against a firm, equally naked body. His lips crashed onto my neck as I fell back against him. With his arm around my waist, he held me in place as my arm traveled to the back of his neck. My entire body felt like it was on fire, a stark contradiction to the cool water surrounding it.

"Tell me this is it, Sav. That there will never be another time where we are apart," he murmured against my neck as he kissed his way along the sensitive skin to my ear, pulling my lobe between his teeth. "Tell me we are forever."

"I'll always be here, Tate," I groaned as a hand swept over my hips, dropping dangerously close to where I craved him the most. "You are and will always be my priority, my number one."

Without warning, he thrust one finger deep in me. Instantly, my body bucked against him and he drove deeper inside me as his mouth continued its assault on my neck. The feeling of his teeth gnawing at my skin and his finger plunging further within me were pushing me to a place only he could take me. Rocking back into his body, I felt the swell of his erection grind against me and heard the break of his breathing.

With one swift movement, I twisted my body to meet his. His hands gripped under my arse and lifted me from my feet, my legs wrapping around his body fiercely and our chests colliding and meeting as one. The water swished around us as we moved to the secluded corner of the pool, hidden away from the rest of the world. My eyes burned into his as the intensity of this moment hit both of us. My heart thundered in my chest; my body ached to be filled with what I had missed for so many months.

"Make love to me, Tate," I begged as he pushed my back up against the edge of the pool.

He filled me without hesitating, his need for me evident from the groan escaping his lips. I cried out and my eyes slammed shut as the sensation of him filling me completely ripped through my body. He stilled, allowing me to adjust. Slowly, he moved, thrusting in and out, his eyes never moving from mine. Our breathing danced in perfect harmony as the rhythm of our bodies moving against each other increased with each movement. My fingernails clawed at his back as his body pounded into me with fevered intensity. I lifted my hips, begging for him to dive deeper.

"Fuck, Sav," he groaned as he met my pleas.

Every word and curse that escaped him only fueled my desire for him. I felt my body succumbing to the pleasure being unleashed on to it.

"I'm so close, Tate," I moaned into his shoulder and bit down into his flesh as the sensation of my impending orgasm drove Tate's body into overdrive, his grip tightening.

"Come for me, Sav," he demanded with assertiveness. With one final thrust, my body succumbed to his and I erupted in a wave of pure ecstasy around him.

Soon, his body fell against mine, and with a moan of my name against my neck, his body relaxed as release swept through him. Pulling his face away from my neck, our breathing heavy and broken, he kissed me ever so lightly and I felt the smile of his lips on mine.

"Well I'm pretty sure that's the best idea you've ever had, Savannah."

My head fell to his shoulder as we remained connected as our breathing settled. He didn't pull out, and I had never experienced anything more sensual in my life. The water remained calm as we stood in silence, his arms around my waist and my arms locked tight around his neck. Being in his arms and feeling protected and loved was what allowed Tate to make me feel like no one else had.

I pulled my head away from his shoulder and my eyes fell on his face as I looked at him completely. The man standing before me was the one who had found me when I was my weakest, even when I was pretending to be my strongest. He was the one who had fought for me time and time again and hadn't stopped until he'd gotten me. This was the man who loved me completely for every shattered piece I was and the one and only man I could never imagine living without. I was stronger because of him. I would never truly be Savannah if I didn't have Tate.

"I figured it out," I whispered against his lips as I rested my forehead against his. He moved his face slightly so his lips tenderly brushed mine. It was a moment we had both been waiting on for almost four long years.

"It's about time, Sav."

Chapter Forty

Tate

SATURDAY MORNING SUNSHINE FILTERED THROUGH the bedroom, illuminating the spray of blonde hair that lay on my bare chest. Saturday mornings were now my favorite. My Saturdays now involved lazing in bed with Savannah until the door of our bedroom would slowly creep open and Max would bounce in and jump on the bed. Looking at the clock beside the bed, I knew we had at least an hour before Max would be joining us.

I still couldn't believe this was my life. My life now involved living completely and utterly for two other people—Savannah and Max. Nothing else mattered but them. The moment we'd gotten home from Las Vegas, everything had changed. I hadn't even given Sav a chance to unpack her things in the spare room. I'd wheeled her suitcase to our room and unpacked her there and then. She had sat cross-legged on the bed with a grin spreading across her face as she'd watched me go through all of her belongings and unpack them into the closet. We had since turned that spare room into an office. My life was almost complete. There was just one last thing to do.

I'd never thought I'd deserve this kind of happiness, but now it was a happiness that I couldn't imagine living without, and it was given to me by a sassy Australian who rocked my world to its core.

"Ahh, it's morning already?" Sav groaned from beside me. As she buried her face into the concave of my chest, her lips kissed my skin. "It's too early."

"It's seven A.M."

"Yep. Too damn early."

I flipped her over and hovered above her as she giggled at my sudden movements. Savannah first thing in the morning was my favorite. Without any makeup, with crazy hair, and dressed in her little panties and cami, she was the perfect specimen to wake up to. A content smile tinkered on her lips as she looked up at me. Fuck, she was beautiful. My fingertips swept off the loose strands of hair that had fallen on her cheek and tucked it behind her ear. Her skin was awash of California glow. *My perfect Aussie girl.*

"What are you thinking?" she asked softly.

"I am thinking how lucky I am."

"Max and I are the lucky ones." She raised her head slightly, allowing her lips to meet mine in a feather light kiss.

With a heavy kiss, I pinned her to the bed under the weight of my body. Her legs parted under us as I ground myself into her, driving my body into hers. My cock stirred to life instantly. Her hand moved between us and I moaned as I felt her fingers wrap around me. I pulled my mouth away from hers and found a look of desire flooding her face. Seriously, she loved morning sex just as much as me. Fuck, I was a lucky prick.

"We have about an hour before Max decides to join us. I want to play with this." Her grip tightened. "And I want you to fuck me 'til I'm moaning your name into the pillow."

"You are the best kind of friend to play with," I growled, my teeth nibbling the flesh of her collarbone. My hand swept down her body with intention roughly pushing aside her lace panties. There was no time to waste.

The moment my fingers slipped through her already wet folds, her back arched from the bed and a low moan escaped her perfect lips. As she pushed hard against my fingers, I increased the intensity of my stroke. With one finger and then two, I pushed into her, pumping, pushing, and stroking her into oblivion. Her pussy tightened around my fingers and her body shuddered in delight. It was the best sight in the fucking world.

Sav pushed on my chest with both hands, pushing me with determination onto my back. Her body slid down mine, her cami caressing every delicious curve of her body. In one movement, our bodies joined together, her eyes closed as her body took mine. She stilled, straddling my body, my cock so deep inside her that my breath caught in the back of my throat. Her eyes were hooded with desire.

"With every day that passes, I fall even more in love with you, Tate."

My hands gripped her hips and lifted her. She took my cue. Her body pounded on top of mine, rising and falling, allowing me deeper and deeper with every crash of her body. Her head flung back, her hair cascading down her back. Her chest heaved, her perfect tits bouncing as her body attacked mine. *Best morning sex ever.*

"Sav, I need to lose myself in you," I moaned from deep within my chest. Her body clenched around mine and it slammed down on me one last time before she fell on my chest. She buried her face in my neck as her muffled groan rang through the room.

Our breathing danced with each other as we desperately tried to get it under control. She didn't move from my chest and I was still inside her. "I want to take you out today," I murmured against the side of her neck.

"Like a date?" she asked, looking up from the confines of my neck.

"Yep. Just like a date."

Santa Monica Pier was splattered with visitors as far as the eye could see. Saturdays were always packed down here, and especially today since California had turned on a perfect day. The shrill of children's laughter floated through the air, the smell of popcorn took over my senses, and the crash of the ocean near me calmed my increasing nerves by the second.

With my hand clasped tightly in Savannah's and my other hand protectively gripping Max's, we walked along the pier looking like the perfect family we were. Everything was finally perfection with us. Even though our relationship was far from easy, it had made us who we were today. It had embraced our stubborn traits and made us work for every part of our relationship. It had made us uniquely perfect for each other, and through everything, I knew this girl beside me was it for me. There was no one else. She was the mother of my child, the owner of my heart, the perfect beam of light that lit up my darkened life.

"Daddy!" Max's voice ripped me from my thoughts.

"What's up, buddy?" I looked between Max and Sav, who was looking at me with an amused expression. Sav turned towards Tanzi and started laughing at something randomly before dropping my hand and walking towards a store hand in hand with Tanzi.

"Uncle Jack said a naughty word."

"What? When? I am on complete Max watch when I am around him!" Jack's shriek caused deep laughter to roar from inside of me. "Do you realize how hard it is not to drop the F-bomb?"

"I heard him say a-s-s the other day," I spelled out. "And he sounded exactly like Savannah with his Aussie twang. It was seriously cute. I couldn't really discipline him for it, considering I laughed so hard."

"He is going to be the biggest lady-killer."

"Yeah, tell me about it."

"I've got a girlfriend," Max suddenly announced. The three of us stopped mid-sentence and looked at the little boy smiling up at us. "Her name is Daisy."

Lucas laughed beside me and mumbled, "Exactly like his mother and father."

My laughter soon joined his. Picking up Max, I placed him on a seat at the table we were sitting at for lunch. "Where did you meet your girlfriend, Max?"

Without missing a beat, he looked me square in the eyes and said, "In my dreams." He nodded self-assuredly and looked between me, Lucas, and Jack with a certain grin. "That's where you met Mummy."

"He did not just say that!" Jack roared with laughter across the table. My son was a fucking Casanova at three years of age. What hope did the future women of the world have?

"Daddy teaches me a lot of things." My eyes shot open at his words.

"I'm sure he does, Maxey." Jack laughed. "I'm sure he does."

"I might have to get locks on the bedroom door," I muttered to Lucas.

Max started talking to Jack about God only knew what, but by the constant laughter coming from Jack, I was sure I would be informed. Max had absolutely no filter, just like his aunt Tanzi. He said what he wanted, when he wanted, and with no consequence. He was going to be a danger to society when he was older, and I knew for a fact that my mom loved every minute of it. The words "Payback is a bitch" had been heard from her on more than one occasion.

Savannah and Tanzi walked towards us, arms full of food and drinks. My eyes drank in Savannah.

"You feeling good about this?" Lucas asked from beside me. I turned to him and nodded. The fact that I now classed him as one of my closest friends shocked even me some days. He was good to my cousin, he was protective of my son, and he loved my girlfriend like a sister. That was more than I could have asked for. And he knew some damn good surf breaks.

My courage barged in as Sav sat beside me. I watched as she tended to Max, giving him half of his cheeseburger and 'chips,' as they both liked to call them. Oh, and of course his 'chips' had to be smothered with 'tomato sauce.' There was no way he would call it ketchup. Seriously, I could swear they were attempting to make me Australian.

"Max, what's this?" Jack asked, holding up the bottle of ketchup.

"Tomato sauce," Max said matter-of-factly.

"No, remember what Uncle Jack taught you yesterday? Ketchup."

"Don't teach my child American," Sav laughed from beside me, throwing one of her fries at him. "He said flip-flops this morning, Jack. They are and will always be thongs."

"Do you really want him to be saying to some chick when he is eighteen, 'Show me your thongs'?"

"Point taken."

"But with parents like you and Tate, this kid is going to be a fucking heartbreaker. Wouldn't surprise me if he pulled out lines like that."

The banter between Sav and Jack continued to fill the table as we all ate our lunch, but I sat in silence. Tanzi's eyes flashed to mine over the table in silent encouragement, and I knew full well that she was reading me like no one else could. I nodded to her, telling her that it had to happen now.

"Maxey, you stay here for a minute while Mommy and Daddy go up there, okay?" I swallowed hard and pointed to the Ferris wheel behind us. Savannah's eyes widened in shock, but the smile on her lips showed her excitement. Why did I have to have a girlfriend who had no fear when it came to heights? Pushing back my chair, I stood and held out my hand to Sav, which she clasped tightly.

"Why are you doing this to yourself?" She laughed as we

walked towards the line. She took her hand from mine and wrapped her arm around my waist before nuzzling into my side.

"It's the thing you do for the girl you love." I smirked. "Either that or I have a death wish."

Sliding into the seat beside her, I watched with petrified eyes as a boy who barely looked like he was old enough to work let alone be responsible for our safety closed the gate. I grabbed hold of the rail and rattled it to make sure we were secured in. *Fuck, I hate heights.* Sav slid on the seat so that she was facing me, her face calm and her eyes looking at me with happiness.

"You didn't have to do this." She grabbed my hands, bringing them to her lips. "I could have gotten someone else to come with me."

All I could do was nod. Once again, my ability to speak had been thrown out the window as fear swept through me. With a jerk, we started the painfully slow rise from the safety of the ground. My eyes locked with Savannah's in a desperate attempt of safety. I could feel the familiar tightening of my chest and the clamminess of my hands against my jeans.

"The things I do for you," I choked out and smiled slightly. "If this isn't love, then I don't know what is."

Sav's attention moved from me to take a glance over the edge. She looked out over the Pacific Ocean as we slowly rose to the peak. The smile gracing her face was pure contentment. If I saw a smile like that on her face every day, then I'd die a happy man.

The Ferris wheel came to a stop as we reached the highest peak. My fear of heights had been stolen by my nerves of the next words that would come out of my mouth. Grabbing both of her hands, Sav shifted in the seat so she was facing me. This was it.

"Savannah Rae, my life changed the moment I first saw you in the lobby. You were the most beautiful girl I had ever seen and I remember that first moment like it was yesterday. You were so different from anyone I had ever seen and my urge to be near you was so strong. I thought that would be it. I thought we would have our moment in the elevator and that would be it, but then fate stepped in and you were my twin's best friend." I took a deep breath, knowing that it was now or never.

This was a moment that had been coming for so long. I loved this girl more than I could have ever imagined, and now, as we sat at the top of the world, I hoped today would be the start of a whole new chapter in the book of Tate Connors and Savannah Rae. I dropped to my knee in the bottom of the carriage and looked up at her through hopeful eyes. Her gasp filled the air around us.

"You made me become a man, Sav. You made me face everything head-on because I was desperate to be the man an amazing woman like you deserved. And until I take my last breath, I will continue to be that man for you. You own my heart completely. I love you like I've never loved before, I crave you like I've never craved before, and I am bound to you for life. Will you be bound to me for life, Sav? Would you take my name and be with me in every sense of the word? Will you marry me, Savannah Maree Rae?

Epilogue

SIX MONTHS LATER

Savannah

I OFTEN FELT LIKE I WAS living a never-ending fairytale, a fairy tale that I was still in the middle of and one I never wanted to finish. It felt like an eternity since I'd left Australia for the first time, and thinking back to the girl I had been when I left caused a shudder to run through my body. The thought of that Savannah was like thinking of someone completely different. She was a stranger, a shadow of who I was today. I had been so utterly and completely screwed up, but I would never have realized that at the time. To me, I had been living the life. Screwing random men into oblivion, partying until the sun came up, drinking 'til I passed out and forgot the world. That had been reality to me. Now I knew that I'd left Australia a shattered and broken young woman. I had been destroyed, hell-bent on self-destruction, and living the life I'd thought I'd deserved. Happiness had been a myth, a legend that I'd thought I would never meet, a legend I'd never wanted to meet. I had been a walking contradiction, a disgrace to my family, and a constant heartache to the only person who had truly accepted me—Mr. Davenport.

Moving to the States had been the best damn decision of my life.

What I hadn't expected when I arrived in the bright lights of Los Angeles was to find love, to find my second chance, to find the other broken, fractured part of my heart. Tate Connors, my stubborn, frustrating, and amazing savior. To find a partner who loved me for all of my faults, who loved me for all of my scars, and who understood loss like I did was something I could never have imagined finding. Never in my wildest dreams had I thought I'd be lucky enough to find the one.

And now today I was going to become Mrs. Tate Connors.

As the sunshine of California beamed through the house, I felt like I was Cinderella living a crazy fairytale, getting ready to meet my prince charming. I was so lovesick that it was pathetic.

The moment Tate had asked me to marry him, everything had fallen into place. I had no idea he was going to do that, and to be honest, he'd shocked the life out of me. But there had been no other answer I could give him. Of course it had been a giant yes.

And that was when the craziness of planning a wedding started. I felt like the past six months had been the craziest ride of my life. Tanzi had gone straight into complete wedding-planner mode the moment we'd gotten off the Ferris wheel and announced our engagement, and since then all I'd had to do was say yes or no and she'd gotten things organised. She had been incredible, and I couldn't have asked for a better maid of honor. Well, besides the three A.M. calls when she got a brilliant idea about flowers or cakes.

All I wanted was a twilight beach wedding, something simple yet elegant, with Tate, Max, and me, surrounded by our family and friends, and that's what we were getting.

"Sav, where are you?" Mr. Davenport's strong voice rumbled through the living area. Wrapping my satin bride-to-be dressing gown around me—a gift from Tanzi and Ali—I walked out of the bathroom and grinned at him. "Well how's the wife-to-be going?"

Walking towards him, I stood on my tiptoes, placing a light kiss on his cheek, and couldn't wipe the smile off my face. "I am feeling good. I don't think it's really hit me yet what today actually is."

"Are you here on your own?" he asked, looking around the empty room.

"Tanzi and Ali have gone to the liquor store. They forgot champagne."

"Well, I just wanted to come here and tell you something, but I don't want you to freak out, okay?" His face looked panicked.

"You cannot start a conversation like that. Has Tate decided he doesn't want to marry me? I knew this was too good to be true. Seriously, could he not have come and told me himself? I am going to kill him!" I groaned in frustration, collapsing on the couch and dropping my head into my hands. Worst-case scenario swamped me.

"Savannah!" His voice rose to grab my frantic attention. "Calm the hell down. Tate is coming. You are getting married today."

Raising my head, I looked at him sheepishly. "Well what do you have to tell me?"

He swallowed hard, his eyes darting away from me quickly as if he were nervous. Mr. Davenport never got nervous—ever. What the hell was going on? "I've met someone."

Did I really just hear that? I felt my lips curving into an excited smile.

I taunted, standing from the couch and walking towards him. "Say again?"

"Jesus, Savannah. I know you heard me." He ran his hands frustratingly through his hair and groaned. "I've met someone and I've invited her today."

I barreled into him, my arms wrapping around him tightly as I nearly squeezed the life out of him. His soft laughter rang through my ears. I had been waiting years for this moment. Mr. Davenport finally had a lady friend! Shit! Tanzi would be devastated.

"What's the lucky lady's name? Where is she from? How did you meet her? Why the hell are you only telling me now? Tanzi will be crushed!" I breathed out at a hundred miles an hour.

"I feel like I'm being interrogated," he scoffed and sat on the couch, grabbing my hand and pulling me down beside him. "Her name is Georgie, she is from England, I met her at a Beautify function, and as for Tanzi, I am sure she will get over her insistent love for me. The reason I haven't told you about Georgie is because I wanted to make sure it was serious before I introduced her to my family."

"I can't wait to meet her," I admitted softly. I had been waiting for him to find someone special for years. Yes, he dated but he had never introduced me to any of them—not one. It was only ever him and me. "I can't believe I'm—"

"Savannah, we are back!" Tanzi shrilled, breaking my conversation with Mr. Davenport.

He stood from the couch, kissing my forehead before walking towards my gawking best friend. Seriously, her obsession with Mr. Davenport was becoming concerning. She fired him a wink before rushing to the kitchen, and the clink of glasses indicated that I was about to be drinking my first glass of champagne.

"I'll leave you girls to get organized. I'll be back soon."

The afternoon was spent in a rush of makeup, flowers, champagne, and laughter. Having Tanzi and Ali excitedly chatting and getting eager by the second as they fussed over my hair and makeup made me forget the nerves that were quickly growing within my butterfly-infested stomach. I was getting married today. Savannah Rae was getting married.

"Let's get you into this beautiful dress." Ali reached for my wedding dressing hanging from the mirror in Tate's and my bedroom. Slipping my robe off my shoulders, I stood in the middle of the room in only my new baby pink lingerie that I had been given on my hens' night.

"I still find it so amusing that you call a bachelorette party a hens' night. You Australians crack me up," Tanzi laughed as she took me in. "You are a vixen, Miss Rae. My brother is going to die when he sees you in this."

"I am hoping I won't be in it for very long once he sees me. I plan on consummating this marriage in every way imaginable." I chuckled at the look of disgust that swept over Tanzi's face. "Your brother's self-imposed 'one week of no sex before the wedding' has almost killed me. I'm sorry, Tanzi, but your brother needs to be between my thighs and fast."

"Fuck, Savannah. Do you seriously need to say that?"

"It's payback for all the Mr. Davenport comments you make."

"Okay, you two. Let's get Sav into this dress. It's almost time!" Ali's calming voice broke my amused gaze at Tanzi as I looked towards the dress Ali was holding.

The satin material slid down my body, caressing my curves perfectly, shimmering over my hips, and falling to the floor. With shaking hands, Tanzi zipped me up and then they both took a step away and focused solely on me.

"Do I look okay?" I asked nervously after neither of them said a word.

"You are absolutely breathtaking," Ali whispered as Tanzi gasped and a single tear ran over her cheek. "I am going to quickly see if everything is okay with the boys and I'll be back to get ready and then watch you marry my cousin."

Ali left shortly after, and I helped Tanzi into her dress in complete silence. The perfect pink Grecian dress clung to her perfect hourglass body and made her gorgeous blue eyes pop. Her chocolate brown hair fell over her shoulders in a waterfall of loose curls. She looked like a goddess.

"Can you believe you are here?" she asked softly as I placed the necklace I had purchased her around her neck.

"Never in my wildest dreams did I think I would get married. Love, babies, and marriage weren't in my cards," I admitted, offering a smile as she turned around towards me.

"I couldn't ask for a better girl for my twin." Her voice cracked under the honesty of her words. Her eyes bored into mine as tears taunted the edges, begging to flow over her cheeks, and soon I felt my own tears forming under the intensity of the moment. "I'll be honest with you, Sav. I was terrified when you two started dating. I was terrified because I had finally found the best friend I had been craving my entire life. The moment we met, I felt like I had not only gained a best friend but I had gained a sister, and I was terrified my brother would screw it up for me. It was selfish, I know."

Tanzi breathed deeply and grabbed both of my hands in hers. "But then I started to witness the most amazing thing. I witnessed my brother growing, loving, and becoming completely devoted to someone in a way I could never have ever wished for. You changed him, Sav. You made him come alive. You made him open his heart and become the man I always knew he could be. You make my brother happy, and for that, I will be forever indebted to you. I thought I had lost Tate, but you found him and gave him back to me. Are you ready to become, Mrs. Tate Connors?"

"I've wanted this from the moment your brother said I had a nice arse."

"That brother of mine is such a damn charmer."

The door swung open, revealing Mr. Davenport standing there with a look of pride over his face. Both Tanzi and I looked him over.

"Fuck, I'd love to ride him."

The champagne I had just sipped came up and the sound of me choking filled the room. Mr. Davenport rushed towards me while Tanzi giggled beside me.

"Something inappropriate, I guess?" Mr. Davenport snickered, firing a knowing look towards Tanzi.

"I just said how handsome you are looking. I don't know what she thought I said."

"Yes, I am sure that's what you said." Mr. Davenport shot a smile at Tanzi and shook his head in amusement. "I am onto you Ms. Connors."

"You are on me? God, Mr. Davenport, that's a bit forward, isn't it?"

"Onto you, Tanzi!" He huffed. "Fuck me dead, girl."

"Seriously, Mr. Davenport. You should just shut up while you can. She will turn everything into a sexual innuendo."

"It's true." Tanzi laughed before leaning up and kissing Mr. Davenport on the cheek. I was watching her like a hawk. Seriously, she cracked me up. "I am going to touch up my makeup and give you two a minute." She smiled sweetly before walking through the apartment and leaving Mr. Davenport and I in the silence of the living room.

"You ready?"

I raised my head to take him in, my eyes instantly glazing over with emotion as I looked at him from head to toe. The crisp black three-piece suit he adorned gave him a 1950s Hollywood vibe, the single pink rose in his top pocket glowing against the black backdrop. His eyes almost broke me as they glistened with tears.

"I think so," I choked out in response.

"You look stunning, Savannah."

My shaking hands ran down the front of my Vera Wang wedding dress, desperately trying to smooth out the non-existent creases. My dress was off white and fit snug to my body and swept out like a mermaid tail at the bottom. The bodice was covered with hundreds of tiny pearls, and it sat off my shoulders. It was everything I had imagined my dream wedding dress to be.

"Okay, girlie. Let's do this. Let's officially make you my sister," Tanzi said, walking out of the bathroom and grabbing her flowers from the table. She hugged me tight and began walking out of the room behind Ali as the sound of music floated through the air.

This was it.

I clasped Mr. Davenport's hand so tight that I knew my nails were digging into his flesh, but he didn't falter once. My thoughts escaped to my parents as I was about to start the next chapter of my life without them. I often wondered what they would think of me, whether they would be proud of their 'little ray of sunshine' as they'd called me. All I wanted in life was to make them proud of their baby girl.

"They would be so proud of you" he whispered softly, knowing exactly that I was thinking about my parents. "I am so proud of you, my girl. I am not your dad, but you are and will always be my little girl, Sav."

"Thank you for being the best dad a girl could ask for." I looked at him and smiled through tears. "Please don't let me fall."

"Have I ever let you fall?" he asked with a smile.

He never had.

Tate

Never in a billion years could I have ever imagined that I would be here, standing beside my best friend and my brother, my son holding my hand proudly while wearing his matching suit, and awaiting the arrival of my future wife.

Tate Connors getting married . . . It was like a fucking comedy movie, and I was sure that the knowledge of my impending nuptials had set raucous laughter to flee from many people around the world. I had been destined to be living the ultimate bachelor lifestyle, spending my days and nights with random women, and engaging in meaningless sex for the rest of my life. It was daily that I pinched myself to make sure this was reality, and I constantly asked Sav to punch me in the face to make sure it was real. She refused, stating that she didn't want to wreck my face. Seriously, that girl does wonders for my ego.

The world as I knew it ceased to exist the moment Max's excited voice echoed through the air, announcing Sav's arrival. Turning eagerly to face the candle-and-lily-lined aisle with our nearest and dearest watching on with excited anticipation, I felt my breath hitch and heard gasps as the beauty of Savannah came into view. I loved this girl. I'd always known that I loved her, but right at this second, as I took her in walking towards me, her heavy eyes bursting with emotion, I knew that I was now experiencing a true love that I never could have thought would ever exist.

"She looks stunning, man," Jack's emotion-laced voice said from beside me. I nodded, my ability to speak swallowed as my eyes took in the vision before me.

With nervousness in her step, she slowly made her way towards me. Her eyes spoke volumes to me and thank fuck I saw excitement floating within them. I had absolutely no second thoughts about this. I'd wanted nothing more than to whisk her away to Vegas and marry her the moment she had said yes to my proposal, but I'd known I'd needed to give her what she deserved and that was a twilight beach wedding on the sand by our home with our family around us. Everything about this day was us.

My eyes bounced from Sav's and I took in my stunning sister. She walked in front of Sav with pride swallowing her face and grace floating around her. My twin, my other half, my constant companion. What the hell would I have done without Tanzi? Everything about today came down to her. I never would have met Sav if it weren't for Tanzi. I wouldn't have chased her if I hadn't been trying to annoy the crap out of Tanzi. I wouldn't have Sav back in my life if it weren't for Tanzi. She'd played cupid so many times when it came to Sav and me, and I would be forever indebted to her. Tanzi and I had survived together, and now with Blake in our lives, we were stronger than I could have ever imagined and it was thanks entirely to my beautiful twin. Tanzi's lips curved into a sweet smile and I knew she was reading me. Twintuition was on full display.

My attention fell back to Sav and my smile took over everything. She was a devastating perfection. This woman walking towards me was the savior of my fears, the healer of my heart, and the owner of my true love. How else could I possibly describe her?

Mr. Davenport stood beside her proudly, a tear brimming on the edge of his eye, begging to fall. I knew this would be a huge moment for him. Over the years, we had clashed on so many occasions. We had thrown words at each. Fuck, I'd wanted to punch him in the face numerous times. But now, as